Don Orsino by F. Marion Crawford

Francis Marion Crawford was born on August 2nd, 1854 at Bagni di Lucca, Italy. An only son and a nephew to Julia Ward Howe, the American poet and writer of 'The Battle Hymn of the Republic'.

His education began at St Paul's School, Concord, New Hampshire, then to Cambridge University; University of Heidelberg; and the University of Rome.

In 1879 Crawford went to India, to study Sanskrit and then edited The Indian Herald. In 1881 he returned to America to continue his Sanskrit studies at Harvard University.

At this time in Boston he lived at his Aunt Julia house and in the company of his Uncle, Sam Ward. His family was concerned about his employment prospects. After a singing career as a baritone was ruled out, he was encouraged to write.

In December 1882 his first novel, 'Mr Isaacs', was an immediate hit which was amplified by 'Dr Claudius' in 1883.

In October 1884 he married Elizabeth Berdan. They went on to have two sons and two daughters.

Encouraged by his excellent start to a literary career he returned to Italy with Elizabeth to make a permanent home, principally in Sant' Agnello, where he bought the Villa Renzi that then became Villa Crawford.

In the late 1890s, he began to write his historical works: 'Ave Roma Immortalis' (1898), 'Rulers of the South' (1900) and 'Gleanings from Venetian History' (1905). The Saracinesca series is perhaps his best work. 'Saracinesca' was followed by 'Sant' Ilario' in 1889, 'Don Orsino' in 1892 and 'Corleone' in 1897, that being the first major treatment of the Mafia in literature.

Francis Marion Crawford died at Sorrento on Good Friday 1909 at Villa Crawford of a heart attack.

Index of Contents

CHAPTER I

Don Orsino Saracinesca is of the younger age and lives in the younger Rome, with his father and mother, under the roof of the vast old palace which has sheltered so many hundreds of Saracinesca in peace and war, but which has rarely in the course of the centuries been the home of three generations at once during one and twenty years.

The lover of romance may lie in the sun, caring not for the time of day and content to watch the butterflies that cross his blue sky on the way from one flower to another. But the historian is an entomologist who must be stirring. He must catch the moths, which are his facts, in the net which is his memory, and he must fasten them upon his paper with sharp pins, which are dates.

By far the greater number of old Prince Saracinesca's contemporaries are dead, and more or less justly forgotten. Old Valdarno died long ago in his bed, surrounded by sons and daughters. The famous dandy of other days, the Duke of Astrardente, died at his young wife's feet some three and twenty years before this chapter of family history opens. Then the primeval Prince Montevarchi came to a violent end at the hands of his librarian, leaving his English princess consolable but unconsoled, leaving also his daughter Flavia married to that other Giovanni Saracinesca who still bears the name of Marchese di San Giacinto; while the younger girl, the fair, brown-eyed Faustina, loved a poor Frenchman, half soldier and all artist. The weak, good-natured Ascanio Bellegra reigns in his father's stead, the timidly extravagant master of all that wealth which the miser's lean and crooked fingers had consigned to a safe keeping. Frangipani too, whose son was to have married Faustina, is gone these many years, and others of the older and graver sort have learned the great secret from the lips of death.

But there have been other and greater deaths, beside which the mortality of a whole society of noblemen sinks into insignificance. An empire is dead and another has arisen in the din of a vast war, begotten in bloodshed, brought forth in strife, baptized with fire. The France we knew is gone, and the

French Republic writes "Liberty, Fraternity, Equality" in great red letters above the gate of its habitation, which within is yet hung with mourning. Out of the nest of kings and princes and princelings, and of all manner of rulers great and small, rises the solitary eagle of the new German Empire and hangs on black wings between sky and earth, not striking again, but always ready, a vision of armed peace, a terror, a problem—perhaps a warning.

Old Rome is dead, too, never to be old Rome again. The last breath has been breathed, the aged eyes are closed for ever, corruption has done its work, and the grand skeleton lies bleaching upon seven hills, half covered with the piecemeal stucco of a modern architectural body. The result is satisfactory to those who have brought it about, if not to the rest of the world. The sepulchre of old Rome is the new capital of united Italy.

The three chief actors are dead also—the man of heart, the man of action and the man of wit, the good, the brave and, the cunning, the Pope, the King and the Cardinal—Pius the Ninth, Victor Emmanuel the Second, Giacomo Antonelli. Rome saw them all dead.

In a poor chamber of the Vatican, upon a simple bed, beside which burned two waxen torches in the cold morning light, lay the body of the man whom none had loved and many had feared, clothed in the violet robe of the cardinal-deacon. The keen face was drawn up on one side with a strange look of mingled pity and contempt. The delicate, thin hands were clasped together on the breast. The chilly light fell upon the dead features, the silken robe and the stone floor. A single servant in a shabby livery stood in a corner, smiling foolishly, while the tears stood in his eyes and wet his unshaven cheeks. Perhaps he cared, as servants will, when no one else cares. The door opened almost directly upon a staircase and the noise of the feet of those passing up and down upon the stone steps disturbed the silence in the death chamber. At night the poor body was thrust unhonoured into a common coach and driven out to its resting-place.

In a vast hall, upon an enormous catafalque, full thirty feet above the floor, lay all that was left of the honest king. Thousands of wax candles cast their light up to the dark, shapeless face, and upon the military accoutrements of the uniform in which the huge body was clothed. A great crowd pressed to the railing to gaze their fill and go away. Behind the division tall troopers in cuirasses mounted guard and moved carelessly about. It was all tawdry, but tawdry on a magnificent scale—all unlike the man in whose honour it was done. For he had been simple and brave.

When he was at last borne to his tomb in the Pantheon, a file of imperial and royal princes marched shoulder to shoulder down the street before him, and the black charger he had loved was led after him.

In a dim chapel of St. Peter's lay the Pope, robed in white, the jewelled tiara upon his head, his white face calm and peaceful. Six torches burned beside him; six nobles of the guard stood like statues with drawn swords, three on his right hand and three on his left. That was all. The crowd passed in single file before the great closed gates of the Julian Chapel.

At night he was borne reverently by loving hands to the deep crypt below. But at another time, at night also, the dead man was taken up and driven towards the gate to be buried without the walls. Then a great crowd assembled in the darkness and fell upon the little band and stoned the coffin of him who never harmed any man, and screamed out curses and blasphemies till all the city was astir with riot. That was the last funeral hymn.

Old Rome is gone. The narrow streets are broad thoroughfares, the Jews' quarter is a flat and dusty building lot, the fountain of Ponte Sisto is swept away, one by one the mighty pines of Villa Ludovisi have fallen under axe and saw, and a cheap, thinly inhabited quarter is built upon the site of the enchanted garden. The network of by-ways from the Jesuits' church to the Sant' Angelo bridge is ploughed up and opened by the huge Corso Vittorio Emmanuele. Buildings which strangers used to search for in the shade, guide-book and map in hand, are suddenly brought into the blaze of light that fills broad streets and sweeps across great squares. The vast Cancelleria stands out nobly to the sun, the curved front of the Massimo palace exposes its black colonnade to sight upon the greatest thoroughfare of the new city, the ancient Arco de' Cenci exhibits its squalor in unshadowed sunshine, the Portico of Octavia once more looks upon the river.

He who was born and bred in the Rome of twenty years ago comes back after a long absence to wander as a stranger in streets he never knew, among houses unfamiliar to him, amidst a population whose speech sounds strange in his ears. He roams the city from the Lateran to the Tiber, from the Tiber to the Vatican, finding himself now and then before some building once familiar in another aspect, losing himself perpetually in unprofitable wastes made more monotonous than the sandy desert by the modern builder's art. Where once he lingered in old days to glance at the river, or to dream of days yet older and long gone, scarce conscious of the beggar at his elbow and hardly seeing the half dozen workmen who laboured at their trades almost in the middle of the public way—where all was once aged and silent and melancholy and full of the elder memories—there, at that very corner, he is hustled and jostled by an eager crowd, thrust to the wall by huge, grinding, creaking carts, threatened with the modern death by the wheel of the modern omnibus, deafened by the yells of the modern newsvendors, robbed, very likely, by the light fingers of the modern inhabitant.

And yet he feels that Rome must be Rome still. He stands aloof and gazes at the sight as upon a play in which Rome herself is the great heroine and actress. He knows the woman and he sees the artist for the first time, not recognising her. She is a dark-eyed, black-haired, thoughtful woman when not upon the stage. How should he know her in the strange disguise, her head decked with Gretchen's fair tresses, her olive cheek daubed with pink and white paint, her stately form clothed in garments that would be gay and girlish but which are only unbecoming? He would gladly go out and wait by the stage door until the performance is over, to see the real woman pass him in the dim light of the street lamps as she enters her carriage and becomes herself again. And so, in the reality, he turns his back upon the crowd and strolls away, not caring whither he goes until, by a mere accident, he finds himself upon the height of Sant' Onofrio, or standing before the great fountains of the Acqua Paola, or perhaps upon the drive which leads through the old Villa Corsini along the crest of the Janiculum. Then, indeed, the scene thus changes, the actress is gone and the woman is before him; the capital of modern Italy sinks like a vision into the earth out of which it was called up, and the capital of the world rises once more, unchanged, unchanging and unchangeable, before the wanderer's eyes. The greater monuments of greater times are there still, majestic and unmoved, the larger signs of a larger age stand out clear and sharp; the tomb of Hadrian frowns on the yellow stream, the heavy hemisphere of the Pantheon turns its single opening to the sky, the enormous dome of the world's cathedral looks silently down upon the sepulchre of the world's masters.

Then the sun sets and the wanderer goes down again through the chilly evening air to the city below, to find it less modern than he had thought. He has found what he sought and he knows that the real will outlast the false, that the stone will outlive the stucco and that the builder of to-day is but a builder of card-houses beside the architects who made Rome.

So his heart softens a little, or at least grows less resentful, for he has realised how small the change really is as compared with the first effect produced. The great house has fallen into new hands and the latest tenant is furnishing the dwelling to his taste. That is all. He will not tear down the walls, for his hands are too feeble to build them again, even if he were not occupied with other matters and hampered by the disagreeable consciousness of the extravagances he has already committed.

Other things have been accomplished, some of which may perhaps endure, and some of which are good in themselves, while some are indifferent and some distinctly bad. The great experiment of Italian unity is in process of trial and the world is already forming its opinion upon the results. Society, heedless as it necessarily is of contemporary history, could not remain indifferent to the transformation of its accustomed surroundings; and here, before entering upon an account of individual doings, the chronicler may be allowed to say a few words upon a matter little understood by foreigners, even when they have spent several seasons in Rome and have made acquaintance with each other for the purpose of criticising the Romans.

Immediately after the taking of the city in 1870, three distinct parties declared themselves, to wit, the Clericals or Blacks, the Monarchists or Whites, and the Republicans or Beds. All three had doubtless existed for a considerable time, but the wine of revolution favoured the expression of the truth, and society awoke one morning to find itself divided into camps holding very different opinions.

At first the mass of the greater nobles stood together for the lost temporal power of the Pope, while a great number of the less important families followed two or three great houses in siding with the Royalists. The Republican idea, as was natural, found but few sympathisers in the highest class, and these were, I believe, in all cases young men whose fathers were Blacks or Whites, and most of whom have since thought fit to modify their opinions in one direction or the other. Nevertheless the Red interest was, and still is, tolerably strong and has been destined to play that powerful part in parliamentary life, which generally falls to the lot of a compact third party, where a fourth does not yet exist, or has no political influence, as is the case in Rome.

For there is a fourth body in Rome, which has little political but much social importance. It was not possible that people who had grown up together in the intimacy of a close caste-life, calling each other "thee" and "thou," and forming the hereditary elements of a still feudal organisation, should suddenly break off all acquaintance and be strangers one to another. The brother, a born and convinced clerical, found that his own sister had followed her husband to the court of the new King. The rigid adherent of the old order met his own son in the street, arrayed in the garb of an Italian officer. The two friends who had stood side by side in good and evil case for a score of years saw themselves suddenly divided by the gulf which lies between a Roman cardinal and a Senator of the Italian Kingdom. The breach was sudden and great, but it was bridged for many by the invention of a fourth, proportional. The points of contact between White and Black became Grey, and a social power, politically neutral and constitutionally indifferent, arose as a mediator between the Contents and the Malcontents. There were families that had never loved the old order but which distinctly disliked the new, and who opened their doors to the adherents of both. There is a house which has become Grey out of a sort of superstition inspired by the unfortunate circumstances which oddly coincided with each movement of its members to join the new order. There is another, and one of the greatest, in which a very high hereditary dignity in the one party, still exercised by force of circumstances, effectually forbids the expression of a sincere sympathy with the opposed power. Another there is, whose members are cousins of the one sovereign and personal friends of the other.

A further means of amalgamation has been found in the existence of the double embassies of the great powers. Austria, France and Spain each send an Ambassador to the King of Italy and an Ambassador to the Pope, of like state and importance. Even Protestant Prussia maintains a Minister Plenipotentiary to the Holy See. Russia has her diplomatic agent to the Vatican, and several of the smaller powers keep up two distinct legations. It is naturally neither possible nor intended that these diplomatists should never meet on friendly terms, though they are strictly interdicted from issuing official invitations to each other. Their point of contact is another grey square on the chess-board.

The foreigner, too, is generally a neutral individual, for if his political convictions lean towards the wrong side of the Tiber his social tastes incline to Court balls; or if he is an admirer of Italian institutions, his curiosity may yet lead him to seek a presentation at the Vatican, and his inexplicable though recent love of feudal princedom may take him, card-case in hand, to that great stronghold of Vaticanism which lies due west of the Piazza di Venezia and due north of the Capitol.

During the early years which followed the change, the attitude of society in Rome was that of protest and indignation on the one hand, of enthusiasm and rather brutally expressed triumph on the other. The line was very clearly drawn, for the adherence was of the nature of personal loyalty on both sides. Eight years and a half later the personal feeling disappeared with the almost simultaneous death of Pius IX. and Victor Emmanuel II. From that time the great strife degenerated by degrees into a difference of opinion. It may perhaps be said also that both parties became aware of their common enemy, the social democrat, soon after the disappearance of the popular King whose great individual influence was of more value to the cause of a united monarchy than all the political clubs and organisations in Italy put together. He was a strong man. He only once, I think, yielded to the pressure of a popular excitement, namely, in the matter of seizing Rome when the French troops were withdrawn, thereby violating a ratified Treaty. But his position was a hard one. He regretted the apparent necessity, and to the day of his death he never would sleep under the roof of Pius the Ninth's Palace on the Quirinal, but had his private apartments in an adjoining building. He was brave and generous. Such faults as he had were no burden to the nation and concerned himself alone. The same praise may be worthily bestowed upon his successor, but the personal influence is no longer the same, any more than that of Leo XIII. can be compared with that of Pius IX., though all the world is aware of the present Pope's intellectual superiority and lofty moral principle.

Let us try to be just. The unification of Italy has been the result of a noble conception. The execution of the scheme has not been without faults, and some of these faults have brought about deplorable, even disastrous, consequences, such as to endanger the stability of the new order. The worst of these attendant errors has been the sudden imposition of a most superficial and vicious culture, under the name of enlightenment and education. The least of the new Government's mistakes has been a squandering of the public money, which, when considered with reference to the country's resources, has perhaps no parallel in the history of nations.

Yet the first idea was large, patriotic, even grand. The men who first steered the ship of the state were honourable, disinterested, devoted—men like Minghetti, who will not soon be forgotten—loyal, conservative monarchists, whose thoughts were free from exaggeration, save that they believed almost too blindly in the power of a constitution to build up a kingdom, and credited their fellows almost too readily with a purpose as pure and blameless as their own. Can more be said for these? I think not. They rest in honourable graves, their doings live in honoured remembrance—would that there had been such another generation to succeed them.

And having said thus much, let us return to the individuals who have played a part in the history of the Saracinesca. They have grown older, some gracefully, some under protest, some most unbecomingly.

In the end of the year 1887 old Leone Saracinesca is still alive, being eighty-two years of age. His massive head has sunk a little between his slightly rounded shoulders, and his white beard is no longer cut short and square, but flows majestically down upon his broad breast. His step is slow, but firm still, and when he looks up suddenly from under his wrinkled lids, the fire is not even yet all gone from his eyes. He is still contradictory by nature, but he has mellowed like rare wine in the long years of prosperity and peace. When the change came in Rome he was in the mountains at Saracinesca, with his daughter-in-law, Corona and her children. His son Giovanni, generally known as Prince of Sant' Ilario, was among the volunteers at the last and sat for half a day upon his horse in the Pincio, listening to the bullets that sang over his head while his men fired stray shots from the parapets of the public garden into the road below. Giovanni is fifty-two years old, but though his hair is grey at the temples and his figure a trifle sturdier and broader than of old, he is little changed. His son, Orsino, who will soon be of age, overtops him by a head and shoulders, a dark youth, slender still, but strong and active, the chief person in this portion of my chronicle. Orsino has three brothers of ranging ages, of whom the youngest is scarcely twelve years old. Not one girl child has been given to Giovanni and Corona and they almost wish that one of the sturdy little lads had been a daughter. But old Saracinesca laughs and shakes his head and says he will not die till his four grandsons are strong enough to bear him to his grave upon their shoulders.

Corona is still beautiful, still dark, still magnificent, though she has reached the age beyond which no woman ever goes until after death. There are few lines in the noble face and such as are there are not the scars of heart wounds. Her life, too, has been peaceful and undisturbed by great events these many years. There is, indeed, one perpetual anxiety in her existence, for the old prince is an aged man and she loves him dearly. The tough strength must give way some day and there will be a great mourning in the house of Saracinesca, nor will any mourn the dead more sincerely than Corona. And there is a shade of bitterness in the knowledge that her marvellous beauty is waning. Can she be blamed for that? She has been beautiful so long. What woman who has been first for a quarter of a century can give up her place without a sigh? But much has been given to her to soften the years of transition, and she knows that also, when she looks from her husband to her four boys.

Then, too, it seems more easy to grow old when she catches a glimpse from time to time of Donna Tullia Del Ferice, who wears her years ungracefully, and who was once so near to becoming Giovanni Saracinesca's wife. Donna Tullia is fat and fiery of complexion, uneasily vivacious and unsure of herself. Her disagreeable blue eyes have not softened, nor has the metallic tone of her voice lost its sharpness. Yet she should not be a disappointed woman, for Del Ferice is a power in the land, a member of parliament, a financier and a successful schemer, whose doors are besieged by parasites and his dinner-table by those who wear fine raiment and dwell in kings' palaces. Del Ferice is the central figure in the great building syndicates which in 1887 are at the height of their power. He juggles with millions of money, with miles of real estate, with thousands of workmen. He is director of a bank, president of a political club, chairman of half a dozen companies and a deputy in the chambers. But his face is unnaturally pale, his body is over-corpulent, and he has trouble with his heart. The Del Ferice couple are childless, to their own great satisfaction.

Anastase Gouache, the great painter, is also in Rome. Sixteen years ago he married the love of his life, Faustina Montevarchi, in spite of the strong opposition of her family. But times had changed. A new law existed and the thrice repeated formal request for consent made by Faustina to her mother, freed her from parental authority and brotherly interference. She and her husband passed through some very lean years in the beginning, but fortune has smiled upon them since that. Anastase is very famous. His character has changed little. With the love of the ideal republic in his heart, he shed his blood at Mentana for the great conservative principle, he fired his last shot for the same cause at the Porta Pia on the twentieth of September 1870; a month later he was fighting for France under the gallant Charette—whether for France imperial, regal or republican he never paused to ask; he was wounded in fighting against the Commune, and decorated for painting the portrait of Gambetta, after which he returned to Rome, cursed politics and married the woman he loved, which was, on the whole, the wisest course he could have followed. He has two children, both girls, aged now respectively fifteen and thirteen. His virtues are many, but they do not include economy. Though his savings are small and he depends upon his brush, he lives in one wing of an historic palace and gives dinners which are famous. He proposes to reform and become a miser when his daughters are married.

"Misery will be the foundation of my second manner, my angel," he says to his wife, when he has done something unusually extravagant.

But Faustina laughs softly and winds her arm about his neck as they look together at the last great picture. Anastase has not grown fat. The gods love him and have promised him eternal youth. He can still buckle round his slim waist the military belt of twenty years ago, and there is scarcely one white thread in his black hair.

San Giacinto, the other Saracinesca, who married Faustina's elder sister Flavia, is in process of making a great fortune, greater perhaps than the one so nearly thrust upon him by old Montevarchi's compact with Meschini the librarian and forger. He had scarcely troubled himself to conceal his opinions before the change of government, being by nature a calm, fearless man, and under the new order he unhesitatingly sided with the Italians, to the great satisfaction of Flavia, who foresaw years of dulness for the mourning party of the Blacks. He had already brought to Rome the two boys who remained to him from his first marriage with Serafina Baldi—the little girl who had been born between the other two children had died in infancy—and the lads had been educated at a military college, and in 1887 are both officers in the Italian cavalry, sturdy and somewhat thick-skulled patriots, but gentlemen nevertheless in spite of the peasant blood. They are tall fellows enough but neither of them has inherited the father's colossal stature, and San Giacinto looks with a very little envy on his young kinsman Orsino who has outgrown his cousins. This second marriage has brought him issue, a boy and a girl, and the fact that he has now four children to provide for has had much to do with his activity in affairs. He was among the first to see that an enormous fortune was to be made in the first rush for land in the city, and he realised all he possessed, and borrowed to the full extent of his credit to pay the first instalments on the land he bought, risking everything with the calm determination and cool judgment which lay at the root of his strong character. He was immensely successful, but though he had been bold to recklessness at the right moment, he saw the great crash looming in the near future, and when the many were frantic to buy and invest, no matter at what loss, his millions were in part safely deposited in national bonds, and in part as securely invested in solid and profitable buildings of which the rents are little liable to fluctuation. Brought up to know what money means, he is not easily carried away by enthusiastic reports. He knows that when the hour of fortune is at hand no price is too great to pay for ready capital, but he understands that when the great rush for success begins the psychological moment of finance is already passed. When he dies, if such strength as his can yield to death, he will die the richest man in Italy, and he will leave what is rare in Italian finance, a stainless name.

Of one person more I must speak, who has played a part in this family history. The melancholy Spicca still lives his lonely life in the midst of the social world. He affects to be a little old-fashioned in his dress. His tall thin body stoops ominously and his cadaverous face is more grave and ascetic than ever. He is said to have been suffering from a mortal disease these fifteen years, but still he goes everywhere, reads everything and knows every one. He is between sixty and seventy years old, but no one knows his precise age. The foils he once used so well hang untouched and rusty above his fireplace, but his reputation survives the lost strength of his supple wrist, and there are few in Rome, brave men or hairbrained youths, who would willingly anger him even now. He is still the great duellist of his day; the emaciated fingers might still find their old grip upon a sword hilt, the long, listless arm might perhaps once more shoot out with lightning speed, the dull eye might once again light up at the clash of steel. Peaceable, charitable when none are at hand to see him give, gravely gentle now in manner, Count Spicca is thought dangerous still. But he is indeed very lonely in his old age, and if the truth be told his fortune seems to have suffered sadly of late years, so that he rarely leaves Rome, even in the hot summer, and it is very long since he spent six weeks in Paris or risked a handful of gold at Monte Carlo. Yet his life is not over, and he has still a part to play, for his own sake and for the sake of another, as shall soon appear more clearly.

CHAPTER II

Orsino Saracinesca's education was almost completed. It had been of the modern kind, for his father had early recognised that it would be a disadvantage to the young man in after life if he did not follow the course of study and pass the examinations required of every Italian subject who wishes to hold office in his own country. Accordingly, though he had not been sent to public schools, Orsino had been regularly entered since his childhood for the public examinations and had passed them all in due order, with great difficulty and indifferent credit. After this preliminary work he had been at an English University for four terms, not with any view to his obtaining a degree after completing the necessary residence, but in order that he might perfect himself in the English language, associate with young men of his own age and social standing, though of different nationality, and acquire that final polish which is so highly valued in the human furniture of society's temples.

Orsino was not more highly gifted as to intelligence than many young men of his age and class. Like many of them he spoke English admirably, French tolerably, and Italian with a somewhat Roman twang. He had learned a little German and was rapidly forgetting it again; Latin and Greek had been exhibited to him as dead languages, and he felt no more inclination to assist in their resurrection than is felt by most boys in our day. He had been taught geography in the practical, continental manner, by being obliged to draw maps from memory. He had been instructed in history, not by parallels, but as it were by tangents, a method productive of odd results, and he had advanced just far enough in the study of mathematics to be thoroughly confused by the terms "differentiation" and "integration." Besides these subjects, a multitude of moral and natural sciences had been made to pass in a sort of panorama before his intellectual vision, including physics, chemistry, logic, rhetoric, ethics and political economy, with a view to cultivating in him the spirit of the age. The Ministry of Public Instruction having decreed that the name of God shall be for ever eliminated from all modern books in use in Italian schools and universities, Orsino's religious instruction had been imparted at home and had at least the advantage of being homogeneous.

It must not be supposed that Orsino's father and mother were satisfied with this sort of education. But it was not easy to foresee what social and political changes might come about before the boy reached mature manhood. Neither Giovanni nor his wife were of the absolutely "intransigent" way of thinking. They saw no imperative reason to prevent their sons from joining at some future time in the public life of their country, though they themselves preferred not to associate with the party at present in power. Moreover Giovanni Saracinesca saw that the abolition of primogeniture had put an end to hereditary idleness, and that although his sons would be rich enough to do nothing if they pleased, yet his grandchildren would probably have to choose between work and genteel poverty, if it pleased the fates to multiply the race. He could indeed leave one half of his wealth intact to Orsino, but the law required that the other half should be equally divided among all; and as the same thing would take place in the second generation, unless a reactionary revolution intervened, the property would before long be divided into very small moieties indeed. For Giovanni had no idea of imposing celibacy upon his younger sons, still less of exerting any influence he possessed to make them enter the Church. He was too broad in his views for that. They promised to turn out as good men in a struggle as the majority of those who would be opposed to them in life, and they should fight their own battles unhampered by parental authority or caste prejudice.

Many years earlier Giovanni had expressed his convictions in regard to the change of order then imminent. He had said that he would fight as long as there was anything to fight for, but that if the change came he would make the best of it. He was now keeping his word. He had fought as far as fighting had been possible and had sincerely wished that his warlike career might have offered more excitement and opportunity for personal distinction than had been afforded him in spending an afternoon on horseback, listening to the singing of bullets overhead. His amateur soldiering was over long ago, but he was strong, brave and intelligent, and if he had been convinced that a second and more radical revolution could accomplish any good result, he would have been capable of devoting himself to its cause with a single-heartedness not usual in these days. But he was not convinced. He therefore lived a quiet life, making the best of the present, improving his lands and doing his best to bring up his sons in such a way as to give them a chance of success when the struggle should come. Orsino was his eldest born and the results of modern education became apparent in him first, as was inevitable.

Orsino was at this time not quite twenty-one years of age, but the important day was not far distant and in order to leave a lasting memorial of the attaining of his majority Prince Saracinesca had decreed that Corona should receive a portrait of her eldest son executed by the celebrated Anastase Gouache. To this end the young man spent three mornings in every week in the artist's palatial studio, a place about as different from the latter's first den in the Via San Basilio as the Basilica of Saint Peter is different from a roadside chapel in the Abruzzi. Those who have seen the successful painter of the nineteenth century in his glory will have less difficulty in imagining the scene of Gouache's labours than the writer finds in describing it. The workroom is a hall, the ceiling is a vault thirty feet high, the pavement is of polished marble; the light enters by north windows which would not look small in a good-sized church, the doors would admit a carriage and pair, the tapestries upon the walls would cover the front of a modern house. Everything is on a grand scale, of the best period, of the most genuine description. Three or four originals of great masters, of Titian, of Reubens, of Van Dyck, stand on huge easels in the most favourable lights. Some scores of matchless antique fragments, both of bronze and marble, are placed here and there upon superb carved tables and shelves of the sixteenth century. The only reproduction visible in the place is a very perfect cast of the Hermes of Olympia. The carpets are all of Shiraz, Sinna, Gjordez or old Baku—no common thing of Smyrna, no unclean aniline production of Russo-Asiatic commerce disturbs the universal harmony. In a full light upon the wall hangs a single silk carpet of wonderful tints, famous in the history of Eastern collections, and upon it is set at a slanting angle a single priceless Damascus blade—a sword to possess which an Arab or a Circassian would commit countless crimes. Anastase Gouache is magnificent in all his tastes and in all his ways. His studio and his dwelling are his only estate, his only capital, his only wealth, and he does not take the trouble to conceal the fact. The very idea of a fixed income is as distasteful to him as the possibility of possessing it is distant and visionary. There is always money in abundance, money for Faustina's horses and carriages, money for Gouache's select dinners, money for the expensive fancies of both. The paint pot is the mine, the brush is the miner's pick, and the vein has never failed, nor the hand trembled in working it. A golden youth, a golden river flowing softly to the red gold sunset of the end—that is life as it seems to Anastase and Faustina.

On the morning which opens this chronicle, Anastase was standing before his canvas, palette and brushes in hand, considering the nature of the human face in general and of young Orsino's face in particular.

"I have known your father and mother for centuries," observed the painter with a fine disregard of human limitations. "Your father is the brown type of a dark man, and your mother is the olive type of a dark woman. They are no more alike than a Red Indian and an Arab, but you are like both. Are you brown or are you olive, my friend? That is the question. I would like to see you angry, or in love, or losing at play. Those things bring out the real complexion."

Orsino laughed and showed a remarkably solid set of teeth. But he did not find anything to say.

"I would like to know the truth about your complexion," said Anastase, meditatively.

"I have no particular reason for being angry," answered Orsino, "and I am not in love—"

"At your age! Is it possible!"

"Quite. But I will play cards with you if you like," concluded the young man.

"No," returned the other. "It would be of no use. You would win, and if you happened to win much, I should be in a diabolical scrape. But I wish you would fall in love. You should see how I would handle the green shadows under your eyes."

"It is rather short notice."

"The shorter the better. I used to think that the only real happiness in life lay in getting into trouble, and the only real interest in getting out."

"And have you changed your mind?"

"I? No. My mind has changed me. It is astonishing how a man may love his wife under favourable circumstances."

Anastase laid down his brushes and lit a cigarette. Reubens would have sipped a few drops of Rhenish from a Venetian glass. Teniers would have lit a clay pipe. Dürer would perhaps have swallowed a pint of Nüremberg beer, and Greuse or Mignard would have resorted to their snuff-boxes. We do not know what Michelangelo or Perugino did under the circumstances, but it is tolerably evident that the man of the nineteenth century cannot think without talking and cannot talk without cigarettes. Therefore Anastase began to smoke and Orsino, being young and imitative, followed his example.

"You have been an exceptionally fortunate man," remarked the latter, who was not old enough to be anything but cynical in his views of life.

"Do you think so? Yes—I have been fortunate. But I do not like to think that my happiness has been so very exceptional. The world is a good place, full of happy people. It must be—otherwise purgatory and hell would be useless institutions."

"You do not suppose all people to be good as well as happy then," said Orsino with a laugh.

"Good? What is goodness, my friend? One half of the theologians tell us that we shall be happy if we are good and the other half assure us that the only way to be good is to abjure earthly happiness. If you will believe me, you will never commit the supreme error of choosing between the two methods. Take the world as it is, and do not ask too many questions of the fates. If you are willing to be happy, happiness will come in its own shape."

Orsino's young face expressed rather contemptuous amusement. At twenty, happiness is a dull word, and satisfaction spells excitement.

"That is the way people talk," he said. "You have got everything by fighting for it, and you advise me to sit still till the fruit drops into my mouth."

"I was obliged to fight. Everything comes to you naturally—fortune, rank—everything, including marriage. Why should you lift a hand?"

"A man cannot possibly be happy who marries before he is thirty years old," answered Orsino with conviction. "How do you expect me to occupy myself during the next ten years?"

"That is true," Gouache replied, somewhat thoughtfully, as though the consideration had not struck him.

"If I were an artist, it would be different."

"Oh, very different. I agree with you." Anastase smiled good-humouredly.

"Because I should have talent—and a talent is an occupation in itself."

"I daresay you would have talent," Gouache answered, still laughing.

"No—I did not mean it in that way—I mean that when a man has a talent it makes him think of something besides himself."

"I fancy there is more truth in that remark than either you or I would at first think," said the painter in a meditative tone.

"Of course there is," returned the youthful philosopher, with more enthusiasm than he would have cared to show if he had been talking to a woman. "What is talent but a combination of the desire to do and the power to accomplish? As for genius, it is never selfish when it is at work."

"Is that reflection your own?"

"I think so," answered Orsino modestly. He was secretly pleased that a man of the artist's experience and reputation should be struck by his remark.

"I do not think I agree with you," said Gouache.

Orsino's expression changed a little. He was disappointed, but he said nothing.

"I think that a great genius is often ruthless. Do you remember how Beethoven congratulated a young composer after the first performance of his opera? 'I like your opera—I will write music to it.' That was a fine instance of unselfishness, was it not. I can see the young man's face—" Anastase smiled.

"Beethoven was not at work when he made the remark," observed Orsino, defending himself.

"Nor am I," said Gouache, taking up his brushes again. "If you will resume the pose—so—thoughtful but bold—imagine that you are already an ancestor contemplating posterity from the height of a nobler age—you understand. Try and look as if you were already framed and hanging in the Saracinesca gallery between a Titian and a Giorgione."

Orsino resumed his position and scowled at Anastase with a good will.

"Not quite such a terrible frown, perhaps," suggested the latter. "When you do that, you certainly look like the gentleman who murdered the Colonna in a street brawl—I forget how long ago. You have his portrait. But I fancy the Princess would prefer—yes—that is more natural. You have her eyes. How the world raved about her twenty years ago—and raves still, for that matter."

"She is the most beautiful woman in the world," said Orsino. There was something in the boy's unaffected admiration of his mother which contrasted pleasantly with his youthful affectation of cynicism and indifference. His handsome face lighted up a little, and the painter worked rapidly.

But the expression was not lasting. Orsino was at the age when most young men take the trouble to cultivate a manner, and the look of somewhat contemptuous gravity which he had lately acquired was already becoming habitual. Since all men in general have adopted the fashion of the mustache, youths who are still waiting for the full crop seem to have difficulty in managing their mouths. Some draw in their lips with that air of unnatural sternness observable in rough weather among passengers on board ship, just before they relinquish the struggle and retire from public life. Others contract their mouths to the shape of a heart, while there are yet others who lose control of the pendant lower lip and are content to look like idiots, while expecting the hairy growth which is to make them look like men. Orsino had chosen the least objectionable idiosyncrasy and had elected to be of a stern countenance. When he forgot himself he was singularly handsome, and Gouache lay in wait for his moments of forgetfulness.

"You are quite right," said the Frenchman. "From the classic point of view your mother was and is the most beautiful dark woman in the world. For myself—well in the first place, you are her son, and secondly I am an artist and not a critic. The painter's tongue is his brush and his words are colours."

"What were you going to say about my mother?" asked Orsino with some curiosity.

"Oh—nothing. Well, if you must hear it, the Princess represents my classical ideal, but not my personal ideal. I have admired some one else more."

"Donna Faustina?" enquired Orsino.

"Ah well, my friend—she is my wife, you see. That always makes a great difference in the degree of admiration—"

"Generally in the opposite direction," Orsino observed in a tone of elderly unbelief.

Gouache had just put his brush into his mouth and held it between his teeth as a poodle carries a stick, while he used his thumb on the canvas. The modern painter paints with everything, not excepting his fingers. He glanced at his model and then at his work, and got his effect before he answered.

"You are very hard upon marriage," he said quietly. "Have you tried it?"

"Not yet. I will wait as long as possible, before I do. It is not every one who has your luck."

"There was something more than luck in my marriage. We loved each other, it is true, but there were difficulties—you have no idea what difficulties there were. But Faustina was brave and I caught a little courage from her. Do you know that when the Serristori barracks were blown up she ran out alone to find me merely because she thought I might have been killed? I found her in the ruins, praying for me. It was sublime."

"I have heard that. She was very brave—"

"And I a poor Zouave—and a poorer painter. Are there such women nowadays? Bah! I have not known them. We used to meet at churches and exchange two words while her maid was gone to get her a chair. Oh, the good old time! And then the separations—the taking of Rome, when the old Princess carried all the family off to England and stayed there while we were fighting for poor France—and the coming back and the months of waiting, and the notes dropped from her window at midnight and the great quarrel with her family when we took advantage of the new law. And then the marriage itself— what a scandal in Rome! But for the Princess, your mother, I do not know what we should have done. She brought Faustina to the church and drove us to the station in her own carriage—in the face of society. They say that Ascanio Bellegra hung about the door of the church while we were being married, but he had not the courage to come in, for fear of his mother. We went to Naples and lived on salad and love—and we had very little else for a year or two. I was not much known, then, except in Rome, and Roman society refused to have its portrait painted by the adventurer who had run away with a daughter of Casa Montevarchi. Perhaps, if we had been rich, we should have hated each other by this time. But we had to live for each other in those days, for every one was against us. I painted, and she kept house—that English blood is always practical in a desert. And it was a desert. The cooking—it would have made a billiard ball's hair stand on end with astonishment. She made the salad, and then evolved the roast from the inner consciousness. I painted a chaudfroid on an old plate. It was well done—the transparent quality of the jelly and the delicate ortolans imprisoned within, imploring dissection. Well, must I tell you? We threw it away. It was martyrdom. Saint Anthony's position was enviable compared with ours. Beside us that good man would have seemed but a humbug. Yet we lived through it all. I repeat it. We lived, and we were happy. It is amazing, how a man may love his wife."

Anastase had told his story with many pauses, working hard while he spoke, for though he was quite in earnest in all he said, his chief object was to distract the young man's attention, so as to bring out his natural expression. Having exhausted one of the colours he needed, he drew back and contemplated his work. Orsino seemed lost in thought.

"What are you thinking about?" asked the painter.

"Do you think I am too old to become an artist?" enquired the young man.

"You? Who knows? But the times are too old. It is the same thing."

"I do not understand."

"You are in love with the life—not with the profession. But the life is not the same now, nor the art either. Bah! In a few years I shall be out of fashion. I know it. Then we will go back to first principles. A garret to live in, bread and salad for dinner. Of course—what do you expect? That need not prevent us from living in a palace as long as we can."

Thereupon Anastase Gouache hummed a very lively little song as he squeezed a few colours from the tubes. Orsino's face betrayed his discontentment.

"I was not in earnest," he said. "At least, not as to becoming an artist. I only asked the question to be sure that you would answer it just as everybody answers all questions of the kind—by discouraging my wish do anything for myself."

"Why should you do anything? You are so rich!"

"What everybody says! Do you know what we rich men, or we men who are to be rich, are expected to be? Farmers. It is not gay."

"It would be my dream—pastoral, you know—Normandy cows, a river with reeds, perpetual Angelus, bread and milk for supper. I adore milk. A nymph here and there—at your age, it is permitted. My dear friend, why not be a farmer?"

Orsino laughed a little, in spite of himself.

"I suppose that is an artist's idea of farming."

"As near the truth as a farmer's idea of art, I daresay," retorted Gouache.

"We see you paint, but you never see us at work. That is the difference—but that is not the question. Whatever I propose, I get the same answer. I imagine you will permit me to dislike farming as a profession."

"For the sake of argument, only," said Gouache gravely.

"Good. For the sake of argument. We will suppose that I am myself in all respects what I am, excepting that I am never to have any land, and only enough money to buy cigarettes. I say, 'Let me take a profession. Let me be a soldier.' Every one rises up and protests against the idea of a Saracinesca serving in the Italian army. Why? Remember that your father was a volunteer officer under Pope Pius Ninth.' It is comic. He spent an afternoon on the Pincio for his convictions, and then retired into private life. 'Let me serve in a foreign army—France, Austria, Russia, I do not care.' They are more horrified than ever. 'You have not a spark of patriotism! To serve a foreign power! How dreadful! And as for the Russians, they are all heretics.' Perhaps they are. I will try diplomacy. 'What? Sacrifice your convictions? Become the blind instrument of a scheming, dishonest ministry? It is unworthy of a Saracinesca!' I will think no more about it. Let me be a lawyer and enter public life. 'A lawyer indeed! Will you wrangle in public with notaries' sons, defend murderers and burglars, and take fees like the old men who write letters for the peasants under a green umbrella in the street? It would be almost better to turn musician and give concerts.' 'The Church, perhaps?' I suggest. 'The Church? Are you not the heir, and will you not be the head of the family some day? You must be mad.' 'Then give me a sum of money and let me try my luck with my cousin San Giacinto.' 'Business? If you make money it is a degradation, and with these new laws you cannot afford to lose it. Besides, you will have enough of business when you have to manage your estates.' So all my questions are answered, and I am condemned at twenty to be a farmer for my natural life. I say so. 'A farmer, forsooth! Have you not the world before you? Have you not received the most liberal education? Are you not rich? How can you take such a narrow view! Come out to the Villa and look at those young thoroughbreds, and afterwards we will drop in at the club before dinner. Then there is that reception at the old Principessa Befana's to-night, and the Duchessa della Seccatura is also at home.' That is my life, Monsieur Gouache. There you have the question, the answer and the result. Admit that it is not gay."

"It is very serious, on the contrary," answered Gouache who had listened to the detached Jeremiah with more curiosity and interest than he often shewed.

"I see nothing for it, but for you to fall in love without losing a single moment."

Orsino laughed a little harshly.

"I am in the humour, I assure you," he answered.

"Well, then—what are you waiting for?" enquired Gouache, looking at him.

"What for? For an object for my affections, of course. That is rather necessary under the circumstances."

"You may not wait long, if you will consent to stay here another quarter of an hour," said Anastase with a laugh. "A lady is coming, whose portrait I am painting—an interesting woman—tolerably beautiful—rather mysterious—here she is, you can have a good look at her, before you make up your mind."

Anastase took the half-finished portrait of Orsino from the easel and put another in its place, considerably further advanced in execution. Orsino lit a cigarette in order to quicken his judgment, and looked at the canvas.

The picture was decidedly striking and one felt at once that it must be a good likeness. Gouache was evidently proud of it. It represented a woman, who was certainly not yet thirty years of age, in full dress, seated in a high, carved chair against a warm, dark background. A mantle of some sort of heavy, claret-coloured brocade, lined with fur, was draped across one of the beautiful shoulders, leaving the other bare, the scant dress of the period scarcely breaking the graceful lines from the throat to the soft white hand, of which the pointed fingers hung carelessly over the carved extremity of the arm of the chair. The lady's hair was auburn, her eyes distinctly yellow. The face was an unusual one and not without attraction, very pale, with a full red mouth too wide for perfect beauty, but well modelled—almost too well, Gouache thought. The nose was of no distinct type, and was the least significant feature in the face, but the forehead was broad and massive, the chin soft, prominent and round, the brows much arched and divided by a vertical shadow which, in the original, might be the first indication of a tiny wrinkle. Orsino fancied that one eye or the other wandered a very little, but he could not tell which— the slight defect made the glance disquieting and yet attractive. Altogether it was one of those faces which to one man say too little, and to another too much.

Orsino affected to gaze upon the portrait with unconcern, but in reality he was oddly fascinated by it, and Gouache did not fail to see the truth.

"You had better go away, my friend," he said, with a smile. "She will be here in a few minutes and you will certainly lose your heart if you see her."

"What is her name?" asked Orsino, paying no attention to the remark.

"Donna Maria Consuelo—something or other—a string of names ending in Aragona. I call her Madame d'Aragona for shortness, and she does not seem to object."

"Married? And Spanish?"

"I suppose so," answered Gouache. "A widow I believe. She is not Italian and not French, so she must be Spanish."

"The name does not say much. Many people put 'd'Aragona' after their names—some cousins of ours, among others—they are Aranjuez d'Aragona—my father's mother was of that family."

"I think that is the name—Aranjuez. Indeed I am sure of it, for Faustina remarked that she might be related to you."

"It is odd. We have not heard of her being in Rome—and I am not sure who she is. Has she been here long?"

"I have known her a month—since she first came to my studio. She lives in a hotel, and she comes alone, except when I need the dress and then she brings her maid, an odd creature who never speaks and seems to understand no known language."

"It is an interesting face. Do you mind if I stay till she comes? We may really be cousins, you know."

"By all means—you can ask her. The relationship would be with her husband, I suppose."

"True. I had not thought of that; and he is dead, you say?"

Gouache did not answer, for at that moment the lady's footfall was heard upon the marble floor, soft, quick and decided. She paused a moment in the middle of the room when she saw that the artist was not alone. He went forward to meet her and asked leave to present Orsino, with that polite indistinctness which leaves to the persons introduced the task of discovering one another's names.

Orsino looked into the lady's eyes and saw that the slight peculiarity of the glance was real and not due to any error of Gouache's drawing. He recognised each feature in turn in the one look he gave at the face before he bowed, and he saw that the portrait was indeed very good. He was not subject to shyness.

"We should be cousins, Madame," he said. "My father's mother was an Aranjuez d'Aragona."

"Indeed?" said the lady with calm indifference, looking critically at the picture of herself.

"I am Orsino Saracinesca," said the young man, watching her with some admiration.

"Indeed?" she repeated, a shade less coldly. "I think I have heard my poor husband say that he was connected with your family. What do you think of my portrait? Every one has tried to paint me and failed, but my friend Monsieur Gouache is succeeding. He has reproduced my hideous nose and my dreadful mouth with a masterly exactness. No—my dear Monsieur Gouache—it is a compliment I pay you. I am in earnest. I do not want a portrait of the Venus of Milo with red hair, nor of the Minerva Medica with yellow eyes, nor of an imaginary Medea in a fur cloak. I want myself, just as I am. That is exactly what you are doing for me. Myself and I have lived so long together that I desire a little memento of the acquaintance."

"You can afford to speak lightly of what is so precious to others," said Gouache, gallantly. Madame d'Aranjuez sank into the carved chair Orsino had occupied.

"This dear Gouache—he is charming, is he not?" she said with a little laugh. Orsino looked at her.

"Gouache is right," he thought, with the assurance of his years. "It would be amusing to fall in love with her."

CHAPTER III

Gouache was far more interested in his work than in the opinions which his two visitors might entertain of each other. He looked at the lady fixedly, moved his easel, raised the picture a few inches higher from the ground and looked again. Orsino watched the proceedings from a little distance, debating whether he should go away or remain. Much depended upon Madame d'Aragona's character, he thought, and of this he knew nothing. Some women are attracted by indifference, and to go away would be to show a disinclination to press the acquaintance. Others, he reflected, prefer the assurance of the man who always stays, even without an invitation, rather than lose his chance. On the other hand a sitting in a studio is not exactly like a meeting in a drawing-room. The painter has a sort of traditional, exclusive right to his sitter's sole attention. The sitter, too, if a woman, enjoys the privilege of sacrificing one-half her good looks in a bad light, to favour the other side which is presented to the artist's view, and the third person, if there be one, has a provoking habit of so placing himself as to receive the least flattering impression. Hence the great unpopularity of the third person—or "the third inconvenience," as the Romans call him.

Orsino stood still for a few moments, wondering whether either of the two would ask him to sit down. As they did not, he was annoyed with them and determined to stay, if only for five minutes. He took up his position, in a deep seat under the high window, and watched Madame d'Aragona's profile. Neither she nor Gouache made any remark. Gouache began to brush over the face of his picture. Orsino felt that the silence was becoming awkward. He began to regret that he had remained, for he discovered from his present position that the lady's nose was indeed her defective feature.

"You do not mind my staying a few minutes?" he said, with a vague interrogation.

"Ask Madame, rather," answered Gouache, brushing away in a lively manner. Madame said nothing, and seemed not to have heard.

"Am I indiscreet?" asked Orsino.

"How? No. Why should you not remain? Only, if you please, sit where I can see you. Thanks. I do not like to feel that some one is looking at me and that I cannot look at him, if I please—and as for me, I am nailed in my position. How can I turn my head? Gouache is very severe."

"You may have heard, Madame, that a beautiful woman is most beautiful in repose," said Gouache.

Orsino was annoyed, for he had of course wished to make exactly the same remark. But they were talking in French, and the Frenchman had the advantage of speed.

"And how about an ugly woman?" asked Madame d'Aragona.

"Motion is most becoming to her—rapid motion—the door," answered the artist.

Orsino had changed his position and was standing behind Gouache.

"I wish you would sit down," said the latter, after a short pause. "I do not like to feel that any one is standing behind me when I am at work. It is a weakness, but I cannot help it. Do you believe in mental suggestion, Madame?"

"What is that?" asked Madame d'Aragona vaguely.

"I always imagine that a person standing behind me when I am at work is making me see everything as he sees," answered Gouache, not attempting to answer the question.

Orsino, driven from pillar to post, had again moved away.

"And do you believe in such absurd superstitions?" enquired Madame d'Aragona with a contemptuous curl of her heavy lips. "Monsieur de Saracinesca, will you not sit down? You make me a little nervous."

Gouache raised his finely marked eyebrows almost imperceptibly at the odd form of address, which betrayed ignorance either of worldly usage or else of Orsino's individuality. He stepped back from the canvas and moved a chair forward.

"Sit here, Prince," he said. "Madame can see you, and you will not be behind me."

Orsino took the proffered seat without any remark. Madame d'Aragona's expression did not change, though she was perfectly well aware that Gouache had intended to correct her manner of addressing the young man. The latter was slightly annoyed. What difference could it make? It was tactless of Gouache, he thought, for the lady might be angry.

"Are you spending the winter in Rome, Madame?" he asked. He was conscious that the question lacked originality, but no other presented itself to him.

"The winter?" repeated Madame d'Aragona dreamily. "Who knows? I am here at present, at the mercy of the great painter. That is all I know. Shall I be here next month, next week? I cannot tell. I know no one. I have never been here before. It is dull. This was my object," she added, after a short pause. "When it is accomplished I will consider other matters. I may be obliged to accompany their Royal Highnesses to Egypt in January. That is next month, is it not?"

It was so very far from clear who the royal highnesses in question might be, that Orsino glanced at Gouache, to see whether he understood. But Gouache was imperturbable.

"January, Madame, follows December," he answered. "The fact is confirmed by the observations of many centuries. Even in my own experience it has occurred forty-seven times in succession."

Orsino laughed a little, and as Madame d'Aragona's eyes met his, the red lips smiled, without parting.

"He is always laughing at me," she said pleasantly.

Gouache was painting with great alacrity. The smile was becoming to her and he caught it as it passed. It must be allowed that she permitted it to linger, as though she understood his wish, but as she was looking at Orsino, he was pleased.

"If you will permit me to say it, Madame," he observed, "I have never seen eyes like yours."

He endeavoured to lose himself in their depths as he spoke. Madame d'Aragona was not in the least annoyed by the remark, nor by the look.

"What is there so very unusual about my eyes?" she enquired. The smile grew a little more faint and thoughtful but did not disappear.

"In the first place, I have never seen eyes of a golden-yellow colour."

"Tigers have yellow eyes," observed Madame d'Aragona.

"My acquaintance with that animal is at second hand—slight, to say the least."

"You have never shot one?"

"Never, Madame. They do not abound in Rome—nor even, I believe, in Albano. My father killed one when he was a young man."

"Prince Saracinesca?"

"Sant' Ilario. My grandfather is still alive."

"How splendid! I adore strong races."

"It is very interesting," observed Gouache, poking the stick of a brush into the eye of his picture. "I have painted three generations of the family, I who speak to you, and I hope to paint the fourth if Don Orsino here can be cured of his cynicism and induced to marry Donna—what is her name?" He turned to the young man.

"She has none—and she is likely to remain nameless," answered Orsino gloomily.

"We will call her Donna Ignota," suggested Madame d'Aragona.

"And build altars to the unknown love," added Gouache.

Madame d'Aragona smiled faintly, but Orsino persisted in looking grave.

"It seems to be an unpleasant subject, Prince."

"Very unpleasant, Madame," answered Orsino shortly.

Thereupon Madame d'Aragona looked at Gouache and raised her brows a little as though to ask a question, knowing perfectly well that Orsino was watching her. The young man could not see the painter's eyes, and the latter did not betray by any gesture that he was answering the silent interrogation.

"Then I have eyes like a tiger, you say. You frighten me. How disagreeable—to look like a wild beast!"

"It is a prejudice," returned Orsino. "One hears people say of a woman that she is beautiful as a tigress."

"An idea!" exclaimed Gouache, interrupting. "Shall I change the damask cloak to a tiger's skin? One claw just hanging over the white shoulder—Omphale, you know—in a modern drawing-room—a small cast of the Farnese Hercules upon a bracket, there, on the right. Decidedly, here is an idea. Do you permit, Madame!"

"Anything you like—only do not spoil the likeness," answered Madame d'Aragona, leaning back in her chair, and looking sleepily at Orsino from beneath her heavy, half-closed lids.

"You will spoil the whole picture," said Orsino, rather anxiously.

Gouache laughed.

"What harm if I do? I can restore it in five minutes—"

"Five minutes!"

"An hour, if you insist upon accuracy of statement," replied Gouache with a shade of annoyance.

He had an idea, and like most people whom fate occasionally favours with that rare commodity he did not like to be disturbed in the realisation of it. He was already squeezing out quantities of tawny colours upon his palette.

"I am a passive instrument," said Madame d'Aragona. "He does what he pleases. These men of genius— what would you have? Yesterday a gown from Worth—to-day a tiger's skin—indeed, I tremble for to-morrow."

She laughed a little and turned her head away.

"You need not fear," answered Gouache, daubing in his new idea with an enormous brush. "Fashions change. Woman endures. Beauty is eternal. There is nothing which may not be made becoming to a beautiful woman."

"My dear Gouache, you are insufferable. You are always telling me that I am beautiful. Look at my nose."

"Yes. I am looking at it."

"And my mouth."

"I look. I see. I admire. Have you any other personal observations to make? How many claws has a tiger, Don Orsino? Quick! I am painting the thing."

"One less than a woman."

Madame d'Aragona looked at the young man a moment, and broke into a laugh.

"There is a charming speech. I like that better than Gouache's flattery."

"And yet you admit that the portrait is like you," said Gouache.

"Perhaps I flatter you, too."

"Ah! I had not thought of that."

"You should be more modest."

"I lose myself—"

"Where?"

"In your eyes, Madame. One, two, three, four—are you sure a tiger has only four claws? Where is the creature's thumb—what do you call it? It looks awkward."

"The dew-claw?" asked Orsino. "It is higher up, behind the paw. You would hardly see it in the skin."

"But a cat has five claws," said Madame d'Aragona. "Is not a tiger a cat? We must have the thing right, you know, if it is to be done at all."

"Has a cat five claws?" asked Anastase, appealing anxiously to Orsino.

"Of course, but you would only see four on the skin."

"I insist upon knowing," said Madame d'Aragona. "This is dreadful! Has no one got a tiger? What sort of studio is this—with no tiger!"

"I am not Sarah Bernhardt, nor the emperor of Siam," observed Gouache, with a laugh.

But Madame d'Aragona was not satisfied.

"I am sure you could procure me one, Prince," she said, turning to Orsino. "I am sure you could, if you would! I shall cry if I do not have one, and it will be your fault."

"Would you like the animal alive or dead?" inquired Orsino gravely, and he rose from his seat.

"Ah, I knew you could procure the thing!" she exclaimed with grateful enthusiasm. "Alive or dead, Gouache? Quick—decide!"

"As you please, Madame. If you decide to have him alive, I will ask permission to exchange a few words with my wife and children, while some one goes for a priest."

"You are sublime, to-day. Dead, then, if you please, Prince. Quite dead—but do not say that I was afraid—"

"Afraid? With, a Saracinesca and a Gouache to defend your life, Madame? You are not serious."

Orsino took his hat.

"I shall be back in a quarter of an hour," he said, as he bowed and went out.

Madame d'Aragona watched his tall young figure till he disappeared.

"He does not lack spirit, your young friend," she observed.

"No member of that family ever did, I think," Gouache answered. "They are a remarkable race."

"And he is the only son?"

"Oh no! He has three younger brothers."

"Poor fellow! I suppose the fortune is not very large."

"I have no means of knowing," replied Gouache indifferently. "Their palace is historic. Their equipages are magnificent. That is all that foreigners see of Roman families."

"But you know them intimately?"

"Intimately—that is saying too much. I have painted their portraits."

Madame d'Aragona wondered why he was so reticent, for she knew that he had himself married the daughter of a Roman prince, and she concluded that he must know much of the Romans.

"Do you think he will bring the tiger?" she asked presently.

"He is quite capable of bringing a whole menagerie of tigers for you to choose from."

"How interesting. I like men who stop at nothing. It was really unpardonable of you to suggest the idea and then to tell me calmly that you had no model for it."

In the meantime Orsino had descended the stairs and was hailing a passing cab. He debated for a moment what he should do. It chanced that at that time there was actually a collection of wild beasts to be seen in the Prati di Castello, and Orsino supposed that the owner might be induced, for a large consideration, to part with one of his tigers. He even imagined that he might shoot the beast and bring it back in the cab. But, in the first place, he was not provided with an adequate sum of money nor did he know exactly how to lay his hand on so large a sum as might be necessary, at a moment's notice. He was still under age, and his allowance had not been calculated with a view to his buying menageries. Moreover he considered that even if his pockets had been full of bank notes, the idea was ridiculous, and he was rather ashamed of his youthful impulse. It occurred to him that what was necessary for the picture was not the carcase of the tiger but the skin, and he remembered that such a skin lay on the floor in his father's private room—the spoil of the animal Giovanni Saracinesca had shot in his youth. It had been well cared for and was a fine specimen.

"Palazzo Saracinesca," he said to the cabman.

Now it chanced, as such things will chance in the inscrutable ways of fate, that Sant' Ilario was just then in that very room and busy with his correspondence. Orsino had hoped to carry off what he wanted, without being questioned, in order to save time, but he now found himself obliged to explain his errand.

Sant' Ilario looked, up in some surprise as his son entered.

"Well, Orsino? Is anything the matter?" he asked.

"Nothing serious, father. I want to borrow your tiger's skin for Gouache. Will you lend it to me?"

"Of course. But what in the world does Gouache want of it? Is he painting you in skins—the primeval youth of the forest?"

"No—not exactly. The fact is, there is a lady there. Gouache talks of painting her as a modern Omphale, with a tiger's skin and a cast of Hercules in the background—"

"Hercules wore a lion's skin—not a tiger's. He killed the Nemean lion."

"Did he?" inquired Orsino indifferently. "It is all the same—they do not know it, and they want a tiger. When I left they were debating whether they wanted it alive or dead. I thought of buying one at the Prati di Castello, but it seemed cheaper to borrow the skin of you. May I take it?"

Sant' Ilario laughed. Orsino rolled up the great hide and carried it to the door.

"Who is the lady, my boy?"

"I never saw her before—a certain Donna Maria d'Aranjuez d'Aragona. I fancy she must be a kind of cousin. Do you know anything about her?"

"I never heard of such a person. Is that her own name?"

"No—she seems to be somebody's widow."

"That is definite. What is she like?"

"Passably handsome—yellow eyes, reddish hair, one eye wanders."

"What an awful picture! Do not fall in love with her, Orsino."

"No fear of that—but she is amusing, and she wants the tiger."

"You seem to be in a hurry," observed Sant' Ilario, considerably amused.

"Naturally. They are waiting for me."

"Well, go as fast as you can—never keep a woman waiting. By the way, bring the skin back. I would rather you bought twenty live tigers at the Prati than lose that old thing."

Orsino promised and was soon in his cab on the way to Gouache's studio, having the skin rolled up on his knees, the head hanging out on one side and the tail on the other, to the infinite interest of the people in the street. He was just congratulating himself on having wasted so little time in conversation with his father, when the figure of a tall woman walking towards him on the pavement, arrested his attention. His cab must pass close by her, and there was no mistaking his mother at a hundred yards' distance. She saw him too and made a sign with her parasol for him to stop.

"Good-morning, Orsino," said the sweet deep voice.

"Good-morning, mother," he answered, as he descended hat in hand, and kissed the gloved fingers she extended to him.

He could not help thinking, as he looked at her, that she was infinitely more beautiful even now than Madame d'Aragona. As for Corona, it seemed to her that there was no man on earth to compare with her eldest son, except Giovanni himself, and there all comparison ceased. Their eyes met affectionately and it would have been, hard to say which was the more proud of the other, the son of his mother, or the mother of her son. Nevertheless Orsino was in a hurry. Anticipating all questions he told her in as few words as possible the nature of his errand, the object of the tiger's skin, and the name of the lady who was sitting to Gouache.

"It is strange," said Corona. "I have never heard your father speak of her."

"He has never heard of her either. He just told me so."

"I have almost enough curiosity to get into your cab and go with you."

"Do, mother." There was not much enthusiasm in the answer.

Corona looked at him, smiled, and shook her head.

"Foolish boy! Did you think I was in earnest? I should only spoil your amusement in the studio, and the lady would see that I had come to inspect her. Two good reasons—but the first is the better, dear. Go—do not keep them waiting."

"Will you not take my cab? I can get another."

"No. I am in no hurry. Good-bye."

And nodding to him with an affectionate smile, Corona passed on, leaving Orsino free at last to carry the skin to its destination.

When he entered the studio he found Madame d'Aragona absorbed in the contemplation of a piece of old tapestry which hung opposite to her, while Gouache was drawing in a tiny Hercules, high up in the right hand corner of the picture, as he had proposed. The conversation seemed to have languished, and Orsino was immediately conscious that the atmosphere had changed since he had left. He unrolled the skin as he entered, and Madame d'Aragona looked at it critically. She saw that the tawny colours would become her in the portrait and her expression grew more animated.

"It is really very good of you," she said, with a grateful glance.

"I have a disappointment in store for you," answered Orsino. "My father says that Hercules wore a lion's skin. He is quite right, I remember all about it."

"Of course," said Gouache. "How could we make such a mistake!"

He dropped the bit of chalk he held and looked at Madame d'Aragona.

"What difference does it make?" asked the latter. "A lion—a tiger! I am sure they are very much alike."

"After all, it is a tiresome idea," said the painter. "You will be much better in the damask cloak. Besides, with the lion's skin you should have the club—imagine a club in your hands! And Hercules should be spinning at your feet—a man in a black coat and a high collar, with a distaff! It is an absurd idea."

"You should not call my ideas absurd and tiresome. It is not civil."

"I thought it had been mine," observed Gouache.

"Not at all. I thought of it—it was quite original."

Gouache laughed a little and looked at Orsino as though asking his opinion.

"Madame is right," said the latter. "She suggested the whole idea—by having yellow eyes."

"You see, Gouache. I told you so. The Prince takes my view. What will you do?"

"Whatever you command—"

"But I do not want to be ridiculous—"

"I do not see—"

"And yet I must have the tiger."

"I am ready."

"Doubtless—but you must think of another subject, with a tiger in it."

"Nothing easier. Noble Roman damsel—Colosseum—tiger about to spring—rose—"

"Just heaven! What an old story! Besides, I have not the type."

"The 'Mysteries of Dionysus,'" suggested Gouache. "Thyrsus, leopard's skin—"

"A Bacchante! Fie, Monsieur—and then, the leopard, when we only have a tiger."

"Indian princess interviewed by a man-eater—jungle—new moon—tropical vegetation—"

"You can think of nothing but subjects for a dark type," said Madame d'Aragona impatiently.

"The fact is, in countries where the tiger walks abroad, the women are generally brunettes."

"I hate facts. You who are enthusiastic, can you not help us?" She turned to Orsino.

"Am I enthusiastic?"

"Yes, I am sure of it. Think of something."

Orsino was not pleased. He would have preferred to be thought cold and impassive.

"What can I say? The first idea was the best. Get a lion instead of a tiger—nothing is simpler."

"For my part I prefer the damask cloak and the original picture," said Gouache with decision. "All this mythology is too complicated—too Pompeian—how shall I say? Besides there is no distinct allusion. A Hercules on a bracket—anybody may have that. If you were the Marchessa di San Giacinto, for instance—oh, then everyone would laugh."

"Why? What is that?"

"She married my cousin," said Orsino. "He is an enormous giant, and they say that she has tamed him."

"Ah no! That would not do. Something else, please."

Orsino involuntarily thought of a sphynx as he looked at the massive brow, the yellow, sleepy eyes, and the heavy mouth. He wondered how the late Aranjuez had lived and what death he had died.

He offered the suggestion.

"It would be appropriate," replied Madame d'Aragona. "The Sphynx in the Desert. Rome is a desert to me."

"It only depends on you—" Orsino began.

"Oh, of course! To make acquaintances, to show myself a little everywhere—it is simple enough. But it wearies me—until one is caught up in the machinery, a toothed wheel going round with the rest, one only bores oneself, and I may leave so soon. Decidedly it is not worth the trouble. Is it?"

She turned her eyes to Orsino as though asking his advice. Orsino laughed.

"How can you ask that question!" he exclaimed. "Only let the trouble be ours."

"Ah! I said you were enthusiastic." She shook her head, and rose from her seat. "It is time for me to go. We have done nothing this morning, and it is all your fault, Prince."

"I am distressed—I will not intrude upon your next sitting."

"Oh—as far as that is concerned—" She did not finish the sentence, but took up the neglected tiger's skin from the chair on which it lay.

She threw it over her shoulders, bringing the grinning head over her hair and holding the forepaws in her pointed white fingers. She came very near to Gouache and looked into his eyes, her closed lips smiling.

"Admirable!" exclaimed Gouache. "It is impossible to tell where the woman ends and the tiger begins. Let me draw you like that."

"Oh no! Not for anything in the world."

She turned away quickly and dropped the skin from her shoulders.

"You will not stay a little longer? You will not let me try?" Gouache seemed disappointed.

"Impossible," she answered, putting on her hat and beginning to arrange her veil before a mirror.

Orsino watched her as she stood, her arms uplifted, in an attitude which is almost always graceful, even for an otherwise ungraceful woman. Madame d'Aragona was perhaps a little too short, but she was justly proportioned and appeared to be rather slight, though the tight-fitting sleeves of her frock betrayed a remarkably well turned arm. Not seeing her face, one might not have singled her out of many as a very striking woman, for she had neither the stateliness of Orsino's mother, nor the enchanting grace which distinguished Gouache's wife. But no one could look into her eyes without feeling that she was very far from being an ordinary woman.

"Quite impossible," she repeated, as she tucked in the ends of her veil and then turned upon the two men. "The next sitting? Whenever you like—to-morrow—the day after—name the time."

"When to-morrow is possible, there is no choice," said Gouache, "unless you will come again to-day."

"To-morrow, then, good-bye." She held out her hand.

"There are sketches on each of my fingers, Madame—principally, of tigers."

"Good-bye then—consider your hand shaken. Are you going, Prince?"

Orsino had taken his hat and was standing beside her.

"You will allow me to put you into your carriage."

"I shall walk."

"So much the better. Good-bye, Monsieur Gouache."

"Why say, Monsieur?"

"As you like—you are older than I."

"I? Who has told you that legend? It is only a myth. When you are sixty years old, I shall still be five-and-twenty."

"And I?" enquired Madame d'Aragona, who was still young enough to laugh at age.

"As old as you were yesterday, not a day older."

"Why not say to-day?"

"Because to-day has a to-morrow—yesterday has none."

"You are delicious, my dear Gouache. Good-bye."

Madame d'Aragona went out with Orsino, and they descended the broad staircase together. Orsino was not sure whether he might not be showing too much anxiety to remain in the company of his new acquaintance, and as he realised how unpleasant it would be to sacrifice the walk with her, he endeavoured to excuse to himself his derogation from his self-imposed character of cool superiority and indifference. She was very amusing, he said to himself, and he had nothing in the world to do. He never had anything to do, since his education had been completed. Why should he not walk with Madame d'Aragona and talk to her? It would be better than hanging about the club or reading a novel at home. The hounds did not meet on that day, or he would not have been at Gouache's at all. But they were to meet to-morrow, and he would therefore not see Madame d'Aragona.

"Gouache is an old friend of yours, I suppose," observed the lady.

"He was a friend of my father's. He is almost a Roman. He married a distant connection of mine, Donna Faustina Montevarchi."

"Ah yes—I have heard. He is a man of immense genius."

"He is a man I envy with all my heart," said Orsino.

"You envy Gouache? I should not have thought—"

"No? Ah, Madame, to me a man who has a career, a profession, an interest, is a god."

"I like that," answered Madame d'Aragona. "But it seems to me you have your choice. You have the world before you. Write your name upon it. You do not lack enthusiasm. Is it the inspiration that you need?"

"Perhaps," said Orsino glancing meaningly at her as she looked at him.

"That is not new," thought she, "but he is charming, all the same. They say," she added aloud, "that genius finds inspiration everywhere."

"Alas, I am not a genius. What I ask is an occupation, and permanent interest. The thing is impossible, but I am not resigned."

"Before thirty everything is possible," said Madame d'Aragona. She knew that the mere mention of so mature an age would be flattering to such a boy.

"The objections are insurmountable," replied Orsino.

"What objections? Remember that I do not know Rome, nor the Romans."

"We are petrified in traditions. Spicca said the other day that there was but one hope for us. The Americans may yet discover Italy, as we once discovered America."

Madame d'Aragona smiled.

"Who is Spicca?" she enquired, with a lazy glance at her companion's face.

"Spicca? Surely you have heard of him. He used to be a famous duellist. He is our great wit. My father likes him very much—he is an odd character."

"There will be all the more credit in succeeding, if you have to break through a barrier of tradition and prejudice," said Madame d'Aragona, reverting rather abruptly to the first subject.

"You do not know what that means." Orsino shook his head incredulously. "You have never tried it."

"No. How could a woman be placed in such a position?"

"That is just it. You cannot understand me."

"That does not follow. Women often understand men—men they love or detest—better than men themselves."

"Do you love me, Madame?" asked Orsino with a smile.

"I have just made your acquaintance," laughed Madame d'Aragona. "It is a little too soon."

"But then, according to you, if you understand me, you detest me."

"Well? If I do?" She was still laughing.

"Then I ought to disappear, I suppose."

"You do not understand women. Anything is better than indifference. When you see that you are disliked, then refuse to go away. It is the very moment to remain. Do not submit to dislike. Revenge yourself."

"I will try," said Orsino, considerably amused.

"Upon me?"

"Since you advise it—"

"Have I said that I detest you?"

"More or less."

"It was only by way of illustration to my argument. I was not serious."

"You have not a serious character, I fancy," said Orsino.

"Do you dare to pass judgment on me after an hour's acquaintance?"

"Since you have judged me! You have said five times that I am enthusiastic."

"That is an exaggeration. Besides, one cannot say a true thing too often."

"How you run on, Madame!"

"And you—to tell me to my face that I am not serious! It is unheard of. Is that the way you talk to your compatriots?"

"It would not be true. But they would contradict me, as you do. They wish to be thought gay."

"Do they? I would like to know them."

"Nothing is easier. Will you allow me the honour of undertaking the matter?"

They had reached the door of Madame d'Aragona's hotel. She stood still and looked curiously at Orsino.

"Certainly not," she answered, rather coldly. "It would be asking too much of you—too much of society, and far too much of me. Thanks. Good-bye."

"May I come and see you?" asked Orsino.

He knew very well that he had gone too far, and his voice was correctly contrite.

"I daresay we shall meet somewhere," she answered, entering the hotel.

CHAPTER IV

The rage of speculation was at its height in Rome. Thousands, perhaps hundreds of thousands of persons were embarked in enterprises which soon afterwards ended in total ruin to themselves and in very serious injury to many of the strongest financial bodies in the country. Yet it is a fact worth recording that the general principle upon which affairs were conducted was an honest one. The land was a fact, the buildings put up were facts, and there was actually a certain amount of capital, of genuine ready money, in use. The whole matter can be explained in a few words.

The population of Rome had increased considerably since the Italian occupation, and house-room was needed for the newcomers. Secondly, the partial execution of the scheme for beautifying the city had destroyed great numbers of dwellings in the most thickly populated parts, and more house-room was needed to compensate the loss of habitations, while extensive lots of land were suddenly set free and offered for sale upon easy conditions in all parts of the town.

Those who availed themselves of these opportunities before the general rush began, realised immense profits, especially when they had some capital of their own to begin with. But capital was not indispensable. A man could buy his lot on credit; the banks were ready to advance him money on notes of hand, in small amounts at high interest, wherewith to build his house or houses. When the building was finished the bank took a first mortgage upon the property, the owner let the house, paid the interest on the mortgage out of the rent and pocketed the difference, as clear gain. In the majority of eases it was the bank itself which sold the lot of land to the speculator. It is clear therefore that the only money which actually changed hands was that advanced in small sums by the bank itself.

As the speculation increased, the banks could not of course afford to lock up all the small notes of hand they received from various quarters. This paper became a circulating medium as far as Vienna, Paris and even London. The crash came when Vienna, Paris and London lost faith in the paper, owing, in the first instance, to one or two small failures, and returned it upon Rome; the banks, unable to obtain cash for it at any price, and being short of ready money, could then no longer discount the speculator's further notes of hand; so that the speculator found himself with half-built houses upon his hands which he could neither let, nor finish, nor sell, and owing money upon bills which he had expected to meet by giving the bank a mortgage on the now valueless property.

That is what took place in the majority of cases, and it is not necessary to go into further details, though of course chance played all the usual variations upon the theme of ruin.

What distinguishes the period of speculation in Rome from most other manifestations of the kind in Europe is the prominent part played in it by the old land-holding families, a number of which were ruined in wild schemes which no sensible man of business would have touched. This was more or less the result of recent changes in the laws regulating the power of persons making a will.

Previous to 1870 the law of primogeniture was as much respected in Rome as in England, and was carried out with considerably greater strictness. The heir got everything, the other children got practically nothing but the smallest pittance. The palace, the gallery of pictures and statues, the lands, the villages and the castles, descended in unbroken succession from eldest son to eldest son, indivisible in principle and undivided in fact.

The new law requires that one half of the total property shall be equally distributed by the testator amongst all his children. He may leave the other half to any one he pleases, and as a matter of practice he of course leaves it to his eldest son.

Another law, however, forbids the alienation of all collections of works of art either wholly or in part, if they have existed as such for a certain length of time, and if the public has been admitted daily or on any fixed days, to visit them. It is not in the power of the Borghese, or the Colonna, for instance, to sell a picture or a statue out of their galleries, nor to raise money upon such an object by mortgage or otherwise.

Yet these works of art figure at a very high valuation, in the total property of which the testator must divide one half amongst his children, though in point of fact they yield no income whatever. But it is of no use to divide them, since none of the heirs could be at liberty to take them away nor realise their value in any manner.

The consequence is, that the principal heir, after the division has taken place, finds himself the nominal master of certain enormously valuable possessions, which in reality yield him nothing or next to nothing. He also foresees that in the next generation the same state of things will exist in a far higher degree, and that the position of the head of the family will go from bad to worse until a crisis of some kind takes place.

Such a case has recently occurred. A certain Roman prince is bankrupt. The sale of his gallery would certainly relieve the pressure, and would possibly free him from debt altogether. But neither he nor his creditors can lay a finger upon the pictures, nor raise a centime upon them. This man, therefore, is permanently reduced to penury, and his creditors are large losers, while he is still de jure and de facto the owner of property probably sufficient to cover all his obligations. Fortunately, he chances to be childless, a fact consoling, perhaps, to the philanthropist, but not especially so to the sufferer himself.

It is clear that the temptation to increase "distributable" property, if one may coin such, an expression, is very great, and accounts for the way in which many Roman gentlemen have rushed headlong into speculation, though possessing none of the qualities necessary for success, and only one of the requisites, namely, a certain amount of ready money, or free and convertible property. A few have been fortunate, while the majority of those who have tried the experiment have been heavy losers. It cannot be said that any one of them all has shown natural talent for finance.

Let the reader forgive these dry explanations if he can. The facts explained have a direct bearing upon the story I am telling, but shall not, as mere facts, be referred to again.

I have already said that Ugo Del Ferice had returned to Rome soon after the change, had established himself with his wife, Donna Tullia, and was at the time I am speaking about, deeply engaged in the speculations of the day. He had once been, tolerably popular in society, having been looked upon as a harmless creature, useful in his way and very obliging. But the circumstances which had attended his flight some years earlier had become known, and most of his old acquaintances turned him the cold shoulder. He had expected this and was neither disappointed nor humiliated. He had made new friends and acquaintances during his exile, and it was to his interest to stand by them. Like many of those who had played petty and dishonourable parts in the revolutionary times, he had succeeded in building up a reputation for patriotism upon a very slight foundation, and had found persons willing to believe him a sufferer who had escaped martyrdom for the cause, and had deserved the crown of election to a constituency as a just reward of his devotion. The Romans cared very little what became of him. The old Blacks confounded Victor Emmanuel with Garibaldi, Cavour with Persiano, and Silvio Pellico with Del Ferice in one sweeping condemnation, desiring nothing so much as never to hear the hated names mentioned in their houses. The Grey party, being also Roman, disapproved of Ugo on general principles and particularly because he had been a spy, but the Whites, not being Romans at all and entertaining an especial detestation for every distinctly Roman opinion, received him at his own estimation, as society receives most people who live in good houses, give good dinners and observe the proprieties in the matter of visiting-cards. Those who knew anything definite of the man's antecedents were mostly persons who had little histories of their own, and they told no tales out of school. The great personages who had once employed him would have been magnanimous enough to acknowledge him in any case, but were agreeably disappointed when they discovered that he was not amongst the common herd of pension hunters, and claimed no substantial rewards save their politeness and a line in the visiting lists of their wives. And as he grew in wealth and importance they found that he could be useful still, as bank directors and members of parliament can be, in a thousand ways. So it came to pass that the Count and Countess Del Ferice became prominent persons in the Roman world.

Ugo was a man of undoubted talent. By his own individual efforts, though with small scruple as to the means he employed, he had raised himself from obscurity to a very enviable position. He had only once in his life been carried away by the weakness of a personal enmity, and he had been made to pay heavily for his caprice. If Donna Tullia had abandoned him when he was driven out of Rome by the influence of the Saracinesca, he might have disappeared altogether from the scene. But she was an odd compound of rashness and foresight, of belief and unbelief, and she had at that time felt herself bound by an oath she dared not break, besides being attached to him by a hatred of Giovanni Saracinesca almost as great as his own. She had followed him and had married him without hesitation; but she had kept the undivided possession of her fortune while allowing him a liberal use of her income. In return, she claimed a certain liberty of action when she chose to avail herself of it. She would not be bound in the choice of her acquaintances nor criticised in the measure of like or dislike she bestowed upon them. She was by no means wholly bad, and if she had a harmless fancy now and then, she required her husband to treat her as above suspicion. On the whole, the arrangement worked very well. Del Ferice, on his part, was unswervingly faithful to her in word and deed, for he exhibited in a high degree that unfaltering constancy which is bred of a permanent, unalienable, financial interest. Bad men are often clever, but if their cleverness is of a superior order they rarely do anything bad. It is true that when they yield to the pressure of necessity their wickedness surpasses that of other men in the same degree as their intelligence. Not only honesty, but all virtue collectively, is the best possible policy, provided that the politician can handle such a tremendous engine of evil as goodness is in the hands of a thoroughly bad man.

Those who desired pecuniary accommodation of the bank in which Del Ferice had an interest, had no better friend than he. His power with the directors seemed to be as boundless as his desire to assist the borrower. But he was helpless to prevent the foreclosure of a mortgage, and had been moved almost to tears in the expression of his sympathy with the debtor and of his horror at the hard-heartedness shown by his partners. To prove his disinterested spirit it only need be said that on many occasions he had actually come forward as a private individual and had taken over the mortgage himself, distinctly stating that he could not hold it for more than a year, but expressing a hope that the debtor might in that time retrieve himself. If this really happened, he earned the man's eternal gratitude; if not, he foreclosed indeed, but the loser never forgot that by Del Fence's kindness he had been offered a last chance at a desperate moment. It could not be said to be Del Ferice's fault that the second case was the more frequent one, nor that the result to himself was profit in either event.

In his dealings with his constituency he showed a noble desire for the public welfare, for he was never known to refuse anything in reason to the electors who applied to him. It is true that in the case of certain applications, he consumed so much time in preliminary enquiries and subsequent formalities that the applicants sometimes died and sometimes emigrated to the Argentine Republic before the matter could be settled; but they bore with them to South America—or to the grave—the belief that the Onorevole Del Ferice was on their side, and the instances of his prompt, decisive and successful action were many. He represented a small town in the Neapolitan Province, and the benefits and advantages he had obtained for it were numberless. The provincial high road had been made to pass through it; all express trains stopped at its station, though the passengers who made use of the inestimable privilege did not average twenty in the month; it possessed a Piazza Vittorio Emmanuela, a Corso Garibaldi, a Via Cavour, a public garden of at least a quarter of an acre, planted with no less than twenty-five acacias and adorned by a fountain representing a desperate-looking character in the act of firing a finely executed revolver at an imaginary oppressor. Pigs were not allowed within the limits of the town, and the uniforms of the municipal brass band were perfectly new. Could civilisation do more? The bank of which Del Ferice was a director bought the octroi duties of the town at the periodical auction, and farmed them skilfully, together with those of many other towns in the same province.

So Del Ferice was a very successful man, and it need scarcely be said that he was now not only independent of his wife's help but very much richer than she had ever been. They lived in a highly decorated, detached modern house in the new part of the city. The gilded gate before the little plot of garden, bore their intertwined initials, surmounted by a modest count's coronet. Donna Tullia would have preferred a coat of arms, or even a crest, but Ugo was sensitive to ridicule, and he was aware that a count's coronet in Rome means nothing at all, whereas a coat of arms means vastly more than in most cities.

Within, the dwelling was somewhat unpleasantly gorgeous. Donna Tullia had always loved red, both for itself and because it made her own complexion seem less florid by contrast, and accordingly red satin predominated in the drawing-rooms, red velvet in the dining-room, red damask in the hall and red carpets on the stairs. Some fine specimens of gilding were also to be seen, and Del Ferice had been one of the first to use electric light. Everything was new, expensive and polished to its extreme capacity for reflection. The servants wore vivid liveries and on formal occasions the butler appeared in short-clothes and black silk stockings. Donna Tullia's equipage was visible at a great distance, but Del Fence's own coachman and groom wore dark green with, black epaulettes.

On the morning which Orsino and Madame d'Aragona had spent in Gouache's studio the Countess Del Ferice entered her husband's study in order to consult him upon a rather delicate matter. He was alone, but busy as usual. His attention was divided between an important bank operation and a petition for his help in obtaining a decoration for the mayor of the town he represented. The claim to this distinction seemed to rest chiefly on the petitioner's unasked evidence in regard to his own moral rectitude, yet Del Ferice was really exercising all his ingenuity to discover some suitable reason for asking the favour. He laid the papers down with a sigh as Donna Tullia came in.

"Good morning, my angel," he said suavely, as he pointed to a chair at his side—the one usually occupied at this hour by seekers for financial support. "Have you rested well?"

He never failed to ask the question.

"Not badly, not badly, thank Heaven!" answered Donna Tullia. "I have a dreadful cold, of course, and a headache—my head is really splitting."

"Rest—rest is what you need, my dear—"

"Oh, it is nothing. This Durakoff is a great man. If he had not made me go to Carlsbad—I really do not know. But I have something to say to you. I want your help, Ugo. Please listen to me."

Ugo's fat white face already expressed anxious attention. To accentuate the expression of his readiness to listen, he now put all his papers into a drawer and turned towards his wife.

"I must go to the Jubilee," said Donna Tullia, coming to the point.

"Of course you must go—"

"And I must have my seat among the Roman ladies"

"Of course you must," repeated Del Ferice with a little less alacrity.

"Ah! You see. It is not so easy. You know it is not. Yet I have as good a right to my seat as any one—better perhaps."

"Hardly that," observed Ugo with a smile. "When you married me, my angel, you relinquished your claims to a seat at the Vatican functions."

"I did nothing of the kind. I never said so, I am sure."

"Perhaps if you could make that clear to the majorduomo—"

"Absurd, Ugo. You know it is. Besides, I will not beg. You must get me the seat. You can do anything with your influence."

"You could easily get into one of the diplomatic tribunes," observed Ugo.

"I will not go there. I mean to assert myself. I am a Roman lady and I will have my seat, and you must get it for me."

"I will do my best. But I do not quite see where I am to begin. It will need time and consideration and much tact."

"It seems to me very simple. Go to one of the clerical deputies and say that you want the ticket for your wife—"

"And then?"

"Give him to understand that you will vote for his next measure. Nothing could be simpler, I am sure."

Del Ferice smiled blandly at his wife's ideas of parliamentary diplomacy.

"There are no clerical deputies in the parliament of the nation. If there were the thing might be possible, and it would be very interesting to all the clericals to read an account of the transaction in the Osservatore Romano. In any case, I am not sure that it will be much to our advantage that the wife of the Onorevole Del Ferice should be seen seated in the midst of the Black ladies. It will produce an unfavourable impression."

"If you are going to talk of impressions—" Donna Tullia shrugged her massive shoulders.

"No, my dear. You mistake me. I am not going to talk of them, because, as I at once told you, it is quite right that you should go to this affair. If you go, you must go in the proper way. No doubt there will be people who will have invitations but will not use them. We can perhaps procure you the use of such a ticket."

"I do not care what name is on the paper, provided I can sit in the right place."

"Very well," answered Del Ferice. "I will do my best."

"I expect it of you, Ugo. It is not often that I ask anything of you, is it? It is the least you can do. The idea of getting a card that is not to be used is good; of course they will all get them, and some of them are sure to be ill."

Donna Tullia went away satisfied that what she wanted would be forthcoming at the right moment. What she had said was true. She rarely asked anything of her husband. But when she did, she gave him to understand that she would have it at any price. It was her way of asserting herself from time to time. On the present occasion she had no especial interest at stake and any other woman might have been satisfied with a seat in the diplomatic tribune, which could probably have been obtained without great difficulty. But she had heard that the seats there were to be very high and she did not really wish to be placed in too prominent a position. The light might be unfavourable, and she knew that she was subject to growing very red in places where it was hot. She had once been a handsome woman and a very vain one, but even her vanity could not survive the daily shock of the looking-glass torture. To sit for four or five hours in a high light, facing fifty thousand people, was more than she could bear with equanimity.

Del Ferice, being left to himself, returned to the question of the mayor's decoration which was of vastly greater importance to him than his wife's position at the approaching function. If he failed to get the man what he wanted, the fellow would doubtless apply to some one of the opposite party, would receive the coveted honour and would take the whole voting population of the town with him at the next general election, to the total discomfiture of Del Ferice. It was necessary to find some valid reason for proposing him for the distinction. Ugo could not decide what to do just then, but he ultimately hit upon a successful plan. He advised his correspondent to write a pamphlet upon the rapid improvement of agricultural interests in his district under the existing ministry, and he even went so far as to enclose with his letter some notes on the subject. These notes proved to be so voluminous and complete that when the mayor had copied them he could not find a pretext for adding a single word or correction. They were printed upon excellent paper, with ornamental margins, under the title of "Onward, Parthenope!" Of course every one knows that Parthenope means Naples, the Neapolitans and the Neapolitan Province, a siren of that name having come to final grief somewhere between the Chiatamone and Posilippo. The mayor got his decoration, and Del Ferice was re-elected; but no one has inquired into the truth of the statements made in the pamphlet upon agriculture.

It is clear that a man who was capable of taking so much trouble for so small a matter would not disappoint his wife when she had set her heart upon such a trifle as a ticket for the Jubilee. Within three days he had the promise of what he wanted. A certain lonely lady of high position lay very ill just then, and it need scarcely be explained that her confidential servant fell upon the invitation as soon as it arrived and sold it for a round sum to the first applicant, who happened to be Count Del Ferice's valet. So the matter was arranged, privately and without scandal.

All Rome was alive with expectation. The date fixed was the first of January, and as the day approached the curious foreigner mustered in his thousands and tens of thousands and took the city by storm. The hotels were thronged. The billiard tables were let as furnished rooms, people slept in the lifts, on the landings, in the porters' lodges. The thrifty Romans retreated to roofs and cellars and let their small dwellings. People reaching the city on the last night slept in the cabs they had hired to take them to St. Peter's before dawn. Even the supplies of food ran low and the hungry fed on what they could get, while the delicate of taste very often did not feed at all. There was of course the usual scare about a revolutionary demonstration, to which the natives paid very little attention, but which delighted the foreigners.

Not more than half of those who hoped to witness the ceremony saw anything of it, though the basilica will hold some eighty thousand people at a pinch, and the crowd on that occasion was far greater than at the opening of the Oecumenical Council in 1869.

Madame d'Aragona had also determined to be present, and she expressed her desire to Gouache. She had spoken the strict truth when she had said that she knew no one in Rome, and so far as general accuracy is concerned it was equally true that she had not fixed the length of her stay. She had not come with any settled purpose beyond a vague idea of having her portrait painted by the French artist, and unless she took the trouble to make acquaintances, there was nothing attractive enough about the capital to keep her. She allowed herself to be driven about the town, on pretence of seeing churches and galleries, but in reality she saw very little of either. She was preoccupied with her own thoughts and subject to fits of abstraction. Most things seemed to her intensely dull, and the unhappy guide who had been selected to accompany her on her excursions, wasted his learning upon her on the first morning, and subsequently exhausted the magnificent catalogue of impossibilities which he had concocted for the especial benefit of the uncultivated foreigner, without eliciting so much as a look of interest or an expression of surprise. He was a young and fascinating guide, wearing a white satin tie, and on the third day he recited some verses of Stecchetti and was about to risk a declaration of worship in ornate prose, when he was suddenly rather badly scared by the lady's yellow eyes, and ran on nervously with a string of deceased popes and their dates.

"Get me a card for the Jubilee," she said abruptly.

"An entrance is very easily procured," answered the guide. "In fact I have one in my pocket, as it happens. I bought it for twenty francs this morning, thinking that one of my foreigners would perhaps take it of me. I do not even gain a franc—my word of honour."

Madame d'Aragona glanced at the slip of paper.

"Not that," she answered. "Do you imagine that I will stand? I want a seat in one of the tribunes."

The guide lost himself in apologies, but explained that he could not get what she desired.

"What are you for?" she inquired.

She was an indolent woman, but when by any chance she wanted anything, Donna Tullia herself was not more restless. She drove at once to Gouache's studio. He was alone and she told him what she needed.

"The Jubilee, Madame? Is it possible that you have been forgotten?"

"Since they have never heard of me! I have not the slightest claim to a place."

"It is you who say that. But your place is already secured. Fear nothing. You will be with the Roman ladies."

"I do not understand—"

"It is simple. I was thinking of it yesterday. Young Saracinesca comes in and begins to talk about you. There is Madame d'Aragona who has no seat, he says. One must arrange that. So it is arranged."

"By Don Orsino?"

"You would not accept? No. A young man, and you have only met once. But tell me what you think of him. Do you like him?"

"One does not like people so easily as that," said Madame d'Aragona, "How have you arranged about the seat?"

"It is very simple. There are to be two days, you know. My wife has her cards for both, of course. She will only go once. If you will accept the one for the first day, she will be very happy."

"You are angelic, my dear friend! Then I go as your wife?" She laughed.

"Precisely. You will be Faustina Gouache instead of Madame d'Aragona."

"How delightful! By the bye, do not call me Madame d'Aragona. It is not my name. I might as well call you Monsieur de Paris, because you are a Parisian."

"I do not put Anastase Gouache de Paris on my cards," answered Gouache with a laugh. "What may I call you? Donna Maria?"

"My name is Maria Consuelo d'Aranjuez."

"An ancient Spanish name," said Gouache.

"My husband was an Italian."

"Ah! Of Spanish descent, originally of Aragona. Of course."

"Exactly. Since I am here, shall I sit for you? You might almost finish to-day."

"Not so soon as that. It is Don Orsino's hour, but as he has not come, and since you are so kind—by all means."

"Ah! Is he punctual?"

"He is probably running after those abominable dogs in pursuit of the feeble fox—what they call the noble sport."

Gouache's face expressed considerable disgust."

"Poor fellow!" said Maria Consuelo. "He has nothing else to do."

"He will get used to it. They all do. Besides, it is really the natural condition of man. Total idleness is his element. If Providence meant man to work, it should have given him two heads, one for his profession and one for himself. A man needs one entire and undivided intelligence for the study of his own individuality."

"What an idea!"

"Do not men of great genius notoriously forget themselves, forget to eat and drink and dress themselves like Christians? That is because they have not two heads. Providence expects a man to do two things at once—an air from an opera and invent the steam-engine at the same moment. Nature rebels. Then Providence and Nature do not agree. What becomes of religion? It is all a mystery. Believe me, Madame, art is easier than, nature, and painting is simpler than theology."

Maria Consuelo listened to Gouache's extraordinary remarks with a smile.

"You are either paradoxical, or irreligious, or both," she said.

"Irreligious? I, who carried a rifle at Mentana? No, Madame, I am a good Catholic."

"What does that mean?"

"I believe in God, and I love my wife. I leave it to the Church to define my other articles of belief. I have only one head, as you see."

Gouache smiled, but there was a note of sincerity in the odd statement which did not escape his hearer.

"You are not of the type which belongs to the end of the century," she said.

"That type was not invented when I was forming myself."

"Perhaps you belong rather to the coming age—the age of simplification."

"As distinguished from the age of mystification—religious, political, scientific and artistic," suggested Gouache. "The people of that day will guess the Sphynx's riddle."

"Mine? You were comparing me to a sphynx the other day."

"Yours, perhaps, Madame. Who knows? Are you the typical woman of the ending century?"

"Why not?" asked Maria Consuelo with a sleepy look.

CHAPTER V

There is something grand in any great assembly of animals belonging to the same race. The very idea of an immense number of living creatures conveys an impression not suggested by anything else. A compact herd of fifty or sixty thousand lions would be an appalling vision, beside which a like multitude of human beings would sink into insignificance. A drove of wild cattle is, I think, a finer sight than a regiment of cavalry in motion, for the cavalry is composite, half man and half horse, whereas the cattle have the advantage of unity. But we can never see so many animals of any species driven together into one limited space as to be equal to a vast throng of men and women, and we conclude naturally enough that a crowd consisting solely of our own kind is the most imposing one conceivable.

It was scarcely light on the morning of New Year's Day when the Princess Sant' Ilario found herself seated in one of the low tribunes on the north side of the high altar in Saint Peter's. Her husband and her eldest son had accompanied her, and having placed her in a position from which they judged she could easily escape at the end of the ceremony, they remained standing in the narrow, winding passage between improvised barriers which led from the tribune to the door of the sacristy, and which had been so arranged as to prevent confusion. Here they waited, greeting their acquaintances when they could recognise them in the dim twilight of the church, and watching the ever-increasing crowd that surged slowly backward and forward outside the barrier. The old prince was entitled by an hereditary office to a place in the great procession of the day, and was not now with them.

Orsino felt as though the whole world were assembled about him within the huge cathedral, as though its heart were beating audibly and its muffled breathing rising and falling in his hearing. The unceasing sound that went up from the compact mass of living beings was soft in quality, but enormous in volume and sustained in tone, a great whispering which, might have been heard a mile away. One hears in mammoth musical festivals the extraordinary effect of four or five thousand voices singing very softly; it is not to be compared to the unceasing whisper of fifty thousand men.

The young fellow was conscious of a strange, irregular thrill of enthusiasm which ran through him from time to time and startled his imagination into life. It was only the instinct of a strong vitality unconsciously longing to be the central point of the vitalities around it. But he could not understand that. It seemed to him like a great opportunity brought "within reach but slipping by untaken, not to return again. He felt a strange, almost uncontrollable longing to spring upon one of the tribunes, to raise his voice, to speak to the great multitude, to fire all those men to break out and carry everything before them. He laughed audibly at himself. Sant' Ilario looked at his son with some curiosity.

"What amuses you?" he asked.

"A dream," answered Orsino, still smiling. "Who knows?" he exclaimed after a pause. "What would happen, if at the right moment the right man could stir such a crowd as this?"

"Strange things," replied Sant' Ilario gravely. "A crowd is a terrible weapon."

"Then my dream was not so foolish after all. One might make history to-day."

Sant' Ilario made a gesture expressive of indifference.

"What is history?" he asked. "A comedy in which the actors have no written parts, but improvise their speeches and actions as best they can. That is the reason why history is so dull and so full of mistakes."

"And of surprises," suggested Orsino.

"The surprises in history are always disagreeable, my boy," answered Sant' Ilario.

Orsino felt the coldness in the answer and felt even more his father's readiness to damp any expression of enthusiasm. Of late he had encountered this chilling indifference at almost every turn, whenever he gave vent to his admiration for any sort of activity.

It was not that Giovanni Saracinesca had any intention of repressing his son's energetic instincts, and he assuredly had no idea of the effect his words often produced. He sometimes wondered at the sudden silence which came over the young man after such conversations, but he did not understand it and on the whole paid little attention to it. He remembered that he himself had been different, and had been wont to argue hotly and not unfrequently to quarrel with his father about trifles. He himself had been headstrong, passionate, often intractable in his early youth, and his father had been no better at sixty and was little improved in that respect even at his present great age. But Orsino did not argue. He suggested, and if any one disagreed with him he became silent. He seemed to possess energy in action, and a number of rather fantastic aspirations, but in conversation he was easily silenced and in outward manner he would have seemed too yielding if he had not often seemed too cold.

Giovanni did not see that Orsino was most like his mother in character, while the contact with a new generation had given him something unfamiliar to the old, an affectation at first, but one which habit was amalgamating with the real nature beneath.

No doubt, it was wise and right to discourage ideas which would tend in any way to revolution. Giovanni had seen revolutions and had been the loser by them. It was not wise and was certainly not necessary to throw cold water on the young fellow's harmless aspirations. But Giovanni had lived for many years in his own way, rich, respected and supremely happy, and he believed that his way was good enough for Orsino. He had, in his youth, tried most things for himself, and had found them failures so far as happiness was concerned. Orsino might make the series of experiments in his turn if he pleased, but there was no adequate reason for such an expenditure of energy. The sooner the boy loved some girl who would make him a good wife, and the sooner he married her, the sooner he would find that calm, satisfactory existence which had not finally come to Giovanni until after thirty years of age.

As for the question of fortune, it was true that there were four sons, but there was Giovanni's mother's fortune, there was Corona's fortune, and there was the great Saracinesca estate behind both. They were all so extremely rich that the deluge must be very distant.

Orsino understood none of these things. He only realised that his father had the faculty and apparently the intention of freezing any originality he chanced to show, and he inwardly resented the coldness, quietly, if foolishly, resolving to astonish those who misunderstood him by seizing the first opportunity of doing something out of the common way. For some time he stood in silence watching the people who came by and glancing from time to time at the dense crowd outside the barrier. He was suddenly aware that his father was observing intently a lady who advanced along the open, way.

"There is Tullia Del Ferice!" exclaimed Sant' Ilario in surprise.

"I do not know her, except by sight," observed Orsino indifferently.

The countess was very imposing in her black veil and draperies. Her red face seemed to lose its colour in the dim church and she affected a slow and stately manner more becoming to her weight than was her natural restless vivacity. She had got what she desired and she swept proudly along to take her old place among the ladies of Rome. No one knew whose card she had delivered up at the entrance to the sacristy, and she enjoyed the triumph of showing that the wife of the revolutionary, the banker, the member of parliament, had not lost caste after all.

She looked Giovanni full in the face with her disagreeable blue eyes as she came up, apparently not meaning to recognise him. Then, just as she passed him, she deigned to make a very slight inclination of the head, just enough to compel Sant' Ilario to return the salutation. It was very well done. Orsino did not know all the details of the past events, but he knew that his father had once wounded Del Ferice in a duel and he looked at Del Fence's wife with some curiosity. He had seldom had an opportunity of being so near to her.

"It was certainly not about her that they fought," he reflected. "It must have been about some other woman, if there was a woman in the question at all."

A moment later he was aware that a pair of tawny eyes was fixed on him. Maria Consuelo was following Donna Tullia at a distance of a dozen yards. Orsino came forward and his new acquaintance held out her hand. They had not met since they had first seen each other.

"It was so kind of you," she said.

"What, Madame?"

"To suggest this to Gouache. I should have had no ticket—where shall I sit?"

Orsino did not understand, for though he had mentioned the subject, Gouache had not told him what he meant to do. But there was no time to be lost in conversation. Orsino led her to the nearest opening in the tribune and pointed to a seat.

"I called," he said quickly. "You did not receive—"

"Come again, I will be at home," she answered in a low voice, as she passed him.

She sat down in a vacant place beside Donna Tullia, and Orsino noticed that his mother was just behind them both. Corona had been watching him unconsciously, as she often did, and was somewhat surprised to see him conducting a lady whom she did not know. A glance told her that the lady was a foreigner; as such, if she were present at all, she should have been in the diplomatic tribune. There was nothing to think of, and Corona tried to solve the small social problem that presented itself. Orsino strolled back to his father's side.

"Who is she?" inquired Sant' Ilario with some curiosity.

"The lady who wanted the tiger's skin—Aranjuez—I told you of her."

"The portrait you gave me was not flattering. She is handsome, if not beautiful."

"Did I say she was not?" asked Orsino with a visible irritation most unlike him.

"I thought so. You said she had yellow eyes, red hair and a squint." Sant' Ilario laughed.

"Perhaps I did. But the effect seems to be harmonious."

"Decidedly so. You might have introduced me."

To this Orsino said nothing, but relapsed into a moody silence. He would have liked nothing better than to bring about the acquaintance, but he had only met Maria Consuelo once, though that interview had been a long one, and he remembered her rather short answer to his offer of service in the way of making acquaintants.

Maria Consuelo on her part was quite unconscious that she was sitting in front of the Princess Sant' Ilario, but she had seen the lady by her side bow to Orsino's companion in passing, and she guessed from a certain resemblance that the dark, middle-aged man might be young Saracinesca's father. Donna Tullia had seen Corona well enough, but as they had not spoken for nearly twenty years she decided not to risk a nod where she could not command an acknowledgment of it. So she pretended to be quite unconscious of her old enemy's presence.

Donna Tullia, however, had noticed as she turned her head in sitting down that Orsino was piloting a strange lady to the tribune, and when the latter sat down beside her, she determined to make her acquaintance, no matter upon what pretext. The time was approaching at which the procession was to make its appearance, and Donna. Tullia looked about for something upon which to open the conversation, glancing from time to time at her neighbour. It was easy to see that the place and the surroundings were equally unfamiliar to the newcomer, who looked with evident interest at the twisted columns of the high altar, at the vast mosaics in the dome, at the red damask hangings of the nave, at the Swiss guards, the chamberlains in court dress and at all the mediæval-looking, motley figures that moved about within the space kept open for the coming function.

"It is a wonderful sight," said Donna Tullia in Trench, very softly, and almost as though speaking to herself.

"Wonderful indeed," answered Maria Consuelo, "especially to a stranger."

"Madame is a stranger, then," observed Donna Tullia with an agreeable smile.

She looked into her neighbour's face and for the first time realised that she was a striking person.

"Quite," replied the latter, briefly, and as though not wishing to press the conversation.

"I fancied so," said Donna Tullia, "though on seeing you in these seats, among us Romans—"

"I received a card through the kindness of a friend."

There was a short pause, during which Donna Tullia concluded that the friend must have been Orsino. But the next remark threw her off the scent.

"It was his wife's ticket, I believe," said Maria Consuelo. "She could not come. I am here on false pretences." She smiled carelessly.

Donna Tullia lost herself in speculation, but failed to solve the problem.

"You have chosen a most favourable moment for your first visit to Rome," she remarked at last.

"Yes. I am always fortunate. I believe I have seen everything worth seeing ever since I was a little girl."

"She is somebody," thought Donna Tullia. "Probably the wife of a diplomatist, though. Those people see everything, and talk of nothing but what they have seen."

"This is historic," she said aloud. "You will have a chance of contemplating the Romans in their glory. Colonna and Orsini marching side by side, and old Saracinesca in all his magnificence. He is eighty-two year old."

"Saracinesca?" repeated Maria Consuelo, turning her tawny eyes upon her neighbour.

"Yes. The father of Sant' Ilario—grandfather of that young fellow who showed you to your seat."

"Don Orsino? Yes, I know him slightly."

Corona, sitting immediately behind them heard her son's name. As the two ladies turned towards each other in conversation she heard distinctly what they said. Donna Tullia was of course aware of this.

"Do you?" she asked. "His father is a most estimable man—just a little too estimable, if you understand! As for the boy—"

Donna Tullia moved, her broad shoulders expressively. It was a habit of which even the irreproachable Del Ferice could not cure her. Corona's face darkened.

"You can hardly call him a boy," observed Maria Consuelo with a smile.

"Ah well—I might have been his mother," Donna Tullia answered with a contempt for the affectation of youth which she rarely showed. But Corona began to understand that the conversation was meant for her ears, and grew angry by degrees. Donna Tullia had indeed been near to marrying Giovanni, and in that sense, too, she might have been Orsino's mother.

"I fancied you spoke rather disparagingly," said Maria Consuelo with a certain degree of interest.

"I? No indeed. On the contrary, Don Orsino is a very fine fellow—but thrown away, positively thrown away in his present surroundings. Of what use is all this English education—but you are a stranger, Madame, you cannot understand our Roman point of view."

"If you could explain it to me, I might, perhaps," suggested the other.

"Ah yes—if I could explain it! But I am far too ignorant myself—no, ignorant is not the word—too prejudiced, perhaps, to make you see it quite as it is. Perhaps I am a little too liberal, and the Saracinesca are certainly far too conservative. They mistake education for progress. Poor Don Orsino, I am sorry for him."

Donna Tullia found no other escape from the difficulty into which she had thrown herself.

"I did not know that he was to be pitied," said Maria Consuelo.

"Oh, not he in particular, perhaps," answered the stout countess, growing more and more vague. "They are all to be pitied, you know. What is to become of young men brought up in that way? The club, the turf, the card-table—to drink, to gamble, to bet, it is not an existence!"

"Do you mean that Don Orsino leads that sort of life?" inquired Maria Consuelo indifferently.

Again Donna Tullia's heavy shoulders moved contemptuously.

"What else is there for him to do?"

"And his father? Did he not do likewise in his youth?"

"His father? Ah, he was different—before he married—full of life, activity, originality!"

"And since his marriage?"

"He has become estimable, most estimable." The smile with which Donna Tullia accompanied the statement was intended to be fine, but was only spiteful. Maria Consuelo, who saw everything with her sleepy glance, noticed the fact.

Corona was disgusted, and leaned back in her seat, as far as possible, in order not to hear more. She could not help wondering who the strange lady might be to whom Donna Tullia was so freely expressing her opinions concerning the Saracinesca, and she determined to ask Orsino after the ceremony. But she wished to hear as little more as she could.

"When a married man becomes what you call estimable," said Donna Tullia's companion, "he either adores his wife or hates her."

"What a charming idea!" laughed the countess. It Was tolerably evident that the remark was beyond her.

"She is stupid," thought Maria Consuelo. "I fancied so from the first. I will ask Don Orsino about her. He will say something amusing. It will be a subject of conversation at all events, in place of that endless tiger I invented the other day. I wonder whether this woman expects me to tell her who I am? That will amount to an acquaintance. She is certainly somebody, or she would not be here. On the other hand, she seems to dislike the only man I know besides Gouache. That may lead to complications. Let us talk of Gouache first, and be guided by circumstances."

"Do you know Monsieur Gouache?" she inquired, abruptly.

"The painter? Yes—I have known him a long time. Is he perhaps painting your portrait?"

"Exactly. It is really for that purpose that I am in Rome. What a charming man!"

"Do you think so? Perhaps he is. He painted me some time ago. I was not very well satisfied. But he has talent."

Donna Tullia had never forgiven the artist for not putting enough soul into the picture he had painted of her when she was a very young widow.

"He has a great reputation," said Maria Consuelo, "and I think he will succeed very well with me. Besides, I am grateful to him. He and his painting have been a pleasant episode in my short stay here."

"Really, I should hardly have thought you could find it worth your while to come all the way to Rome to be painted by Gouache," observed Donna Tullia. "But of course, as I say, he has talent."

"This woman is rich," she said to herself. "The wives of diplomatists do not allow themselves such caprices, as a rule. I wonder who she is?"

"Great talent," assented Maria Consuelo. "And great charm, I think."

"Ah well—of course—I daresay. We Romans cannot help thinking that for an artist he is a little too much occupied in being a gentleman—and for a gentleman he is quite too much an artist."

The remark was not original with Donna Tullia, but had been reported to her as Spicca's, and Spicca had really said something similar about somebody else.

"I had not got that impression," said Maria Consuelo, quietly.

"She hates him, too," she thought. "She seems to hate everybody. That either means that she knows everybody, or is not received in society."

"But of course you know him better than I do," she added aloud, after a little pause.

At that moment a strain of music broke out above the great, soft, muffled whispering that filled the basilica. Some thirty chosen voices of the choir of Saint Peter's had begun the hymn "Tu es Petrus," as the procession began to defile from the south aisle into the nave, close by the great door, to traverse the whole distance thence to the high altar. The Pope's own choir, consisting solely of the singers of the Sixtine Chapel, waited silently behind the lattice under the statue of Saint Veronica.

The song rang out louder and louder, simple and grand. Those who have heard Italian singers at their best know that thirty young Roman throats can emit a volume of sound equal to that which a hundred men of any other nation could produce. The stillness around them increased, too, as the procession lengthened. The great, dark crowd stood shoulder to shoulder, breathless with expectation, each man and woman feeling for a few short moments that thrill of mysterious anxiety and impatience which Orsino had felt. No one who was there can ever forget what followed. More than forty cardinals filed out in front from the Chapel of the Pietà. Then the hereditary assistants of the Holy See, the heads of the Colonna and the Orsini houses, entered the nave, side by side for the first time, I believe, in history. Immediately after them, high above all the procession and the crowd, appeared the great chair of state, the huge white feathered fans moving slowly on each side, and upon the throne, the central figure of that vast display, sat the Pope, Leo the Thirteenth.

Then, without warning and without hesitation, a shout went up such as has never been heard before in that dim cathedral, nor will, perhaps, be heard again.

"Viva il Papa-Rè! Long life to the Pope-King!"

At the same instant, as though at a preconcerted signal—utterly impossible in such a throng—in the twinkling of an eye, the dark crowd was as white as snow. In every hand a white handkerchief was raised, fluttering and waving above every head.

And the shout once taken up, drowned the strong voices of the singers as long-drawn thunder drowns the pattering of the raindrops and the sighing of the wind.

The wonderful face, that seemed to be carved out of transparent alabaster, smiled and slowly turned from side to side as it passed by. The thin, fragile hand moved unceasingly, blessing the people.

Orsino Saracinesca saw and heard, and his young face turned pale while his lips set themselves. By his side, a head shorter than he, stood his father, lost in thought as he gazed at the mighty spectacle of what had been, and of what might still have been, but for one day of history's surprises.

Orsino said nothing, but he glanced at Sant' Ilario's face as though to remind his father of what he had said half an hour earlier; and the elder man knew that there had been truth in the boy's words. There were soldiers in the church, and they were not Italian soldiers—some thousands of them in all, perhaps. They were armed, and there were at the very least computation thirty thousand strong, grown men in the crowd. And the crowd was on fire. Had there been a hundred, nay a score, of desperate, devoted leaders there, who knows what bloody work might not have been done in the city before the sun went down? Who knows what new surprises history might have found for her play? The thought must have crossed many minds at that moment. But no one stirred; the religious ceremony remained a religious ceremony and nothing more; holy peace reigned within the walls, and the hour of peril glided away undisturbed to take its place among memories of good.

"The world is worn out!" thought Orsino. "The days of great deeds are over. Let us eat and drink, for to-morrow we die—they are right in teaching me their philosophy."

A gloomy, sullen melancholy took hold of the boy's young nature, a passing mood, perhaps, but one which left its mark upon him. For he was at that age when a very little thing will turn the balance of a character, when an older man's thoughtless words may direct half a lifetime in a good or evil channel, being recalled and repeated for a score of years. Who is it that does not remember that day when an impatient "I will," or a defiant "I will not," turned the whole current of his existence in the one direction or the other, towards good or evil, or towards success or failure? Who, that has fought his way against odds into the front rank, has forgotten the woman's look that gave him courage, or the man's sneer that braced nerve and muscle to strike the first of many hard blows?

The depression which fell upon Orsino was lasting, for that morning at least. The stupendous pageant went on before him, the choirs sang, the sweet boys' voices answered back, like an angel's song, out of the lofty dome, the incense rose in columns through the streaming sunlight as the high mass proceeded. Again the Pope was raised upon the chair and borne out into the nave, whence in the solemn silence the thin, clear, aged voice intoned the benediction three times, slowly rising and falling, pausing and beginning again. Once more the enormous shout broke out, louder and deeper than ever, as the procession moved away. Then all was over.

Orsino saw and heard, but the first impression was gone, and the thrill did not come back.

"It was a fine sight," he said to his father, as the shout died away.

"A fine sight? Have you no stronger expression than that?"

"No," answered Orsino, "I have not."

The ladies were already coming out of the tribunes, and Orsino saw his father give his arm to Corona to lead her through the crowd. Naturally enough, Maria Consuelo and Donna Tullia came out together very soon after her. Orsino offered to pilot the former through the confusion, and she accepted gratefully. Donna Tullia walked beside them.

"You do not know me, Don Orsino," said she with a gracious smile.

"I beg your pardon—you are the Countess Del Ferice—I have not been back from England long, and have not had an opportunity of being presented."

Whatever might be Orsino's weaknesses, shyness was certainly not one of them, and as he made the civil answer he calmly looked at Donna Tullia as though to inquire what in the world she wished to accomplish in making his acquaintance. He had been so situated during the ceremony as not to see that the two ladies had fallen into conversation.

"Will you introduce me?" said Maria Consuelo. "We have been talking together."

She spoke in a low voice, but the words could hardly have escaped Donna Tullia. Orsino was very much surprised and not by any means pleased, for he saw that the elder woman had forced the introduction by a rather vulgar trick. Nevertheless, he could not escape.

"Since you have been good enough to recognise me," he said rather stiffly to Donna Tullia, "permit me to make you acquainted with Madame d'Aranjuez d'Aragona."

Both ladies nodded and smiled the smile of the newly introduced. Donna Tullia at once began to wonder how it was that a person with such a name should have but a plain "Madame" to put before it. But her curiosity was not satisfied on this occasion.

"How absurd society is!" she exclaimed. "Madame d'Aranjuez and I have been talking all the morning, quite like old friends—and now we need an introduction!"

Maria Consuelo glanced at Orsino as though, expecting him to make some remark. But he said nothing.

"What should we do without conventions!" she said, for the sake of saying something.

By this time they were threading the endless passages of the sacristy building, on their way to the Piazza Santa, Marta. Sant' Ilario and Corona were not far in front of them. At a turn in the corridor Corona looked back.

"There is Orsino talking to Tullia Del Ferice!" she exclaimed in great surprise. "And he has given his arm to that other lady who was next to her in the tribune."

"What does it matter?" asked Sant' Ilario indifferently. "By the bye, the other lady is that Madame d'Aranjuez he talks about."

"Is she any relation of your mother's family, Giovanni?"

"Not that I am aware of. She may have married some younger son of whom I never heard."

"You do not seem to care whom Orsino knows," said Corona rather reproachfully.

"Orsino is grown up, dear. You must not forget that."

"Yes—I suppose he is," Corona answered with a little sigh. "But surely you will not encourage him to cultivate the Del Ferice!"

"I fancy it would take a deal of encouragement to drive him to that," said Sant' Ilario with a laugh. "He has better taste."

There was some confusion outside. People were waiting for their carriages, and as most of them knew each other intimately every one was talking at once. Donna Tullia nodded here and there, but Maria Consuelo noticed that her salutations were coldly returned. Orsino and his two companions stood a little aloof from the crowd. Just then the Saracinesca carriage drove up.

"Who is that magnificent woman?" asked Maria Consuelo, as Corona got in.

"My mother," said Orsino. "My father is getting in now."

"There comes my carriage! Please help me."

A modest hired brougham made its appearance. Orsino hoped that Madame d'Aranjuez would offer him a seat. But he was mistaken.

"I am afraid mine is miles away," said Donna Tullia. "Good-bye, I shall be so glad if you will come and see me." She held out her hand.

"May I not take you home?" asked Maria Consuelo. "There is just room—it will be better than waiting here."

Donna Tullia hesitated a moment, and then accepted, to Orsino's great annoyance. He helped the two ladies to get in, and shut the door.

"Come soon," said Maria Consuelo, giving him her hand out of the window.

He was inclined to be angry, but the look that accompanied the invitation did its work satisfactorily.

"He is very young," thought Maria Consuelo, as she drove away.

"She can be very amusing. It is worth while," said Orsino to himself as he passed in front of the next carriage, and walked out upon the small square.

He had not gone far, hindered as he was at every step, when some one touched his arm. It was Spicca, looking more cadaverous and exhausted than usual.

"Are you going home in a cab?" he asked. "Then let us go together."

They got out of the square, scarcely knowing how they had accomplished the feat. Spicca seemed nervous as well as tired, and he leaned on Orsino's arm.

"There was a chance lost this morning," said the latter when they were under the colonnade. He felt sure of a bitter answer from the keen old man.

"Why did you not seize it then?" asked Spicca. "Do you expect old men like me to stand up and yell for a republic, or a restoration, or a monarchy, or whichever of the other seven plagues of Egypt you desire? I have not voice enough left to call a cab, much less to howl down a kingdom."

"I wonder what would have happened, if I, or some one else, had tried."

"You would have spent the night in prison with a few kindred spirits. After all, that would have been better than making love to old Donna Tullia and her young friend."

Orsino laughed.

"You have good eyes," he said.

"So have you, Orsino. Use them. You will see something odd if you look where you were looking this morning. Do you know what sort of a place this world is?"

"It is a dull place. I have found that out already."

"You are mistaken. It is hell. Do you mind calling that cab?"

Orsino stared a moment at his companion, and then hailed the passing conveyance.

CHAPTER VI

Orsino had shown less anxiety to see Madame d'Aranjuez than might perhaps have been expected. In the ten days which had elapsed between the sitting at Gouache's studio and the first of January he had only once made an attempt to find her at home, and that attempt had failed. He had not even seen her passing in the street, and he had not been conscious of any uncontrollable desire to catch a glimpse of her at any price.

But he had not forgotten her existence as he would certainly have forgotten that of a wholly indifferent person in the same time. On the contrary, he had thought of her frequently and had indulged in many speculations concerning her, wondering among other matters why he did not take more trouble to see her since she occupied his thoughts so much. He did not know that he was in reality hesitating, for he would not have acknowledged to himself that he could be in danger of falling seriously in love. He was too young to admit such a possibility, and the character which he admired and meant to assume was altogether too cold and superior to such weaknesses. To do him justice, he was really not of the sort to fall in love at first sight. Persons capable of a self-imposed dualism rarely are, for the second nature they build up on the foundation of their own is never wholly artificial. The disposition to certain modes of thought and habits of bearing is really present, as is sufficiently proved by their admiration of both. Very shy persons, for instance, invariably admire very self-possessed ones, and in trying to imitate them occasionally exhibit a cold-blooded arrogance which is amazing. Timothy Titmouse secretly looks up to Don Juan as his ideal, and after half a lifetime of failure outdoes his model, to the horror of his friends. Dionysus masks as Hercules, and the fox is sometimes not unsuccessful in his saint's disguise. Those who have been intimate with a great actor know that the characters he plays best are not all assumed; there is a little of each in his own nature. There is a touch of the real Othello in Salvini—there is perhaps a strain of the melancholy Scandinavian in English Irving.

To be short, Orsino Saracinesca was too enthusiastic to be wholly cold, and too thoughtful to be thoroughly enthusiastic. He saw things differently according to his moods, and being dissatisfied, he tried to make one mood prevail constantly over the other. In a mean nature the double view often makes an untruthful individual; in one possessing honourable instincts it frequently leads to unhappiness. Affectation then becomes aspiration and the man's failure to impose on others is forgotten in his misery at failing to impose upon himself.

The few words Orsino had exchanged with Maria Consuelo on the morning of the great ceremony recalled vividly the pleasant hour he had spent with her ten days earlier, and he determined to see her as soon as possible. He was out of conceit with himself and consequently with all those who knew him, and he looked forward with pleasure to the conversation of an attractive woman who could have no preconceived opinion of him, and who could take him at his own estimate. He was curious, too, to find out something more definite in regard to her. She was mysterious, and the mystery pleased him. She had admitted that her deceased husband had spoken of being connected with the Saracinesca, but he could not discover where the relationship lay. Spicca's very odd remark, too, seemed to point to her, in some way which Orsino could not understand, and he remembered her having said that she had heard of Spicca. Her husband had doubtless been an Italian of Spanish descent, but she had given no clue to her own nationality, and she did not look Spanish, in spite of her name, Maria Consuelo. As no one in Rome knew her it was impossible to get any information whatever. It was all very interesting.

Accordingly, late on the afternoon of the second of January, Orsino called and was led to the door of a small sitting-room on the second floor of the hotel. The servant shut the door behind him and Orsino found himself alone. A lamp with a pretty shade was burning on the table and beside it an ugly blue glass vase contained a few flowers, common roses, but fresh and fragrant. Two or three new books in yellow paper covers lay scattered upon the hideous velvet table cloth, and beside one of them Orsino noticed a magnificent paper cutter of chiselled silver, bearing a large monogram done in brilliants and rubies. The thing contrasted oddly with its surroundings and attracted the light. An easy chair was drawn up to the table, an abominable object covered with perfectly new yellow satin. A small red morocco cushion, of the kind used in travelling, was balanced on the back, and there was a depression in it, as though some one's head had lately rested there.

Orsino noticed all these details as he stood waiting for Madame d'Aranjuez to appear, and they were not without interest to him, for each one told a story, and the stories were contradictory. The room was not encumbered with those numberless objects which most women scatter about them within an hour after reaching a hotel. Yet Madame d'Aranjuez must have been at least a month in Rome. The room smelt neither of perfume nor of cigarettes, but of the roses, which was better, and a little of the lamp, which was much worse. The lady's only possessions seemed to be three books, a travelling cushion and a somewhat too gorgeous paper cutter; and these few objects were perfectly new. He glanced at the books; they were of the latest, and only one had been cut. The cushion might have been bought that morning. Not a breath had tarnished the polished blade of the silver knife.

A door opened softly and Orsino drew himself up as some one pushed in the heavy, vivid curtains. But it was not Madame d'Aranjuez. A small dark woman of middle age, with downcast eyes and exceedingly black hair, came forward a step.

"The signora will come presently," she said in Italian, in a very low voice, as though she were almost afraid of hearing herself speak.

She was gone in a moment, as noiselessly as she had come. This was evidently the silent maid of whom Gouache had spoken. The few words she had spoken had revealed to Orsino the fact that she was an Italian from the north, for she had the unmistakable accent of the Piedmontese, whose own language is comprehensible only by themselves.

Orsino prepared to wait some time, supposing that the message could hardly have been sent without an object. But another minute had not elapsed before Maria Consuelo herself appeared. In the soft lamplight her clear white skin looked very pale and her auburn hair almost red. She wore one of those nondescript garments which we have elected to call tea-gowns, and Orsino, who had learned to criticise dress as he had learned Latin grammar, saw that the tea-gown was good and the lace real. The colours produced no impression upon him whatever. As a matter of fact they were dark, being combined in various shades of olive.

Maria Consuelo looked at her visitor and held out her hand, but said nothing. She did not even smile, and Orsino began to fancy that he had chosen an unfortunate moment for his visit.

"It was very good of you to let me come," he said, waiting for her to sit down.

Still she said nothing. She placed the red morocco cushion carefully in the particular position which would be most comfortable, turned the shade of the lamp a little, which, of course, produced no change whatever in the direction of the light, pushed one of the books half across the table and at last sat down in the easy chair. Orsino sat down near her, holding his hat upon his knee. He wondered whether she had heard him speak, or whether she might not be one of those people who are painfully shy when there is no third person present.

"I think it was very good of you to come," she said at last, when she was comfortably settled.

"I wish goodness were always so easy," answered Orsino with alacrity.

"Is it your ambition to be good?" asked Maria Consuelo with a smile.

"It should be. But it is not a career."

"Then you do not believe in Saints?"

"Not until they are canonised and made articles of belief—unless you are one, Madame."

"I have thought of trying it," answered Maria Consuelo, calmly. "Saintship is a career, even in society, whatever you may say to the contrary. It has attractions, after all."

"Not equal to those of the other side. Every one admits that. The majority is evidently in favour of sin, and if we are to believe in modern institutions, we must believe that majorities are right."

"Then the hero is always wrong, for he is the enthusiastic individual who is always for facing odds, and if no one disagrees with him he is very unhappy. Yet there are heroes—"

"Where?" asked Orsino. "The heroes people talk of ride bronze horses on inaccessible pedestals. When the bell rings for a revolution they are all knocked down and new ones are set up in their places—also executed by the best artists—and the old ones are cast into cannon to knock to pieces the ideas they invented. That is called history."

"You take a cheerful and encouraging view of the world's history, Don Orsino."

"The world is made for us, and we must accept it. But we may criticise it. There is nothing to the contrary in the contract."

"In the social contract? Are you going to talk to me about Jean-Jacques?"

"Have you read him, Madame?"

"'No woman who respects herself—'" began Maria Consuelo, quoting the famous preface.

"I see that you have," said Orsino, with a laugh. "I have not."

"Nor I."

To Orsino's surprise, Madame d'Aranjuez blushed. He could not have told why he was pleased, nor why her change of colour seemed so unexpected.

"Speaking of history," he said, after a very slight pause, "why did you thank me yesterday for having got you a card?"

"Did you not speak to Gouache about it?"

"I said something—I forget what. Did he manage it?"

"Of course. I had his wife's place. She could not go. Do you dislike being thanked for your good offices? Are you so modest as that?"

"Not in the least, but I hate misunderstandings, though I will get all the credit I can for what I have not done, like other people. When I saw that you knew the Del Ferice, I thought that perhaps she had been exerting herself."

"Why do you hate her so?" asked Maria Consuelo.

"I do not hate her. She does not exist—that is all."

"Why does she not exist, as you call it? She is a very good-natured woman. Tell me the truth. Everybody hates her—I saw that by the way they bowed to her while we were waiting—why? There must be a reason. Is she a—an incorrect person?"

Orsino laughed.

"No. That is the point at which existence is more likely to begin than to end."

"How cynical you are! I do not like that. Tell me about Madame Del Ferice."

"Very well. To begin with, she is a relation of mine."

"Seriously?"

"Seriously. Of course that gives me a right to handle the whole dictionary of abuse against her."

"Of course. Are you going to do that?"

"No. You would call me cynical. I do not like you to call me by bad names, Madame."

"I had an idea that men liked it," observed Maria Consuelo gravely.

"One does not like to hear disagreeable truths."

"Then it is the truth? Go on. You have forgotten what we were talking about."

"Not at all Donna Tullia, my second, third or fourth cousin, was married once upon a time to a certain Mayer."

"And left him. How interesting!"

"No, Madame. He left her—very suddenly, I believe—for another world. Better or worse? Who can say? Considering his past life, worse, I suppose; but considering that he was not obliged to take Donna Tullia with him, decidedly better."

"You certainly hate her. Then she married Del Ferice."

"Then she married Del Ferice—before I was born. She is fabulously old. Mayer left her very rich, and without conditions. Del Ferice was an impossible person. My father nearly killed him in a duel once—also before I was born. I never knew what it was about. Del Ferice was a spy, in the old days when spies got a living in a Rome—"

"Ah! I see it all now!" exclaimed Maria Consuelo. "Del Ferice is white, and you are black. Of course you hate each other. You need not tell me any more."

"How you take that for granted!"

"Is it not perfectly clear? Do not talk to me of like and dislike when your dreadful parties have anything to do with either! Besides, if I had any sympathy with either side it would be for the whites. But the whole thing is absurd, complicated, mediaeval, feudal—anything you like except sensible. Your intolerance is—intolerable."

"True tolerance should tolerate even intolerance," observed Orsino smartly.

"That sounds like one of the puzzles of pronunciation like 'in un piatto poco cupo poco pepe pisto cape,'" laughed Maria Consuelo. "Tolerably tolerable tolerance tolerates tolerable tolerance intolerably—"

"You speak Italian?" asked Orsino, surprised by her glib enunciation of the difficult sentence she had quoted. "Why are we talking a foreign language?"

"I cannot really speak Italian. I have an Italian maid, who speaks French. But she taught me that puzzle."

"It is odd—your maid is a Piedmontese and you have a good accent."

"Have I? I am very glad. But tell me, is it not absurd that you should hate these people as you do—you cannot deny it—merely because they are whites?"

"Everything in life is absurd if you take the opposite point of view. Lunatics find endless amusement in watching sane people."

"And of course, you are the sane people," observed Maria Consuelo.

"Of course."

"What becomes of me? I suppose I do not exist? You would not be rude enough to class me with the lunatics."

"Certainly not. You will of course choose to be a black."

"In order to be discontented, as you are?"

"Discontented?"

"Yes. Are you not utterly out of sympathy with your surroundings? Are you not hampered at every step by a network of traditions which have no meaning to your intelligence, but which are laid on you like a harness upon a horse, and in which you are driven your daily little round of tiresome amusement—or dissipation? Do you not hate the Corso as an omnibus horse hates it? Do you not really hate the very faces of all those people who effectually prevent you from using your own intelligence, your own strength—your own heart? One sees it in your face. You are too young to be tired of life. No, I am not going to call you a boy, though I am older than you, Don Orsino. You will find people enough in your own surroundings to call you a boy—because you are not yet so utterly tamed and wearied as they are, and for no other reason. You are a man. I do not know your age, but you do not talk as boys do. You are a man—then be a man altogether, be independent—use your hands for something better than throwing mud at other people's houses merely because they are new!"

Orsino looked at her in astonishment. This was certainly not the sort of conversation he had anticipated when he had entered the room.

"You are surprised because I speak like this," she said after a short pause. "You are a Saracinesca and I am—a stranger, here to-day and gone to-morrow, whom you will probably never see again. It is amusing, is it not? Why do you not laugh?"

Maria Consuelo smiled and as usual her strong red lips closed as soon as she had finished speaking, a habit which lent the smile something unusual, half-mysterious, and self-contained.

"I see nothing to laugh at," answered Orsino. "Did the mythological personage whose name I have forgotten laugh when the sphynx proposed the riddle to him?"

"That is the third time within the last few days that I have been compared to a sphynx by you or Gouache. It lacks originality in the end."

"I was not thinking of being original. I was too much interested. Your riddle is the problem of my life."

"The resemblance ceases there. I cannot eat you up if you do not guess the answer—or if you do not take my advice. I am not prepared to go so far as that."

"Was it advice? It sounded more like a question."

"I would not ask one when I am sure of getting no answer. Besides, I do not like being laughed at."

"What has that to do with the matter? Why imagine anything so impossible?"

"After all—perhaps it is more foolish to say, 'I advise you to do so and so,' than to ask, 'Why do you not do so and so?' Advice is always disagreeable and the adviser is always more or less ridiculous. Advice brings its own punishment."

"Is that not cynical?" asked Orsino.

"No. Why? What is the worst thing you can do to your social enemy? Prevail upon him to give you his counsel, act upon it—it will of course turn out badly—then say, "I feared this would happen, but as you advised me I did not like—" and so on! That is simple and always effectual. Try it."

"Not for worlds!"

"I did not mean with me," answered Maria Consuelo with a laugh.

"No. I am afraid there are other reasons which will prevent me from making a career for myself," said Orsino thoughtfully.

Maria Consuelo saw by his face that the subject was a serious one with him, as she had already guessed that it must be, and one which would always interest him. She therefore let it drop, keeping it in reserve in case the conversation flagged.

"I am going to see Madame Del Ferice to-morrow," she observed, changing the subject.

"Do you think that is necessary?"

"Since I wish it! I have not your reasons for avoiding her."

"I offended you the other day, Madame, did I not? You remember—when I offered my services in a social way."

"No—you amused me," answered Maria Consuelo coolly, and watching to see how he would take the rebuke.

But, young as Orsino was, he was a match for her in self-possession.

"I am very glad," he answered without a trace of annoyance. "I feared you were displeased."

Maria Consuelo smiled again, and her momentary coldness vanished. The answer delighted her, and did more to interest her in Orsino than fifty clever sayings could have done. She resolved to push the question a little further.

"I will be frank," she said.

"It is always best," answered Orsino, beginning to suspect that something very tortuous was coming. His disbelief in phrases of the kind, though originally artificial, was becoming profound.

"Yes, I will be quite frank," she repeated. "You do not wish me to know the Del Ferice and their set, and you do wish me to know the people you like."

"Evidently."

"Why should I not do as I please?"

She was clearly trying to entrap him into a foolish answer, and he grew more and more wary.

"It would be very strange if you did not," answered Orsino without hesitation.

"Why, again?"

"Because you are absolutely free to make your own choice."

"And if my choice does not meet with your approval?" she asked.

"What can I say, Madame? I and my friends will be the losers, not you."

Orsino had kept his temper admirably, and he did not suffer a hasty word to escape his lips nor a shadow of irritation to appear in his face. Yet she had pressed him in a way which was little short of rude. She was silent for a few seconds, during which Orsino watched her face as she turned it slightly away from him and from the lamp. In reality he was wondering why she was not more communicative about herself, and speculating as to whether her silence in that quarter proceeded from the consciousness of a perfectly assured position in the world, or from the fact that she had something to conceal; and this idea led him to congratulate himself upon not having been obliged to act immediately upon his first proposal by bringing about an acquaintance between Madame d'Aranjuez and his mother. This uncertainty lent a spice of interest to the acquaintance. He knew enough of the world already to be sure that Maria Consuelo was born and bred in that state of life to which it has pleased Providence to call the social elect. But the peculiar people sometimes do strange things and afterwards establish themselves in foreign cities where their doings are not likely to be known for some time. Not that Orsino cared what this particular stranger's past might have been. But he knew that his mother would care very much indeed, if Orsino wished her to know the mysterious lady, and would sift the matter very thoroughly before asking her to the Palazzo Saracinesca. Donna Tullia, on the other hand, had committed herself to the acquaintance on her own responsibility, evidently taking it for granted that if Orsino knew Madame d'Aranjuez, the latter must be socially irreproachable. It amused Orsino to imagine the fat countess's rage if she turned out to have made a mistake.

"I shall be the loser too," said Maria Consuelo, in a different tone, "if I make a bad choice. But I cannot draw back. I took her to her house in my carriage. She seemed to take a fancy to me—" she laughed a little.

Orsino smiled as though to imply that the circumstance did not surprise him.

"And she said she would come to see me. As a stranger I could not do less than insist upon making the first visit, and I named the day—or rather she did. I am going to-morrow."

"To-morrow? Tuesday is her day. You will meet all her friends."

"Do you mean to say that people still have days in Rome?" Maria Consuelo did not look pleased.

"Some people do—very few. Most people prefer to be at home one evening in the week."

"What sort of people are Madame Del Ferice's friends?"

"Excellent people."

"Why are you so cautious?"

"Because you are about to be one of them, Madame."

"Am I? No, I will not begin another catechism! You are too clever—I shall never get a direct answer from you."

"Not in that way," answered Orsino with a frankness that made his companion smile.

"How then?"

"I think you would know how," he replied gravely, and he fixed his young black eyes on her with an expression that made her half close her own.

"I should think you would make a good actor," she said softly.

"Provided that I might be allowed to be sincere between the acts."

"That sounds well. A little ambiguous perhaps. Your sincerity might or might not take the same direction as the part you had been acting."

"That would depend entirely upon yourself, Madame."

This time Maria Consuelo opened her eyes instead of closing them.

"You do not lack—what shall I say? A certain assurance—you do not waste time!"

She laughed merrily, and Orsino laughed with her.

"We are between the acts now," he said. "The curtain goes up to-morrow, and you join the enemy."

"Come with me, then."

"In your carriage? I shall be enchanted."

"No. You know I do not mean that. Come with me to the enemy's camp. It will be very amusing."

Orsino shook his head.

"I would rather die—if possible at your feet, Madame."

"Are you afraid to call upon Madame Del Ferice?"

"More than of death itself."

"How can you say that?"

"The conditions of the life to come are doubtful—there might be a chance for me. There is no doubt at all as to what would happen if I went to see Madame Del Ferice."

"Is your father so severe with you?" asked Maria Consuelo with a little scorn.

"Alas, Madame, I am not sensitive to ridicule," answered Orsino, quite unmoved. "I grant that there is something wanting in my character."

Maria Consuelo had hoped to find a weak point, and had failed, though indeed there were many in the young man's armour. She was a little annoyed, both at her own lack of judgment and because it would have amused her to see Orsino in an element so unfamiliar to him as that in which Donna Tullia lived.

"And there is nothing which would induce you to go there?" she asked.

"At present—nothing," Orsino answered coldly.

"At present—but in the future of all possible possibilities?"

"I shall undoubtedly go there. It is only the unforeseen which invariably happens."

"I think so too."

"Of course. I will illustrate the proverb by bidding you good evening," said Orsino, laughing as he rose. "By this time the conviction must have formed itself in your mind that I was never going. The unforeseen happens. I go."

Maria Consuelo would have been glad if he had stayed even longer, for he amused her and interested her, and she did not look forward with pleasure to the lonely evening she was to spend in the hotel.

"I am generally at home at this hour," she said, giving him her hand.

"Then, if you will allow me? Thanks. Good evening, Madame."

Their eyes met for a moment, and then Orsino left the room. As he lit his cigarette in the porch of the hotel, he said to himself that he had not wasted his hour, and he was pleasantly conscious of tha inward and spiritual satisfaction which every very young man feels when he is aware of having appeared at his best in the society of a woman alone. Youth without vanity is only premature old age after all.

"She is certainly more than pretty," he said to himself, affecting to be critical when he was indeed convinced. "Her mouth is fabulous, but it is well shaped and the rest is perfect—no, the nose is insignificant, and one of those yellow eyes wanders a little. These are not perfections. But what does it matter? The whole is charming, whatever the parts may be. I wish she would not go to that horrible fat woman's tea to-morrow."

Such were the observations which Orsino thought fit to make to himself, but which by no means represented all that he felt, for they took no notice whatever of that extreme satisfaction at having talked well with Maria Consuelo, which in reality dominated every other sensation just then. He was well enough accustomed to consideration, though his only taste of society had been enjoyed during the winter vacations of the last two years. He was not the greatest match in the Roman matrimonial market for nothing, and he was perfectly well aware of his advantages in this respect. He possessed that keen, business-like appreciation of his value as a marriageable man which seems to characterise the young generation of to-day, and he was not mistaken in his estimate. It was made sufficiently clear to him at every turn that he had but to ask in order to receive. But he had not the slightest intention of marrying at one and twenty as several of his old school-fellows were doing, and he was sensible enough to foresee that his position as a desirable son-in-law would soon cause him more annoyance than amusement.

Madame d'Aranjuez was doubtless aware that she could not marry him if she wished to do so. She was several years older than he—he admitted the fact rather reluctantly—she was a widow, and she seemed to have no particular social position. These were excellent reasons against matrimony, but they were also equally excellent reasons for being pleased with himself at having produced a favourable impression on her.

He walked rapidly along the crowded street, glancing carelessly at the people who passed and at the brilliantly lighted windows of the shops. He passed the door of the club, where he was already becoming known for rather reckless play, and he quite forgot that a number of men were probably spending an hour at the tables before dinner, a fact which would hardly have escaped his memory if he had not been more than usually occupied with pleasant thoughts. He did not need the excitement of baccarat nor the stimulus of brandy and soda, for his brain was already both excited and stimulated, though he was not at once aware of it. But it became clear to him when he suddenly found himself standing before the steps of the Capitol in the gloomy square of the Ara Coeli, wondering what in the world had brought him so far out of his way.

"What a fool I am!" he exclaimed impatiently, as he turned back and walked in the direction of his home. "And yet she told me that I would make a good actor. They say that an actor should never be carried away by his part."

At dinner that evening he was alternately talkative and very silent.

"Where have you been to-day, Orsino?" asked his father, looking at him curiously.

"I spent half an hour with Madame d'Aranjuez, and then went for a walk," answered Orsino with sudden indifference.

"What is she like?" asked Corona.

"Clever—at least in Rome." There was an odd, nervous sharpness about the answer.

Old Saracinesca raised his keen eyes without lifting his head and looked hard at his grandson. He was a little bent in his great old age.

"The boy is in love!" he exclaimed abruptly, and a laugh that was still deep and ringing followed the words. Orsino recovered his self-possession and smiled carelessly.

Corona was thoughtful during the remainder of the meal.

CHAPTER VII

The Princess Sant' Ilario's early life had been deeply stirred by the great makers of human character, sorrow and happiness. She had suffered profoundly, she had borne her trials with a rare courage, and her reward, if one may call it so, had been very great. She had seen the world and known it well, and the knowledge had not been forgotten in the peaceful prosperity of later years. Gifted with a beauty not equalled, perhaps, in those times, endowed with a strong and passionate nature under a singularly cold and calm outward manner, she had been saved from many dangers by the rarest of commonplace qualities, common sense. She had never passed for an intellectual person, she had never been very brilliant in conversation, she had even been thought old-fashioned in her prejudices concerning the books she read. But her judgment had rarely failed her at critical moments. Once only, she remembered having committed a great mistake, of which the sudden and unexpected consequences had almost wrecked her life. But in that case she had suffered her heart to lead her, an innocent girl's good name had been at stake, and she had rashly taken a responsibility too heavy for love itself to bear. Those days were long past now; twenty years separated Corona, the mother of four tall sons, from the Corona who had risked all to save poor little Faustina Montevarchi.

But even she knew that a state of such perpetual and unclouded happiness could hardly last a lifetime, and she had forced herself, almost laughing at the thought, to look forward to the day when Orsino must cease to be a boy and must face the world of strong loves and hates through which most men have to pass, and which all men must have known in order to be men indeed.

The people whose lives are full of the most romantic incidents, are not generally, I think, people of romantic disposition. Romance, like power, will come uncalled for, and those who seek it most, are often those who find it least. And the reason is simple enough. The man of heart is not perpetually burrowing in his surroundings for affections upon which his heart may feed, any more than the very strong man is naturally impelled to lift every weight he sees or to fight with every man he meets. The persons whom others call romantic are rarely conscious of being so. They are generally far too much occupied with the one great thought which make their strongest, bravest and meanest actions seem perfectly commonplace to themselves. Corona Del Carmine, who had heroically sacrificed herself in her earliest girlhood to save her father from ruin and who a few years later had risked a priceless happiness to shield a foolish girl, had not in her whole life been conscious of a single romantic instinct. Brave, devoted, but unimaginative by nature, she had followed her heart's direction in most worldly matters.

She was amazed to find that she was becoming romantic now, in her dreams for Orsino's future. All sorts of ideas which she would have laughed at in her own youth flitted through her brain from morning till night. Her fancy built up a life for her eldest son, which she knew to be far from the possibility of realisation, but which had for her a new and strange attraction.

She planned for him the most unimaginable happiness, of a kind which would perhaps have hardly satisfied his more modern instincts. She saw a maiden of indescribable beauty, brought up in unapproachable perfections, guarded by the all but insuperable jealousy of an ideal home. Orsino was to love this vision, and none other, from the first meeting to the term of his natural life, and was to win her in the face or difficulties such as would have made even Giovanni, the incomparable, look grave. This radiant creature was also to love Orsino, as a matter of course, with a love vastly more angelic than human, but not hastily nor thoughtlessly, lest Orsino should get her too easily and not value her as he ought. Then she saw the two betrothed, side by side on shady lawns and moonlit terraces, in a perfectly beautiful intimacy such as they would certainly never enjoy in the existing conditions of their own society. But that mattered little. The wooing, the winning and the marrying of the exquisite girl were to make up Orsino's life, and fifty or sixty years of idyllic happiness were to be the reward of their mutual devotion. Had she not spent twenty such years herself? Then why should not all the rest be possible?

The dreams came and went and she was too sensible not to laugh at them. That was not the youth of Giovanni, her husband, nor of men who even faintly resembled him in her estimation. Giovanni had wandered far, had seen much, and had undoubtedly indulged more than one passing affection, before he had been thirty years of age and had loved Corona. Giovanni would laugh too, if she told him of her vision of two young and beautiful married saints. And his laugh would be more sincere than her own. Nevertheless, her dreams haunted her, as they have haunted many a loving mother, ever since Althaea plucked from the flame the burning brand that measured Meleager's life, and smothered the sparks upon it and hid it away among her treasures.

Such things seem foolish, no doubt, in the measure of fact, in the glaring light of our day. The thought is none the less noble. The dream of an untainted love, the vision of unspotted youth and pure maiden, the glory of unbroken faith kept whole by man and wife in holy wedlock, the pride of stainless name and stainless race—these things are not less high because there is a sublimity in the strength of a great sin which may lie the closer to our sympathy, as the sinning is the nearer to our weakness.

When old Saracinesca looked up from under his bushy brows and laughed and said that his grandson was in love, he thought no more of what he said than if he had remarked that Orsino's beard was growing or that Giovanni's was turning grey. But Corona's pretty fancies received a shock from which they never recovered again, and though she did her best to call them back they lost all their reality from that hour. The plain fact that at one and twenty years the boy is a man, though a very young one, was made suddenly clear to her, and she was faced by another fact still more destructive of her ideals, namely, that a man is not to be kept from falling in love, when and where he is so inclined, by any personal influence whatsoever. She knew that well enough, and the supposition that his first young passion might be for Madame d'Aranjuez was by no means comforting. Corona immediately felt an interest in that lady which she had not felt before and which was not altogether friendly.

It seemed to her necessary in the first place to find out something definite concerning Maria Consuelo, and this was no easy matter. She communicated her wish to her husband when they were alone that evening.

"I know nothing about her," answered Giovanni. "And I do not know any one who does. After all it is of very little importance."

"What if he falls seriously in love with this woman?"

"We will send him round the world. At his age that will cure anything. When he comes back Madame d'Aranjuez will have retired to the chaos of the unknown out of which Orsino has evolved her."

"She does not look the kind of woman to disappear at the right moment," observed Corona doubtfully.

Giovanni was at that moment supremely comfortable, both in mind and body. It was late. The old prince had gone to his own quarters, the boys were in bed, and Orsino was presumably at a party or at the club. Sant' Ilario was enjoying the delight of spending an hour alone in his wife's society. They were in Corona's old boudoir, a place full of associations for them both. He did not want to be mentally disturbed. He said nothing in answer to his wife's remark. She repeated it in a different form.

"Women like her do not disappear when one does not want them," she said.

"What makes you think so?" inquired Giovanni with a man's irritating indolence when he does not mean to grasp a disagreeable idea.

"I know it," Corona answered, resting her chin upon her hand and staring at the fire.

Giovanni surrendered unconditionally.

"You are probably right, dear. You always are about people."

"Well—then you must see the importance of what I say," said Corona pushing her victory.

"Of course, of course," answered Giovanni, squinting at the flames with one eye between his outstretched fingers.

"I wish you would wake up!" exclaimed Corona, taking the hand in hers and drawing it to her. "Orsino is probably making love to Madame d'Aranjuez at this very moment."

"Then I will imitate him, and make love to you, my dear. I could not be better occupied, and you know it. You used to say I did it very well."

Corona laughed in her deep, soft voice.

"Orsino is like you. That is what frightens me. He will make love too well. Be serious, Giovanni. Think of what I am saying."

"Let us dismiss the question then, for the simple reason that there is absolutely nothing to be done. We cannot turn this good woman out of Rome, and we cannot lock Orsino up in his room. To tell a boy not to bestow his affections in a certain quarter is like ramming a charge into a gun and then expecting that it will not come out by the same way. The harder you ram it down the more noise it makes—that is all. Encourage him and he may possibly tire of it. Hinder him and he will become inconveniently heroic."

"I suppose that is true," said Corona. "Then at least find out who the woman is," she added, after a pause.

"I will try," Giovanni answered. "I will even go to the length of spending an hour a day at the club, if that will do any good—and you know how I detest clubs. But if anything whatever is known of her, it will be known there."

Giovanni kept his word and expended more energy in attempting to find out something about Madame d'Aranjuez during the next few days than he had devoted to anything connected with society for a long time. Nearly a week elapsed before his efforts met with any success.

He was in the club one afternoon at an early hour, reading the papers, and not more than three or four other men were present. Among them were Frangipani and Montevarchi, who was formerly known as

Ascanio Bellegra. There was also a certain young foreigner, a diplomatist, who, like Sant' Ilario, was reading a paper, most probably in search of an idea for the next visit on his list.

Giovanni suddenly came upon a description of a dinner and reception given by Del Ferice and his wife. The paragraph was written in the usual florid style with a fine generosity in the distribution of titles to unknown persons.

"The centre of all attraction," said the reporter, "was a most beautiful Spanish princess, Donna Maria Consuelo d'A—z d'A—a, in whose mysterious eyes are reflected the divine fires of a thousand triumphs, and who was gracefully attired in olive green brocade—"

"Oh! Is that it?" said Sant' Ilario aloud, and in the peculiar tone always used by a man who makes a discovery in a daily paper.

"What is it?" inquired Frangipani and Montevarchi in the same breath. The young diplomatist looked up with an air of interrogation.

Sant' Ilario read the paragraph aloud. All three listened as though the fate of empires depended on the facts reported.

"Just like the newspapers!" exclaimed Frangipani. "There probably is no such person. Is there, Ascanio?"

Montevarchi had always been a weak fellow, and was reported to be at present very deep in the building speculations of the day. But there was one point upon which he justly prided himself. He was a superior authority on genealogy. It was his passion and no one ever disputed his knowledge or decision. He stroked his fair beard, looked out of the window, winked his pale blue eyes once or twice and then gave his verdict.

"There is no such person," he said gravely.

"I beg your pardon, prince," said the young diplomatist, "I have met her. She exists."

"My dear friend," answered Montevarchi, "I do not doubt the existence of the woman, as such, and I would certainly not think of disagreeing with you, even if I had the slightest ground for doing so, which, I hasten to say, I have not. Nor, of course, if she is a friend of yours, would I like to say more on the subject. But I have taken some little interest in genealogy and I have a modest library—about two thousand volumes, only—consisting solely of works on the subject, all of which I have read and many of which I have carefully annotated. I need not say that they are all at your disposal if you should desire to make any researches."

Montevarchi had much of his murdered father's manner, without the old man's strength. The young secretary of embassy was rather startled at the idea of searching through two thousand volumes in pursuit of Madame d'Aranjuez's identity. Sant' Ilario laughed.

"I only mean that I have met the lady," said the young man. "Of course you are right. I have no idea who she may really be. I have heard odd stories about her."

"Oh—have you?" asked Sant' Ilario with renewed interest.

"Yes, very odd." He paused and looked round the room to assure himself that no one else was present. "There are two distinct stories about her. The first is this. They say that she is a South American prima donna, who sang only a few months, at Rio de Janeiro and then at Buenos Ayres. An Italian who had gone out there and made a fortune married her from the stage. In coming to Europe, he unfortunately fell overboard and she inherited all his money. People say that she was the only person who witnessed the accident. The man's name was Aragno. She twisted it once and made Aranjuez of it, and she turned it again and discovered that it spelled Aragona. That is the first story. It sounds well at all events."

"Very," said Sant' Ilario, with a laugh.

"A profoundly interesting page in genealogy, if she happens to marry somebody," observed Montevarchi, mentally noting all the facts.

"What is the other story?" asked Frangipani.

"The other story is much less concise and detailed. According to this version, she is the daughter of a certain royal personage and of a Polish countess. There is always a Polish countess in those stories! She was never married. The royal personage has had her educated in a convent and has sent her out into the wide world with a pretty fancy name of his own invention, plentifully supplied with money and regular documents referring to her union with the imaginary Aranjuez, and protected by a sort of body-guard of mutes and duennas who never appear in public. She is of course to make a great match for herself, and has come to Rome to do it. That is also a pretty tale."

"More interesting than the other," said Montevarchi. "These side lights of genealogy, these stray rivulets of royal races, if I may so poetically call them, possess an absorbing interest for the student. I will make a note of it."

"Of course, I do not vouch for the truth of a single word in either story," observed the young man. "Of the two the first is the less improbable. I have met her and talked to her and she is certainly not less than five and twenty years old. She may be more. In any case she is too old to have been just let out of a convent."

"Perhaps she has been loose for some years," observed Sant' Ilario, speaking of her as though she were a dangerous wild animal.

"We should have heard of her," objected the other. "She has the sort of personality which is noticed anywhere and which makes itself felt."

"Then you incline to the belief that she dropped the Signor Aragno quietly overboard in the neighbourhood of the equator?"

"The real story may be quite different from either of those I have told you."

"And she is a friend of poor old Donna Tullia!" exclaimed Montevarchi regretfully. "I am sorry for that. For the sake of her history I could almost have gone to the length of making her acquaintance."

"How the Del Ferice would rave if she could hear you call her poor old Donna Tullia," observed Frangipani. "I remember how she danced at the ball when I came of age!"

"That was a long time ago, Filippo," said Montevarchi thoughtfully, "a very long time ago. We were all young once, Filippo—but Donna Tullia is really only fit to fill a glass case in a museum of natural history now."

The remark was not original, and had been in circulation some time. But the three men laughed a little and Montevarchi was much pleased by their appreciation. He and Frangipani began to talk together, and Sant' Ilario took up his paper again. When the young diplomatist laid his own aside and went out, Giovanni followed him, and they left the club together.

"Have you any reason to believe that there is anything irregular about this Madame d'Aranjuez?" asked Sant' Ilario.

"No. Stories of that kind are generally inventions. She has not been presented at Court—but that means nothing here. And there is a doubt about her nationality—but no one has asked her directly about it."

"May I ask who told you the stories?"

The young man's face immediately lost all expression.

"Really—I have quite forgotten," he said. "People have been talking about her."

Sant' Ilario justly concluded that his companion's informant was a lady, and probably one in whom the diplomatist was interested. Discretion is so rare that it can easily be traced to its causes. Giovanni left the young man and walked away in the opposite direction, inwardly meditating a piece of diplomacy quite foreign to his nature. He said to himself that he would watch the man in the world and that it would be easy to guess who the lady in question was. It would have been clear to any one but himself that he was not likely to learn anything worth knowing, by his present mode of procedure.

"Gouache," he said, entering the artist's studio a quarter of an hour later, "do you know anything about Madame d'Aranjuez?"

"That is all I know," Gouache answered, pointing to Maria Consuelo's portrait which stood finished upon an easel before him, set in an old frame. He had been touching it when Giovanni entered. "That is all I know, and I do not know that thoroughly. I wish I did. She is a wonderful subject."

Sant' Ilario gazed at the picture in silence.

"Are her eyes really like these?" he asked at length.

"Much finer."

"And her mouth?"

"Much larger," answered Gouache with a smile.

"She is bad," said Giovanni with conviction, and he thought of the Signor Aragno.

"Women are never bad," observed Gouache with a thoughtful air. "Some are less angelic than others. You need only tell them all so to assure yourself of the fact."

"I daresay. What is this person? French, Spanish—South American?"

"I have not the least idea. She is not French, at all events."

"Excuse me—does your wife know her?"

Gouache glanced quickly at his visitor's face.

"No."

Gouache was a singularly kind man, and he did his best perhaps for reasons of his own, to convey nothing by the monosyllable beyond the simple negation of a fact. But the effort was not altogether successful. There was an almost imperceptible shade of surprise in the tone which did not escape Giovanni. On the other hand it was perfectly clear to Gouache that Sant' Ilario's interest in the matter was connected with Orsino.

"I cannot find any one who knows anything definite," said Giovanni after a pause.

"Have you tried Spicca?" asked the artist, examining his work critically.

"No. Why Spicca?"

"He always knows everything," answered Gouache vaguely. "By the way, Saracinesca, do you not think there might be a little more light just over the left eye?"

"How should I know?"

"You ought to know. What is the use of having been brought up under the very noses of original portraits, all painted by the best masters and doubtless ordered by your ancestors at a very considerable expense—if you do not know?"

Giovanni laughed.

"My dear old friend," he said good-humouredly, "have you known us nearly five and twenty years without discovering that it is our peculiar privilege to be ignorant without reproach?"

Gouache laughed in his turn.

"You do not often make sharp remarks—but when you do!"

Giovanni left the studio very soon, and went in search of Spicca. It was no easy matter to find the peripatetic cynic on a winter's afternoon, but Gouache's remark had seemed to mean something, and Sant' Ilario saw a faint glimmer of hope in the distance. He knew Spicca's habits very well, and was aware that when the sun was low he would certainly turn into one of the many houses where he was intimate, and spend an hour over a cup of tea. The difficulty lay in ascertaining which particular fireside he would select on that afternoon. Giovanni hastily sketched a route for himself and asked the porter at each of his friends' houses if Spicca had entered. Fortune favoured him at last. Spicca was drinking his tea with the Marchesa di San Giacinto.

Giovanni paused a moment before the gateway of the palace in which San Giacinto had inhabited a large hired apartment for many years. He did not see much of his cousin, now, on account of differences in political opinion, and he had no reason whatever for calling on Flavia, especially as formal New Year's visits had lately been exchanged. However, as San Giacinto was now a leading authority on questions of landed property in the city, it struck him that he could pretend a desire to see Flavia's husband, and make that an excuse for staying a long time, if necessary, in order to wait for him.

He found Flavia and Spicca alone together, with a small tea-table between them. The air was heavy with the smoke of cigarettes, which clung to the oriental curtains and hung in clouds about the rare palms and plants. Everything in the San Giacinto house was large, comfortable and unostentatious. There was not a chair to be seen which might not have held the giant's frame. San Giacinto was a wonderful judge of what was good. If he paid twice as much as Montevarchi for a horse, the horse turned out to be capable of four times the work. If he bought a picture at a sale, it was discovered to be by some good master and other people wondered why they had lost courage in the bidding for a trifle of a hundred francs. Nothing ever turned out badly with him, but no success had the power to shake his solid prudence. No one knew how rich he was, but those who had watched him understood that he would never let the world guess at half his fortune. He was a giant in all ways and he had shown what he could do when he had dominated Flavia during the first year of their marriage. She had at first been proud of him, but about the time when she would have wearied of another man, she discovered that she feared him in a way she certainly did not fear the devil. Yet lie had never spoken a harsh, word to her in his life. But there was something positively appalling to her in his enormous strength, rarely exhibited and never without good reason, but always quietly present, as the outline of a vast mountain reflected in a placid lake. Then she discovered to her great surprise that he really loved her, which she had not expected, and at the end of three years he became aware that she loved him, which was still more astonishing. As usual, his investment had turned out well.

At the time of which I am speaking Flavia was a slight, graceful woman of forty years or thereabouts, retaining much of the brilliant prettiness which served her for beauty, and conspicuous always for her extremely bright eyes. She was of the type of women who live to a great age.

She had not expected to see Sant' Ilario, and as she gave her hand, she looked up at him with an air of inquiry. It would have been like him to say that he had come to see her husband and not herself, for he had no tact with persons whom he did not especially like. There are such people in the world.

"Will you give me a cup of tea, Flavia?" he asked, as he sat down, after shaking hands with Spicca.

"Have you at last heard that your cousin's tea is good?" inquired the latter, who was surprised by Giovanni's coming.

"I am afraid it is cold," said Flavia, looking into the teapot, as though she could discover the temperature by inspection.

"It is no matter," answered Giovanni absently.

He was wondering how he could lead the conversation to the discussion of Madame d'Aranjuez.

"You belong to the swallowers," observed Spicca, lighting a fresh cigarette. "You swallow something, no matter what, and you are satisfied."

"It is the simplest way—one is never disappointed."

"It is a pity one cannot swallow people in the same way," said Flavia with a laugh.

"Most people do," answered Spicca viciously.

"Were you at the Jubilee on the first day?" asked Giovanni, addressing Flavia.

"Of course I was—and you spoke to me."

"That is true. By the bye, I saw that excellent Donna Tullia there. I wonder whose ticket she had."

"She had the Princess Befana's," answered Spicca, who knew everything. "The old lady happened to be dying—she always dies at the beginning of the season—it used to be for economy, but it has become a habit—and so Del Ferice bought her card of her servant for his wife."

"Who was the lady who sat with her?" asked Giovanni, delighted with his own skill.

"You ought to know!" exclaimed Flavia. "We all saw Orsino take her out. That is the famous, the incomparable Madame d'Aranjuez—the most beautiful of Spanish princesses according to to-day's paper. I daresay you have seen the account of the Del Ferice party. She is no more Spanish than Alexander the Great. Is she, Spicca?"

"No, she is not Spanish," answered the latter.

"Then what in the world is she?" asked Giovanni impatiently.

"How should I know? Of course it is very disagreeable for you." It was Flavia who spoke.

"Disagreeable? How?"

"Why, about Orsino of course. Everybody says he is devoted to her."

"I wish everybody would mind his and her business," said Giovanni sharply. "Because a boy makes the acquaintance of a stranger at a studio—"

"Oh—it was at a studio? I did not know that."

"Yes, at Gouache's—I fancied your sister might have told you that," said Giovanni, growing more and more irritable, and yet not daring to change the subject, lest he should lose some valuable information. "Because Orsino makes her acquaintance accidentally, every one must say that he is in love with her."

Flavia laughed.

"My dear Giovanni," she answered. "Let us be frank. I used never to tell the truth under any circumstances, when I was a girl, but Giovanni—my Giovanni—did not like that. Do you know what he did? He used to cut off a hundred francs of my allowance for every fib I told—laughing at me all the time. At the end of the first quarter I positively had not a pair of shoes, and all my gloves had been cleaned twice. He used to keep all the fines in a special pocket-book—if you knew how hard I tried to steal it! But I could not. Then, of course, I reformed. There was nothing else to be done—that or rags—fancy! And do you know? I have grown quite used to being truthful. Besides, it is so original, that I pose with it."

Flavia paused, laughed a little, and puffed at her cigarette.

"You do not often come to see me, Giovanni," she said, "and since you are here I am going to tell you the truth about your visit. You are beside yourself with rage at Orsino's new fancy, and you want to find out all about this Madame d'Aranjuez. So you came here, because we are Whites and you saw that she had been at the Del Ferice party, and you know that we know them—and the rest is sung by the organ, as we say when high mass is over. Is that the truth, or not?"

"Approximately," said Giovanni, smiling in spite of himself.

"Does Corona cut your allowance when you tell fibs?" asked Flavia. "No? Then why say that it is only approximately true?"

"I have my reasons. And you can tell me nothing?"

"Nothing. I believe Spicca knows all about her. But he will not tell what he knows."

Spicca made no answer to this, and Giovanni determined to outstay him, or rather, to stay until he rose to go and then go with him. It was tedious work for he was not a man who could talk against time on all occasions. But he struggled bravely and Spicca at last got up from his deep chair. They went out together, and stopped as though by common consent upon the brilliantly lighted landing of the first floor.

"Seriously, Spicca," said Giovanni, "I am afraid Orsino is falling in love with this pretty stranger. If you can tell me anything about her, please do so."

Spicca stared at the wall, hesitated a moment, and then looked straight into his companion's eyes.

"Have you any reason to suppose that I, and I especially, know anything about this lady?" he asked.

"No—except that you know everything."

"That is a fable." Spicca turned from him and began to descend the stairs.

Giovanni followed and laid a hand upon his arm.

"You will not do me this service?" he asked earnestly.

Again Spicca stopped and looked at him.

"You and I are very old friends, Giovanni," he said slowly. "I am older than you, but we have stood by each other very often—in places more slippery than these marble steps. Do not let us quarrel now, old friend. When I tell you that my omniscience exists only in the vivid imaginations of people whose tea I like, believe me, and if you wish to do me a kindness—for the sake of old times—do not help to spread the idea that I know everything."

The melancholy Spicca had never been given to talking about friendship or its mutual obligations. Indeed, Giovanni could not remember having ever heard him speak as he had just spoken. It was perfectly clear that he knew something very definite about Maria Consuelo, and he probably had no intention of deceiving Giovanni in that respect. But Spicca also knew his man, and he knew that his appeal for Giovanni's silence would not be vain.

"Very well," said Sant' Ilario.

They exchanged a few indifferent words before parting, and then Giovanni walked slowly homeward, pondering on the things he had heard that day.

CHAPTER VIII

While Giovanni was exerting himself to little purpose in attempting to gain information concerning Maria Consuelo, she had launched herself upon the society of which the Countess Del Ferice was an important and influential member. Chance, and probably chance alone, had guided her in the matter of this acquaintance, for it could certainly not be said that she had forced herself upon Donna Tullia, nor even shown any uncommon readiness to meet the latter's advances. The offer of a seat in her carriage had seemed natural enough, under the circumstances, and Donna Tullia had been perfectly free to refuse it if she had chosen to do so.

Though possessing but the very slightest grounds for believing herself to be a born diplomatist, the Countess had always delighted in petty plotting and scheming. She now saw a possibility of annoying all Orsino's relations by attracting the object of Orsino's devotion to her own house. She had no especial reason for supposing that the young man was really very much in love with Madame d'Aranjuez, but her woman's instinct, which far surpassed her diplomatic talents in acuteness, told her that Orsino was certainly not indifferent to the interesting stranger. She argued, primitively enough, that to annoy Orsino must be equivalent to annoying his people, and she supposed that she could do nothing more disagreeable to the young man's wishes than to induce Madame d'Aranjuez to join that part of society from which all the Saracinesca were separated by an insuperable barrier.

And Orsino indeed resented the proceeding, as she had expected; but his family were at first more inclined to look upon Donna Tullia as a good angel who had carried off the tempter at the right moment to an unapproachable distance. It was not to be believed that Orsino could do anything so monstrous as to enter Del Ferice's house or ask a place in Del Ferice's circle, and it was accordingly a relief to find that Madame d'Aranjuez had definitely chosen to do so, and had appeared in olive-green brocade at the Del

Ferice's last party. The olive-green brocade would now assuredly not figure in the gatherings of the Saracinesca's intimate friends.

Like every one else, Orsino read the daily chronicle of Roman life in the papers, and until he saw Maria Consuelo's name among the Del Ferice's guests, he refused to believe that she had taken the irrevocable step he so much feared. He had still entertained vague notions of bringing about a meeting between her and his mother, and he saw at a glance that such a meeting was now quite out of the question. This was the first severe shock his vanity had ever received and he was surprised at the depth of his own annoyance. Maria Consuelo might indeed have been seen once with Donna Tullia, and might have gone once to the latter's day. That was bad enough, but might be remedied by tact and decision in her subsequent conduct. But there was no salvation possible after a person had been advertised in the daily paper as Madame d'Aranjuez had been. Orsino was very angry. He had been once to see her since his first visit, and she had said nothing about this invitation, though Donna Tullia's name had been mentioned. He was offended with her for not telling him that she was going to the dinner, as though he had any right to be made acquainted with her intentions. He had no sooner made the discovery than he determined to visit his anger upon her, and throwing the paper aside went straight to the hotel where she was stopping.

Maria Consuelo was at home and he was ushered into the little sitting-room without delay. To his inexpressible disgust he found Del Ferice himself installed upon the chair near the table, engaged in animated conversation with Madame d'Aranjuez. The situation was awkward in the extreme. Orsino hoped that Del Ferice would go at once, and thus avoid the necessity of an introduction. But Ugo did nothing of the kind. He rose, indeed, but did not take his hat from the table, and stood smiling pleasantly while Orsino shook hands with Maria Consuelo.

"Let me make you acquainted," she said with exasperating calmness, and she named the two men to each other.

Ugo put out his hand quietly and Orsino was obliged to take it, which he did coldly enough. Ugo had more than his share of tact, and he never made a disagreeable impression upon any one if he could help it. Maria Consuelo seemed to take everything for granted, and Orsino's appearance did not disconcert her in the slightest degree. Both men sat down and looked at her as though expecting that she would choose a subject of conversation for them.

"We were talking of the change in Rome," she said. "Monsieur Del Ferice takes a great interest in all that is doing, and he was explaining to me some of the difficulties with which he has to contend."

"Don Orsino knows what they are, as well as I, though we might perhaps differ as to the way of dealing with them," said Del Ferice.

"Yes," answered Orsino, more coldly than was necessary. "You play the active part, and we the passive."

"In a certain sense, yes," returned the other, quite unruffled. "You have exactly defined the situation, and ours is by far the more disagreeable and thankless part to play. Oh—I am not going to defend all we have done! I only defend what we mean to do. Change of any sort is execrable to the man of taste, unless it is brought about by time—and that is a beautifier which we have not at our disposal. We are half Vandals and half Americans, and we are in a terrible hurry."

Maria Consuelo laughed, and Orsino's face became a shade less gloomy. He had expected to find Del Ferice the arrogant, self-satisfied apostle of the modern, which he was represented to be.

"Could you not have taken a little more time?" asked Orsino.

"I cannot see how. Besides it is our time which takes us with it. So long as Rome was the capital of an idea there was no need of haste in doing anything. But when it became the capital of a modern kingdom, it fell a victim to modern facts—which are not beautiful. The most we can hope to do is to direct the current, clumsily enough, I daresay. We cannot stop it. Nothing short of Oriental despotism could. We cannot prevent people from flocking to the centre, and where there is a population it must be housed."

"Evidently," said Madame d'Aranjuez.

"It seems to me that, without disturbing the old city, a new one might have been built beside it," observed Orsino.

"No doubt. And that is practically what we have done. I say 'we,' because you say 'you.' But I think you will admit that, as far as personal activity is concerned, the Romans of Rome are taking as active a share in building ugly houses as any of the Italian Romans. The destruction of the Villa Ludovisi, for instance, was forced upon the owner not by the national government but by an insane municipality, and those who have taken over the building lots are largely Roman princes of the old stock."

The argument was unanswerable, and Orsino knew it, a fact which did not improve his temper. It was disagreeable enough to be forced into a conversation with Del Ferice, and it was still worse to be obliged to agree with him. Orsino frowned and said nothing, hoping that the subject would drop. But Del Ferice had only produced an unpleasant impression in order to remove it and thereby improve the whole situation, which was one of the most difficult in which he had found himself for some time.

"I repeat," he said, with a pleasant smile, "that it is hopeless to defend all of what is actually done in our day in Rome. Some of your friends and many of mine are building houses which even age and ruin will never beautify. The only defensible part of the affair is the political change which has brought about the necessity of building at all, and upon that point I think that we may agree to differ. Do you not think so, Don Orsino?"

"By all means," answered the young man, conscious that the proposal was both just and fitting.

"And for the rest, both your friends and mine—for all I know, your own family and certainly I myself— have enormous interests at stake. We may at least agree to hope that none of us may be ruined."

"Certainly—though we have had nothing to do with the matter. Neither my father nor my grandfather have entered into any such speculation."

"It is a pity," said Del Ferice thoughtfully.

"Why a pity?"

"On the one hand my instincts are basely commercial," Del Ferice answered with a frank laugh. "No matter how great a fortune may be, it may be doubled and trebled. You must remember that I am a banker in fact if not exactly in designation, and the opportunity is excellent. But the greater pity is that such men as you, Don Orsino, who could exercise as much influence as it might please you to use, leave it to men—very unlike you, I fancy—to murder the architecture of Rome and prepare the triumph of the hideous."

Orsino did not answer the remark, although he was not altogether displeased with the idea it conveyed. Maria Consuelo looked at him.

"Why do you stand aloof and let things go from bad to worse when you might really do good by joining in the affairs of the day?" she asked.

"I could not join in them, if I would," answered Orsino.

"Why not?"

"Because I have not command of a hundred francs in the world, Madame. That is the simplest and best of all reasons."

Del Ferice laughed incredulously.

"The eldest son of Casa Saracinesca would not find that a practical obstacle," he said, taking his hat and rising to go. "Besides, what is needed in these transactions is not so much ready money as courage, decision and judgment. There is a rich firm of contractors now doing a large business, who began with three thousand francs as their whole capital—what you might lose at cards in an evening without missing it, though you say that you have no money at your command."

"Is that possible?" asked Orsino with some interest.

"It is a fact. There were three men, a tobacconist, a carpenter and a mason, and they each had a thousand francs of savings. They took over a contract last week for a million and a half, on which they will clear twenty per cent. But they had the qualities—the daring and the prudence combined. They succeeded."

"And if they had failed, what would have happened?"

"They would have lost their three thousand francs. They had nothing else to lose, and there was nothing in the least irregular about their transactions. Good evening, Madame—I have a private meeting of directors at my house. Good evening, Don Orsino."

He went out, leaving behind him an impression which was not by any means disagreeable. His appearance was against him, Orsino thought. His fat white face and dull eyes were not pleasant to look at. But he had shown tact in a difficult situation, and there was a quiet energy about him, a settled purpose which could not fail to please a young man who hated his own idleness.

Orsino found that his mood had changed. He was less angry than he had meant to be, and he saw extenuating circumstances where he had at first only seen a wilful mistake. He sat down again.

"Confess that he is not the impossible creature you supposed," said Maria Consuelo with a laugh.

"No, he is not. I had imagined something very different. Nevertheless, I wish—one never has the least right to wish what one wishes—" He stopped in the middle of the sentence.

"That I had not gone to his wife's party, you would say? But my dear Don Orsino, why should I refuse pleasant things when they come into my life?"

"Was it so pleasant?"

"Of course it was. A beautiful dinner—half a dozen clever men, all interested in the affairs of the day, and all anxious to explain them to me because I was a stranger. A hundred people or so in the evening, who all seemed to enjoy themselves as much as I did. Why should I refuse all that? Because my first acquaintance in Rome—who was Gouache—is so 'indifferent,' and because you—my second—are a pronounced clerical? That is not reasonable."

"I do not pretend to be reasonable," said Orsino. "To be reasonable is the boast of people who feel nothing."

"Then you are a man of heart?" Maria Consuelo seemed amused.

"I make no pretence to being a man of head, Madame."

"You are not easily caught."

"Nor Del Ferice either."

"Why do you talk of him?"

"The opportunity is good, Madame. As he is just gone, we know that he is not coming."

"You can be very sarcastic, when you like," said Maria Consuelo. "But I do not believe that you are as bitter as you make yourself out to be. I do not even believe that you found Del Ferice so very disagreeable as you pretend. You were certainly interested in what he said."

"Interest is not always agreeable. The guillotine, for instance, possesses the most lively interest for the condemned man at an execution."

"Your illustrations are startling. I once saw an execution, quite by accident, and I would rather not think of it. But you can hardly compare Del Ferice to the guillotine."

"He is as noiseless, as keen and as sure," said Orsino smartly.

"There is such a thing as being too clever," answered Maria Consuelo, without a smile.

"Is Del Ferice a case of that?"

"No. You are. You say cutting things merely because they come into your head, though I am sure that you do not always mean them. It is a bad habit."

"Because it makes enemies, Madame?" Orsino was annoyed by the rebuke.

"That is the least good of good reasons."

"Another, then?"

"It will prevent people from loving you," said Maria Consuelo gravely.

"I never heard that—"

"No? It is true, nevertheless."

"In that case I will reform at once," said Orsino, trying to meet her eyes. But she looked away from him.

"You think that I am preaching to you," she answered. "I have not the right to do that, and if I had, I would certainly not use it. But I have seen something of the world. Women rarely love a man who is bitter against any one but himself. If he says cruel things of other women, the one to whom he says them believes that he will say much worse of her to the next he meets; if he abuses the men she knows, she likes it even less—it is an attack on her judgment, on her taste and perhaps upon a half-developed sympathy for the man attacked. One should never be witty at another person's expense, except with one's own sex." She laughed a little.

"What a terrible conclusion!"

"Is it? It is the true one."

"Then the way to win a woman's love is to praise her acquaintances? That is original."

"I never said that."

"No? I misunderstood. What is the best way?"

"Oh—it is very simple," laughed Maria Consuelo.

"Tell her you love her, and tell her so again and again—you will certainly please her in the end."

"Madame—" Orsino stopped, and folded his hands with an air of devout supplication.

"What?"

"Oh, nothing! I was about to begin. It seemed so simple, as you say."

They both laughed and their eyes met for a moment.

"Del Ferice interests me very much," said Maria Consuelo, abruptly returning to the original subject of conversation. "He is one of those men who will be held responsible for much that is now doing. Is it not true? He has great influence."

"I have always heard so." Orsino was not pleased at being driven to talk of Del Ferice again.

"Do you think what he said about you so altogether absurd?"

"Absurd, no—impracticable, perhaps. You mean his suggestion that I should try a little speculation? Frankly, I had no idea that such things could be begun with so little capital. It seems incredible. I fancy that Del Ferice was exaggerating. You know how carelessly bankers talk of a few thousands, more or less. Nothing short of a million has much meaning for them. Three thousand or thirty thousand—it is much the same in their estimation."

"I daresay. After all, why should you risk anything? I suppose it is simpler to play cards, though I should think it less amusing. I was only thinking how easy it would be for you to find a serious occupation if you chose."

Orsino was silent for a moment, and seemed to be thinking over the matter.

"Would you advise me to enter upon such a business without my father's knowledge?" he asked presently.

"How can I advise you? Besides, your father would let you do as you please. There is nothing dishonourable in such things. The prejudice against business is old-fashioned, and if you do not break through it your children will."

Orsino looked thoughtfully at Maria Consuelo. She sometimes found an oddly masculine bluntness with which to express her meaning, and which produced a singular impression on the young man. It made him feel what he supposed to be a sort of weakness, of which he ought to be ashamed.

"There is nothing dishonourable in the theory," he answered, "and the practice depends on the individual."

Maria Consuelo laughed.

"You see—you can be a moralist when you please," she said.

There was a wonderful attraction in her yellow eyes just at that moment.

"To please you, Madame, I could do something much worse—or much better."

He was not quite in earnest, but he was not jesting, and his face was more serious than his voice. Maria Consuelo's hand was lying on the table beside the silver paper-cutter. The white, pointed fingers were very tempting and he would willingly have touched them. He put out his hand. If she did not draw hers away he would lay his own upon it. If she did, he would take up the paper-cutter. As it turned out, he had to content himself with the latter. She did not draw her hand away as though she understood what he was going to do, but quietly raised it and turned the shade of the lamp a few inches.

"I would rather not be responsible for your choice," she said quietly.

"And yet you have left me none," he answered with, sudden boldness.

"No? How so?"

He held up the silver knife and smiled.

"I do not understand," she said, affecting a look of surprise.

"I was going to ask your permission to take your hand."

"Indeed? Why? There it is." She held it out frankly.

He took the beautiful fingers in his and looked at them for a moment. Then he quietly raised them to his lips.

"That was not included in the permission," she said, with a little laugh and drawing back. "Now you ought to go away at once."

"Why?"

"Because that little ceremony can belong only to the beginning or the end of a visit."

"I have only just come."

"Ah? How long the time has seemed! I fancied you had been here half an hour."

"To me it has seemed but a minute," answered Orsino promptly.

"And you will not go?"

There was nothing of the nature of a peremptory dismissal in the look which accompanied the words.

"No—at the most, I will practise leave-taking."

"I think not," said Maria Consuelo with sudden coldness. "You are a little too—what shall I say?—too enterprising, prince. You had better make use of the gift where it will be a recommendation—in business, for instance."

"You are very severe, Madame," answered Orsino, deeming it wiser to affect humility, though a dozen sharp answers suggested themselves to his ready wit.

Maria Consuelo was silent for a few seconds. Her head was resting upon the little red morocco cushion, which heightened the dazzling whiteness of her skin and lent a deeper colour to her auburn hair. She was gazing at the hangings above the door. Orsino watched her in quiet admiration. She was beautiful as he saw her there at that moment, for the irregularities of her features were forgotten in the brilliancy of her colouring and in the grace of the attitude. Her face was serious at first. Gradually a smile stole over it, beginning, as it seemed, from the deeply set eyes and concentrating itself at last in the full, red mouth. Then she spoke, still looking upwards and away from him.

"What would you think if I were not a little severe?" she asked. "I am a woman living—travelling, I should say—quite alone, a stranger here, and little less than a stranger to you. What would you think if I were not a little severe, I say? What conclusion would you come to, if I let you take my hand as often as you pleased, and say whatever suggested itself to your imagination—your very active imagination?"

"I should think you the most adorable of women—"

"But it is not my ambition to be thought the most adorable of women by you, Prince Orsino."

"No—of course not. People never care for what they get without an effort."

"You are absolutely irrepressible!" exclaimed Maria Consuelo, laughing in spite of herself.

"And you do not like that! I will be meekness itself—a lamb, if you please."

"Too playful—it would not suit your style."

"A stone—"

"I detest geology."

"A lap-dog, then. Make your choice, Madame. The menagerie of the universe is at your disposal. When Adam gave names to the animals, he could have called a lion a lap-dog—to reassure the Africans. But he lacked imagination—he called a cat, a cat."

"That had the merit of simplicity, at all events."

"Since you admire his system, you may call me either Cain or Abel," suggested Orsino. "Am I humble enough? Can submission go farther?"

"Either would be flattery—for Abel was good and Cain was interesting."

"And I am neither—you give me another opportunity of exhibiting my deep humility. I thank you sincerely. You are becoming more gracious than I had hoped."

"You are very like a woman, Don Orsino. You always try to have the last word."

"I always hope that the last word may be the best. But I accept the criticism—or the reproach, with my usual gratitude. I only beg you to observe that to let you have the last word would be for me to end the conversation, after which I should be obliged to go away. And I do not wish to go, as I have already said."

"You suggest the means of making you go," answered Maria Consuelo, with a smile. "I can be silent—if you will not."

"It will be useless. If you do not interrupt me, I shall become eloquent—"

"How terrible! Pray do not!"

"You see! I have you in my power. You cannot get rid of me."

"I would appeal to your generosity, then."

"That is another matter, Madame," said Orsino, taking his hat.

"I only said that I would—" Maria Consuelo made a gesture to stop him.

But he was wise enough to see that the conversation had reached its natural end, and his instinct told him that he should not outstay his welcome. He pretended not to see the motion of her hand, and rose to take his leave.

"You do not know me," he said. "To point out to me a possible generous action, is to ensure my performing it without hesitation. When may I be so fortunate as to see you again, Madame?"

"You need not be so intensely ceremonious. You know that I am always at home at this hour."

Orsino was very much struck by this answer. There was a shade of irritation in the tone, which he had certainly not expected, and which flattered him exceedingly. She turned her face away as she gave him her hand and moved a book on the table with the other as though she meant to begin reading almost before he should be out of the room. He had not felt by any means sure that she really liked his society, and he had not expected that she would so far forget herself as to show her inclination by her impatience. He had judged, rightly or wrongly, that she was a woman who weighed every word and gesture beforehand, and who would be incapable of such an oversight as an unpremeditated manifestation of feeling.

Very young men are nowadays apt to imagine complications of character where they do not exist, often overlooking them altogether where they play a real part. The passion for analysis discovers what it takes for new simple elements in humanity's motives, and often ends by feeding on itself in the effort to decompose what is not composite. The greatest analysers are perhaps the young and the old, who, being respectively before and behind the times, are not so intimate with them as those who are actually making history, political or social, ethical or scandalous, dramatic or comic.

It is very much the custom among those who write fiction in the English language to efface their own individuality behind the majestic but rather meaningless plural, "we," or to let the characters created express the author's view of mankind. The great French novelists are more frank, for they say boldly "I," and have the courage of their opinions. Their merit is the greater, since those opinions seem to be rarely complimentary to the human race in general, or to their readers in particular. Without introducing any comparison between the fiction of the two languages, it may be said that the tendency of the method is identical in both cases and is the consequence of an extreme preference for analysis, to the detriment of the romantic and very often of the dramatic element in the modern novel. The result may or may not be a volume of modern social history for the instruction of the present and the future generation. If it is not, it loses one of the chief merits which it claims; if it is, then we must admit the rather strange deduction, that the political history of our times has absorbed into itself all the romance and the tragedy at the disposal of destiny, leaving next to none at all in the private lives of the actors and their numerous relations.

Whatever the truth may be, it is certain that this love of minute dissection is exercising an enormous influence in our time; and as no one will pretend that a majority of the young persons in society who analyse the motives of their contemporaries and elders are successful moral anatomists, we are forced to the conclusion that they are frequently indebted to their imaginations for the results they obtain and not seldom for the material upon which they work. A real Chemistry may some day grow out of the failures of this fanciful Alchemy, but the present generation will hardly live to discover the philosopher's stone, though the search for it yield gold, indirectly, by the writing of many novels. If fiction is to be counted among the arts at all, it is not yet time to forget the saying of a very great man: "It is the mission of all art to create and foster agreeable illusions."

Orsino Saracinesca was no further removed from the action of the analytical bacillus than other men of his age. He believed and desired his own character to be more complicated than it was, and he had no sooner made the acquaintance of Maria Consuelo than he began to attribute to her minutest actions such a tortuous web of motives as would have annihilated all action if it had really existed in her brain. The possible simplicity of a strong and much tried character, good or bad, altogether escaped him, and even an occasional unrestrained word or gesture failed to convince him that he was on the wrong track. To tell the truth, he was as yet very inexperienced. His visits to Maria Consuelo passed in making light conversation. He tried to amuse her, and succeeded fairly well, while at the same time he indulged in endless and fruitless speculations as to her former life, her present intentions and her sentiments with regard to himself. He would have liked to lead her into talking of herself, but he did not know where to begin. It was not a part of his system to believe in mysteries concerning people, but when he reflected upon the matter he was amazed at the impenetrability of the barrier which cut him off from all knowledge of her life. He soon heard the tales about her which were carelessly circulated at the club, and he listened to them without much interest, though he took the trouble to deny their truth on his own responsibility, which surprised the men who knew him and gave rise to the story that he was in love with Madame d'Aranjuez. The most annoying consequence of the rumour was that every woman to whom he spoke in society overwhelmed him with questions which he could not answer except in the vaguest terms. In his ignorance he did his best to evolve a satisfactory history for Maria Consuelo out of his imagination, but the result was not satisfactory.

He continued his visits to her, resolving before each meeting that he would risk offending her by putting some question which she must either answer directly or refuse to answer altogether. But he had not counted upon his own inherent hatred of rudeness, nor upon the growth of an attachment which he had not foreseen when he had coldly made up his mind that it would be worth while to make love to her, as Gouache had laughingly suggested. Yet he was pleased with what he deemed his own coldness. He assuredly did not love her, but he knew already that he would not like to give up the half hours he spent with her. To offend her seriously would be to forfeit a portion of his daily amusement which he could not spare.

From time to time he risked a careless, half-jesting declaration such as many a woman might have taken seriously. But Maria Consuelo turned such advances with a laugh or by an answer that was admirably tempered with quiet dignity and friendly rebuke.

"If she is not good," he said to himself at last, "she must be enormously clever. She must be one or the other."

CHAPTER IX

Orsino's twenty-first birthday fell in the latter part of January, when the Roman season was at its height, but as the young man's majority did not bring him any of those sudden changes in position which make epochs in the lives of fatherless sons, the event was considered as a family matter and no great social celebration of it was contemplated. It chanced, too, that the day of the week was the one appropriated by the Montevarchi for their weekly dance, with which it would have been a mistake to interfere. The old Prince Saracinesca, however, insisted that a score of old friends should be asked to dinner, to drink the health of his eldest grandson, and this was accordingly done.

Orsino always looked back to that banquet as one of the dullest at which he ever assisted. The friends were literally old, and their conversation was not brilliant. Each one on arriving addressed to him a few congratulatory and moral sentiments, clothed in rounded periods and twanging of Cicero in his most sermonising mood. Each drank his especial health at the end of the dinner in a teaspoonful of old "vin santo," and each made a stiff compliment to Corona on her youthful appearance. The men were almost all grandees of Spain of the first class and wore their ribbons by common consent, which lent the assembly an imposing appearance; but several of them were of a somnolent disposition and nodded after dinner, which did not contribute to prolong the effect produced. Orsino thought their stories and anecdotes very long-winded and pointless, and even the old prince himself seemed oppressed by the solemnity of the affair, and rarely laughed. Corona, with serene good humour did her best to make conversation, and a shade of animation occasionally appeared at her end of the table; but Sant' Ilario was bored to the verge of extinction and talked of nothing but archaeology and the trial of the Cenci, wondering inwardly why he chose such exceedingly dry subjects. As for Orsino, the two old princesses between whom he was placed paid very little attention to him, and talked across him about the merits of their respective confessors and directors. He frivolously asked them whether they ever went to the theatre, to which they replied very coldly that they went to their boxes when the piece was not on the Index and when there was no ballet. Orsino understood why he never saw them at the opera, and relapsed into silence. The butler, a son of the legendary Pasquale of earlier days, did his best to cheer the youngest of his masters with a great variety of wines; but Orsino would not be comforted either by very dry champagne or very mellow claret. But he vowed a bitter revenge and swore to dance till three in the morning at the Montevarchi's and finish the night with a rousing baccarat at the club, which projects he began to put into execution as soon as was practicable.

In due time the guests departed, solemnly renewing their expressions of good wishes, and the Saracinesca household was left to itself. The old prince stood before the fire in the state drawing-room, rubbing his hands and shaking his head. Giovanni and Corona sat on opposite sides of the fireplace, looking at each other and somewhat inclined to laugh. Orsino was intently studying a piece of historical tapestry which had never interested him before.

The silence lasted some time. Then old Saracinesca raised his head and gave vent to his feelings, with all his old energy.

"What a museum!" he exclaimed. "I would not have believed that I should live to dine in my own house with a party of stranded figure-heads, set up in rows around my table! The paint is all worn off and the brains are all worn out and there is nothing left but a cracked old block of wood with a ribbon around its neck. You will be just like them, Giovanni, in a few years, for you will be just like me—we all turn into the same shape at seventy, and if we live a dozen years longer it is because Providence designs to make us an awful example to the young."

"I hope you do not call yourself a figure-head," said Giovanni.

"They are calling me by worse names at this very minute as they drive home. 'That old Methuselah of a Saracinesca, how has he the face to go on living?' That is the way they talk. 'People ought to die decently when other people have had enough of them, instead of sitting up at the table like death's-heads to grin at their grandchildren and great-grandchildren!' They talk like that, Giovanni. I have known some of those old monuments for sixty years and more—since they were babies and I was of Orsino's age. Do you suppose I do not know how they talk? You always take me for a good, confiding old fellow, Giovanni. But then, you never understood human nature."

Giovanni laughed and Corona smiled. Orsino turned round to enjoy the rare delight of seeing the old gentleman rouse himself in a fit of temper.

"If you were ever confiding it was because you were too good," said Giovanni affectionately.

"Yes—good and confiding—that is it! You always did agree with me as to my own faults. Is it not true, Corona? Can you not take my part against that graceless husband of yours? He is always abusing me—as though I were his property, or his guest. Orsino, my boy, go away—we are all quarrelling here like a pack of wolves, and you ought to respect your elders. Here is your father calling me by bad names—"

"I said you were too good," observed Giovanni.

"Yes—good and confiding! If you can find anything worse to say, say it—and may you live to hear that good-for-nothing Orsino call you good and confiding when you are eighty-two years old. And Corona is laughing at me. It is insufferable. You used to be a good girl, Corona—but you are so proud of having four sons that there is no possibility of talking to you any longer. It is a pity that you have not brought them up better. Look at Orsino. He is laughing too."

"Certainly not at you, grandfather," the young man hastened to say.

"Then you must be laughing at your father or your mother, or both, since there is no one else here to laugh at. You are concocting sharp speeches for your abominable tongue. I know it. I can see it in your eyes. That is the way you have brought up your children, Giovanni. I congratulate you. Upon my word, I congratulate you with all my heart! Not that I ever expected anything better. You addled your own brains with curious foreign ideas on your travels—the greater fool I for letting you run about the world when you were young. I ought to have locked you up in Saracinesca, on bread and water, until you understood the world well enough to profit by it. I wish I had."

None of the three could help laughing at this extraordinary speech. Orsino recovered his gravity first, by the help of the historical tapestry. The old gentleman noticed the fact.

"Come here, Orsino, my boy," he said. "I want to talk to you."

Orsino came forward. The old prince laid a hand on his shoulder and looked up into his face.

"You are twenty-one years old to-day," he said, "and we are all quarrelling in honour of the event. You ought to be flattered that we should take so much trouble to make the evening pass pleasantly for you, but you probably have not the discrimination to see what your amusement costs us."

His grey beard shook a little, his rugged features twitched, and then a broad good-humoured smile lit up the old face.

"We are quarrelsome people," he continued in his most Cheerful and hearty tone. "When Giovanni and I were young—we were young together, you know—we quarrelled every day as regularly as we ate and drank. I believe it was very good for us. We generally made it up before night—for the sake of beginning again with a clear conscience. Anything served us—the weather, the soup, the colour of a horse."

"You must have led an extremely lively life," observed Orsino, considerably amused.

"It was very well for us, Orsino. But it will not do for you. You are not so much like your father, as he was like me at your age. We fought with the same weapons, but you two would not, if you fought at all. We fenced for our own amusement and we kept the buttons on the foils. You have neither my really angelic temper nor your father's stony coolness—he is laughing again—no matter, he knows it is true. You have a diabolical tongue. Do not quarrel with your father for amusement, Orsino. His calmness will exasperate you as it does me, but you will not laugh at the right moment as I have done all my life. You will bear malice and grow sullen and permanently disagreeable. And do not say all the cutting things you think of, because with your disposition you will get into serious trouble. If you have really good cause for being angry, it is better to strike than to speak, and in such cases I strongly advise you to strike first. Now go and amuse yourself, for you must have had enough of our company. I do not think of any other advice to give you on your coming of age."

Thereupon he laughed again and pushed his grandson away, evidently delighted with the lecture he had given him. Orsino was quick to profit by the permission and was soon in the Montevarchi ballroom, doing his best to forget the lugubrious feast in his own honour at which he had lately assisted.

He was not altogether successful, however. He had looked forward to the day for many months as one of rejoicing as well as of emancipation, and he had been grievously disappointed. There was something of ill augury, he thought, in the appalling dulness of the guests, for they had congratulated him upon his entry into a life exactly similar to their own. Indeed, the more precisely similar it proved to be, the more he would be respected when he reached their advanced age. The future unfolded to him was not gay. He was to live forty, fifty or even sixty years in the same round of traditions and hampered by the same net of prejudices. He might have his romance, as his father had had before him, but there was nothing beyond that. His father seemed perfectly satisfied with his own unruffled existence and far from desirous of any change. The feudalism of it all was still real in fact, though abolished in theory, and the old prince was as much a great feudal lord as ever, whose interests were almost tribal in their narrowness, almost sordid in their detail, and altogether uninteresting to his presumptive heir in the third generation. What was the peasant of Aquaviva, for instance, to Orsino? Yet Sant' Ilario and old Saracinesca took a lively interest in his doings and in the doings of four or five hundred of his kind, whom they knew by name and spoke of as belongings, much as they would have spoken of books in the library. To collect rents from peasants and to ascertain in person whether their houses needed repair was not a career. Orsino thought enviously of San Giacinto's two sons, leading what seemed to him a life of comparative activity and excitement in the Italian army, and having the prospect of distinction by their own merits. He thought of San Giacinto himself, of his ceaseless energy and of the great position he was building up. San Giacinto was a Saracinesca as well as Orsino, bearing the same name and perhaps not less respected than the rest by the world at large, though he had sullied his hands with finance. Even Del Ferice's position would have been above criticism, but for certain passages in his earlier life not immediately connected with his present occupation. And as if such instances were not enough there were, to Orsino's certain knowledge, half a dozen men of his father's rank even now deeply engaged in the speculations of the day. Montevarchi was one of them, and neither he nor the others made any secret of their doings.

"Surely," thought Orsino, "I have as good a head as any of them, except, perhaps, San Giacinto."

And he grew more and more discontented with his lot, and more and more angry at himself for submitting to be bound hand and foot and sacrificed upon the altar of feudalism. Everything had disappointed and irritated him on that day, the weariness of the dinner, the sight of his parents' placid felicity, the advice his grandfather had given him—good of its kind, but lamentably insufficient, to say the least of it. He was rapidly approaching that state of mind in which young men do the most unexpected things for the mere pleasure of surprising their relations.

He grew tired of the ball, because Madame d'Aranjuez was not there. He longed to dance with her and he wished that he were at liberty to frequent the houses la which she was asked. But as yet she saw only the Whites and had not made the acquaintance of a single Grey family, in spite of his entreaties. He could not tell whether she had any fixed reason in making her choice, or whether as yet it had been the result of chance, but he discovered that he was bored wherever he went because she was not present. At supper-time on this particular evening, he entered into a conspiracy with certain choice spirits to leave the party and adjourn to the club and cards.

The sight of the tables revived him and he drew a long breath as he sat down with a cigarette in his mouth and a glass at his elbow. It seemed as though the day were beginning at last.

Orsino was no more a born gambler than he was disposed to be a hard drinker. He loved excitement in any shape, and being so constituted as to bear it better than most men, he took it greedily in whatever form it was offered to him. He neither played nor drank every day, but when he did either he was inclined to play more than other people and to consume more strong liquor. Yet his judgment was not remarkable, nor his head much stronger than the heads of his companions. Great gamblers do not drink, and great drinkers are not good players, though they are sometimes amazingly lucky when in their cups.

It is of no use to deny the enormous influence of brandy and games of chance on the men of the present day, but there is little profit in describing such scenes as take place nightly in many clubs all over Europe. Something might be gained, indeed, if we could trace the causes which have made gambling especially the vice of our generation, for that discovery might show us some means of influencing the next. But I do not believe that this is possible. The times have undoubtedly grown more dull, as civilisation has made them more alike, but there is, I think, no truth in the common statement that vice is bred of idleness. The really idle man is a poor creature, incapable of strong sins. It is far more often the man of superior gifts, with faculties overwrought and nerves strained above concert pitch by excessive mental exertion, who turns to vicious excitement for the sake of rest, as a duller man falls asleep. Men whose lives are spent amidst the vicissitudes, surprises and disappointments of the money market are assuredly less idle than country gentlemen; the busy lawyer has less time to spare than the equally gifted fellow of a college; the skilled mechanic works infinitely harder, taking the average of the whole year, than the agricultural labourer; the life of a sailor on an ordinary merchant ship is one of rest, ease and safety compared with that of the collier. Yet there can hardly be a doubt as to which individual in each example is the one to seek relaxation in excitement, innocent or the reverse, instead of in sleep. The operator in the stock market, the barrister, the mechanic, the miner, in every case the men whose faculties are the more severely strained, are those who seek strong emotions in their daily leisure, and who are the more inclined to extend that leisure at the expense of bodily rest. It may be objected that the worst vice is found in the highest grades of society, that is to say, among men who have no settled occupation. I answer that, in the first place, this is not a known fact, but a matter of speculation, and that the conclusion is principally drawn from the circumstance that the evil deeds of such persons, when they become known, are very severely criticised by those whose criticism has the most weight, namely by the equals of the sinners in question—as well as by writers of fiction whose opinions may or may not be worth considering. For one Zola, historian of the Rougon-Macquart family, there are a hundred would-be Zolas, censors of a higher class, less unpleasantly fond of accurate detail, perhaps, but as merciless in intention. But even if the case against society be proved, which is possible, I do not think that society can truly be called idle, because many of those who compose it have no settled occupation. The social day is a long one. Society would not accept the eight hours' system demanded by the labour unions. Society not uncommonly works at a high pressure for twelve, fourteen and even sixteen hours at a stretch. The mental strain, though, not of the most intellectual order, is incomparably more severe than that required for success in many lucrative professions or crafts. The general absence of a distinct aim sharpens the faculties in the keen pursuit of details, and lends an importance to trifles which overburdens at every turn the responsibility borne by the nerves. Lazy people are not favourites in drawing-rooms, and still less at the dinner-table. Consider also that the average man of the world, and many women, daily sustain an amount of bodily fatigue equal perhaps to that borne by many mechanics and craftsmen and much greater than that required in the liberal professions, and that, too, under far less favourable conditions. Recapitulate all these points. Add together the physical effort, the mental activity, the nervous strain. Take the sum and compare it with that got by a similar process from other conditions of existence. I think there can be little doubt of the verdict. The force exerted is wasted, if you please, but it is enormously great, and more than sufficient to prove that those who daily exert it are by no means idle. Besides, none of the inevitable outward and visible results of idleness are apparent in the ordinary society man or woman. On the contrary, most of them exhibit the peculiar and unmistakable signs of physical exhaustion, chief of which is cerebral anæmia. They are overtrained and overworked. In the language of training they are "stale."

Men like Orsino Saracinesca are not vicious at his age, though they may become so. Vice begins when the excitement ceases to be a matter of taste and turns into a necessity. Orsino gambled because it amused him when no other amusement was obtainable, and he drank while he played because it made the amusement seem more amusing. He was far too young and healthy and strong to feel an irresistible longing for anything not natural.

On the present occasion he cared very little, at first, whether he won or lost, and as often happens to a man in that mood he won a considerable sum during the first hour. The sight of the notes before him strengthened an idea which had crossed his mind more than once of late, and the stimulants he drank suddenly fixed it into a purpose. It was true that he did not command any sum of money which could be dignified by the name of capital, but he generally had enough in his pocket to play with, and to-night he had rather more than usual. It struck him that if he could win a few thousands by a run of luck, he would have more than enough to try his fortune in the building speculations of which Del Ferice had talked. The scheme took shape and at once lent a passionate interest to his play.

Orsino had no system and generally left everything to chance, but he had no sooner determined that he must win than he improvised a method, and began to play carefully. Of course he lost, and as he saw his heap of notes diminishing, he filled his glass more and more often. By two o'clock he had but five hundred francs left, his face was deadly pale, the lights dazzled him and his hands moved uncertainly. He held the bank and he knew that if he lost on the card he must borrow money, which he did not wish to do.

He dealt himself a five of spades, and glanced at the stakes. They were considerable. A last sensation of caution prevented him from taking another card. The table turned up a six and he lost.

"Lend me some money, Filippo," he said to the man nearest him, who immediately counted out a number of notes.

Orsino paid with the money and the bank passed. He emptied his glass and lit a cigarette. At each succeeding deal he staked a small sum and lost it, till the bank came to him again. Once more he held a five. The other men saw that he was losing and put up all they could. Orsino hesitated. Some one observed justly that he probably held a five again. The lights swam indistinctly before him and he drew another card. It was a four. Orsino laughed nervously as he gathered the notes and paid back what he had borrowed.

He did not remember clearly what happened afterwards. The faces of the cards grew less distinct and the lights more dazzling. He played blindly and won almost without interruption until the other men dropped off one by one, having lost as much as they cared to part with at one sitting. At four o'clock in the morning Orsino went home in a cab, having about fifteen thousand francs in his pockets. The men he had played with were mostly young fellows like himself, having a limited allowance of pocket money, and Orsino's winnings were very large under the circumstances.

The night air cooled his head and he laughed gaily to himself as he drove through the deserted streets. His hand was steady enough now, and the gas lamps did not move disagreeably before his eyes. But he had reached the stage of excitement in which a fixed idea takes hold of the brain, and if it had been possible he would undoubtedly have gone as he was, in evening dress, with his winnings in his pocket, to rouse Del Ferice, or San Giacinto, or any one else who could put him in the way of risking his money on a building lot. He reluctantly resigned himself to the necessity of going to bed, and slept as one sleeps at twenty-one until nearly eleven o'clock on the following morning.

While he dressed he recalled the circumstances of the previous night and was surprised to find that his idea was as fixed as ever. He counted the money. There was five times as much as the Del Ferice's carpenter, tobacconist and mason had been able to scrape together amongst them. He had therefore, according to his simple calculation, just five times as good a chance of succeeding as they. And they had been successful. His plan fascinated him, and he looked forward to the constant interest and occupation with a delight which was creditable to his character. He would be busy and the magic word "business" rang in his ears. It was speculation, no doubt, but he did not look upon it as a form of gambling; if he had done so, he would not have cared for it on two consecutive days. It was something much better in his eyes. It was to do something, to be some one, to strike out of the everlastingly dull road which lay before him and which ended in the vanishing point of an insignificant old age.

He had not the very faintest conception of what that business was with which he aspired to occupy himself. He was totally ignorant of the methods of dealing with money, and he no more knew what a draft at three months meant than he could have explained the construction of the watch he carried in his pocket. Of the first principles of building he knew, if possible, even less and he did not know whether land in the city were worth a franc or a thousand francs by the square foot. But he said to himself that those things were mere details, and that he could learn all he needed of them in a fortnight. Courage and judgment, Del Ferice had said, were the chief requisites for success. Courage he possessed, and he believed himself cool. He would avail himself of the judgment of others until he could judge for himself.

He knew very well what his father would think of the whole plan, but he had no intention of concealing his project. Since yesterday, he was of age and was therefore his own master to the extent of his own small resources. His father had not the power to keep him from entering upon any honourable undertaking, though he might justly refuse to be responsible for the consequences. At the worst, thought Orsino, those consequences might be the loss of the money he had in hand. Since he had nothing else to risk, he had nothing else to lose. That is the light in which most inexperienced people regard speculation. Orsino therefore went to his father and unfolded his scheme, without mentioning Del Ferice.

Sant' Ilario listened rather impatiently and laughed when Orsino had finished. He did not mean to be unkind, and if he had dreamed of the effect his manner would produce, he would have been more careful. But he did not understand his son, as he himself had been understood by his own father.

"This is all nonsense, my boy," he answered. "It is a mere passing fancy. What do you know of business or architecture, or of a dozen other matters which you ought to understand thoroughly before attempting anything like what you propose?"

Orsino was silent, and looked out of the window, though he was evidently listening.

"You say you want an occupation. This is not one. Banking is an occupation, and architecture is a career, but what we call affairs in Rome are neither one nor the other. If you want to be a banker you must go into a bank and do clerk's work for years. If you mean to follow architecture as a profession you must spend four or five years in study at the very least."

"San Giacinto has not done that," observed Orsino coldly.

"San Giacinto has a very much better head on his shoulders than you, or I, or almost any other man in Rome. He has known how to make use of other men's talents, and he had a rather more practical education than I would have cared to give you. If he were not one of the most honest men alive he would certainly have turned out one of the greatest scoundrels."

"I do not see what that has to do with it," said Orsino.

"Not much, I confess. But his early life made him understand men as you and I cannot understand them, and need not, for that matter."

"Then you object to my trying this?"

"I do nothing of the kind. When I object to the doing of anything I prevent it, by fair words or by force. I am not inclined for a pitched battle with you, Orsino, and I might not get the better of you after all. I will be perfectly neutral. I will have nothing to do with this business. If I believed in it, I would give you all the capital you could need, but I shall not diminish your allowance in order to hinder you from throwing it away. If you want more money for your amusements or luxuries, say so. I am not fond of counting small expenses, and I have not brought you up to count them either. Do not gamble at cards any more than you can help, but if you lose and must borrow, borrow of me. When I think you are going too far, I will tell you so. But do not count upon me for any help in this scheme of yours. You will not get it. If you find yourself in a commercial scrape, find your own way out of it. If you want better advice than mine, go to San Giacinto. He will give you a practical man's view of the case."

"You are frank, at all events," said Orsino, turning from the window and facing his father.

"Most of us are in this house," answered Sant' Ilario. "That will make it all the harder for you to deal with the scoundrels who call themselves men of business."

"I mean to try this, father," said the young man. "I will go and see San Giacinto, as you suggest, and I will ask his opinion. But if he discourages me I will try my luck all the same. I cannot lead this life any longer. I want an occupation and I will make one for myself."

"It is not an occupation that you want, Orsino. It is another excitement. That is all. If you want an occupation, study, learn something, find out what work means. Or go to Saracinesca and build houses for the peasants—you will do no harm there, at all events. Go and drain that land in Lombardy—I can do nothing with it and would sell it if I could. But that is not what you want. You want an excitement for the hours of the morning. Very well. You will probably find more of it than you like. Try it, that is all I have to say."

Like many very just men Giovanni could state a case with alarming unfairness when thoroughly convinced that he was right. Orsino stood still for a moment and then walked towards the door without another word. His father called him back.

"What is it?" asked Orsino coldly.

Sant' Ilario held out his hand with a kindly look in his eyes.

"I do not want you to think that I am angry, my boy. There is to be no ill feeling between us about this."

"None whatever," said the young man, though without much alacrity, as he shook hands with his father. "I see you are not angry. You do not understand me, that is all."

He went out, more disappointed with the result of the interview than he had expected, though he had not looked forward to receiving any encouragement. He had known very well what his father's views were but he had not foreseen that he would be so much irritated by the expression of them. His determination hardened and he resolved that nothing should hinder him. But he was both willing and ready to consult San Giacinto, and went to the latter's house immediately on leaving Sant' Ilario's study.

As for Giovanni, he was dimly conscious that he had made a mistake, though he did not care to acknowledge it. He was a good horseman and he was aware that he would have used a very different method with a restive colt. But few men are wise enough to see that there is only one universal principle to follow in the exertion of strength, moral or physical; and instead of seeking analogies out of actions familiar to them as a means of accomplishing the unfamiliar, they try to discover new theories of motion at every turn and are led farther and farther from the right line by their own desire to reach the end quickly.

"At all events," thought Sant' Ilario, "the boy's new hobby will take him to places where he is not likely to meet that woman."

And with this discourteous reflection upon Madame d'Aranjuez he consoled himself. He did not think it necessary to tell Corona of Orsino's intentions, simply because he did not believe that they would lead to anything serious, and there was no use in disturbing her unnecessarily with visions of future annoyance. If Orsino chose to speak of it to her, he was at liberty to do so.

CHAPTER X

Orsino went directly to San Giacinto's house, and found him in the room which he used for working and in which he received the many persons whom he was often obliged to see on business. The giant was alone and was seated behind a broad polished table, occupied in writing. Orsino was struck by the extremely orderly arrangement of everything he saw. Papers were tied together in bundles of exactly like shape, which lay in two lines of mathematical precision. The big inkstand was just in the middle of the rows and a paper-cutter, a pen-rack and an erasing knife lay side by side in front of it. The walls were lined with low book-cases of a heavy and severe type, filled principally with documents neatly filed in volumes and marked on the back in San Giacinto's clear handwriting. The only object of beauty in the room was a full-length portrait of Flavia by a great artist, which hung above the fireplace. The rigid symmetry of everything was made imposing by the size of the objects—the table was larger than ordinary tables, the easy-chairs were deeper, broader and lower than common, the inkstand was bigger, even the penholder in San Giacinto's fingers was longer and thicker than any Orsino had ever seen. And yet the latter felt that there was no affectation about all this. The man to whom these things belonged and who used them daily was himself created on a scale larger than other men.

Though he was older than Sant' Ilario and was, in fact, not far from sixty years of age San Giacinto might easily have passed for less than fifty. There was hardly a grey thread in his short, thick, black hair, and he was still as lean and strong, and almost as active, as he had been thirty years earlier. The large features were perhaps a little more bony and the eyes somewhat deeper than they had been, but these changes lent an air of dignity rather than of age to the face.

He rose to meet Orsino and then made him sit down beside the table. The young man suddenly felt an unaccountable sense of inferiority and hesitated as to how he should begin.

"I suppose you want to consult me about something," said San Giacinto quietly.

"Yes. I want to ask your advice, if you will give it to me—about a matter of business."

"Willingly. What is it?"

Orsino was silent for a moment and stared at the wall. He was conscious that the very small sum of which he could dispose must seem even smaller in the eyes of such a man, but this did not disturb him. He was oppressed by San Giacinto's personality and prepared himself to speak as though he had been a student undergoing oral examination. He stated his case plainly, when he at last spoke. He was of age and he looked forward with dread to an idle life. All careers were closed to him. He had fifteen thousand francs in his pocket. Could San Giacinto help him to occupy himself by investing the sum in a building speculation? Was the sum sufficient as a beginning? Those were the questions.

San Giacinto did not laugh as Sant' Ilario had done. He listened very attentively to the end and then deliberately offered Orsino a cigar and lit one himself, before he delivered his answer.

"You are asking the same question which is put to me very often," he said at last. "I wish I could give you any encouragement. I cannot."

Orsino's face fell, for the reply was categorical. He drew back a little in his chair, but said nothing.

"That is my answer," continued San Giacinto thoughtfully, "but when one says 'no' to another the subject is not necessarily exhausted. On the contrary, in such a case as this I cannot let you go without giving you my reasons. I do not care to give my views to the public, but such as they are, you are welcome to them. The time is past. That is why I advise you to have nothing to do with any speculation of this kind. That is the best of all reasons."

"But you yourself are still engaged in this business," objected Orsino.

"Not so deeply as you fancy. I have sold almost everything which I do not consider a certainty, and am selling what little I still have as fast as I can. In speculation there are only two important moments—the moment to buy and the moment to sell. In my opinion, this is the time to sell, and I do not think that the time for buying will come again without a crisis."

"But everything is in such a flourishing state—"

"No doubt it is—to-day. But no one can tell what state business will be in next week, nor even to-morrow."

"There is Del Ferice—"

"No doubt, and a score like him," answered San Giacinto, looking quietly at Orsino. "Del Ferice is a banker, and I am a speculator, as you wish to be. His position is different from ours. It is better to leave him out of the question. Let us look at the matter logically. You wish to speculate—"

"Excuse me," said Orsino, interrupting him. "I want to try what I can do in business."

"You wish to risk money, in one way or another. You therefore wish one or more of three things—money for its own sake, excitement or occupation. I can hardly suppose that you want money. Eliminate that. Excitement is not a legitimate aim, and you can get it more safely in other ways. Therefore you want occupation."

"That is precisely what I said at the beginning," observed Orsino with a shade of irritation.

"Yes. But I like to reach my conclusions in my own way. You are then a young man in search of an occupation. Speculation, and what you propose is nothing else, is no more an occupation than playing at the public lottery and much less one than playing at baccarat. There at least you are responsible for your own mistakes and in decent society you are safe from the machinations of dishonest people. That would matter less if the chances were in your favour, as they might have been a year ago and as they were in mine from the beginning. They are against you now, because it is too late, and they are against me. I would as soon buy a piece of land on credit at the present moment, as give the whole sum in cash to the first man I met in the street."

"Yet there is Montevarchi who still buys—"

"Montevarchi is not worth the paper on which he signs his name," said San Giacinto calmly.

Orsino uttered an exclamation of surprise and incredulity.

"You may tell him so, if you please," answered the giant with perfect indifference. "If you tell any one what I have said, please to tell him first, that is all. He will not believe you. But in six months he will know it, I fancy, as well as I know it now. He might have doubled his fortune, but he was and is totally ignorant of business. He thought it enough to invest all he could lay hands on and that the returns would be sure. He has invested forty millions and owns property which he believes to be worth sixty, but which will not bring ten in six months, and those remaining ten millions he owes on all manner of paper, on mortgages on his original property, in a dozen ways which he has forgotten himself."

"I do not see how that is possible!" exclaimed Orsino.

"I am a plain man, Orsino, and I am your cousin. You may take it for granted that I am right. Do not forget that I was brought up in a hand-to-hand struggle for fortune such as you cannot dream of. When I was your age I was a practical man of business, and I had taught myself, and it was all on such a small scale that a mistake of a hundred francs made the difference between profit and loss. I dislike details, but I have been a man of detail all my life, by force of circumstances. Successful business implies the comprehension of details. It is tedious work, and if you mean to try it you must begin at the beginning. You ought to do so. There is an enormous business before you, with considerable capabilities in it. If I were in your place, I would take what fell naturally to my lot."

"What is that?"

"Farming. They call it agriculture in parliament, because they do not know what farming means. The men who think that Italy can live without farmers are fools. We are not a manufacturing people any more than we are a business people. The best dictator for us would be a practical farmer, a ploughman like Cincinnatus. Nobody who has not tried to raise wheat on an Italian mountain-side knows the great difficulties or the great possibilities of our country. Do you know that bad as our farming is, and absurd as is our system of land taxation, we are food exporters, to a small extent? The beginning is there. Take my advice, be a farmer. Manage one of the big estates you have amongst you for five or six years. You will not do much good to the land in that time, but you will learn what land really means. Then go into parliament and tell people facts. That is an occupation and a career as well, which cannot be said of speculation in building lots, large or small. If you have any ready money keep it in government bonds until you have a chance of buying something worth keeping."

Orsino went away disappointed and annoyed. San Giacinto's talk about farming seemed very dull to him. To bury himself for half a dozen years in the country in order to learn the rotation of crops and the principles of land draining did not present itself as an attractive career. If San Giacinto thought farming the great profession of the future, why did he not try it himself? Orsino dismissed the idea rather indignantly, and his determination to try his luck became stronger by the opposition it met. Moreover he had expected very different language from San Giacinto, whose sober view jarred on Orsino's enthusiastic impulse.

But he now found himself in considerable difficulty. He was ignorant even of the first steps to be taken, and knew no one to whom he could apply for information. There was Prince Montevarchi indeed, who though he was San Giacinto's brother-in-law, seemed by the latter's account to have got into trouble. He did not understand how San Giacinto could allow his wife's brother to ruin himself without lending him a helping hand, but San Giacinto was not the kind of man of whom people ask indiscreet questions, and Orsino had heard that the two men were not on the best of terms. Possibly good advice had been offered and refused. Such affairs generally end in a breach of friendship. However that might be, Orsino would not go to Montevarchi.

He wandered aimlessly about the streets, and the money seemed to burn in his pocket, though he had carefully deposited it in a place of safety at home. Again and again Del Ferice's story of the carpenter and his two companions recurred to his mind. He wondered how they had set about beginning, and he wished he could ask Del Ferice himself. He could not go to the man's house, but he might possibly meet him at Maria Consuelo's. He was surprised to find that he had almost forgotten her in his anxiety to become a man of business. It was too early to call yet, and in order to kill the time he went home, got a horse from the stables and rode out into the country for a couple of hours.

At half-past five o'clock he entered the familiar little sitting-room in the hotel. Madame d'Aranjuez was alone, cutting a new book with the jewelled knife which continued to be the only object of the kind visible in the room. She smiled as Orsino entered, and she laid aside the volume as he sat down in his accustomed place.

"I thought you were not coming," she said.

"Why?"

"You always come at five. It is half-past to-day." Orsino looked at his watch.

"Do you notice whether I come or not?" he asked.

Maria Consuelo glanced at his face, and laughed.

"What have you been doing to-day?" she asked. "That is much more interesting."

"Is it? I am afraid not. I have been listening to those disagreeable things which are called truths by the people who say them. I have listened to two lectures delivered by two very intelligent men for my especial benefit. It seems to me that as soon as I make a good resolution it becomes the duty of sensible people to demonstrate that I am a fool."

"You are not in a good humour. Tell me all about it."

"And weary you with my grievances? No. Is Del Ferice coming this afternoon?"

"How can I tell? He does not come often."

"I thought he came almost every day," said Orsino gloomily.

He was disappointed, but Maria Consuelo did not understand what was the matter. She leaned forward in her low seat, her chin resting upon one hand, and her tawny eyes fixed on Orsino's.

"Tell me, my friend—are you unhappy? Can I do anything? Will you tell me?"

It was not easy to resist the appeal. Though the two had grown intimate of late, there had hitherto always been something cold and reserved behind her outwardly friendly manner. To-day she seemed suddenly willing to be different. Her easy, graceful attitude, her soft voice full of promised sympathy, above all the look in her strange eyes revealed a side of her character which Orsino had not suspected and which affected him in a way he could not have described.

Without hesitation he told her his story, from beginning to end, simply, without comment and without any of the cutting phrases which came so readily to his tongue on most occasions. She listened very thoughtfully to the end.

"Those things are not misfortunes," she said. "But they may be the beginnings of unhappiness. To be unhappy is worse than any misfortune. What right has your father to laugh at you? Because he never needed to do anything for himself, he thinks it absurd that his son should dislike the lazy life that is prepared for him. It is not reasonable—it is not kind!"

"Yet he means to be both, I suppose," said Orsino bitterly.

"Oh, of course! People always mean to be the soul of logic and the paragon of charity! Especially where their own children are concerned."

Maria Consuelo added the last words with more feeling than seemed justified by her sympathy for Orsino's woes. The moment was perhaps favourable for asking a leading question about herself, and her answer might have thrown light on her problematic past. But Orsino was too busy with his own troubles to think of that, and the opportunity slipped by and was lost.

"You know now why I want to see Del Ferice," he said. "I cannot go to his house. My only chance of talking to him lies here."

"And that is what brings you? You are very flattering!"

"Do not be unjust! We all look forward to meeting our friends in heaven."

"Very pretty. I forgive you. But I am afraid that you will not meet Del Ferice. I do not think he has left the Chambers yet. There was to be a debate this afternoon in which he had to speak."

"Does he make speeches?"

"Very good ones. I have heard him."

"I have never been inside the Chambers," observed Orsino.

"You are not very patriotic. You might go there and ask for Del Ferice. You could see him without going to his house—without compromising your dignity."

"Why do you laugh?"

"Because it all seems to me so absurd. You know that you are perfectly free to go and see him when and where you will. There is nothing to prevent you. He is the one man of all others whose advice you need. He has an unexceptional position in the world—no doubt he has done strange things, but so have dozens of people whom you know—his present reputation is excellent, I say. And yet, because some twenty years ago, when you were a child, he held one opinion and your father held another, you are interdicted from crossing his threshold! If you can shake hands with him here, you can take his hand in his own house. Is not that true?"

"Theoretically, I daresay, but not in practice. You see it yourself. You have chosen one side from the first, and all the people on the other side know it. As a foreigner, you are not bound to either, and you can know everybody in time, if you please. Society is not so prejudiced as to object to that. But because you begin with the Del Ferice in a very uncompromising way, it would take a long time for you to know the Montevarchi, for instance."

"Who told you that I was a foreigner?" asked Maria Consuelo, rather abruptly.

"You yourself—"

"That is good authority!" She laughed. "I do not remember—ah! because I do not speak Italian? You mean that? One may forget one's own language, or for that matter one may never have learned it."

"Are you Italian, then, Madame?" asked Orsino, surprised that she should lead the conversation so directly to a point which he had supposed must be reached by a series of tactful approaches.

"Who knows? I am sure I do not. My father was Italian. Does that constitute nationality?"

"Yes. But the woman takes the nationality of her husband, I believe," said Orsino, anxious to hear more.

"Ah yes—poor Aranjuez!" Maria Consuelo's voice suddenly took that sleepy tone which Orsino had heard more than once. Her eyelids drooped a little and she lazily opened and shut her hand, and spread out the fingers and looked at them.

But Orsino was not satisfied to let the conversation drop at this point, and after a moment's pause he put a decisive question.

"And was Monsieur d'Aranjuez also Italian?" he asked.

"What does it matter?" she asked in the same indolent tone. "Yes, since you ask me, he was Italian, poor man."

Orsino was more and more puzzled. That the name did not exist in Italy he was almost convinced. He thought of the story of the Signor Aragno, who had fallen overboard in the south seas, and then he was suddenly aware that he could not believe in anything of the sort. Maria Consuelo did not betray a shade of emotion, either, at the mention of her deceased husband. She seemed absorbed in the contemplation of her hands. Orsino had not been rebuked for his curiosity and would have asked another question if he had known how to frame it. An awkward silence followed. Maria Consuelo raised her eyes slowly and looked thoughtfully into Orsino's face.

"I see," she said at last. "You are curious. I do not know whether you have any right to be—have you?"

"I wish I had!" exclaimed Orsino thoughtlessly.

Again she looked at him in silence for some moments.

"I have not known you long enough," she said. "And if I had known you longer, perhaps it would not be different. Are other people curious, too? Do they talk about me?"

"The people I know do—but they do not know you. They see your name in the papers, as a beautiful Spanish princess. Yet everybody is aware that there is no Spanish nobleman of your name. Of course they are curious. They invent stories about you, which I deny. If I knew more, it would be easier."

"Why do you take the trouble to deny such things?"

She asked the question with a change of manner. Once more she leaned forward and her face softened wonderfully as she looked at him.

"Can you not guess?" he asked.

He was conscious of a very unusual emotion, not at all in harmony with the imaginary character he had chosen for himself, and which he generally maintained with considerable success. Maria Consuelo was one person when she leaned back in her chair, laughing or idly listening to his talk, or repulsing the insignificant declarations of devotion which were not even meant to be taken altogether in earnest. She was pretty then, attractive, graceful, feminine, a little artificial, perhaps, and Orsino felt that he was free to like her or not, as he pleased, but that he pleased to like her for the present. She was quite another woman to-day, as she bent forward, her tawny eyes growing darker and more mysterious every moment, her auburn hair casting wonderful shadows upon her broad pale forehead, her lips not closed as usual, but slightly parted, her fragrant breath just stirring the quiet air Orsino breathed. Her features might be irregular. It did not matter. She was beautiful for the moment with a kind of beauty Orsino had never seen, and which produced a sudden and overwhelming effect upon him.

"Do you not know?" he asked again, and his voice trembled unexpectedly.

"Thank you," she said softly and she touched his hand almost caressingly.

But when he would have taken it, she drew back instantly and was once more the woman whom he saw every day, careless, indifferent, pretty.

"Why do you change so quickly?" he asked in a low voice, bending towards her. "Why do you snatch your hand away? Are you afraid of me?"

"Why should I be afraid? Are you dangerous?"

"You are. You may be fatal, for all I know."

"How foolish!" she exclaimed, with a quick glance.

"You are Madame d'Aranjuez, now," he answered. "We had better change the subject."

"What do you mean?"

"A moment ago you were Consuelo," he said boldly.

"Have I given you any right to say that?"

"A little."

"I am sorry. I will be more careful. I am sure I cannot imagine why you should think of me at all, unless when you are talking to me, and then I do not wish to be called by my Christian name. I assure you, you are never anything in my thoughts but His Excellency Prince Orsino Saracinesca—with as many titles after that as may belong to you."

"I have none," said Orsino.

Her speech irritated him strongly, and the illusion which had been so powerful a few moments earlier all but disappeared.

"Then you advise me to go and find Del Ferice at Monte Citorio," he observed.

"If you like." She laughed. "There is no mistaking your intention when you mean to change the subject," she added.

"You made it sufficiently clear that the other was disagreeable to you."

"I did not mean to do so."

"Then in heaven's name, what do you mean, Madame?" he asked, suddenly losing his head in his extreme annoyance.

Maria Consuelo raised her eyebrows in surprise.

"Why are you so angry?" she asked. "Do you know that it is very rude to speak like that?"

"I cannot help it. What have I done to-day that you should torment me as you do?"

"I? I torment you? My dear friend, you are quite mad."

"I know I am. You make me so."

"Will you tell me how? What have I done? What have I said? You Romans are certainly the most extraordinary people. It is impossible to please you. If one laughs, you become tragic. If one is serious, you grow gay! I wish I understood you better."

"You will end by making it impossible for me to understand myself," said Orsino. "You say that I am changeable. Then what are you?"

"Very much the same to-day as yesterday," said Maria Consuelo calmly. "And I do not suppose that I shall be very different to-morrow."

"At least I will take my chance of finding that you are mistaken," said Orsino, rising suddenly, and standing before her.

"Are you going?" she asked, as though she were surprised.

"Since I cannot please you."

"Since you will not."

"I do not know how."

"Be yourself—the same that you always are. You are affecting to be some one else, to-day."

"I fancy it is the other way," answered Orsino, with more truth than he really owned to himself.

"Then I prefer the affectation to the reality."

"As you will, Madame. Good evening."

He crossed the room to go out. She called him back.

"Don Orsino!"

He turned sharply round.

"Madame?"

Seeing that he did not move, she rose and went to him. He looked down into her face and saw that it was changed again.

"Are you really angry?" she asked. There was something girlish in the way she asked the question, and, for a moment, in her whole manner.

Orsino could not help smiling. But he said nothing.

"No, you are not," she continued. "I can see it. Do you know? I am very glad. It was foolish of me to tease you. You will forgive me? This once?"

"If you will give me warning the next time." He found that he was looking into her eyes.

"What is the use of warning?" she asked.

They were very close together, and there was a moment's silence. Suddenly Orsino forgot everything and bent down, clasping her in his arms and kissing her again and again. It was brutal, rough, senseless, but he could not help it.

Maria Consuelo uttered a short, sharp cry, more of surprise, perhaps, than of horror. To Orsino's amazement and confusion her voice was immediately answered by another, which was that of the dark and usually silent maid, whom he had seen once or twice. The woman ran into the room, terrified by the cry she had heard.

"Madame felt faint in crossing the room, and was falling when I caught her," said Orsino, with a coolness that did him credit.

And, in fact, Maria Consuelo closed her eyes as he let her sink into the nearest chair. The maid fell on her knees beside her mistress and began chafing her hands.

"The poor Signora!" she exclaimed. "She should never be left alone! She has not been herself since the poor Signore died. You had better leave us, sir—I will put her to bed when she revives. It often happens—pray do not be anxious!"

Orsino picked up his hat and left the room.

"Oh—it often happens, does it?" he said to himself as he closed the door softly behind him and walked down the corridor of the hotel.

He was more amazed at his own boldness than he cared to own. He had not supposed that scenes of this description produced themselves so very unexpectedly, and, as it were, without any fixed intention on the part of the chief actor. He remembered that he had been very angry with Madame d'Aranjuez, that she had spoken half a dozen words, and that he had felt an irresistible impulse to kiss her. He had done so, and he thought with considerable trepidation of their next meeting. She had screamed, which showed that she was outraged by his boldness. It was doubtful whether she would receive him again. The best thing to be done, he thought, was to write her a very humble letter of apology, explaining his conduct as best he could. This did not accord very well with his principles, but he had already transgressed them in being so excessively hasty. Her eyes had certainly been provoking in the extreme, and it had been impossible to resist the expression on her lips. But at all events, he should have begun by kissing her hand, which she would certainly not have withdrawn again—then he might have put his arm round her and drawn her head to his shoulder. These were preliminaries in the matter of kissing which it was undoubtedly right to observe, and he had culpably neglected them. He had been abominably brutal, and he ought to apologise. Nevertheless, he would not have forfeited the recollection of that moment for all the other recollections of his life, and he knew it. As he walked along the street he felt a wild exhilaration such as he had never known before. He owned gladly to himself that he loved Maria Consuelo, and resolutely thrust away the idea that his boyish vanity was pleased by the snatching of a kiss.

Whatever the real nature of his delight might be it was for the time so sincere that he even forgot to light a cigarette in order to think over the circumstances.

Walking rapidly up the Corso he came to the Piazza Colonna, and the glare of the electric light somehow recalled him to himself.

"Great speech of the Honourable Del Ferice!" yelled a newsboy in his ear. "Ministerial crisis! Horrible murder of a grocer!"

Orsino mechanically turned to the right in the direction of the Chambers. Del Ferice had probably gone home, since his speech was already in print. But fate had ordained otherwise. Del Ferice had corrected his proofs on the spot and had lingered to talk with his friends before going home. Not that it mattered much, for Orsino could have found him as well on the following day. His brougham was standing in front of the great entrance and he himself was shaking hands with a tall man under the light of the lamps. Orsino went up to him.

"Could you spare me a quarter of an hour?" asked the young man in a voice constrained by excitement. He felt that he was embarked at last upon his great enterprise.

Del Ferice looked up in some astonishment. He had reason to dread the quarrelsome disposition of the Saracinesca as a family, and he wondered what Orsino wanted.

"Certainly, certainly, Don Orsino," he answered, with a particularly bland smile. "Shall we drive, or at least sit in my carriage? I am a little fatigued with my exertions to-day."

The tall man bowed and strolled away, biting the end of an unlit cigar.

"It is a matter of business," said Orsino, before entering the carriage. "Can you help me to try my luck— in a very small way—in one of the building enterprises you manage?"

"Of course I can, and will," answered Del Ferice, more and more astonished. "After you, my dear Don Orsino, after you," he repeated, pushing the young man into the brougham. "Quiet streets—till I stop you," he said to the footman, as he himself got in.

CHAPTER XI

Del Ferice was surprised beyond measure at Orsino's request, and was not guilty of any profoundly nefarious intention when he so readily acceded to it. His own character made him choose as a rule to refuse nothing that was asked of him, though his promises were not always fulfilled afterwards. To express his own willingness to help those who asked, was of course not the same as asserting his power to give assistance when the time should come. In the present case he did not even make up his mind which of two courses he would ultimately pursue. Orsino came to him with a small sum of ready money in his hand. Del Ferice had it in his power to make him lose that sum, and a great deal more besides, thereby causing the boy endless trouble with his family; or else the banker could, if he pleased, help him to a very considerable success. His really superior talent for diplomacy inclined him to choose the latter plan, but he was far too cautious to make any hasty decision.

The brougham rolled on through quiet and ill-lighted streets, and Del Ferice leaned back in his corner, not listening at all to Orsino's talk, though he occasionally uttered a polite though utterly unintelligible syllable or two which might mean anything agreeable to his companion's views. The situation was easy enough to understand, and he had grasped it in a moment. What Orsino might say was of no importance whatever, but the consequences of any action on Del Ferice's part might be serious and lasting.

Orsino stated his many reasons for wishing to engage in business, as he had stated them more than once already during the day and during the past weeks, and when he had finished he repeated his first question.

"Can you help me to try my luck?" he asked.

Del Ferice awoke from his reverie with characteristic readiness and realised that he must say something. His voice had never been strong and he leaned out of his corner of the carriage in order to speak near Orsino's ear.

"I am delighted with all you say," he began, "and I scarcely need repeat that my services are altogether at your disposal. The only question is, how are we to begin? The sum you mention is certainly not large, but that does not matter. You would have little difficulty in raising as many hundreds of thousands as you have thousands, if money were necessary. But in business of this kind the only ready money needed is for stamp duty and for the wages of workmen, and the banks advance what is necessary for the latter purpose, in small sums on notes of hand guaranteed by a general mortgage. When you have paid the stamp duties, you may go to the club and lose the balance of your capital at baccarat if you please. The loss in that direction will not affect your credit as a contractor. All that is very simple. You wish to succeed, however, not at cards, but at business. That is the difficulty."

Del Ferice paused.

"That is not very clear to me," observed Orsino.

"No—no," answered Del Ferice thoughtfully. "No—I daresay it is not so very clear. I wish I could make it clearer. Speculation means gambling only when the speculator is a gambler. Of course there are successful gamblers in the world, but there are not many of them. I read somewhere the other day that business was the art of handling other people's-money. The remark is not particularly true. Business is the art of creating a value where none has yet existed. That is what you wish to do. I do not think that a Saracinesca would take pleasure in turning over money not belonging to him."

"Certainly not!" exclaimed Orsino. "That is usury."

"Not exactly, but it is banking; and banking, it is quite true, is usury within legal bounds. There is no question of that here. The operation is simple in the extreme. I sell you a piece of land on the understanding that you will build upon it, and instead of payment you give me a mortgage. I lend you money from month to month in small sums at a small interest, to pay for material and labour. You are only responsible upon one point. The money is to be used for the purpose stated. When the building is finished you sell it. If you sell it for cash, you pay off the mortgage, and receive the difference. If you sell it with the mortgage, the buyer becomes the mortgager and only pays you the difference, which remains yours, out and out. That is the whole process from beginning to end."

"How wonderfully simple!"

"It is almost primitive in its simplicity," answered Del Ferice gravely. "But in every case two difficulties present themselves, and I am bound to tell you that they are serious ones."

"What are they?"

"You must know how to buy in the right part of the city and you must have a competent assistant. The two conditions are indispensable."

"What sort of an assistant?" asked Orsino.

"A practical man. If possible, an architect, who will then have a share of the profits instead of being paid for his work."

"Is it very hard to find such a person?"

"It is not easy."

"Do you think you could help me?"

"I do not know. I am assuming a great responsibility in doing so. You do not seem to realise that, Don Orsino."

Del Ferice laughed a little in his quiet way, but Orsino was silent. It was the first time that the banker had reminded him of the vast difference in their social and political positions.

"I do not think it would be very wise of me to help you into such a business as this," said Del Ferice cautiously. "I speak quite selfishly and for my own sake. Success is never certain, and it would be a great injury to me if you failed."

He was beginning to make up his mind.

"Why?" asked Orsino. His own instincts of generosity were aroused. He would certainly not do Del Ferice an injury if he could help it, nor allow him to incur the risk of one.

"If you fail," answered the other, "all Rome will say that I have intentionally brought about your failure. You know how people talk. Thousands will become millions and I shall be accused of having plotted the destruction of your family, because your father once wounded me in a duel, nearly five and twenty years ago."

"How absurd!"

"No, no. It is not absurd. I am afraid I have the reputation of being vindictive. Well, well—it is in bad taste to talk of oneself. I am good at hating, perhaps, but I have always felt that I preferred peace to war, and now I am growing old. I am not what I once was, Don Orsino, and I do not like quarrelling. But I would not allow people to say impertinent things about me, and if you failed and lost money, I should be abused by your friends, and perhaps censured by my own. Do you see? Yes, I am selfish. I admit it. You must forgive that weakness in me. I like peace."

"It is very natural," said Orsino, "and I have no right to put you in danger of the slightest inconvenience. But, after all, why need I appear before the public?"

Del Ferice smiled in the dark.

"True," he answered. "You could establish an anonymous firm, so to say, and the documents would be a secret between you and me and the notary. Of course there are many ways of managing such an affair quietly."

He did not add that the secret could only be kept so long as Orsino was successful. It seemed a pity to damp so much good enthusiasm.

"We will do that, then, if you will show me how. My ambition is not to see my name on a door-plate, but to be really occupied."

"I understand, I understand," said Del Ferice thoughtfully. "I must ask you to give me until to-morrow to consider the matter. It needs a little thought."

"Where can I find you, to hear your decision?"

Del Ferice was silent for a moment.

"I think I once met you late in the afternoon at Madame d'Aranjuez's. We might manage to meet there to-morrow and come away together. Shall we name an hour? Would it suit you?"

"Perfectly," answered Orsino with alacrity.

The idea of meeting Maria Consuelo alone was very disturbing in his present state of mind. He felt that he had lost his balance in his relations with her, and that in order to regain it he must see her in the presence of a third person, if only for a quarter of an hour. It would be easier, then, to resume the former intercourse and to say whatever he should determine upon saying. If she were offended, she would at least not show it in any marked way before Del Ferice. Orsino's existence, he thought, was becoming complicated for the first time, and though he enjoyed the vague sensation of impending difficulty, he wanted as many opportunities as possible of reviewing the situation and of meditating upon each new move.

He got out of Del Ferice's carriage at no great distance from his own home, and after a few words of very sincere thanks walked slowly away. He found it very hard to arrange his thoughts in any consecutive order, though he tried several methods of self-analysis, and repeated to himself that he had experienced a great happiness and was probably on the threshold of a great success. These two reflections did not help him much. The happiness had been of the explosive kind, and the success in the business matter was more than problematic, as well as certainly distant in the future.

He was very restless and craved the immediate excitement of further emotions, so that he would certainly have gone to the club that night, had not the fear of losing his small and precious capital deterred him. He thought of all that was coming and he determined to be careful, even sordid if necessary, rather than lose his chance of making the great attempt. Besides, he would cut a poor figure on the morrow if he were obliged to admit to Del Ferice that he had lost his fifteen thousand francs and was momentarily penniless. He accordingly shut himself up in his own room at an early hour, and smoked in solitude until he was sleepy, reviewing the various events of the day, or trying to do so, though his mind reverted constantly to the one chief event of all, to the unaccountable outburst of passion by which he had perhaps offended Maria Consuelo beyond forgiveness. With all his affectation of cynicism he had not learned that sin is easy only because it meets with such very general encouragement. Even if he had been aware of that undeniable fact, the knowledge might not have helped him very materially.

The hours passed very slowly during the next day, and even when the appointed time had come, Orsino allowed another quarter of an hour to go by before he entered the hotel and ascended to the little sitting-room in which Maria Consuelo received. He meant to be sure that Del Ferice was there before entering, but he was too proud to watch for the latter's coming, or to inquire of the porter whether Maria Consuelo were alone or not. It seemed simpler in every way to appear a little late.

But Del Ferice was a busy man and not always punctual, so that to Orsino's considerable confusion, he found Maria Consuelo alone, in spite of his precaution. He was so much surprised as to become awkward, for the first time in his life, and he felt the blood rising in his face, dark as he was.

"Will you forgive me?" he asked, almost timidly, as he held out his hand.

Maria Consuelo's tawny eyes looked curiously at him. Then she smiled suddenly.

"My dear child," she said, "you should not do such things! It is very foolish, you know."

The answer was so unexpected and so exceedingly humiliating, as Orsino thought at first, that he grew pale and drew back a little. But Maria Consuelo took no notice of his behaviour, and settled herself in her accustomed chair.

"Did you find Del Ferice last night?" she asked, changing the subject without the least hesitation.

"Yes," answered Orsino.

Almost before the word was spoken there was a knock at the door and Del Ferice appeared. Orsino's face cleared, as though something pleasant had happened, and Maria Consuelo observed the fact. She concluded, naturally enough, that the two men had agreed to meet in her sitting-room, and she resented the punctuality which she supposed they had displayed in coming almost together, especially after what had happened on the preceding day. She noted the cordiality with which they greeted each other and she felt sure that she was right. On the other hand she could not afford to show the least coldness to Del Ferice, lest he should suppose that she was annoyed at being disturbed in her conversation with Orsino. The situation was irritating to her, but she made the best of it and began to talk to Del Ferice about the speech he had made on the previous evening. He had spoken well, and she found it easy to be just and flattering at the same time.

"It must be an immense satisfaction to speak as you do," said Orsino, wishing to say something at least agreeable.

Del Ferice acknowledged the compliment by a deprecatory gesture.

"To speak as some of my colleagues can—yes—it must be a great satisfaction. But Madame d'Aranjuez exaggerates. And, besides, I only make speeches when I am called upon to do so. Speeches are wasted in nine cases out of ten, too. They are, if I may say so, the music at the political ball. Sometimes the guests will dance, and sometimes they will not, but the musicians must try and suit the taste of the great invited. The dancing itself is the thing."

"Deeds not words," suggested Maria Consuelo, glancing at Orsino, who chanced to be looking at her.

"That is a good motto enough," he said gloomily.

"Deeds may need explanation, post facto," remarked Del Ferice, unconsciously making such a direct allusion to recent events that Orsino looked sharply at him, and Maria Consuelo smiled.

"That is true," she said.

"And when you need any one to help you, it is necessary to explain your purpose beforehand," observed Del Ferice. "That is what happens so often in politics, and in other affairs of life as well. If a man takes money from me without my consent, he steals, but if I agree to his taking it, the transaction becomes a gift or a loan. A despotic government steals, a constitutional one borrows or receives free offerings. The fact that the despot pays interest on a part of what he steals raises him to the position of the magnanimous brigand who leaves his victims just enough money to carry them to the nearest town. Possibly it is after all a quibble of definitions, and the difference may not be so great as it seems at first sight. But then, all morality is but the shadow cast on one side or the other of a definition."

"Surely that is not your political creed!" said Maria Consuelo.

"Certainly not, Madame, certainly not," answered Del Ferice in gentle protest. "It is not a creed at all, but only a very poor explanation of the way in which most experienced people look upon the events of their day. The idea in which we believe is very different from the results it has brought about, and very much higher, and very much better. But the results are not all bad either. Unfortunately the bad ones are on the surface, and the good ones, which are enduring, must be sought in places where the honest sunshine has not yet dispelled the early shadows."

Maria Consuelo smiled faintly, and the slight cast in her eyes was more than usually apparent, as though her attention were wandering. Orsino said nothing, and wondered why Del Ferice continued to talk. The latter, indeed, was allowing himself to run on because neither of his hearers seemed inclined to make a remark which might serve to turn the conversation, and he began to suspect that something had occurred before his coming which had disturbed their equanimity.

He presently began to talk of people instead of ideas, for he had no intention of being thought a bore by Madame d'Aranjuez, and the man who is foolish enough to talk of anything but his neighbours, when he has more than one hearer, is in danger of being numbered with the tormentors.

Half an hour passed quickly enough after the common chord had been struck, and Del Ferice and Orsino exchanged glances of intelligence, meaning to go away together as had been agreed. Del Ferice rose first, and Orsino took up his hat. To his surprise and consternation Maria Consuelo made a quick and imperative sign to him to remain. Del Ferice's dull blue eyes saw most things that happened within the range of their vision, and neither the gesture nor the look that accompanied it escaped him.

Orsino's position was extremely awkward. He had put Del Ferice to some inconvenience on the understanding that they were to go away together and did not wish to offend him by not keeping his engagement. On the other hand it was next to impossible to disobey Maria Consuelo, and to explain his difficulty to Del Ferice was wholly out of the question. He almost wished that the latter might have seen and understood the signal. But Del Ferice made no sign and took Maria Consuelo's offered hand, in the act of leavetaking. Orsino grew desperate and stood beside the two, holding his hat. Del Ferice turned to shake hands with him also.

"But perhaps you are going too," he said, with a distinct interrogation.

Orsino glanced at Maria Consuelo as though imploring her permission to take his leave, but her face was impenetrable, calm and indifferent.

Del Ferice understood perfectly what was taking place, but he found a moment while Orsino hesitated. If the latter had known how completely he was in Del Ferice's power throughout the little scene, he would have then and there thrown over his financial schemes in favour of Maria Consuelo. But Del Ferice's quiet, friendly manner did not suggest despotism, and he did not suffer Orsino's embarrassment to last more than five seconds.

"I have a little proposition to make," said the fat count, turning again to Maria Consuelo. "My wife and I are alone this evening. Will you not come and dine with us, Madame? And you, Don Orsino, will you not come too? We shall just make a party of four, if you will both come."

"I shall be enchanted!" exclaimed Maria Consuelo without hesitation.

"I shall be delighted!" answered Orsino with an alacrity which surprised himself.

"At eight then," said Del Ferice, shaking hands with him again, and in a moment he was gone.

Orsino was too much confused, and too much delighted at having escaped so easily from his difficulty to realise the importance of the step he was taking in going to Del Fence's house, or to ask himself why the latter had so opportunely extended the invitation. He sat down in his place with a sigh of relief.

"You have compromised yourself for ever," said Maria Consuelo with a scornful laugh. "You, the blackest of the Black, are to be numbered henceforth with the acquaintances of Count Del Ferice and Donna Tullia."

"What difference does it make? Besides, I could not have done otherwise."

"You might have refused the dinner."

"I could not possibly have done that. To accept was the only way out of a great difficulty."

"What difficulty?" asked Maria Consuelo relentlessly.

Orsino was silent, wondering how he could explain, as explain he must, without offending her.

"You should not do such things," she said suddenly. "I will not always forgive you."

A gleam of light which, indeed, promised little forgiveness, flashed in her eyes.

"What things?" asked Orsino.

"Do not pretend that you think me so simple," she said, in a tone of irritation. "You and Del Ferice come here almost at the same moment. When he goes, you show the utmost anxiety to go too. Of course you have agreed to meet here. It is evident. You might have chosen the steps of the hotel for your place of meeting instead of my sitting-room."

The colour rose slowly in her cheeks. She was handsome when she was angry.

"If I had imagined that you could be displeased—"

"Is it so surprising? Have you forgotten what happened yesterday? You should be on your knees, asking my forgiveness for that—and instead, you make a convenience of your visit to-day in order to meet a man of business. You have very strange ideas of what is due to a woman."

"Del Fence suggested it," said Orsino, "and I accepted the suggestion."

"What is Del Ferice to me, that I should be made the victim of his suggestions, as you call them? Besides, he does not know anything of your folly of yesterday, and he has no right to suspect it."

"I cannot tell you how sorry I am."

"And yet you ought to tell me, if you expect that I will forget all this. You cannot? Then be so good as to do the only other sensible thing in your power, and leave me as soon as possible."

"Forgive me, this once!" Orsino entreated in great distress, but not finding any words to express his sense of humiliation.

"You are not eloquent," she said scornfully. "You had better go. Do not come to the dinner this evening, either. I would rather not see you. You can easily make an excuse."

Orsino recovered himself suddenly.

"I will not go away now, and I will not give up the dinner to-night," he said quietly.

"I cannot make you do either—but I can leave you," said Maria Consuelo, with a movement as though she were about to rise from her chair.

"You will not do that," Orsino answered.

She raised her eyebrows in real or affected surprise at his persistence.

"You seem very sure of yourself," she said. "Do not be so sure of me."

"I am sure that I love you. Nothing else matters." He leaned forward and took her hand, so quickly that she had not time to prevent him. She tried to draw it away, but he held it fast.

"Let me go!" she cried. "I will call, if you do not!"

"Call all Rome if you will, to see me ask your forgiveness. Consuelo—do not be so hard and cruel—if you only knew how I love you, you would be sorry for me, you would see how I hate myself, how I despise myself for all this—"

"You might show a little more feeling," she said, making a final effort to disengage her hand, and then relinquishing the struggle.

Orsino wondered whether he were really in love with her or not. Somehow, the words he sought did not rise to his lips, and he was conscious that his speech was not of the same temperature, so to say, as his actions. There was something in Maria Consuelo's manner which disturbed him disagreeably, like a cold draught blowing unexpectedly through a warm room. Still he held her hand and endeavoured to rise to the occasion.

"Consuelo!" he cried in a beseeching tone. "Do not send me away—see how I am suffering—it is so easy for you to say that you forgive!"

She looked at him a moment, and her eyelids drooped suddenly.

"Will you let me go, if I forgive you?" she asked in a low voice.

"Yes."

"I forgive you then. Well? Do you still hold my hand?"

"Yes."

He leaned forward and tried to draw her toward him, looking into her eyes. She yielded a little, and their faces came a little nearer to each other, and still a little nearer. All at once a deep blush rose in her cheeks, she turned her head away and drew back quickly.

"Not for all the world!" she exclaimed, in a tone that was new to Orsino's ear.

He tried to take her hand again, but she would not give it.

"No, no! Go—you are not to be trusted!" she cried, avoiding him.

"Why are you so unkind?" he asked, almost passionately.

"I have been kind enough for this day," she answered. "Pray go—do not stay any longer—I may regret it."

"My staying?"

"No—my kindness. And do not come again for the present. I would rather see you at Del Ferice's than here."

Orsino was quite unable to understand her behaviour, and an older and more experienced man might have been almost as much puzzled as he. A long silence followed, during which he sat quite still and she looked steadily at the cover of a book which lay on the table.

"Please go," she said at last, in a voice which was not unkind.

Orsino rose from his seat and prepared to obey her, reluctantly enough and feeling that he was out of tune with himself and with everything.

"Will you not even tell me why you send me away?" he asked.

"Because I wish to be alone," she answered. "Good-bye."

She did not look up as he left the room, and when he was gone she did not move from her place, but sat as she had sat before, staring at the yellow cover of the novel on the table.

Orsino went home in a very unsettled frame of mind, and was surprised to find that the lighted streets looked less bright and cheerful than on the previous evening, and his own immediate prospects far less pleasing. He was angry with himself for having been so foolish as to make his visit to Maria Consuelo a mere appointment with Del Ferice, and he was surprised beyond measure to find himself suddenly engaged in a social acquaintance with the latter, when he had only meant to enter into relations of business with him. Yet it did not occur to him that Del Ferice had in any way entrapped him into accepting the invitation. Del Ferice had saved him from a very awkward situation. Why? Because Del Ferice had seen the gesture Maria Consuelo had made, and had understood it, and wished to give Orsino another opportunity of discussing his project. But if Del Ferice had seen the quick sign, he had probably interpreted it in a way compromising to Madame d'Aranjuez. This was serious, though it was assuredly not Orsino's fault if she compromised herself. She might have let him go without question, and since an explanation of some sort was necessary she might have waited until the next day to demand it of him. He resented what she had done, and yet within the last quarter of an hour, he had been making a declaration of love to her. He was further conscious that the said declaration had been wholly lacking in spirit, in passion and even in eloquence. He probably did not love her after all, and with an attempt at his favourite indifference he tried to laugh at himself.

But the effort was not successful, and he felt something approaching to pain as he realised that there was nothing to laugh at. He remembered her eyes and her face and the tones of her voice, and he imagined that if he could turn back now and see her again, he could say in one breath such things as would move a statue to kisses. The very phrases rose to his lips and he repeated them to himself as he walked along.

Most unaccountable of all had been Maria Consuelo's own behaviour. Her chief preoccupation seemed to have been to get rid of him as soon as possible. She had been very seriously offended with him to-day, much more deeply, indeed, than yesterday, though, the cause appeared to his inexperience to be a far less adequate one. It was evident, he thought, that she had not really pardoned his want of tact, but had yielded to the necessity of giving a reluctant forgiveness, merely because she did not wish to break off her acquaintance with him. On the other hand, she had allowed him to say again and again that he loved her, and she had not forbidden him to call her by her name.

He had always heard that it was hard to understand women, and he began to believe it. There was one hypothesis which he had not considered. It was faintly possible that she loved him already, though he was slow to believe that, his vanity lying in another direction. But even if she did, matters were not clearer. The supposition could not account for her sending him away so abruptly and with such evident intention. If she loved him, she would naturally, he supposed, wish him to stay as long as possible. She had only wished to keep him long enough to tell him how angry she was. He resented that again, for he was in the humour to resent most things.

It was all extremely complicated, and Orsino began to think that he might find the complication less interesting than he had expected a few hours earlier. He had little time for reflection either, since he was to meet both Maria Consuelo and Del Ferice at dinner. He felt as though the coming evening were in a measure to decide his future existence, and it was indeed destined to exercise a great influence upon his life, as any person not disturbed by the anxieties which beset him might easily have foreseen.

Before leaving the house he made an excuse to his mother, saying that he had unexpectedly been asked to dine with friends, and at the appointed hour he rang at Del Ferice's door.

CHAPTER XII

Orsino looked about him with some curiosity as he entered Del Fence's abode. He had never expected to find himself the guest of Donna Tullia and her husband and when he took the robust countess's hand he was inclined to wish that the whole affair might turn out to be a dream. In vain he repeated to himself that he was no longer a boy, but a grown man, of age in the eyes of the law to be responsible for his own actions, and old enough in fact to take what steps he pleased for the accomplishment of his own ends. He found no solace in the reflection, and he could not rid himself of the idea that he had got himself into a very boyish scrape. It would indeed have been very easy to refuse Del Ferice's invitation and to write him a note within the hour explaining vaguely that circumstances beyond his control obliged him to ask another interview for the discussion of business matters. But it was too late now. He was exchanging indifferent remarks with Donna Tullia, while Del Ferice looked on benignantly, and all three waited for Madame d'Aranjuez.

Five minutes had not elapsed before she came, and her appearance momentarily dispelled Orsino's annoyance at his own rashness. He had never before seen her dressed for the evening, and he had not realised how much to her advantage the change from the ordinary costume, or the inevitable "tea-garment," to a dinner gown would be. She was assuredly not over-dressed, for she wore black without colours and her only ornament was a single string of beautiful pearls which Donna Tullia believed to be false, but which Orsino accepted as real. Possibly he knew even more about pearls than the countess, for his mother had many and wore them often, whereas Donna Tullia preferred diamonds and rubies. But his eyes did not linger on the necklace, for Maria Consuelo's whole presence affected him strangely. There was something light-giving and even dazzling about her which he had not expected, and he understood for the first time that the language of the newspaper paragraphs was not so grossly flattering as he had supposed. In spite of the great artistic defects of feature, which could not long escape an observer of ordinary taste, it was clear that Maria Consuelo must always be a striking and central figure in any social assembly, great or small. There had been moments in Orsino's acquaintance with her, when he had thought her really beautiful; as she now appeared, one of those moments seemed to have become permanent. He thought of what he had dared on the preceding day, his vanity was pleased and his equanimity restored. With a sense of pride which was very far from being delicate and was by no means well founded, he watched her as she walked in to dinner before him, leaning on Del Ferice's arm.

"Beautiful—eh? I see you think so," whispered Donna Tullia in his ear.

The countess treated him at once as an old acquaintance, which put him at his ease, while it annoyed his conscience.

"Very beautiful," he answered, with a grave nod.

"And so mysterious," whispered the countess again, just as they reached the door of the dining-room. "She is very fascinating—take care!"

She tapped his arm familiarly with her fan and laughed, as he left her at her seat.

"What are you two laughing at?" asked Del Ferice, smiling pleasantly as he surveyed the six oysters he found upon his plate, and considered which should be left until the last as the crowning tit-bit. He was fond of good eating, and especially fond of oysters as an introduction to the feast.

"What we were laughing at? How indiscreet you are, Ugo! You always want to find out all my little secrets. Consuelo, my dear, do you like oysters, or do you not? That is the question. You do, I know—a little lemon and a very little red pepper—I love red, even to adoring cayenne!"

Orsino glanced at Madame d'Aranjuez, for he was surprised to hear Donna Tullia call her by her first name. He had not known that the two women had reached the first halting place of intimacy.

Maria Consuelo smiled rather vaguely as she took the advice in the shape of lemon juice and pepper. Del Ferice could not interrupt his enjoyment of the oysters by words, and Orsino waited for an opportunity of saying something witty.

"I have lately formed the highest opinion of the ancient Romans," said Donna Tullia, addressing him. "Do you know why?"

Orsino professed his ignorance.

"Ugo tells me that in a recent excavation twenty cartloads of oyster shells were discovered behind one house. Think of that! Twenty cartloads to a single house! What a family must have lived there—indeed the Romans were a great people!"

Orsino thought that Donna Tullia herself might pass for a heroine in future ages, provided that the shells of her victims were deposited together in a safe place. He laughed politely and hoped that the conversation might not turn upon archaeology, which was not his strong point.

"I wonder how long it will be before modern Rome is excavated and the foreigner of the future pays a franc to visit the ruins of the modern house of parliament," suggested Maria Consuelo, who had said nothing as yet.

"At the present rate of progress, I should think about two years would be enough," answered Donna Tullia. "But Ugo says we are a great nation. Ask him."

"Ah, my angel, you do not understand those things," said Del Ferice. "How shall I explain? There is no development without decay of the useless parts. The snake casts its old skin before it appears with a new one. And there can be no business without an occasional crisis. Unbroken fair weather ends in a dead calm. Why do you take such a gloomy view, Madame?"

"One should never talk of things—only people are amusing," said Donna Tullia, before Madame d'Aranjuez could answer. "Whom have you seen to-day, Consuelo? And you, Don Orsino? And you, Ugo? Are we to talk for ever of oysters, and business and snakes? Come, tell me, all of you, what everybody has told you. There must be something new. Of course that poor Carantoni is going to be married again, and the Princess Befana is dying, as usual, and the same dear old people have run away with each other, and all that. Of course. I wish things were not always just going to happen. One would like to hear what is said on the day after the events which never come off. It would be a novelty."

Donna Tullia loved talk and noise, and gossip above all things, and she was not quite at her ease. The news that Orsino was to come to dinner had taken her breath away. Ugo had advised her to be natural, and she was doing her best to follow his advice.

"As for me," he said, "I have been tormented all day, and have spent but one pleasant half hour. I was so fortunate as to find Madame d'Aranjuez at home, but that was enough to indemnify me for many sacrifices."

"I cannot do better than say the same," observed Orsino, though with far less truth. "I believe I have read through a new novel, but I do not remember the title and I have forgotten the story."

"How satisfactory!" exclaimed Maria Consuelo, with a little scorn.

"It is the only way to read novels," answered Orsino, "for it leaves them always new to you, and the same one may be made to last several weeks."

"I have heard it said that one should fear the man of one book," observed Maria Consuelo, looking at him.

"For my part, I am more inclined to fear the woman of many."

"Do you read much, my dear Consuelo?" asked Donna Tullia, laughing.

"Perpetually."

"And is Don Orsino afraid of you?"

"Mortally," answered Orsino. "Madame d'Aranjuez knows everything."

"Is she blue, then?" asked Donna Tullia.

"What shall I say, Madame?" inquired Orsino, turning to Maria Consuelo. "Is it a compliment to compare you to the sky of Italy?"

"For blueness?"

"No—for brightness and serenity."

"Thanks. That is pretty. I accept."

"And have you nothing for me?" asked Donna Tullia, with an engaging smile.

The other two looked at Orsino, wondering what he would say in answer to such a point-blank demand for flattery.

"Juno is still Minerva's ally," he said, falling back upon mythology, though it struck him that Del Ferice would make a poor Jupiter, with his fat white face and dull eyes.

"Very good!" laughed Donna Tullia. "A little classic, but I pressed you hard. You are not easily caught. Talking of clever men," she added with another meaning glance at Orsino, "I met your friend to-day, Consuelo."

"My friend? Who is he?"

"Spicca, of course. Whom did you think I meant? We always laugh at her," she said, turning to Orsino, "because she hates him so. She does not know him, and has never spoken to him. It is his cadaverous face that frightens her. One can understand that—we of old Rome, have been used to him since the deluge. But a stranger is horrified at the first sight of him. Consuelo positively dreads to meet him in the street. She says that he makes her dream of all sorts of horrors."

"It is quite true," said Maria Consuelo, with a slight movement of her beautiful shoulders. "There are people one would rather not see, merely because they are not good to look at. He is one of them and if I see him coming I turn away."

"I know, I told him so to-day," continued Donna Tullia cheerfully. "We are old friends, but we do not often meet nowadays. Just fancy! It was in that little antiquary's shop in the Monte Brianzo—the first on the left as you go, he has good things—and I saw a bit of embroidery in the window that took my fancy, so I stopped the carriage and went in. Who should be there but Spicca, hat and all, looking like old

Father Time. He was bargaining for something—a wretched old bit of brass—bargaining, my dear! For a few sous! One may be poor, but one has no right to be mean—I thought he would have got the miserable antiquary's skin."

"Antiquaries can generally take care of themselves," observed Orsino incredulously.

"Oh, I daresay—but it looks so badly, you know. That is all I mean. When he saw me he stopped wrangling and we talked a little, while I had the embroidery wrapped up. I will show it to you after dinner. It is sixteenth century, Ugo says—a piece of a chasuble—exquisite flowers on claret-coloured satin, a perfect gem, so rare now that everything is imitated. However, that is not the point. It was Spicca. I was forgetting my story. He said the usual things, you know—that he had heard that I was very gay this year, but that it seemed to agree with me, and so on. And I asked him why he never came to see me, and as an inducement I told him of our great beauty here—that is you, Consuelo, so please look delighted instead of frowning—and I told him that she ought to hear him talk, because his face had frightened her so that she ran away when she saw him coming towards her in the street. You see, if one flatters his cleverness he does not mind being called ugly—or at least I thought not, until to-day. But to my consternation he seemed angry, and he asked me almost savagely if it were true that the Countess d'Aranjuez—that is what he called you, my dear—really tried to avoid him in the street. Then I laughed and said I was only joking, and he began to bargain again for the little brass frame and I went away. When I last heard his voice he was insisting upon seventy-five centimes, and the antiquary was jeering at him and asking a franc and a half. I wonder which got the better of the fight in the end. I will ask him the next time I see him."

Del Ferice supported his wife with a laugh at her story, but it was not very genuine. He had unpleasant recollections of Spicca in earlier days, and his name recalled events which Ugo would willingly have forgotten. Orsino smiled politely, but resented the way in which Donna Tullia spoke of his father's old friend. As for Maria Consuelo, she was a little pale, and looked tired. But the countess was irrepressible, for she feared lest Orsino should go away and think her dull.

"Of course we all really like Spicca," she said. "Every one does."

"I do, for my part," said Orsino gravely. "I have a great respect for him, for his own sake, and he is one of my father's oldest friends."

Maria Consuelo looked at him very suddenly, as though she were surprised by what he said. She did not remember to have heard him mention the melancholy old duellist. She seemed about to say something, but changed her mind.

"Yes," said Ugo, turning the subject, "he is one of the old tribe that is dying out. What types there were in those days, and how those who are alive have changed! Do you remember, Tullia? But of course you cannot, my angel, it was far before your time."

One of Ugo's favourite methods of pleasing his wife was to assert that she was too young to remember people who had indeed played a part as lately as after the death of her first husband. It always soothed her.

"I remember them all," he continued. "Old Montevarchi, and Frangipani, and poor Casalverde—and a score of others."

He had been on the point of mentioning old Astrardente, too, but checked himself.

"Then there were the young ones, who are in middle age now," he went on, "such as Valdarno and the Montevarchi whom you know, as different from their former selves as you can well imagine. Society was different too."

Del Ferice spoke thoughtfully and slowly, as though wishing that some one would interrupt him or take up the subject, for he felt that his wife's long story about Spicca and the antiquary had not been a success, and his instinct told him that Spicca had better not be mentioned again, since he was a friend of Orsino's and since his name seemed to exert a depressing influence on Maria Consuelo. Orsino came to the rescue and began to talk of current social topics in a way which showed that he was not so profoundly prejudiced by traditional ideas as Del Ferice had expected. The momentary chill wore off quickly enough, and when the dinner ended Donna Tullia was sure that it had been a success. They all returned to the drawing-room and then Del Ferice, without any remark, led Orsino away to smoke with him in a distant apartment.

"We can smoke again, when we go back," he said. "My wife does not mind and Madame d'Aranjuez likes it. But it is an excuse to be alone together for a little while, and besides, my doctor makes me lie down for a quarter of an hour after dinner. You will excuse me?"

Del Ferice extended himself upon a leathern lounge, and Orsino sat down in a deep easy-chair.

"I was so sorry not to be able to come away with you to-day," said Orsino. "The truth is, Madame d'Aranjuez wanted some information and I was just going to explain that I would stay a little longer, when you asked us both to dinner. You must have thought me very forgetful."

"Not at all, not at all," answered Del Ferice. "Indeed, I quite supposed that you were coming with me, when it struck me that this would be a much more pleasant place for talking. I cannot imagine why I had not thought of it before—but I have so many details to think of."

Not much could be said for the veracity of either of the statements which the two men were pleased to make to each other, but Orsino had the small advantage of being nearer to the letter, if not to the spirit of the truth. Each, however, was satisfied with the other's tact.

"And so, Don Orsino," continued Del Ferice after a short pause, "you wish to try a little operation in business. Yes. Very good. You have, as we said yesterday, a sum of money ample for a beginning. You have the necessary courage and intelligence. You need a practical assistant, however, and it is indispensable that the point selected for the first venture should be one promising speedy profit. Is that it?"

"Precisely."

"Very good, very good. I think I can offer you both the land and the partner, and almost guarantee your success, if you will be guided by me."

"I have come to you for advice," said Orsino. "I will follow it gratefully. As for the success of the undertaking, I will assume the responsibility."

"Yes. That is better. After all, everything is uncertain in such matters, and you would not like to feel that you were under an obligation to me. On the other hand, as I told you, I am selfish and cautious. I would rather not appear in the transaction."

If any doubt as to Del Ferice's honesty of purpose crossed Orsino's mind at that moment, it was fully compensated by the fact that he himself distinctly preferred not to be openly associated with the banker.

"I quite agree with you," he said.

"Very well. Now for business. Do you know that it is sometimes more profitable to take over a half-finished building, than to begin a new one? Often, I assure you, for the returns are quicker and you get a great deal at half price. Now, the man whom I recommend to you is a practical architect, and was employed by a certain baker to build a tenement building in one of the new quarters. The baker dies, the house is unfinished, the heirs wish to sell it as it is—there are at least a dozen of them—and meanwhile the work is stopped. My advice is this. Buy this house, go into partnership with the unemployed architect, agreeing to give him a share of the profits, finish the building and sell it as soon as it is habitable. In six months you will get a handsome return."

"That sounds very tempting," answered Orsino, "but it would need more capital than I have."

"Not at all, not at all. It is a mere question of taking over a mortgage and paying stamp duty."

"And how about the difference in ready money, which ought to go to the present owners?"

"I see that you are already beginning to understand the principles of business," said Del Ferice, with an encouraging smile. "But in this case the owners are glad to get rid of the house on any terms by which they lose nothing, for they are in mortal fear of being ruined by it, as they probably will be if they hold on to it."

"Then why should I not lose, if I take it?"

"That is just the difference. The heirs are a number of incapable persons of the lower class, who do not understand these matters. If they attempted to go on they would soon find themselves entangled in the greatest difficulties. They would sink where you will almost certainly swim."

Orsino was silent for a moment. There was something despicable, to his thinking, in profiting by the loss of a wretched baker's heirs.

"It seems to me," he said presently, "that if I succeed in this, I ought to give a share of the profits to the present owners."

Not a muscle of Del Ferice's face moved, but his dull eyes looked curiously at Orsino's young face.

"That sort of thing is not commonly done in business," he said quietly, after a short pause. "As a rule, men who busy themselves with affairs do so in the hope of growing rich, but I can quite understand that where business is a mere pastime, as it is to be in your case, a man of generous instincts may devote the proceeds to charity."

"It looks more like justice than charity to me," observed Orsino.

"Call it what you will, but succeed first and consider the uses of your success afterwards. That is not my affair. The baker's heirs are not especially deserving people, I believe. In fact they are said to have hastened his death in the hope of inheriting his wealth and are disappointed to find that they have got nothing. If you wish to be philanthropic you might wait until you have cleared a large sum and then give it to a school or a hospital."

"That is true," said Orsino. "In the meantime it is important to begin."

"We can begin to-morrow, if you please. You will find me at the bank at mid-day. I will send for the architect and the notary and we can manage everything in forty-eight hours. Before the week is out you can be at work."

"So soon as that?"

"Certainly. Sooner, by hurrying matters a little."

"As soon as possible then. And I will go to the bank at twelve o'clock to-morrow. A thousand thanks for all your good offices, my dear count."

"It is a pleasure, I assure you."

Orsino was so much pleased with Del Ferice's quick and business-like way of arranging matters that he began to look upon him as a model to imitate, so far as executive ability was concerned. It was odd enough that any one of his name should feel anything like admiration for Ugo, but friendship and hatred are only the opposite points at which the social pendulum pauses before it swings backward, and they who live long may see many oscillations.

The two men went back to the drawing-room where Donna Tullia and Maria Consuelo were discussing the complicated views of the almighty dressmaker. Orsino knew that there was little chance of his speaking a word alone with Madame d'Aranjuez and resigned himself to the effort of helping the general conversation. Fortunately the time to be got over in this way was not long, as all four had engagements in the evening. Maria Consuelo rose at half-past ten, but Orsino determined to wait five minutes longer, or at least to make a show of meaning to do so. But Donna Tullia put out her hand as though she expected him to take his leave at the same time. She was going to a ball and wanted at least an hour in which to screw her magnificence up to the dancing pitch.

The consequence was that Orsino found himself helping Maria Consuelo into the modest hired conveyance which awaited her at the gate. He hoped that she would offer him a seat for a short distance, but he was disappointed.

"May I come to-morrow?" he asked, as he closed the door of the carriage. The night was not cold and the window was down.

"Please tell the coachman to take me to the Via Nazionale," she said quickly.

"What number?"

"Never mind—he knows—I have forgotten. Good-night."

She tried to draw up the window, but Orsino held his hand on it.

"May I come to-morrow?" he asked again.

"No."

"Are you angry with me still?"

"No."

"Then why—"

"Let me shut the window. Take your hand away."

Her voice was very imperative in the dark. Orsino relinquished his hold on the frame, and the pane ran up suddenly into its place with a rattling noise. There was obviously nothing more to be said.

"Via Nazionale. The Signora says you know the house," he called to the driver.

The man looked surprised, shrugged his shoulders after the manner of livery stable coachmen and drove slowly off in the direction indicated. Orsino stood looking after the carriage and a few seconds later he saw that the man drew rein and bent down to the front window as though asking for orders. Orsino thought he heard Maria Consuelo's voice, answering the question, but he could not distinguish what she said, and the brougham drove on at once without taking a new direction.

He was curious to know whither she was going, and the idea of following her suggested itself but he instantly dismissed it, partly because it seemed unworthy and partly, perhaps, because he was on foot, and no cab was passing within hail.

Orsino was very much puzzled. During the dinner she had behaved with her usual cordiality but as soon as they were alone she spoke and acted as she had done in the afternoon. Orsino turned away and walked across the deserted square. He was greatly disturbed, for he felt a sense of humiliation and disappointment quite new to him. Young as he was, he had been accustomed already to a degree of consideration very different from that which Maria Consuelo thought fit to bestow, and it was certainly the first time in his life that a door—even the door of a carriage—had been shut in his face without ceremony. What would have been an unpardonable insult, coming from a man, was at least an indignity when it came from a woman. As Orsino walked along, his wrath rose, and he wondered why he had not been angry at once.

"Very well," he said to himself. "She says she does not want me. I will take her at her word and I will not go to see her any more. We shall see what happens. She will find out that I am not a child, as she was good enough to call me to-day, and that I am not in the habit of having windows put up in my face. I have much more serious business on hand than making love to Madame d'Aranjuez."

The more he reflected upon the situation, the more angry he grew, and when he reached the door of the club he was in a humour to quarrel with everything and everybody. Fortunately, at that early hour, the place was in the sole possession of half a dozen old gentlemen whose conversation diverted his thoughts though it was the very reverse of edifying. Between the stories they told and the considerable number of cigarettes he smoked while listening to them he was almost restored to his normal frame of mind by midnight, when four or five of his usual companions straggled in and proposed baccarat. After his recent successes he could not well refuse to play, so he sat down rather reluctantly with the rest. Oddly enough he did not lose, though he won but little.

"Lucky at play, unlucky in love," laughed one of the men carelessly.

"What do you mean?" asked Orsino, turning sharply upon the speaker.

"Mean? Nothing," answered the latter in great surprise. "What is the matter with you, Orsino? Cannot one quote a common proverb?"

"Oh—if you meant nothing, let us go on," Orsino answered gloomily.

As he took up the cards again, he heard a sigh behind him and turning round saw that Spicca was standing at his shoulder. He was shocked by the melancholy count's face, though he was used to meeting him almost every day. The haggard and cadaverous features, the sunken and careworn eyes, contrasted almost horribly with the freshness and gaiety of Orsino's companions, and the brilliant light in the room threw the man's deadly pallor into strong relief.

"Will you play, Count?" asked Orsino, making room for him.

"Thanks—no. I never play nowadays," answered Spicca quietly.

He turned and left the room. With all his apparent weakness his step was not unsteady, though it was slower than in the old days.

"He sighed in that way because we did not quarrel," said the man whose quoted proverb had annoyed Orsino.

"I am ready and anxious to quarrel with everybody to-night," answered Orsino. "Let us play baccarat—that is much better."

Spicca left the club alone and walked slowly homewards to his small lodging in the Via della Croce. A few dying embers smouldered in the little fireplace which warmed his sitting-room. He stirred them slowly, took a stick of wood from the wicker basket, hesitated a moment, and then put it back again instead of burning it. The night was not cold and wood was very dear. He sat down under the light of the old lamp which stood upon the mantelpiece, and drew a long breath. But presently, putting his hand into the pocket of his overcoat in search of his cigarette case, he drew out something else which he had almost forgotten, a small something wrapped in coarse paper. He undid it and looked at the little frame of chiselled brass which Donna Tullia had found him buying in the afternoon, turning it over and over, absently, as though thinking of something else.

Then he fumbled in his pockets again and found a photograph which he had also bought in the course of the day—the photograph of Gouache's latest portrait, obtained in a contraband fashion and with some difficulty from the photographer.

Without hesitation Spicca took a pocket-knife and began to cut the head out, with that extraordinary neatness and precision which characterised him when he used any sharp instrument. The head just fitted the frame. He fastened it in with drops of sealing-wax and carefully burned the rest of the picture in the embers.

The face of Maria Consuelo smiled at him in the lamplight, as he turned it in different ways so as to find the best aspect of it. Then he hung it on a nail above the mantelpiece just under a pair of crossed foils.

"That man Gouache is a very clever fellow," he said aloud. "Between them, he and nature have made a good likeness."

He sat down again and it was a long time before he made up his mind to take away the lamp and go to bed.

CHAPTER XIII

Del Ferice kept his word and arranged matters for Orsino with a speed and skill which excited the latter's admiration. The affair was not indeed very complicated though it involved a deed of sale, the transfer of a mortgage and a deed of partnership between Orsino Saracinesca and Andrea Contini, architect, under the style "Andrea Contini and Company," besides a contract between this firm of the one party and the bank in which Del Ferice was a director, of the other, the partners agreeing to continue the building of the half-finished house, and the bank binding itself to advance small sums up to a certain amount for current expenses of material and workmen's wages. Orsino signed everything required of him after reading the documents, and Andrea Contini followed his example.

The architect was a tall man with bright brown eyes, a dark and somewhat ragged beard, close cropped hair, a prominent, bony forehead and large, coarsely shaped, thin ears oddly set upon his head. He habitually wore a dark overcoat, of which the collar was generally turned up on one side and not on the other. Judging from the appearance of his strong shoes he had always been walking a long distance over bad roads, and when it had rained within the week his trousers were generally bespattered with mud to a considerable height above the heel. He habitually carried an extinguished cigar between his teeth of which he chewed the thin black end uneasily. Orsino fancied that he might be about eight and twenty years old, and was not altogether displeased with his appearance. He was not at all like the majority of his kind, who, in Rome at least, usually affect a scrupulous dandyism of attire and an uncommon refinement of manner. Whatever Contini's faults might prove to be, Orsino did not believe that they would turn out to be those of idleness or vanity. How far he was right in his judgment will appear before long, but he conceived his partner to be gifted, frank, enthusiastic and careless of outward forms.

As for the architect himself, he surveyed Orsino with a sort of sympathetic curiosity which the latter would have thought unpleasantly familiar if he had understood it. Contini had never spoken before with any more exalted personage than Del Ferice, and he studied the young aristocrat as though he were a being from another world. He hesitated some time as to the proper mode of addressing him and at last decided to call him "Signor Principe." Orsino seemed quite satisfied with this, and the architect was inwardly pleased when the young man said "Signor Contini" instead of Contini alone. It was quite clear that Del Ferice had already acquainted him with all the details of the situation, for he seemed to understand all the documents at a glance, picking out and examining the important clauses with unfailing acuteness, and pointing with his finger to the place where Orsino was to sign his name.

At the end of the interview Orsino shook hands with Del Ferice and thanked him warmly for his kindness, after which, he and his partner went out together. They stood side by side upon the pavement for a few seconds, each wondering what the other was going to say.

"Perhaps we had better go and look at the house, Signor Principe," observed Contini, in the midst of an ineffectual effort to light the stump of his cigar.

"I think so, too," answered Orsino, realising that since he had acquired the property it would be as well to know how it looked. "You see I have trusted my adviser entirely in the matter, and I am ashamed to say I do not know where the house is."

Andrea Contini looked at him curiously.

"This is the first time that you have had anything to do with business of this kind, Signor Principe," he observed. "You have fallen into good hands."

"Yours?" inquired Orsino, a little stiffly.

"No. I mean that Count Del Ferice is a good adviser in this matter."

"I hope so."

"I am sure of it," said Contini with conviction. "It would be a great surprise to me if we failed to make a handsome profit by this contract."

"There is luck and ill-luck in everything," answered Orsino, signalling to a passing cab.

The two men exchanged few words as they drove up to the new quarter in the direction indicated to the driver by Contini. The cab entered a sort of broad lane, the sketch of a future street, rough with the unrolled metalling of broken stones, the space set apart for the pavement being an uneven path of trodden brown earth. Here and there tall detached houses rose out of the wilderness, mostly covered by scaffoldings and swarming with workmen, but hideous where so far finished as to be visible in all the isolation of their six-storied nakedness. A strong smell of lime, wet earth and damp masonry was blown into Orsino's nostrils by the scirocco wind. Contini stopped the cab before an unpromising and deserted erection of poles, boards and tattered matting.

"This is our house," he said, getting out and immediately making another attempt to light his cigar.

"May I offer you a cigarette?" asked Orsino, holding out his case.

Contini touched his hat, bowed a little awkwardly and took one of the cigarettes, which he immediately transferred to his coat pocket.

"If you will allow me I will smoke it by and by," he said. "I have not finished my cigar."

Orsino stood on the slippery ground beside the stones and contemplated his purchase. All at once his heart sank and he felt a profound disgust for everything within the range of his vision. He was suddenly aware of his own total and hopeless ignorance of everything connected with building, theoretical or practical. The sight of the stiff, angular scaffoldings, draped with torn straw mattings that flapped fantastically in the south-east wind, the apparent absence of anything like a real house behind them, the blades of grass sprouting abundantly about the foot of each pole and covering the heaps of brown pozzolana earth prepared for making mortar, even the detail of a broken wooden hod before the boarded entrance—all these things contributed at once to increase his dismay and to fill him with a bitter sense of inevitable failure. He found nothing to say, as he stood with his hands in his pockets staring at the general desolation, but he understood for the first time why women cry for disappointment. And moreover, this desolation was his own peculiar property, by deed of purchase, and he could not get rid of it.

Meanwhile Andrea Contini stood beside him, examining the scaffoldings with his bright brown eyes, in no way disconcerted by the prospect.

"Shall we go in?" he asked at last.

"Do unfinished houses always look like this?" inquired Orsino, in a hopeless tone, without noticing his companion's proposition.

"Not always," answered Contini cheerfully. "It depends upon the amount of work that has been done, and upon other things. Sometimes the foundations sink and the buildings collapse."

"Are you sure nothing of the kind has happened here?" asked Orsino with increasing anxiety.

"I have been several times to look at it since the baker died and I have not noticed any cracks yet," answered the architect, whose coolness seemed almost exasperating.

"I suppose you understand these things, Signor Contini?"

Contini laughed, and felt in his pockets for a crumpled paper box of wax-lights.

"It is my profession," he answered. "And then, I built this house from the foundations. If you will come in, Signor Principe, I will show you how solidly the work is done."

He took a key from his pocket and thrust it into a hole in the boarding, which latter proved to be a rough door and opened noisily upon rusty hinges. Orsino followed him in silence. To the young man's inexperienced eye the interior of the building was even more depressing than the outside. It smelt like a vault, and a dim grey light entered the square apertures from the curtained scaffoldings without, just sufficient to help one to find a way through the heaps of rubbish that covered the unpaved floors.

Contini explained rapidly and concisely the arrangement of the rooms, calling one cave familiarly a dining-room and another a "conjugal bedroom," as he expressed it, and expatiating upon the facilities of communication which he himself had carefully planned. Orsino listened in silence and followed his guide patiently from place to place, in and out of dark passages and up flights of stairs as yet unguarded by any rail, until they emerged upon a sort of flat terrace intersected by low walls, which was indeed another floor and above which another story and a garret were yet to be built to complete the house. Orsino looked gloomily about him, lighted a cigarette and sat down upon a bit of masonry.

"To me, it looks very like failure," he remarked. "But I suppose there is something in it."

"It will not look like failure next month," said Contini carelessly. "Another story is soon built, and then the attic, and then, if you like, a Gothic roof and a turret at one corner. That always attracts buyers first and respectable lodgers afterwards."

"Let us have a turret, by all means," answered Orsino, as though his tailor had proposed to put an extra button on the cuff of his coat. "But how in the world are you going to begin? Everything looks to me as though it were falling to pieces."

"Leave all that to me, Signor Principe. We will begin to-morrow. I have a good overseer and there are plenty of workmen to be had. We have material for a week at least, and paid for, excepting a few cartloads of lime. Come again in ten days and you will see something worth looking at."

"In ten days? And what am I to do in the meantime?" asked Orsino, who fancied that he had found an occupation.

Andrea Contini looked at him in some surprise, not understanding in the least what he meant.

"I mean, am I to have nothing to do with the work?" asked Orsino.

"Oh—as far as that goes, you will come every day, Signor Principe, if it amuses you, though as you are not a practical architect, your assistance is not needed until questions of taste have to be considered, such as the Gothic roof for instance. But there are the accounts to be kept, of course, and there is the business with the bank from week to week, office work of various kinds. That becomes naturally your department, as the practical superintendence of the building is mine, but you will of course leave it to the steward of the Signor Principe di Sant' Ilario, who is a man of affairs."

"I will do nothing of the kind!" exclaimed Orsino. "I will do it myself. I will learn how it is done. I want occupation."

"What an extraordinary wish!" Andrea Contini opened his eyes in real astonishment.

"Is it? You work. Why should not I?"

"I must, and you need not, Signor Principe," observed the architect. "But if you insist, then you had better get a clerk to explain the details to you at first."

"Do you not understand them? Can you not teach me?" asked Orsino, displeased with the idea of employing a third person.

"Oh yes—I have been a clerk myself. I should be too much honoured but—the fact is, my spare time—"

He hesitated and seemed reluctant to explain.

"What do you do with your spare time?" asked Orsino, suspecting some love affair.

"The fact is—I play a second violin at one of the theatres—and I give lessons on the mandolin, and sometimes I do copying work for my uncle who is a clerk in the Treasury. You see, he is old, and his eyes are not as good as they were."

Orsino began to think that his partner was a very odd person. He could not help smiling at the enumeration of his architect's secondary occupations.

"You are very fond of music, then?" he asked.

"Eh—yes—as one can be, without talent—a little by necessity. To be an architect one must have houses to build. You see the baker died unexpectedly. One must live somehow."

"And could you not—how shall I say? Would you not be willing to give me lessons in book-keeping instead of teaching some one else to play the mandolin?"

"You would not care to learn the mandolin yourself, Signor Principe? It is a very pretty instrument, especially for country parties, as well as for serenading."

Orsino laughed. He did not see himself in the character of a mandolinist.

"I have not the slightest ear for music," he answered. "I would much rather learn something about business."

"It is less amusing," said Andrea Contini regretfully.

"But I am at your service. I will come to the office when work is over and we will do the accounts together. You will learn in that way very quickly."

"Thank you. I suppose we must have an office. It is necessary, is it not?"

"Indispensable—a room, a garret—anything. A habitation, a legal domicile, so to say."

"Where do you live, Signor Contini? Would not your lodging do?"

"I am afraid not, Signor Principe. At least not for the present. I am not very well lodged and the stairs are badly lighted."

"Why not here, then?" asked Orsino, suddenly growing desperately practical, for he felt unaccountably reluctant to hire an office in the city.

"We should pay no rent," said Contini. "It is an idea. But the walls are dry downstairs, and we only need a pavement, and plastering, and doors and windows, and papering and some furniture to make one of the rooms quite habitable. It is an idea, undoubtedly. Besides, it would give the house an air of being inhabited, which is valuable."

"How long will all that take? A month or two?"

"About a week. It will be a little fresh, but if you are not rheumatic, Signor Principe, we can try it."

"I am not rheumatic," laughed Orsino, who was pleased with the idea of having his office on the spot, and apparently in the midst of a wilderness. "And I suppose you really do understand architecture, Signor Contini, though you do play the fiddle."

In this exceedingly sketchy way was the firm of Andrea Contini and Company established and lodged, being at the time in a very shadowy state, theoretically and practically, though it was destined to play a more prominent part in affairs than either of the young partners anticipated. Orsino discovered before long that his partner was a man of skill and energy, and his spirits rose by degrees as the work began to advance. Contini was restless, untiring and gifted, such a character as Orsino had not yet met in his limited experience of the world. The man seemed to understand his business to the smallest details and could show the workmen how to mix mortar in the right proportions, or how to strengthen a scaffolding at the weak point much better than the overseer or the master builder. At the books he seemed to be infallible, and he possessed, moreover, such a power of stating things clearly and neatly that Orsino actually learnt from him in a few weeks what he would have needed six months to learn anywhere else. As soon as the first dread of failure wore off, Orsino discovered that he was happier than he had ever been in the course of his life before. What he did was not, indeed, of much use in the progress of the office work and rather hindered than helped Contini, who was obliged to do everything slowly and sometimes twice over in order to make his pupil understand; but Orsino had a clear and practical mind, and did not forget what he had learned once. An odd sort of friendship sprang up between the two men, who under ordinary circumstances would never have met, or known each other by sight. The one had expected to find in his partner an overbearing, ignorant patrician; the other had supposed that his companion would turn out a vulgar, sordid, half-educated builder. Both were equally surprised when each discovered the truth about the other.

Though Orsino was reticent by nature, he took no especial pains to conceal his goings and comings, but as his occupation took him out of the ordinary beat followed by his idle friends, it was a long time before any of them discovered that he was engaged in practical business. In his own home he was not questioned, and he said nothing. The Saracinesca were considered eccentric, but no one interfered with them nor ventured to offer them suggestions. If they chose to allow their heir absolute liberty of action, merely because he had passed his twenty-first birthday, it was their own concern, and his ruin would be upon their own heads. No one cared to risk a savage retort from the aged prince, or a cutting answer from Sant' Ilario for the questionable satisfaction of telling either that Orsino was going to the bad. The only person who really knew what Orsino was about, and who could have claimed the right to speak to his family of his doings was San Giacinto, and he held his peace, having plenty of important affairs of his own to occupy him and being blessed with an especial gift for leaving other people to themselves.

Sant' Ilario never spied upon his son, as many of his contemporaries would have done in his place. He preferred to trust him to his own devices so long as these led to no great mischief. He saw that Orsino was less restless than formerly, that he was less at the club, and that he was stirring earlier in the morning than had been his wont, and he was well satisfied.

It was not to be expected, however, that Orsino should take Maria Consuelo literally at her word, and cease from visiting her all at once. If not really in love with her, he was at least so much interested in her that he sorely missed the daily half hour or more which he had been used to spend in her society.

Three several times he went to her hotel at the accustomed hour, and each time he was told by the porter that she was at home; but on each occasion, also, when he sent up his card, the hotel servant returned with a message from the maid to the effect that Madame d'Aranjuez was tired and did not receive. Orsino's pride rebelled equally against making a further attempt and against writing a letter requesting an explanation. Once only, when he was walking alone she passed him in a carriage, and she acknowledged his bow quietly and naturally, as though nothing had happened. He fancied she was paler than usual, and that there were shadows under her eyes which he had not formerly noticed. Possibly, he thought, she was really not in good health, and the excuses made through her maid were not wholly invented. He was conscious that his heart beat a little faster as he watched the back of the brougham disappearing in the distance, but he did not feel an irresistible longing to make another and more serious attempt to see her. He tried to analyse his own sensations, and it seemed to him that he rather dreaded a meeting than desired it, and that he felt a certain humiliation for which he could not account. In the midst of his analysis, his cigarette went out and he sighed. He was startled by such an expression of feeling, and tried to remember whether he had ever sighed before in his life, but if he had, he could not recall the circumstances. He tried to console himself with the absurd supposition that he was sleepy and that the long-drawn breath had been only a suppressed yawn. Then he walked on, gazing before him into the purple haze that filled the deep street just as the sun was setting, and a vague sadness and longing touched him which had no place in his catalogue of permissible emotions and which were as far removed from the cold cynicism which he admired in others and affected in himself as they were beyond the sphere of his analysis.

There is an age, not always to be fixed exactly, at which the really masculine nature craves the society of womankind, in one shape or another, as a necessity of existence, and by the society of womankind no one means merely the daily and hourly social intercourse which consists in exchanging the same set of remarks half a dozen times a day with as many beings of gentle sex who, to the careless eye of ordinary man, differ from each other in dress rather than in face or thought. There are eminently manly men, that is to say men fearless, strong, honourable and active, to whom the common five o'clock tea presents as much distraction and offers as much womanly sympathy as they need; who choose their intimate friends among men, rather than among women, and who die at an advanced age without ever having been more than comfortably in love—and of such is the Kingdom of Heaven. The masculine man may be as brave, as strong and as scrupulously just in all his dealings, but on the other hand he may be weak, cowardly and a cheat, and he is apt to inherit the portion of sinners, whatever his moral characteristics may be, good or bad.

Orsino was certainly not unmanly, but he was also eminently masculine and he began to suffer from the loss of Maria Consuelo's conversation in a way that surprised himself. His acquaintance with her, to give it a mild name, had been the first of the kind which he had enjoyed, and it contrasted too strongly with the crude experiences of his untried youth not to be highly valued by him and deeply regretted. He might pretend to laugh at it, and repeat to himself that his Egeria had been but a very superficial person, fervent in the reading of the daily novel and possibly not even worldly wise; he did not miss her any the less for that. A little sympathy and much patience in listening will go far to make a woman of small gifts indispensable even to a man of superior talent, especially when he thinks himself misunderstood in his ordinary surroundings. The sympathy passes for intelligence and the patience for assent and encouragement—a touch of the hand, and there is friendship, a tear, a sigh, and devotion stands upon the stage, bearing in her arms an infant love who learns to walk his part at the first suspicion of a kiss.

Orsino did not imagine that he had exhausted the world's capabilities of happiness. The age of Byronism, as it used to be called, is over. Possibly tragedies are more real and frequent in our day than when the century was young; at all events those which take place seem to draw a new element of horror from those undefinable, mechanical, prosaic, psuedo-scientific conditions which make our lives so different from those of our fathers. Everything is terribly sudden nowadays, and alarmingly quick. Lovers make love across Europe by telegraph, and poetic justice arrives in less than forty-eight hours by the Oriental Express. Divorce is our weapon of precision, and every pack of cards at the gaming table can distil a poison more destructive than that of the Borgia. The unities of time and place are preserved by wire and rail in a way which would have delighted the hearts of the old French tragics. Perhaps men seek dramatic situations in their own lives less readily since they have found out means of making the concluding act more swift, sudden and inevitable. At all events we all like tragedy less and comedy more than our fathers did, which, I think, shows that we are sadder and possibly wiser men than they.

However this may be, Orsino was no more inclined to fancy himself unhappy than any of his familiar companions, though he was quite willing to believe that he understood most of life's problems, and especially the heart of woman. He continued to go into the world, for it was new to him and if he did not find exactly the sort of sympathy he secretly craved, he found at least a great deal of consideration, some flattery and a certain amount of amusement. But when he was not actually being amused, or really engaged in the work which he had undertaken with so much enthusiasm, he felt lonely and missed Maria Consuelo more than ever. By this time she had taken a position in society from which there could be no drawing back, and he gave up for ever the hope of seeing her in his own circle. She seemed to avoid even the grey houses where they might have met on neutral ground, and Orsino saw that his only chance of finding her in the world lay in going frequently and openly to Del Ferice's house. He had called on Donna Tullia after the dinner, of course, but he was not prepared to do more, and Del Ferice did not seem to expect it.

Three or four weeks after he had entered into partnership with Andrea Contini, Orsino found himself alone with his mother in the evening. Corona was seated near the fire in her favourite boudoir, with a book in her hand, and Orsino stood warming himself on one side of the chimney-piece, staring into the flames and occasionally glancing at his mother's calm, dark face. He was debating whether he should stay at home or not.

Corona became conscious that he looked at her from time to time and dropped her novel upon her knee.

"Are you going out, Orsino?" she asked.

"I hardly know," he answered. "There is nothing particular to do, and it is too late for the theatre."

"Then stay with me. Let us talk." She looked at him affectionately and pointed to a low chair near her.

He drew it up until he could see her face as she spoke, and then sat down.

"What shall we talk about, mother?" he asked, with a smile.

"About yourself, if you like, my dear. That is, if you have anything that you know I would like to hear. I am not curious, am I, Orsino? I never ask you questions about yourself."

"No, indeed. You never tease me with questions—nor does my father either, for that matter. Would you really like to know what I am doing?"

"If you will tell me."

"I am building a house," said Orsino, looking at her to see the effect of the announcement.

"A house?" repeated Corona in surprise. "Where? Does your father know about it?"

"He said he did not care what I did." Orsino spoke rather bitterly.

"That does not sound like him, my dear. Tell me all about it. Have you quarrelled with him, or had words together?"

Orsino told his story quickly, concisely and with a frankness he would perhaps not have shown to any one else in the world, for he did not even conceal his connection with Del Ferice. Corona listened intently, and her deep eyes told him plainly enough that she was interested. On his part he found an unexpected pleasure in telling her the tale, and he wondered why it had never struck him that his mother might sympathise with his plans and aspirations. When he had finished, he waited for her first word almost as anxiously as he would have waited for an expression of opinion from Maria Consuelo.

Corona did not speak at once. She looked into his eyes, smiled, patted his lean brown hand lovingly and smiled again before she spoke.

"I like it," she said at last. "I like you to be independent and determined. You might perhaps have chosen a better man than Del Ferice for your adviser. He did something once—well, never mind! It was long ago and it did us no harm."

"What did he do, mother? I know my father wounded him in a duel before you were married—"

"It was not that. I would rather not tell you about it—it can do no good, and after all, it has nothing to do with the present affair. He would not be so foolish as to do you an injury now. I know him very well. He is far too clever for that."

"He is certainly clever," said Orsino. He knew that it would be quite useless to question his mother further after what she had said. "I am glad that you do not think I have made a mistake in going into this business."

"No. I do not think you have made a mistake, and I do not believe that your father will think so either when he knows all about it."

"He need not have been so icily discouraging," observed Orsino.

"He is a man, my dear, and I am a woman. That is the difference. Was San Giacinto more encouraging than he? No. They think alike, and San Giacinto has an immense experience besides. And yet they are both wrong. You may succeed, or you may fail—I hope you will succeed—but I do not care much for the result. It is the principle I like, the idea, the independence of the thing. As I grow old, I think more than I used to do when I was young."

"How can you talk of growing old!" exclaimed Orsino indignantly.

"I think more," said Corona again, not heeding him. "One of my thoughts is that our old restricted life was a mistake for us, and that to keep it up would be a sin for you. The world used to stand still in those days, and we stood at the head of it, or thought we did. But it is moving now and you must move with it or you will not only have to give up your place, but you will be left behind altogether."

"I had no idea that you were so modern, dearest mother," laughed Orsino. He felt suddenly very happy and in the best of humours with himself.

"Modern—no, I do not think that either your father or I could ever be that. If you had lived our lives you would see how impossible it is. The most I can hope to do is to understand you and your brothers as you grow up to be men. But I hate interference and I hate curiosity—the one breeds opposition and the other dishonesty—and if the other boys turn out to be as reticent as you, Orsino, I shall not always know when they want me. You do not realise how much you have been away from me since you were a boy, nor how silent you have grown when you are at home."

"Am I, mother? I never meant to be."

"I know it, dear, and I do not want you to be always confiding in me. It is not a good thing for a young man. You are strong and the more you rely upon yourself, the stronger you will grow. But when you want sympathy, if you ever do, remember that I have my whole heart full of it for you. For that, at least, come to me. No one can give you what I can give you, dear son."

Orsino was touched and pressed her hand, kissing it more than once. He did not know whether in her last words she had meant any allusion to Maria Consuelo, or whether, indeed, she had been aware of his intimacy with the latter. But he did not ask the question of her nor of himself. For the moment he felt that a want in his nature had been satisfied, and he wondered again why he had never thought of confiding in his mother.

They talked of his plans until it was late, and from that time they were more often together than before, each growing daily more proud of the other, though perhaps Orsino had better reasons for his pride than Corona could have found, for the love of mother for son is more comprehensive and not less blind than the passion of woman for man.

CHAPTER XIV

The short Roman season was advancing rapidly to its premature fall, which is on Ash Wednesday, after which it struggles to hold up its head against the overwhelming odds of a severely observed Lent, to revive only spasmodically after Easter and to die a natural death on the first warm day. In that year, too, the fatal day fell on the fifteenth of February, and progressive spirits talked of the possibility of fixing the movable Feasts and Fasts of the Church in a more convenient part of the calendar. Easter might be made to fall in June, for instance, and society need not be informed of its inevitable and impending return to dust and ashes until it had enjoyed a good three months, or even four, of what an eminent American defines as "brass, sass, lies and sin."

Rome was very gay that year, to compensate for the shortness of its playtime. Everything was successful, and every one was rich. People talked of millions less soberly than they had talked of thousands a few years earlier, and with less respect than they mentioned hundreds twelve months later. Like the vanity-struck frog, the franc blew itself up to the bursting point, in the hope of being taken for the louis, and momentarily succeeded, even beyond its own expectations. No one walked, though horse-flesh was enormously dear and a good coachman's wages amounted to just twice the salary of a government clerk. Men who, six months earlier, had climbed ladders with loads of brick or mortar, were now transformed into flourishing sub-contractors, and drove about in smart pony-carts, looking the picture of Italian prosperity, rejoicing in the most flashy of ties and smoking the blackest and longest of long black cigars. During twenty hours out of the twenty-four the gates of the city roared with traffic. From all parts of the country labourers poured in, bundle in hand and tools on shoulder to join in the enormous work and earn their share of the pay that was distributed so liberally. A certain man who believed in himself stood up and said that Rome was becoming one of the greatest of cities, and he smacked his lips and said that he had done it, and that the Triple Alliance was a goose which would lay many golden eggs. The believing bulls roared everything away before them, opposition, objections, financial experience, and the vanquished bears hibernated in secret places, sucking their paws and wondering what, in the name of Ursa Major and Ursa Minor, would happen next. Distinguished men wrote pamphlets in the most distinguished language to prove that wealth was a baby capable of being hatched artificially and brought up by hand. Every unmarried swain who could find a bride, married her forthwith; those who could not followed the advice of an illustrious poet and, being over-anxious to take wives, took those of others. Everybody was decorated. It positively rained decorations and hailed grand crosses and enough commanders' ribbons were reeled out to have hanged half the population. The periodical attempt to revive the defunct carnival in the Corso was made, and the yet unburied corpse of ancient gaiety was taken out and painted, and gorgeously arrayed, and propped up in its seat to be a posthumous terror to its enemies, like the dead Cid. Society danced frantically and did all those things which it ought not to have done—and added a few more, unconsciously imitating Pico della Mirandola.

Even those comparatively few families who, like the Saracinesca, had scornfully declined to dabble in the whirlpool of affairs, did not by any means refuse to dance to the music of success which filled the city with, such enchanting strains. The Princess Befana rose from her deathbed with more than usual vivacity and went to the length of opening her palace on two evenings in two successive weeks, to the intense delight of her gay and youthful heirs, who earnestly hoped that the excitement might kill her at last, and kill her beyond resurrection this time. But they were disappointed. She still dies periodically in winter and blooms out again in spring with the poppies, affording a perpetual and edifying illustration of the changes of the year, or, as some say, of the doctrine of immortality. On one of those memorable occasions she walked through a quadrille with the aged Prince Saracinesca, whereupon Sant' Ilario slipped his arm round Corona's waist and waltzed with her down the whole length of the ballroom and back again amidst the applause of his contemporaries and their children. If Orsino had had a wife he would have followed their example. As it was, he looked rather gloomily in the direction of a silent and high-born damsel with whom he was condemned to dance the cotillon at a later hour.

So all went gaily on until Ash Wednesday extinguished the social flame, suddenly and beyond relighting. And still Orsino did not meet Maria Consuelo, and still he hesitated to make another attempt to find her at home. He began to wonder whether he should ever see her again, and as the days went by he almost wished that Donna Tullia would send him a card for her lenten evenings, at which Maria Consuelo regularly assisted as he learned from the papers. After that first invitation to dinner, he had expected that Del Ferice's wife would make an attempt to draw him into her circle; and, indeed, she would probably have done so had she followed her own instinct instead of submitting to the higher policy dictated by her husband. Orsino waited in vain, not knowing whether to be annoyed at the lack of consideration bestowed upon him, or to admire the tact which assumed that he would never wish to enter the Del Ferice circle.

It is presumably clear that Orsino was not in love with Madame d'Aranjuez, and he himself appreciated the fact with a sense of disappointment. He was amazed at his own coldness and at the indifference with which he had submitted to what amounted to a most abrupt dismissal. He even went so far as to believe that Maria Consuelo had repulsed him designedly in the hope of kindling a more sincere passion. In that case she had been egregiously mistaken, he thought. He felt a curiosity to see her again before she left Rome, but it was nothing more than that. A new and absorbing interest had taken possession of him which at first left little room in his nature for anything else. His days were spent in the laborious study of figures and plans, broken only by occasional short but amusing conversations with Andrea Contini. His evenings were generally passed among a set of people who did not know Maria Consuelo except by sight and who had long ceased to ask him questions about her. Of late, too, he had missed his daily visits to her less and less, until he hardly regretted them at all, nor so much as thought of the possibility of renewing them. He laughed at the idea that his mother should have taken the place of a woman whom he had begun to love, and yet he was conscious that it was so, though he asked himself how long such a condition of things could last. Corona was far too wise to discuss his affairs with his father. He was too like herself for her to misunderstand him, and if she regarded the whole matter as perfectly harmless and as a legitimate subject for general conversation, she yet understood perfectly that having been once rebuffed by Sant' Ilario, Orsino must wish to be fully successful in his attempt before mentioning it again to the latter. And she felt so strongly in sympathy with her son that his work gradually acquired an intense interest for her, and she would have sacrificed much rather than see it fail. She did not on that account blame Giovanni for his discouraging view when Orsino had consulted him. Giovanni was the passion of her life and was not fallible in his impulses, though his judgment might sometimes be at fault in technical matters for which he cared nothing. But her love for her son was as great and sincere in its own way, and her pride in him was such as to make his success a condition of her future happiness.

One of the greatest novelists of this age begins one of his greatest novels with the remark that "all happy families resemble each other, but that every unhappy family is unhappy in its own especial way." Generalities are dangerous in proportion as they are witty or striking, or both, and it may be asked whether the great Tolstoi has not fallen a victim to his own extraordinary power of striking and witty generalisations. Does the greatest of all his generalisations, the wide disclaimer of his early opinions expressed in the postscript subsequently attached by him to his Kreutzer Sonata, include also the words I have quoted, and which were set up, so to say, as the theme of his Anna Karjenina? One may almost hope so. I am no critic, but those words somehow seem to me to mean that only unhappiness can be interesting. It is not pleasant to think of the consequences to which the acceptance of such a statement might lead.

There are no statistics to tell us whether the majority of living men and women are to be considered as happy or unhappy. But it does seem true that whereas a single circumstance can cause very great and lasting unhappiness, felicity is always dependent upon more than one condition and often upon so many as to make the explanation of it a highly difficult and complicated matter.

Corona had assuredly little reason to complain of her lot during the past twenty years, but unruffled and perfect as it had seemed to her she began to see that there were sources of sorrow and satisfaction before her which had not yet poured their bitter or sweet streams into the stately river of her mature life. The new interest which Orsino had created for her became more and more absorbing, and she watched it and tended it, and longed to see it grow to greater proportions. The situation was strange in one way at least. Orsino was working and his mother was helping him to work in the hope of a financial success which neither of them wanted or cared for. Possibly the certainty that failure could entail no serious consequences made the game a more amusing if a less exciting one to play.

"If I lose," said Orsino to her, "I can only lose the few thousands I invested. If I win, I will give you a string of pearls as a keepsake."

"If you lose, dear boy," answered Corona, "it must be because you had not enough to begin with. I will give you as much as you need, and we will try again."

They laughed happily together. Whatever chanced, things must turn out well. Orsino worked very hard, and Corona was very rich in her own right and could afford to help to any extent she thought necessary. She could, indeed, have taken the part of the bank and advanced him all the money he needed, but it seemed useless to interfere with the existing arrangements.

In Lent the house had reached an important point in its existence. Andrea Contini had completed the Gothic roof and the turret which appeared to him in the first vision of his dream, but to which the defunct baker had made objections on the score of expense. The masons were almost all gone and another set of workmen were busy with finer tools moulding cornices and laying on the snow-white stucco. Within, the joiners and carpenters kept up a ceaseless hammering.

One day Andrea Contini walked into the office after a tour of inspection, with a whole cigar, unlighted and intact, between his teeth. Orsino was well aware from this circumstance that something unusually fortunate had happened or was about to happen, and he rose from his books, as soon as he recognised the fair-weather signal.

"We can sell the house whenever we like," said the architect, his bright brown eyes sparkling with satisfaction.

"Already!" exclaimed Orsino who, though equally delighted at the prospect of such speedy success, regretted in his heart the damp walls and the constant stir of work which he had learned to like so well.

"Already—yes. One needs luck like ours! The count has sent a man up in a cab to say that an acquaintance of his will come and look at the building to-day between twelve and one with a view to buying. The sooner we look out for some fresh undertaking, the better. What do you say, Don Orsino?"

"It is all your doing, Contini. Without you I should still be standing outside and watching the mattings flapping in the wind, as I did on that never-to-be-forgotten first day."

"I conceive that a house cannot be built without an architect," answered Contini, laughing, "and it has always been plain to me that there can be no architects without houses to build. But as for any especial credit to me, I refute the charge indignantly. I except the matter of the turret, which is evidently what has attracted the buyer. I always thought it would. You would never have thought of a turret, would you, Don Orsino?"

"Certainly not, nor of many other things," answered Orsino, laughing. "But I am sorry to leave the place. I have grown into liking it."

"What can one do? It is the way of the world—'lieto ricordo d'un amor che fù,'" sang Contini in the thin but expressive falsetto which seems to be the natural inheritance of men who play upon stringed instruments. He broke off in the middle of a bar and laughed, out of sheer delight at his own good fortune.

In due time the purchaser came, saw and actually bought. He was a problematic personage with a disquieting nose, who spoke few words but examined everything with an air of superior comprehension. He looked keenly at Orsino but seemed to have no idea who he was and put all his questions to Contini.

After agreeing to the purchase he inquired whether Andrea Contini and Company had any other houses of the same description building and if so where they were situated, adding that he liked the firm's way of doing things. He stipulated for one or two slight improvements, made an appointment for a meeting with the notaries on the following day and went off with a rather unceremonious nod to the partners. The name he left was that of a well-known capitalist from the south, and Contini was inclined to think he had seen him before, but was not certain.

Within a week the business was concluded, the buyer took over the mortgage as Orsino and Contini had done and paid the difference in cash into the bank, which deducted the amounts due on notes of hand before handing the remainder to the two young men. The buyer also kept back a small part of the purchase money to be paid on taking possession, when the house was to be entirely finished. Andrea Contini and Company had realised a considerable sum of money.

"The question is, what to do next," said Orsino thoughtfully.

"We had better look about us for something promising," said his partner. "A corner lot in this same quarter. Corner houses are more interesting to build and people like them to live in because they can see two or three ways at once. Besides, a corner is always a good place for a turret. Let us take a walk— smoking and strolling, we shall find something."

"A year ago, no doubt," answered Orsino, who was becoming worldly wise. "A year ago that would have been well enough. But listen to me. That house opposite to ours has been finished some time, yet nobody has bought it. What is the reason?"

"It faces north and not south, as ours does, and it has not a Gothic roof."

"My dear Contini, I do not mean to say that the Gothic roof has not helped us very much, but it cannot have helped us alone. How about those two houses together at the end of the next block. Balconies, travertine columns, superior doors and windows, spaces for hydraulic lifts and all the rest of it. Yet no one buys. Dry, too, and almost ready to live in, and all the joinery of pitch pine. There is a reason for their ill luck."

"What do you think it is?" asked Contini, opening his eyes.

"The land on which they are built was not in the hands of Del Ferice's bank, and the money that built them was not advanced by Del Ferice's bank, and Del Ferice's bank has no interest in selling the houses themselves. Therefore they are not sold."

"But surely there are other banks in Rome, and private individuals—"

"No, I do not believe that there are," said Orsino with conviction. "My cousin of San Giacinto thinks that the selling days are over, and I fancy he is right, except about Del Ferice, who is cleverer than any of us. We had better not deceive ourselves, Contini. Del Ferice sold our house for us, and unless we keep with him we shall not sell another so easily. His bank has a lot of half-finished houses on its hands secured by mortgages which are worthless until the houses are habitable. Del Ferice wants us to finish those houses for him, in order to recover their value. If we do it, we shall make a profit. If we attempt anything on our own account we shall fail. Am I right or not?"

"What can I say? At all events you are on the safe side. But why has not the count given all this work to some old established firm of his acquaintance?"

"Because he cannot trust any one as he can trust us, and he knows it."

"Of course I owe the count a great deal for his kindness in introducing me to you. He knew all about me before the baker died, and afterwards I waited for him outside the Chambers one evening and asked him if he could find anything for me to do, but he did not give me much encouragement. I saw you speak to him and get into his carriage—was it not you?"

"Yes—it was I," answered Orsino, remembering the tall man in an overcoat who had disappeared in the dusk on the evening when he himself had first sought Del Ferice. "Yes, and you see we are both under a sort of obligation to him which is another reason for taking his advice."

"Obligations are humiliating!" exclaimed Contini impatiently. "We have succeeded in increasing our capital—your capital, Don Orsino—let us strike out for ourselves."

"I think my reasons are good," said Orsino quietly. "And as for obligations, let us remember that we are men of business."

It appears from this that the low-born Andrea Contini and the high and mighty Don Orsino Saracinesca were not very far from exchanging places so far as prejudice was concerned. Contini noticed the fact and smiled.

"After all," he said, "if you can accept the situation, I ought to accept it, too."

"It is a matter of business," said Orsino, returning to his argument. "There is no such thing as obligation where money is borrowed on good security and a large interest is regularly paid."

It was clear that Orsino was developing commercial instincts. His grandfather would have died of rage on the spot if he could have listened to the young fellow's cool utterances. But Contini was not pleased and would not abandon his position so easily.

"It is very well for you, Don Orsino," he said, vainly attempting to light his cigar. "You do not need the money as I do. You take it from Del Ferice because it amuses you to do so, not because you are obliged to accept it. That is the difference. The count knows It too, and knows that he is not conferring a favour but receiving one. You do him an honour in borrowing his money. He lays me under an obligation in lending it."

"We must get money somewhere," answered Orsino with indifference. "If not from Del Ferice, then from some other bank. And as for obligations, as you call them, he is not the bank himself, and the bank does not lend its money in order to amuse me or to humiliate you, my friend. But if you insist, I shall say that the convenience is not on one side only. If Del Ferice supports us it is because we serve his interests. If he has done us a good turn, it is a reason why we should do him one, and build his houses rather than those of other people. You talk about my conferring a favour upon him. Where will he find another Andrea Contini and Company to make worthless property valuable for him? In that sense you and I are earning his gratitude, by the simple process of being scrupulously honest. I do not feel in the least humiliated, I assure you."

"I cannot help it," replied Contini, biting his cigar savagely. "I have a heart, and it beats with good blood. Do you know that there is blood of Cola di Rienzo in my veins?"

"No. You never told me," answered Orsino, one of whose forefathers had been concerned in the murder of the tribune, a fact to which he thought it best not to refer at the present moment.

"And the blood of Cola di Rienzo burns under the shame of an obligation!" cried Contini, with a heat hardly warranted by the circumstances. "It is humiliating, it is base, to submit to be the tool of a Del Ferice—we all know who and what Del Ferice was, and how he came by his title of count, and how he got his fortune—a spy, an intriguer! In a good cause? Perhaps. I was not born then, nor you either, Signor Principe, and we do not know what the world was like, when it was quite another world. That is not a reason for serving a spy!"

"Calm yourself, my friend. We are not in Del Ferice's service."

"Better to die than that! Better to kill him at once and go to the galleys for a few years! Better to play the fiddle, or pick rags, or beg in the streets than that, Signor Principe. One must respect oneself. You see it yourself. One must be a man, and feel as a man. One must feel those things here, Signor Principe, here in the heart!"

Contini struck his breast with his clenched fist and bit the end of his cigar quite through in his anger. Then he suddenly seized his hat and rushed out of the room.

Orsino was less surprised at the outburst than might have been expected, and did not attach any great weight to his partner's dramatic rage. But he lit a cigarette and carefully thought over the situation, trying to find out whether there were really any ground for Contini's first remarks. He was perfectly well aware that as Orsino Saracinesca he would cut his own throat with enthusiasm rather than borrow a louis of Ugo Del Ferice. But as Andrea Contini and Company he was another person, and so Del Ferice was not Count Del Ferice, nor the Onorevole Del Ferice, but simply a director in a bank with which he had business. If the interests of Andrea Contini and Company were identical with those of the bank, there was no reason whatever for interrupting relations both amicable and profitable, merely because one member of the firm claimed to be descended from Cola di Bienzo, a defunct personage in whom Orsino felt no interest whatever. Andrea Contini, considering his social relations, might be on terms of friendship with his hatter, for instance, or might have personal reasons for disliking him. In neither case could the buying of a hat from that individual be looked upon as an obligation conferred or received by either party. This was quite clear, and Orsino was satisfied.

"Business is business," he said to himself, "and people who introduce personal considerations into a financial transaction will get the worst of the bargain."

Andrea Contini was apparently of the same opinion, for when he entered the room again at the end of an hour his excitement had quite disappeared.

"If we take another contract from the count," he said, "is there any reason why we should not take a larger one, if it is to be had? We could manage three or four buildings now that you have become such a good bookkeeper."

"I am quite of your opinion," Orsino answered, deciding at once to make no reference to what had gone before.

"The only question is, whether we have capital enough for a margin."

"Leave that to me."

Orsino determined to consult his mother, in whose judgment he felt a confidence which he could not explain but which was not misplaced. The fact was simple enough. Corona understood him thoroughly, though her comprehension of his business was more than limited, and she did nothing in reality but encourage his own sober opinion when it happened to be at variance with some enthusiastic inclination which momentarily deluded him. That quiet pushing of a man's own better reason against his half considered but often headstrong impulses, is after all one of the best and most loving services which a wise woman can render to a man whom she loves, be he husband, son or brother. Many women have no other secret, and indeed there are few more valuable ones, if well used and well kept. But let not graceless man discover that it is used upon him. He will resent being led by his own reason far more than being made the senseless slave of a foolish woman's wildest caprice. To select the best of himself for his own use is to trample upon his free will. To send him barefoot to Jericho in search of a dried flower is to appeal to his heart. Man is a reasoning animal.

Corona, as was to be expected, was triumphant in Orsino's first success, and spent as much time in talking over the past and the future with him as she could command during his own hours of liberty. He needed no urging to continue in the same course, but he enjoyed her happiness and delighted in her encouragement.

"Contini wishes to take a large contract," he said to her, after the interview last described. "I agree with him, in a way. We could certainly manage a larger business."

"No doubt," Corona answered thoughtfully, for she saw that there was some objection to the scheme in his own mind.

"I have learned a great deal," he continued, "and we have much more capital than we had. Besides, I suppose you would lend me a few thousands if we needed them, would you not, mother?"

"Certainly, my dear. You shall not be hampered by want of money."

"And then, it is possible that we might make something like a fortune in a short time. It would be a great satisfaction. But then, too—" He stopped.

"What then?" asked Corona, smiling.

"Things may turn out differently. Though I have been successful this time, I am much more inclined to believe that San Giacinto was right than I was before I began. All this movement does not rest on a solid basis."

A financier of thirty years' standing could not have made the statement more impressively, and Orsino was conscious that he was assuming an elderly tone. He laughed the next moment.

"That is a stock phrase, mother," he continued. "But it means something. Everything is not what it should be. If the demand were as great as people say it is, there would not be half a dozen houses—better houses than ours—unsold in our street. That is why I am afraid of a big contract. I might lose all my money and some of yours."

"It would not be of much consequence if you did," answered Corona. "But of course you will be guided by your own judgment, which, is much better than mine. One must risk something, of course, but there is no use in going into danger."

"Nevertheless, I should enjoy a big venture immensely."

"There is no reason why you should not try one, when the moment comes, my dear. I suppose that a few months will decide whether there is to be a crisis or not. In the meantime you might take something moderate, neither so small as the last, nor so large as you would like. You will get more experience, risk less and be better prepared for a crash if it comes, or to take advantage of anything favourable if business grows safer."

Orsino was silent for a moment.

"You are very wise, mother," he said. "I will take your advice."

Corona had indeed acted as wisely as she could. The only flaw in her reasoning was her assertion that a few months would decide the fate of Roman affairs. If it were possible to predict a crisis even within a few months, speculation would be a less precarious business than it is.

Orsino and his mother might have talked longer and perhaps to better purpose, but they were interrupted by the entrance of a servant, bearing a note. Corona instinctively put out her hand to receive it.

"For Don Orsino," said the man, stopping before him.

Orsino took the letter, looked at it and turned it over.

"I think it is from Madame d'Aranjuez," he remarked, without emotion. "May I read it?"

"There is no answer, Eccellenza," said the servant, whose curiosity was satisfied.

"Read it, of course," said Corona, looking at him.

She was surprised that Madame d'Aranjuez should write to him, but she was still more astonished to see the indifference with which he opened the missive. She had imagined that he was more or less in love with Maria Consuelo.

"I fancy it is the other way," she thought. "The woman wants to marry him. I might have suspected it."

Orsino read the note, and tossed it into the fire without volunteering any information.

"I will take your advice, mother," he said, continuing the former conversation, as though nothing had happened.

But the subject seemed to be exhausted, and before long Orsino made an excuse to his mother and went out.

CHAPTER XV

There was nothing in the note burnt by Orsino which he might not have shown to his mother, since he had already told her the name of the writer. It contained the simple statement that Maria Consuelo was about to leave Rome, and expressed the hope that she might see Orsino before her departure as she had a small request to make of him, in the nature of a commission. She hoped he would forgive her for putting him to so much inconvenience.

Though he betrayed no emotion in reading the few lines, he was in reality annoyed by them, and he wished that he might be prevented from obeying the summons. Maria Consuelo had virtually dropped the acquaintance, and had refused repeatedly and in a marked way to receive him. And now, at the last moment, when she needed something of him, she chose to recall him by a direct invitation. There was nothing to be done but to yield, and it was characteristic of Orsino that, having submitted to necessity, he did not put off the inevitable moment, but went to her at once.

The days were longer now than they had been during the time when he had visited her every day, and the lamp was not yet on the table when Orsino entered the small sitting-room. Maria Consuelo was standing by the window, looking out into the street, and her right hand rested against the pane while her fingers tapped it softly but impatiently. She turned quickly as he entered, but the light was behind her and he could hardly see her face. She came towards him and held out her hand.

"It is very kind of you to have come so soon," she said, as she took her old accustomed place by the table.

Nothing was changed, excepting that the two or three new books at her elbow were not the same ones which had been there two months earlier. In one of them was thrust the silver paper-cutter with the jewelled handle, which Orsino had never missed. He wondered whether there were any reason for the unvarying sameness of these details.

"Of course I came," he said. "And as there was time to-day, I came at once."

He spoke rather coldly, still resenting her former behaviour and expecting that she would immediately say what she wanted of him. He would promise to execute the commission, whatever it might be, and after ten minutes of conversation he would take his leave. There was a short pause, during which he looked at her. She did not seem well. Her face was pale and her eyes were deep with shadows. Even her auburn hair had lost something of its gloss. Yet she did not look older than before, a fact which proved her to be even younger than Orsino had imagined. Saving the look of fatigue and suffering in her face, Maria Consuelo had changed less than Orsino during the winter, and she realised the fact at a glance. A determined purpose, hard work, the constant exertion of energy and will, and possibly, too, the giving up to a great extent of gambling and strong drinks, had told in Orsino's face and manner as a course of training tells upon a lazy athlete. The bold black eyes had a more quiet glance, the well-marked features had acquired strength and repose, the lean jaw was firmer and seemed more square. Even physically, Orsino had improved, though the change was undefinable. Young as he was, something of the power of mature manhood was already coming over his youth.

"You must have thought me very—rude," said Maria Consuelo, breaking the silence and speaking with a slight hesitation which Orsino had never noticed before.

"It is not for me to complain, Madame," he answered. "You had every right—"

He stopped short, for he was reluctant to admit that she had been justified in her behaviour towards him.

"Thanks," she said, with an attempt to laugh. "It is pleasant to find magnanimous people now and then. I do not want you to think that I was capricious. That is all."

"I certainly do not think that. You were most consistent. I called three times and always got the same answer."

He fancied that he heard her sigh, but she tried to laugh again.

"I am not imaginative," she answered. "I daresay you found that out long go. You have much more imagination than I."

"It is possible, Madame—but you have not cared to develop it."

"What do you mean?"

"What does it matter? Do you remember what you said when I bade you good-night at the window of your carriage after Del Ferice's dinner? You said that you were not angry with me. I was foolish enough to imagine that you were in earnest. I came again and again, but you would not see me. You did not encourage my illusion."

"Because I would not receive you? How do you know what happened to me? How can you judge of my life? By your own? There is a vast difference."

"Yes, indeed!" exclaimed Orsino almost impatiently. "I know what you are going to say. It will be flattering to me of course. The unattached young man is dangerous to the reputation. The foreign lady is travelling alone. There is the foundation of a vaudeville in that!"

"If you must be unjust, at least do not be brutal," said Maria Consuelo in a low voice, and she turned her face away from him.

"I am evidently placed in the world to offend you, Madame. Will you believe that I am sorry for it, though I only dimly comprehend my fault? What did I say? That you were wise in breaking off my visits, because you are alone here, and because I am young, unmarried and unfortunately a little conspicuous in my native city. Is it brutal to suggest that a young and beautiful woman has a right not to be compromised? Can we not talk freely for half an hour, as we used to talk, and then say good-bye and part good friends until you come to Rome again?"

"I wish we could!" There was an accent of sincerity in the tone which pleased Orsino.

"Then begin by forgiving me all my sins, and put them down to ignorance, want of tact, the inexperience of youth or a naturally weak understanding. But do not call me brutal on such slight provocation."

"We shall never agree for a long time," answered Maria Consuelo thoughtfully.

"Why not?"

"Because, as I told you, there is too great a difference between our lives. Do not answer me as you did before, for I am right. I began by admitting that I was rude. If that is not enough I will say more—I will even ask you to forgive me—can I do more?"

She spoke so earnestly that Orsino was surprised and almost touched. Her manner now was even less comprehensible than her repeated refusals to see him had been.

"You have done far too much already," he said gravely. "It is mine to ask your forgiveness for much that I have done and said. I only wish that I understood you better."

"I am glad you do not," replied Maria Consuelo, with a sigh which this time was not to be mistaken. "There is a sadness which it is better not to understand," she added softly.

"Unless one can help to drive it away." He, too, spoke gently, his voice being attracted to the pitch and tone of hers.

"You cannot do that—and if you could, you would not."

"Who can tell?"

The charm which he had formerly felt so keenly in her presence but which he had of late so completely forgotten, was beginning to return and he submitted to it with a sense of satisfaction which he had not anticipated. Though the twilight was coming on, his eyes had become accustomed to the dimness in the room and he saw every change in her pale, expressive face. She leaned back in her chair with eyes half closed.

"I like to think that you would, if you knew how," she said presently.

"Do you not know that I would?"

She glanced quickly at him, and then, instead of answering, rose from her seat and called to her maid through one of the doors, telling her to bring the lamp. She sat down again, but being conscious that they were liable to interruption, neither of the two spoke. Maria Consuelo's fingers played with the silver knife, drawing it out of the book in which it lay and pushing it back again. At last she took it up and looked closely at the jewelled monogram on the handle.

The maid entered, set the shaded lamp upon the table and glanced sharply at Orsino. He could not help noticing the look. In a moment she was gone, and the door closed behind her. Maria Consuelo looked over her shoulder to see that it had not been left ajar.

"She is a very extraordinary person, that elderly maid of mine," she said.

"So I should imagine from her face."

"Yes. She looked at you as she passed and I saw that you noticed it. She is my protector. I never have travelled without her and she watches over me—as a cat watches a mouse."

The little laugh that accompanied the words was not one of satisfaction, and the shade of annoyance did not escape Orsino.

"I suppose she is one of those people to whose ways one submits because one cannot live without them," he observed.

"Yes. That is it. That is exactly it," repeated Maria Consuelo. "And she is very strongly attached to me," she added after an instant's hesitation. "I do not think she will ever leave me. In fact we are attached to each other."

She laughed again as though amused by her own way of stating the relation, and drew the paper-cutter through her hand two or three times. Orsino's eyes were oddly fascinated by the flash of the jewels.

"I would like to know the history of that knife," he said, almost thoughtlessly.

Maria Consuelo started and looked at him, paler even than before. The question seemed to be a very unexpected one.

"Why?" she asked quickly.

"I always see it on the table or in your hand," answered Orsino. "It is associated with you—I think of it when I think of you. I always fancy that it has a story."

"You are right. It was given to me by a person who loved me."

"I see—I was indiscreet."

"No—you do not see, my friend. If you did you—you would understand many things, and perhaps it is better that you should not know them."

"Your sadness? Should I understand that, too?"

"No. Not that."

A slight colour rose in her face, and she stretched out her hand to arrange the shade of the lamp, with a gesture long familiar to him.

"We shall end by misunderstanding each other," she continued in a harder tone. "Perhaps it will be my fault. I wish you knew much more about me than you do, but without the necessity of telling you the story. But that is impossible. This paper-cutter—for instance, could tell the tale better than I, for it made people see things which I did not see."

"After it was yours?"

"Yes. After it was mine."

"It pleases you to be very mysterious," said Orsino with a smile.

"Oh no! It does not please me at all," she answered, turning her face away again. "And least of all with you—my friend."

"Why least with me?"

"Because you are the first to misunderstand. You cannot help it. I do not blame you."

"If you would let me be your friend, as you call me, it would be better for us both."

He spoke as he had assuredly not meant to speak when he had entered the room, and with a feeling that surprised himself far more than his hearer. Maria Consuelo turned sharply upon him.

"Have you acted like a friend towards me?" she asked.

"I have tried to," he answered, with more presence of mind than truth.

Her tawny eyes suddenly lightened.

"That is not true. Be truthful! How have you acted, how have you spoken with me? Are you ashamed to answer?"

Orsino raised his head rather haughtily, and met her glance, wondering whether any man had ever been forced into such a strange position before. But though her eyes were bright, their look was neither cold nor defiant.

"You know the answer," he said. "I spoke and acted as though I loved you, Madame, but since you dismissed me so very summarily, I do not see why you wish me to say so."

"And you, Don Orsino, have you ever been loved—loved in earnest—by any woman?"

"That is a very strange question, Madame."

"I am discreet. You may answer it safely."

"I have no doubt of that."

"But you will not? No—that is your right. But it would be kind of you—I should be grateful if you would tell me—has any woman ever loved you dearly?"

Orsino laughed, almost in spite of himself. He had little false pride.

"It is humiliating, Madame. But since you ask the question and require a categorical answer, I will make my confession. I have never been loved. But you will observe, as an extenuating circumstance, that I am young. I do not give up all hope."

"No—you need not," said Maria Consuelo in a low voice, and again she moved the shade of the lamp.

Though Orsino was by no means fatuous, he must have been blind if he had not seen by this time that Madame d'Aranjuez was doing her best to make him speak as he had formerly spoken to her, and to force him into a declaration of love. He saw it, indeed, and wondered; but although he felt her charm upon him, from time to time, he resolved that nothing should induce him to relax even so far as he had done already more than once during the interview. She had placed him in a foolish position once before, and he would not expose himself to being made ridiculous again, in her eyes or his. He could not discover what intention she had in trying to lead him back to her, but he attributed it to her vanity. She regretted, perhaps, having rebuked him so soon, or perhaps she had imagined that he would have made further and more determined efforts to see her. Possibly, too, she really wished to ask a service of him, and wished to assure herself that she could depend upon him by previously extracting an avowal of his devotion. It was clear that one of the two had mistaken the other's character or mood, though it was impossible to say which was the one deceived.

The silence which followed lasted some time, and threatened to become awkward. Maria Consuelo could not or would not speak and Orsino did not know what to say. He thought of inquiring what the commission might be with which, according to her note, she had wished to entrust him. But an instant's reflection told him that the question would be tactless. If she had invented the idea as an excuse for seeing him, to mention it would be to force her hand, as card-players say, and he had no intention of doing that. Even if she really had something to ask of him, he had no right to change the subject so suddenly. He bethought him of a better question.

"You wrote me that you were going away," he said quietly. "But you will come back next winter, will you not, Madame?"

"I do not know," she answered, vaguely. Then she started a little, as though understanding his words. "What am I saying!" she exclaimed. "Of course I shall come back."

"Have you been drinking from the Trevi fountain by moonlight, like those mad English?" he asked, with a smile.

"It is not necessary. I know that I shall come back—if I am alive."

"How you say that! You are as strong as I—"

"Stronger, perhaps. But then—who knows! The weak ones sometimes last the longest."

Orsino thought she was growing very sentimental, though as he looked at her he was struck again by the look of suffering in her eyes. Whatever weakness she felt was visible there, there was nothing in the full, firm little hand, in the strong and easy pose of the head, in the softly coloured ear half hidden by her hair, that could suggest a coming danger to her splendid health.

"Let us take it for granted that you will come back to us," said Orsino cheerfully.

"Very well, we will take it for granted. What then?"

The question was so sudden and direct that Orsino fancied there ought to be an evident answer to it.

"What then?" he repeated, after a moment's hesitation. "I suppose you will live in these same rooms again, and with your permission, a certain Orsino Saracinesca will visit you from time to time, and be rude, and be sent away into exile for his sins. And Madame d'Aranjuez will go a great deal to Madame Del Ferice's and to other ultra-White houses, which will prevent the said Orsino from meeting her in society. She will also be more beautiful than ever, and the daily papers will describe a certain number of gowns which she will bring with her from Paris, or Vienna, or London, or whatever great capital is the chosen official residence of her great dressmaker. And the world will not otherwise change very materially in the course of eight months."

Orsino laughed lightly, not at his own speech, which he had constructed rather clumsily under the spur of necessity, but in the hope that she would laugh, too, and begin to talk more carelessly. But Maria Consuelo was evidently not inclined for anything but the most serious view of the world, past, present and future.

"Yes," she answered gravely. "I daresay you are right. One comes, one shows one's clothes, and one goes away again—and that is all. It would be very much the same if one did not come. It is a great mistake to think oneself necessary to any one. Only things are necessary—food, money and something to talk about."

"You might add friends to the list," said Orsino, who was afraid of being called brutal again if he did not make some mild remonstrance to such a sweeping assertion.

"Friends are included under the head of 'something to talk about,'" answered Maria Consuelo.

"That is an encouraging view."

"Like all views one gets by experience."

"You grow more and more bitter."

"Does the world grow sweeter as one grows older?"

"Neither you nor I have lived long enough to know," answered Orsino.

"Facts make life long—not years."

"So long as they leave no sign of age, what does it matter?"

"I do not care for that sort of flattery."

"Because it is not flattery at all. You know the truth too well. I am not ingenious enough to flatter you, Madame. Perfection is not flattered when it is called perfect."

"It is at all events impossible to exaggerate better than you can," answered Maria Consuelo, laughing at last at the overwhelming compliment. "Where did you learn that?"

"At your feet, Madame. The contemplation of great masterpieces enlarges the intelligence and deepens the power of expression."

"And I am a masterpiece—of what? Of art? Of caprice? Of consistency?"

"Of nature," answered Orsino promptly.

Again Maria Consuelo laughed a little, at the mere quickness of the answer. Orsino was delighted with himself, for he fancied he was leading her rapidly away from the dangerous ground upon which she had been trying to force him. But her next words showed him that he had not yet succeeded.

"Who will make me laugh during all these months!" she exclaimed with a little sadness.

Orsino thought she was strangely obstinate, and wondered what she would say next.

"Dear me, Madame," he said, "if you are so kind as to laugh at my poor wit, you will not have to seek far to find some one to amuse you better!"

He knew how to put on an expression of perfect simplicity when he pleased, and Maria Consuelo looked at him, trying to be sure whether he were in earnest or not. But his face baffled her.

"You are too modest," she said.

"Do you think it is a defect? Shall I cultivate a little more assurance of manner?" he asked, very innocently.

"Not to-day. Your first attempt might lead you into extremes."

"There is not the slightest fear of that, Madame," he answered with some emphasis.

She coloured a little and her closed lips smiled in a way he had often noticed before. He congratulated himself upon these signs of approaching ill-temper, which promised an escape from his difficulty. To take leave of her suddenly was to abandon the field, and that he would not do. She had determined to force him into a confession of devotion, and he was equally determined not to satisfy her. He had tried to lead her off her track with frivolous talk and had failed. He would try and irritate her instead, but without incurring the charge of rudeness. Why she was making such an attack upon him, was beyond his understanding, but he resented it, and made up his mind neither to fly nor yield. If he had been a hundredth part as cynical as he liked to fancy himself, he would have acted very differently. But he was young enough to have been wounded by his former dismissal, though he hardly knew it, and to seek almost instinctively to revenge his wrongs. He did not find it easy. He would not have believed that such a woman as Maria Consuelo could so far forget her pride as to go begging for a declaration of love.

"I suppose you will take Gouache's portrait away with you," he observed, changing the subject with a directness which he fancied would increase her annoyance.

"What makes you think so?" she asked, rather drily.

"I thought it a natural question."

"I cannot imagine what I should do with it. I shall leave it with him."

"You will let him send it to the Salon in Paris, of course?"

"If he likes. You seem interested in the fate of the picture."

"A little. I wondered why you did not have it here, as it has been finished so long."

"Instead of that hideous mirror, you mean? There would be less variety. I should always see myself in the same dress."

"No—on the opposite wall. You might compare truth with fiction in that way."

"To the advantage of Gouache's fiction, you would say. You were more complimentary a little while ago."

"You imagine more rudeness than even I am capable of inventing."

"That is saying much. Why did you change the subject just now?"

"Because I saw that you were annoyed at something. Besides, we were talking about myself, if I remember rightly."

"Have you never heard that a man should always talk to a woman about himself or herself?"

"No. I never heard that. Shall we talk of you, then, Madame?"

"Do you care to talk of me?" asked Maria Consuelo.

Another direct attack, Orsino thought.

"I would rather hear you talk of yourself," he answered without the least hesitation.

"If I were to tell you my thoughts about myself at the present moment, they would surprise you very much."

"Agreeably or disagreeably?"

"I do not know. Are you vain?"

"As a peacock!" replied Orsino quickly.

"Ah—then what I am thinking would not interest you."

"Why not?"

"Because if it is not flattering it would wound you, and if it is flattering it would disappoint you—by falling short of your ideal of yourself."

"Yet I confess that I would like to know what you think of me, though I would much rather hear what you think of yourself."

"On one condition, I will tell you."

"What is that?"

"That you will give me your word to give me your own opinion of me afterwards."

"The adjectives are ready, Madame, I give you my word."

"You give it so easily! How can I believe you?"

"It is so easy to give in such a case, when one has nothing disagreeable to say."

"Then you think me agreeable?"

"Eminently!"

"And charming?"

"Perfectly!"

"And beautiful?"

"How can you doubt it?"

"And in all other respects exactly like all the women in society to whom you repeat the same commonplaces every day of your life?"

The feint had been dexterous and the thrust was sudden, straight and unexpected.

"Madame!" exclaimed Orsino in the deprecatory tone of a man taken by surprise.

"You see—you have nothing to say!" She laughed a little bitterly.

"You take too much for granted," he said, recovering himself. "You suppose that because I agree with you upon one point after another, I agree with you in the conclusion. You do not even wait to hear my answer, and you tell me that I am checkmated when I have a dozen moves from which to choose. Besides, you have directly infringed the conditions. You have fired before the signal and an arbitration would go against you. You have done fifty things contrary to agreement, and you accuse me of being dumb in my own defence. There is not much justice in that. You promise to tell me a certain secret on condition that I will tell you another. Then, without saying a word on your own part you stone me with quick questions and cry victory because I protest. You begin before I have had so much as—"

"For heaven's sake stop!" cried Maria Consuelo, interrupting a speech which threatened to go on for twenty minutes. "You talk of chess, duelling and stoning to death, in one sentence—I am utterly confused! You upset all my ideas!"

"Considering how you have disturbed mine, it is a fair revenge. And since we both admit that we have disturbed that balance upon which alone depends all possibility of conversation, I think that I can do nothing more graceful—pardon me, nothing less ungraceful—than wish you a pleasant journey, which I do with all my heart, Madame."

Thereupon Orsino rose and took his hat.

"Sit down. Do not go yet," said Maria Consuelo, growing a shade paler, and speaking with an evident effort.

"Ah—true!" exclaimed Orsino. "We were forgetting the little commission you spoke of in your note. I am entirely at your service."

Maria Consuelo looked at him quickly and her lips trembled.

"Never mind that," she said unsteadily. "I will not trouble you. But I do not want you to go away as—as you were going. I feel as though we had been quarrelling. Perhaps we have. But let us say we are good friends—if we only say it."

Orsino was touched and disturbed. Her face was very white and her hand trembled visibly as she held it out. He took it in his own without hesitation.

"If you care for my friendship, you shall have no better friend in the world than I," he said, simply and naturally.

"Thank you—good-bye. I shall leave to-morrow."

The words were almost broken, as though she were losing control of her voice. As he closed the door behind him, the sound of a wild and passionate sob came to him through the panel. He stood still, listening and hesitating. The truth which would have long been clear to an older or a vainer man, flashed upon him suddenly. She loved him very much, and he no longer cared for her. That was the reason why she had behaved so strangely, throwing her pride and dignity to the winds in her desperate attempt to get from him a single kind and affectionate word—from him, who had poured into her ear so many words of love but two months earlier, and from whom to draw a bare admission of friendship to-day she had almost shed tears.

To go back into the room would be madness; since he did not love her, it would almost be an insult. He bent his head and walked slowly down the corridor. He had not gone far, when he was confronted by a small dark figure that stopped the way. He recognised Maria Consuelo's elderly maid.

"I beg your pardon, Signore Principe," said the little black-eyed woman. "You will allow me to say a few words? I thank you, Eccellenza. It is about my Signora, in there, of whom I have charge."

"Of whom, you have charge?" repeated Orsino, not understanding her.

"Yes—precisely. Of course, I am only her maid. You understand that. But I have charge of her though she does not know it. The poor Signora has had terrible trouble during the last few years, and at times—you understand? She is a little—yes—here." She tapped her forehead. "She is better now. But in my position I sometimes think it wiser to warn some friend of hers—in strict confidence. It sometimes saves some little unnecessary complication, and I was ordered to do so by the doctors we last consulted in Paris. You will forgive me, Eccellenza, I am sure."

Orsino stared at the woman for some seconds in blank astonishment. She smiled in a placid, self-confident way.

"You mean that Madame d'Aranjuez is—mentally deranged, and that you are her keeper? It is a little hard to believe, I confess."

"Would you like to see my certificates, Signor Principe? Or the written directions of the doctors? I am sure you are discreet."

"I have no right to see anything of the kind," answered Orsino coldly. "Of course, if you are acting under instructions it is no concern of mine."

He would have gone forward, but she suddenly produced a small bit of note-paper, neatly folded, and offered it to him.

"I thought you might like to know where we are until we return," she said, continuing to speak in a very low voice. "It is the address."

Orsino made an impatient gesture. He was on the point of refusing the information which he had not taken the trouble to ask of Maria Consuelo herself. But he changed his mind and felt in his pocket for something to give the woman. It seemed the easiest and simplest way of getting rid of her. The only note he had, chanced to be one of greater value than necessary.

"A thousand thanks, Eccellenza!" whispered the maid, overcome by what she took for an intentional piece of generosity.

Orsino left the hotel as quickly as he could.

"For improbable situations, commend me to the nineteenth century and the society in which we live!" he said to himself as he emerged into the street.

CHAPTER XVI

It was long before Orsino saw Maria Consuelo again, but the circumstances of his last meeting with her constantly recurred to his mind during the following months. It is one of the chief characteristics of Rome that it seems to be one of the most central cities in Europe during the winter, whereas in the summer months it appears to be immensely remote from the rest of the civilised world. From having been the prey of the inexpressible foreigner in his shooting season, it suddenly becomes, and remains during about five months, the happy hunting ground of the silent flea, the buzzing fly and the insinuating mosquito. The streets are, indeed, still full of people, and long lines of carriages may be seen towards sunset in the Villa Borghesa and in the narrow Corso. Rome and the Romans are not easily parted as London and London society, for instance. May comes—the queen of the months in the south. June follows. Southern blood rejoices in the first strong sunshine. July trudges in at the gates, sweating under the cloudless sky, heavy, slow of foot, oppressed by the breath of the coming dog-star. Still the nights are cool. Still, towards sunset, the refreshing breeze sweeps up from the sea and fills the streets. Then behind closely fastened blinds, the glass windows are opened and the weary hand drops the fan at last. Then men and women array themselves in the garments of civilisation and sally forth, in carriages, on foot, and in trams, according to the degrees of social importance which provide that in old countries the middle term shall be made to suffer for the priceless treasure of a respectability which is a little higher than the tram and financially not quite equal to the cab. Then, at that magic touch of the west wind the house-fly retires to his own peculiar Inferno, wherever that may be, the mosquito and the gnat pause in their work of darkness and blood to concert fresh and more bloodthirsty deeds, and even the joyous and wicked flea tires of the war dance and lays down his weary head to snatch a hard-earned nap. July drags on, and terrible August treads the burning streets bleaching the very dust up on the pavement, scourging the broad campagna with fiery lashes of heat. Then the white-hot sky reddens in the evening when it cools, as the white iron does when it is taken from the forge. Then at last, all those who can escape from the condemned city flee for their lives to the hills, while those who must face the torment of the sun and the poison of the air turn pale in their sufferings, feebly curse their fate and then grow listless, weak and irresponsible as over-driven galley slaves, indifferent to everything, work, rest, blows, food, sleep and the hope of release. The sky darkens suddenly. There is a sort of horror in the stifling air. People do not talk much, and if they do are apt to quarrel and sometimes to kill one another without warning. The plash of the fountains has a dull sound like the pouring out of molten lead. The horses' hoofs strike visible sparks out of the grey stones in broad daylight. Many houses are shut, and one fancies that there must be a dead man in each whom no one will bury. A few great drops of rain make ink-stains on the pavement at noon, and there is an exasperating, half-sulphurous smell abroad. Late in the afternoon they fall again. An evil wind comes in hot blasts from all quarters at once—then a low roar like an earthquake and presently a crash that jars upon the overwrought nerves—great and plashing drops again, a sharp short flash—then crash upon crash, deluge upon deluge, and the worst is over. Summer has received its first mortal wound. But its death is more fatal than its life. The noontide heat is fierce and drinks up the moisture of the rain and the fetid dust with it. The fever-wraith rises in the damp, cool night, far out in the campagna, and steals up to the walls of the city, and over them and under them and into the houses. If there are any yet left in Rome who can by any possibility take themselves out of it, they are not long in going. Till that moment, there has been only suffering to be borne; now, there is danger of something worse. Now, indeed, the city becomes a desert inhabited by white-faced ghosts. Now, if it be a year of cholera, the dead carts rattle through the streets all night on their way to the gate of Saint Lawrence, and the workmen count their numbers when they meet at dawn. But the bad days are not many, if only there be rain enough, for a little is worse than none. The nights lengthen and the September gales sweep away the poison-mists with kindly strength. Body and soul revive, as the ripe grapes appear in their vine-covered baskets at the street corners. Rich October is coming, the month in which the small citizens of Rome take their wives and the children to the near towns, to Marino, to Froscati, to Albano and Aricia, to eat late fruits and drink new must, with songs and laughter, and small miseries and great delights such as are remembered a whole year. The first clear breeze out of the north shakes down the dying leaves and brightens the blue air. The brown campagna turns green again, and the heart of the poor lame cab-horse is lifted up. The huge porter of the palace lays aside his linen coat and his pipe, and opens wide the great gates; for the masters are coming back, from their castles and country places, from the sea and from the mountains, from north and south, from the magic shore of Sorrento, and from distant French bathing places, some with brides or husbands, some with rosy Roman babies making their first trumphal entrance into Rome—and some, again, returning companionless to the home they had left in companionship. The great and complicated machinery of social life is set in order and repaired for the winter; the lost or damaged pieces in the engine are carefully replaced with new ones which will do as well or better, the joints and bearings are lubricated, the whistle of the first invitation is heard, there is some puffing and a little creaking at first, and then the big wheels begin to go slowly round, solemnly and regularly as ever, while all the little wheels run as fast as they can and set fire to their axles in the attempt to keep up the speed, and are finally jammed and caught up and smashed, as little wheels are sure to be when they try to act like big ones. But unless something happens to one of the very biggest the machine does not stop until the end of the season, when it is taken to pieces again for repairs.

That is the brief history of a Roman year, of which the main points are very much like those of its predecessor and successor. The framework is the same, but the decorations change, slowly, surely and not, perhaps, advantageously, as the younger generation crowds into the place of the older—as young acquaintances take the place of old friends, as faces strange to us hide faces we have loved.

Orsino Saracinesca, in his new character as a contractor and a man of business, knew that he must either spend the greater part of the summer in town, or leave his affairs in the hands of Andrea Contini. The latter course was repugnant to him, partly because he still felt a beginner's interest in his first success, and partly because he had a shrewd suspicion that Contini, if left to himself in the hot weather, might be tempted to devote more time to music than to architecture. The business, too, was now on a much larger scale than before, though Orsino had taken his mother's advice in not at once going so far as he might have gone. It needed all his own restless energy, all Contini's practical talents, and perhaps more of Del Ferice's influence than either of them suspected, to keep it going on the road to success.

In July Orsino's people made ready to go up to Saracinesca. The old prince, to every one's surprise, declared his intention of going to England, and roughly refused to be accompanied by any one of the family. He wanted to find out some old friends, he said, and desired the satisfaction of spending a couple of months in peace, which was quite impossible at home, owing to Giovanni's outrageous temper and Orsino's craze for business. He thereupon embraced them all affectionately, indulged in a hearty laugh and departed in a special carriage with his own servants.

Giovanni objected to Orsino's staying in Rome during the great heat. Though Orsino had not as yet entered into any explanation with his father, but the latter understood well enough that the business had turned out better than had been expected and began to feel an interest in its further success, for his son's sake. He saw the boy developing into a man by a process which he would naturally have supposed to be the worst possible one, judging from his own point of view. But he could not find fault with the result. There was no disputing the mental superiority of the Orsino of July over the Orsino of the preceding January. Whatever the sensation which Giovanni experienced as he contemplated the growing change, it was not one of anxiety nor of disappointment. But he had a Roman's well-founded prejudice against spending August and September in town. His objections gave rise to some discussion, in which Corona joined.

Orsino enlarged upon the necessity of attending in person to the execution of his contracts. Giovanni suggested that he should find some trustworthy person to take his place. Corona was in favour of a compromise. It would be easy, she said, for Orsino to spend two or three days of every week in Rome and the remainder in the country with his father and mother. They were all three quite right according to their own views, and they all three knew it. Moreover they were all three very obstinate people. The consequence was that Orsino, who was in possession, so to say, since the other two were trying to make him change his mind, got the best of the argument, and won his first pitched battle. Not that there was any apparent hostility, or that any of the three spoke hotly or loudly. They were none of them like old Saracinesca, whose feats of argumentation were vehement, eccentric and fiery as his own nature. They talked with apparent calm through a long summer's afternoon, and the vanquished retired with a fairly good grace, leaving Orsino master of the field. But on that occasion Giovanni Saracinesca first formed the opinion that his son was a match for him, and that it would be wise in future to ascertain the chances of success before incurring the risk of a humiliating defeat.

Giovanni and his wife went out together and talked over the matter as their carriage swept round the great avenues of Villa Borghesa.

"There is no question of the fact that Orsino is growing up—is grown up already," said Sant' Ilario, glancing at Corona's calm, dark face.

She smiled with a certain pride, as she heard the words.

"Yes," she answered, "he is a man. It is a mistake to treat him as a boy any longer."

"Do you think it is this sudden interest in business that has changed him so?"

"Of course—what else?"

"Madame d'Aranjuez, for instance," Giovanni suggested.

"I do not believe she ever had the least influence over him. The flirtation seems to have died a natural death. I confess, I hoped it might end in that way, and I am glad if it has. And I am very glad that Orsino is succeeding so well. Do you know, dear? I am glad, because you did not believe it possible that he should."

"No, I did not. And now that I begin to understand it, he does not like to talk to me about his affairs. I suppose that is only natural. Tell me—has he really made money? Or have you been giving him money to lose, in order that he may buy experience."

"He has succeeded alone," said Corona proudly. "I would give him whatever he needed, but he needs nothing. He is immensely clever and immensely energetic. How could he fail?"

"You seem to admire our firstborn, my dear," observed Giovanni with a smile.

"To tell the truth, I do. I have no doubt that he does all sorts of things which he ought not to do, and of which I know nothing. You did the same at his age, and I shall be quite satisfied if he turns out like you. I would not like to have a lady-like son with white hands and delicate sensibilities, and hypocritical affectations of exaggerated morality. I think I should be capable of trying to make such a boy bad, if it only made him manly—though I daresay that would be very wrong."

"No doubt," said Giovanni. "But we shall not be placed in any such position by Orsino, my dear. You remember that little affair last year, in England? It was very nearly a scandal. But then—the English are easily led into temptation and very easily scandalised afterwards. Orsino will not err in the direction of hypocritical morality. But that is not the question. I wish to know, from you since he does not confide in me, how far he is really succeeding."

Corona gave her husband a remarkably clear statement of Orsino's affairs, without exaggeration so far as the facts were concerned, but not without highly favourable comment. She did not attempt to conceal her triumph, now that success had been in a measure attained, and she did not hesitate to tell Giovanni that he ought to have encouraged and supported the boy from the first.

Giovanni listened with very great interest, and bore her affectionate reproaches with equanimity. He felt in his heart that he had done right, and he somehow still believed that things were not in reality all that they seemed to be. There was something in Orsino's immediate success against odds apparently heavy, which disturbed his judgment. He had not, it was true, any personal experience of the building speculations in the city, nor of financial transactions in general, as at present understood, and he had recently heard of cases in which individuals had succeeded beyond their own wildest expectations. There was, perhaps, no reason why Orsino should not do as well as other people, or even better, in spite of his extreme youth. Andrea Contini was probably a man of superior talent, well able to have directed the whole affair alone, if other circumstances had been favourable to him, and there was on the whole nothing to prove that the two young men had received more than their fair share of assistance or accommodation from the bank. But Giovanni knew well enough that Del Ferice was the most influential personage in the bank in question, and the mere suggestion of his name lent to the whole affair a suspicious quality which disturbed Orsino's father. In spite of all reasonable reflexions there was an air of unnatural good fortune in the case which he did not like, and he had enough experience of Del Ferice's tortuous character to distrust his intentions. He would have preferred to see his son lose money through Ugo rather than that Orsino should owe the latter the smallest thanks. The fact that he had not spoken with the man for over twenty years did not increase the confidence he felt in him. In that time Del Ferice had developed into a very important personage, having much greater power to do harm than he had possessed in former days, and it was not to be supposed that he had forgotten old wounds or given up all hope of avenging them. Del Ferice was not very subject to that sort of forgetfulness.

When Corona had finished speaking, Giovanni was silent for a few moments.

"Is it not splendid?" Corona asked enthusiastically. "Why do you not say anything? One would think that you were not pleased."

"On the contrary, as far as Orsino is concerned, I am delighted. But I do not trust Del Ferice."

"Del Ferice is far too clever a man to ruin Orsino," answered Corona.

"Exactly. That is the trouble. That is what makes me feel that though Orsino has worked hard and shown extraordinary intelligence—and deserves credit for that—yet he would not have succeeded in the same way if he had dealt with any other bank. Del Ferice has helped him. Possibly Orsino knows that, as well as we do, but he certainly does not know what part Del Ferice played in our lives, Corona. If he did, he would not accept his help."

In her turn Corona was silent and a look of disappointment came into her face. She remembered a certain afternoon in the mountains when she had entreated Giovanni to let Del Ferice escape, and Giovanni had yielded reluctantly and had given the fugitive a guide to take him to the frontier. She wondered whether the generous impulse of that day was to bear evil fruit at last.

"Orsino knows nothing about it at all," she said at last. "We kept the secret of Del Ferice's escape very carefully—for there were good reasons to be careful in those days. Orsino only knows that you once fought a duel with the man and wounded him."

"I think it is time that he knew more."

"Of what use can it be to tell him those old stories?" asked Corona. "And after all, I do not believe that Del Ferice has done so much. If you could have followed Orsino's work, day by day and week by week, as I have, you would see how much is really due to his energy. Any other banker would have done as much as he. Besides, it is in Del Ferice's own interest—"

"That is the trouble," interrupted Giovanni. "It is bad enough that he should help Orsino. It is much worse that he should help him in order to make use of him. If, as you say, any other bank would do as much, then let him go to another bank. If he owes Del Ferice money at the present moment, we will pay it for him."

"You forget that he has bought the buildings he is now finishing, from Del Ferice, on a mortgage."

Giovanni laughed a little.

"How you have learned to talk about mortgages and deeds and all sorts of business!" he exclaimed. "But what you say is not an objection. We can pay off these mortgages, I suppose, and take the risk ourselves."

"Of course we could do that," Corona answered, thoughtfully. "But I really think you exaggerate the whole affair. For the time being, Del Ferice is not a man, but a banker. His personal character and former doings do not enter into the matter."

"I think they do," said Giovanni, still unconvinced.

"At all events, do not make trouble now, dear," said Corona in earnest tones. "Let the present contract be executed and finished, and then speak to Orsino before he makes another. Whatever Del Ferice may have done, you can see for yourself that Orsino is developing in a way we had not expected, and is becoming a serious, energetic man. Do not step in now, and check the growth of what is good. You will regret it as much as I shall. When he has finished these buildings he will have enough experience to make a new departure."

"I hate the idea of receiving a favour from Del Ferice, or of laying him under an obligation. I think I will go to him myself."

"To Del Ferice?" Corona started and looked round at Giovanni as she sat. She had a sudden vision of new trouble.

"Yes. Why not? I will go to him and tell him that I would rather wind up my son's business with him, as our former relations were not of a nature to make transactions of mutual profit either fitting or even permissible between any of our family and Ugo Del Ferice."

"For Heaven's sake, Giovanni, do not do that."

"And why not?" He was surprised at her evident distress.

"For my sake, then—do not quarrel with Del Ferice—it was different then, in the old days. I could not bear it now—" she stopped, and her lower lip trembled a little.

"Do you love me better than you did then, Corona?"

"So much better—I cannot tell you."

She touched his hand with hers and her dark eyes were a little veiled as they met his. Both were silent for a moment.

"I have no intention of quarrelling with Del Ferice, dear," said Giovanni, gently.

His face had grown a shade paler as she spoke. The power of her hand and voice to move him, had not diminished in all the years of peaceful happiness that had passed so quickly.

"I do not mean any such thing," he said again. "But I mean this. I will not have it said that Del Ferice has made a fortune for Orsino, nor that Orsino has helped Del Ferice's interests. I see no way but to interfere myself. I can do it without the suspicion of a quarrel."

"It will be a great mistake, Giovanni. Wait till there is a new contract."

"I will think of it, before doing anything definite."

Corona well knew that she should get no greater concession than this. The point of honour had been touched in Giovanni's sensibilities and his character was stubborn and determined where his old prejudices were concerned. She loved him very dearly, and this very obstinacy of his pleased her. But she fancied that trouble of some sort was imminent. She understood her son's nature, too, and dreaded lest he should be forced into opposing his father.

It struck her that she might herself act as intermediary. She could certainly obtain concessions from Orsino which Giovanni could not hope to extract by force or stratagem. But the wisdom of her own proposal in the matter seemed unassailable. The business now in hand should be allowed to run its natural course before anything was done to break off the relations between Orsino and Del Ferice.

In the evening she found an opportunity of speaking with Orsino in private. She repeated to him the details of her conversation with Giovanni during the drive in the afternoon.

"My dear mother," answered Orsino, "I do not trust Del Ferice any more than you and my father trust him. You talk of things which he did years ago, but you do not tell me what those things were. So far as I understand, it all happened before you were married. My father and he quarrelled about something, and I suppose there was a lady concerned in the matter. Unless you were the lady in question, and unless what he did was in the nature of an insult to you, I cannot see how the matter concerns me. They fought and it ended there, as affairs of honour do. If it touched you, then tell me so, and I will break with Del Ferice to-morrow morning."

Corona was silent, for Orsino's speech was very plain, and if she answered it all, the answer must be the truth. There could be no escape from that. And the truth would be very hard to tell. At that time she had been still the wife of old Astrardente, and Del Ferice's offence had been that he had purposely concealed himself in the conservatory of the Frangipan's palace in order to overhear what Giovanni Saracinesca was about to say to another man's wife. The fact that on that memorable night she had bravely resisted a very great temptation did not affect the difficulty of the present case in any way. She asked herself rather whether Del Ferice's eavesdropping would appear to Orsino to be in the nature of an insult to her, to use his own words, and she had no doubt but that it would seem so. At the same time she would find hard to explain to her son why Del Ferice suspected that there was to be anything said to her worth overhearing, seeing that she bore at that time the name of another man then still living. How could Orsino understand all that had gone before? Even now, though she knew that she had acted well, she humbly believed that she might have done much better. How would her son judge her? She was silent, waiting for him to speak again.

"That would be the only conceivable reason for my breaking with Del Ferice," said Orsino. "We only have business relations, and I do not go to his house. I went once. I saw no reason for telling you so at the time, and I have not been there again. It was at the beginning of the whole affair. Outside of the bank, we are the merest acquaintances. But I repeat what I said. If he ever did anything which makes it dishonourable for me to accept even ordinary business services from him, let me know it. I have some right to hear the truth."

Corona hesitated, and laid the case again before her own conscience, and tried to imagine herself in her son's position. It was hard to reach a conclusion. There was no doubt but that when she had learned the truth, long after the event, she had felt that she had been insulted and justly avenged. If she said nothing now, Orsino would suspect something and would assuredly go to his father, from whom he would get a view of the case not conspicuous for its moderation. And Giovanni would undoubtedly tell his son the details of what had followed, how Del Ferice had attempted to hinder the marriage when it was at last possible, and all the rest of the story. At the same time, she felt that so far as her personal sensibilities were concerned, she had not the least objection to the continuance of a mere business relation between Orsino and Del Ferice. She was more forgiving than Giovanni.

"I will tell you this much, my dear boy," she said, at last. "That old quarrel did concern me and no one else. Your father feels more strongly about it than I do, because he fought for me and not for himself. You trust me, Orsino. You know that I would rather see you dead than doing anything dishonourable. Very well. Do not ask any more questions, and do not go to your father about it. Del Ferice has only advanced you money, in a business way, on good security and at a high interest. So far as I can judge of the point of honour involved, what happened long ago need not prevent your doing what you are doing now. Possibly, when you have finished the present contract, you may think it wiser to apply to some other bank, or to work on your own account with my money."

Corona believed that she had found the best way out of the difficulty, and Orsino seemed satisfied, for he nodded thoughtfully and said nothing. The day had been filled with argument and discussion about his determination to stay in town, and he was weary of the perpetual question and answer. He knew his mother well, and was willing to take her advice for the present. She, on her part, told Giovanni what she had done, and he consented to consider the matter a little longer before interfering. He disliked even the idea of a business relation extremely, but he feared that there was more behind the appearances of commercial fairness than either he or Orsino himself could understand. The better Orsino succeeded, the less his father was pleased, and his suspicions were not unfounded. He knew from San Giacinto that success was becoming uncommon, and he knew that all Orsino's industry and energy could not have sufficed to counterbalance his inexperience. Andrea Contini, too, had been recommended by Del Ferice, and was presumably Del Ferice's man.

On the following day Giovanni and Corona with the three younger boys went up to Saracinesca leaving Orsino alone in the great palace, to his own considerable satisfaction. He was well pleased with himself and especially at having carried his point. At his age, and with his constitution, the heat was a matter of supreme indifference to him, and he looked forward with delight to a summer of uninterrupted work in the not uncongenial society of Andrea Contini. As for the work itself, it was beginning to have a sort of fascination for him as he understood it better. The love of building, the passion for stone and brick and mortar, is inherent in some natures, and is capable of growing into a mania little short of actual insanity. Orsino began to ask himself seriously whether it were too late to study architecture as a profession and in the meanwhile he learned more of it in practice from Contini than he could have acquired in twice the time at any polytechnic school in Europe.

He liked Contini himself more and more as the days went by. Hitherto he had been much inclined to judge his own countrymen from his own class. He was beginning to see that he had understood little or nothing of the real Italian nature when uninfluenced by foreign blood. The study interested and pleased him. Only one unpleasant memory occasionally disturbed his peace of mind. When he thought of his last meeting with Maria Consuelo he hated himself for the part he had played, though he was quite unable to account logically, upon his assumed principles, for the severity of his self-condemnation.

CHAPTER XVII

Orsino necessarily led a monotonous life, though, his occupation was an absorbing one. Very early in the morning he was with Contini where the building was going on. He then passed the hot hours of the day in the office, which, as before, had been established in one of the unfinished houses. Towards evening, he went down into the city to his home, refreshed himself after his long day's work, and then walked or drove until half past eight, when he went to dinner in the garden of a great restaurant in the Corso. Here he met a few acquaintances who, like himself, had reasons for staying in town after their families had left. He always sat at the same small table, at which there was barely room for two persons, for he preferred to be alone, and he rarely asked a passing friend to sit down with him.

On a certain hot evening in the beginning of August he had just taken his seat, and was trying to make up his mind whether he were hungry enough to eat anything or whether it would not be less trouble to drink a glass of iced coffee and go away, when he was aware of a lank shadow cast across the white cloth by the glaring electric light. He looked up and saw Spicca standing there, apparently uncertain where to sit down for the place was fuller than usual. He liked the melancholy old man and spoke to him, offering to share his table.

Spicca hesitated a moment and then accepted the invitation. He deposited his hat upon a chair beside him and leaned back, evidently exhausted either in mind or body, if not in both.

"I am very much obliged to you, my dear Orsino," he said. "There is an abominable crowd here, which means an unusual number of people to avoid—just as many as I know, in fact, excepting yourself."

"I am glad you do not wish to avoid me, too," observed Orsino, by way of saying something.

"You are a less evil—so I choose you in preference to the greater," Spicca answered. But there was a not unkindly look in his sunken eyes as he spoke.

He tipped the great flask of Chianti that hung in its swinging plated cradle in the middle of the table, and filled two glasses.

"Since all that is good has been abolished, let us drink to the least of evils," he said, "in other words, to each other."

"To the absence of friends," answered Orsino, touching the wine with his lips.

Spicca emptied his glass slowly and then looked at him.

"I like that toast," he said. "To the absence of friends. I daresay you have heard of Adam and Eve in the garden of Eden. Do they still teach the dear old tale in these modern schools? No. But you have heard it—very well. You will remember that if they had not allowed the serpent to scrape acquaintance with them, on pretence of a friendly interest in their intellectual development, Adam and Eve would still be inventing names for the angelic little wild beasts who were too well-behaved to eat them. They would still be in paradise. Moreover Orsino Saracinesca and John Nepomucene Spicca would not be in daily danger of poisoning in this vile cookshop. Summary ejection from Eden was the first consequence of friendship, and its results are similar to this day. What nauseous mess are we to swallow to-night? Have you looked at the card?"

Orsino laughed a little. He foresaw that Spicca would not be dull company on this particular evening. Something unusually disagreeable had probably happened to him during the day. After long and melancholy hesitation he ordered something which he believed he could eat, and Orsino followed his example.

"Are all your people out of town?" Spicca asked, after a pause.

"Yes. I am alone."

"And what in the world is the attraction here? Why do you stay? I do not wish to be indiscreet, and I was never afflicted with curiosity. But cases of mental alienation grow more common every day, and as an old friend of your father's I cannot overlook symptoms of madness in you. A really sane person avoids Rome in August."

"It strikes me that I might say the same to you," answered Orsino. "I am kept here by business. You have not even that excuse."

"How do you know?" asked Spicca, sharply. "Business has two main elements—credit and debit. The one means the absence of the other. I leave it to your lively intelligence to decide which of the two means Rome in August, and which means Trouville or St. Moritz."

"I had not thought of it in that light."

"No? I daresay not. I constantly think of it."

"There are other places, nearer than St. Moritz," suggested Orsino. "Why not go to Sorrento?"

"There was such a place once—but my friends have found it out. Nevertheless, I might go there. It is better to suffer friendship in the spirit than fever in the body. But I have a reason for staying here just at present—a very good one."

"Without indiscretion—?"

"No, certainly not without considerable indiscretion. Take some more wine. When intoxication is bliss it is folly to be sober, as the proverb says. I cannot get tipsy, but you may, and that will be almost as amusing. The main object of drinking wine is that one person should make confidences for the other to laugh at—the one enjoys it quite as much as the other."

"I would rather be the other," said Orsino with a laugh.

"In all cases in life it is better to be the other person," observed Spicca, thoughtfully, though the remark lacked precision.

"You mean the patient and not the agent, I suppose?"

"No. I mean the spectator. The spectator is a well fed, indifferent personage who laughs at the play and goes home to supper—perdition upon him and his kind! He is the abomination of desolation in a front stall, looking on while better men cut one another's throats. He is a fat man with a pink complexion and small eyes, and when he has watched other people's troubles long enough, he retires to his comfortable vault in the family chapel in the Campo Varano, which is decorated with coloured tiles, embellished with a modern altar piece and adorned with a bust of himself by a good sculptor. Even in death, he is still the spectator, grinning through the window of his sanctuary at the rows of nameless graves outside. He is happy and self-satisfied still—even in marble. It is worth living to be such a man."

"It is not an exciting life," remarked Orsino.

"No. That is the beauty of it. Look at me. I have never succeeded in imitating that well-to-do, thoroughly worthy villain. I began too late. Take warning, Orsino. You are young. Grow fat and look on—then you will die happy. All the philosophy of life is there. Farinaceous food, money and a wife. That is the recipe. Since you have money you can purchase the gruel and the affections. Waste no time in making the investment."

"I never heard you advocate marriage before. You seem to have changed your mind, of late."

"Not in the least. I distinguish between being married and taking a wife, that is all."

"Rather a fine distinction."

"The only difference between a prisoner and his gaoler is that they are on opposite sides of the same wall. Take some more wine. We will drink to the man on the outside."

"May you never be inside," said Orsino.

Spicca emptied his glass and looked at him, as he set it down again.

"May you never know what it is to have been inside," he said.

"You speak as though you had some experience."

"Yes, I have—through an acquaintance of mine."

"That is the most agreeable way of gaining experience."

"Yes," answered Spicca with a ghastly smile. "Perhaps I may tell you the story some day. You may profit by it. It ended rather dramatically—so far as it can be said to have ended at all. But we will not speak of it just now. Here is another dish of poison—do you call that thing a fish, Checco? Ah—yes. I perceive that you are right. The fact is apparent at a great distance. Take it away. We are all mortal, Checco, but we do not like to be reminded of it so very forcibly. Give me a tomato and some vinegar."

"And the birds, Signore? Do you not want them any more?"

"The birds—yes, I had forgotten. And another flask of wine, Checco."

"It is not empty yet, Signore," observed the waiter lifting the rush-covered bottle and shaking it a little.

Spicca silently poured out two glasses and handed him the empty flask. He seemed to be very thirsty. Presently he got his birds. They proved eatable, for quails are to be had all through the summer in Italy, and he began to eat in silence. Orsino watched him with some curiosity wondering whether the quantity of wine he drank would not ultimately produce some effect. As yet, however, none was visible; his cadaverous face was as pale and quiet as ever, and his sunken eyes had their usual expression.

"And how does your business go on, Orsino?" he asked, after a long silence.

Orsino answered him willingly enough and gave him some account of his doings. He grew somewhat enthusiastic as he compared his present busy life with his former idleness.

"I like the way you did it, in spite of everybody's advice," said Spicca, kindly. "A man who can jump through the paper ring of Roman prejudice without stumbling must be nimble and have good legs. So nobody gave you a word of encouragement?"

"Only one person, at first. I think you know her—Madame d'Aranjuez. I used to see her often just at that time."

"Madame d'Aranjuez?" Spicca looked up sharply, pausing with his glass in his hand.

"You know her?"

"Very well indeed," answered the old man, before he drank. "Tell me, Orsino," he continued, when he had finished the draught, "are you in love with that lady?"

Orsino was surprised by the directness of the question, but he did not show it.

"Not in the least," he answered, coolly.

"Then why did you act as though you were?" asked Spicca looking him through and through.

"Do you mean to say that you were watching me all winter?" inquired Orsino, bending his black eyebrows rather angrily.

"Circumstances made it inevitable that I should know of your visits. There was a time when you saw her every day."

"I do not know what the circumstances, as you call them, were," answered Orsino. "But I do not like to be watched—even by my father's old friends."

"Keep your temper, Orsino," said Spicca quietly. "Quarrelling is always ridiculous unless somebody is killed, and then it is inconvenient. If you understood the nature of my acquaintance with Maria Consuelo—with Madame d'Aranjuez, you would see that while not meaning to spy upon you in the least, I could not be ignorant of your movements."

"Your acquaintance must be a very close one," observed Orsino, far from pacified.

"So close that it has justified me in doing very odd things on her account. You will not accuse me of taking a needless and officious interest in the affairs of others, I think. My own are quite enough for me. It chances that they are intimately connected with the doings of Madame d'Aranjuez, and have been so for a number of years. The fact that I do not desire the connexion to be known does not make it easier for me to act, when I am obliged to act at all. I did not ask an idle question when I asked you if you loved her."

"I confess that I do not at all understand the situation," said Orsino.

"No. It is not easy to understand, unless I give you the key to it. And yet you know more already than any one in Rome. I shall be obliged if you will not repeat what you know."

"You may trust me," answered Orsino, who saw from Spicca's manner that the matter was very serious.

"Thank you. I see that you are cured of the idea that I have been frivolously spying upon you for my own amusement."

Orsino was silent. He thought of what had happened after he had taken leave of Maria Consuelo. The mysterious maid who called herself Maria Consuelo's nurse, or keeper, had perhaps spoken the truth. It was possible that Spicca was one of the guardians responsible to an unknown person for the insane lady's safety, and that he was consequently daily informed by the maid of the coming and going of visitors, and of other minor events. On the other hand it seemed odd that Maria Consuelo should be at liberty to go whithersoever she pleased. She could not reasonably be supposed to have a guardian in every city of Europe. The more he thought of this improbability the less he understood the truth.

"I suppose I cannot hope that you will tell me more," he said.

"I do not see why I should," answered Spicca, drinking again. "I asked you an indiscreet question and I have given you an explanation which you are kind enough to accept. Let us say no more about it. It is better to avoid unpleasant subjects."

"I should not call Madame d'Aranjuez an unpleasant subject," observed Orsino.

"Then why did you suddenly cease to visit her?" asked Spicca.

"For the best of all reasons. Because she repeatedly refused to receive me." He was less inclined to take offence now than five minutes earlier. "I see that your information was not complete."

"No. I was not aware of that. She must have had a good reason for not seeing you."

"Possibly."

"But you cannot guess what the reason was?"

"Yes—and no. It depends upon her character, which I do not pretend to understand."

"I understand it well enough. I can guess at the fact. You made love to her, and one fine day, when she saw that you were losing your head, she quietly told her servant to say that she was not at home when you called. Is that it?"

"Possibly. You say you know her well—then you know whether she would act in that way or not."

"I ought to know. I think she would. She is not like other women—she has not the same blood."

"Who is she?" asked Orsino, with a sudden hope that he might learn the truth.

"A woman—rather better than the rest—a widow, too, the widow of a man who never was her husband—thank God!"

Spicca slowly refilled and emptied his goblet for the tenth time.

"The rest is a secret," he added, when he had finished drinking.

The dark, sunken eyes gazed into Orsino's with an expression so strange and full of a sort of inexplicable horror, as to make the young man think that the deep potations were beginning to produce an effect upon the strong old head. Spicca sat quite still for several minutes after he had spoken, and then leaned back in his cane chair with a deep sigh. Orsino sighed too, in a sort of unconscious sympathy, for even allowing for Spicca's natural melancholy the secret was evidently an unpleasant one. Orsino tried to turn the conversation, not, however, without a hope of bringing it back unawares to the question which interested him.

"And so you really mean to stay here all summer," he remarked, lighting a cigarette and looking at the people seated at a table behind Spicca.

Spicca did not answer at first, and when he did his reply had nothing to do with Orsino's interrogatory observation.

"We never get rid of the things we have done in our lives," he said, dreamily. "When a man sows seed in a ploughed field some of the grains are picked out by birds, and some never sprout. We are much more perfectly organised than the earth. The actions we sow in our souls all take root, inevitably and fatally—and they all grow to maturity sooner or later."

Orsino stared at him for a moment.

"You are in a philosophising mood this evening," he said.

"We are only logic's pawns," continued Spicca without heeding the remark. "Or, if you like it better, we are the Devil's chess pieces in his match against God. We are made to move each in our own way. The one by short irregular steps in every direction, the other in long straight lines between starting point and goal—the one stands still, like the king-piece, and never moves unless he is driven to it, the other jumps unevenly like the knight. It makes no difference. We take a certain number of other pieces, and then we are taken ourselves—always by the adversary—and tossed aside out of the game. But then, it is easy to carry out the simile, because the game itself was founded on the facts of life, by the people who invented it."

"No doubt," said Orsino, who was not very much interested.

"Yes. You have only to give the pieces the names of men and women you know, and to call the pawns society—you will see how very like real life chess can be. The king and queen on each side are a married couple. Of course, the object of each queen is to get the other king, and all her friends help her—knights, bishops, rooks and her set of society pawns. Very like real life, is it not? Wait till you are married."

Spicca smiled grimly and took more wine.

"There at least you have no personal experience," objected Orsino.

But Spicca only smiled again, and vouchsafed no answer.

"Is Madame d'Aranjuez coming back next winter?" asked the young man.

"Madame d'Aranjuez will probably come back, since she is free to consult her own tastes," answered Spicca gravely.

"I hope she may be out of danger by that time," said Orsino quietly. He had resolved upon a bolder attack than he had hitherto made.

"What danger is she in now?" asked Spicca quietly.

"Surely, you must know."

"I do not understand you. Please speak plainly if you are in earnest."

"Before she went away I called once more. When I was coming away her maid met me in the corridor of the hotel and told me that Madame d'Aranjuez was not quite sane, and that she, the maid, was in reality her keeper, or nurse—or whatever you please to call her."

Spicca laughed harshly. No one could remember to have heard him laugh many times.

"Oh—she said that, did she?" He seemed very much amused. "Yes," he added presently, "I think Madame d'Aranjuez will be quite out of danger before Christmas."

Orsino was more puzzled than ever. He was almost sure that Spicca did not look upon the maid's assertion as serious, and in that case, if his interest in Maria Consuelo was friendly, it was incredible that he should seem amused at what was at least a very dangerous piece of spite on the part of a trusted servant.

"Then is there no truth in that woman's statement?" asked Orsino.

"Madame d'Aranjuez seemed perfectly sane when I last saw her," answered Spicca indifferently.

"Then what possible interest had the maid in inventing the lie?"

"Ah—what interest? That is quite another matter, as you say. It may not have been her own interest."

"You think that Madame d'Aranjuez had instructed her?"

"Not necessarily. Some one else may have suggested the idea, subject to the lady's own consent."

"And she would have consented? I do not believe that."

"My dear Orsino, the world is full of such apparently improbable things that it is always rash to disbelieve anything on the first hearing. It is really much less trouble to accept all that one is told without question."

"Of course, if you tell me positively that she wishes to be thought mad—"

"I never say anything positively, especially about a woman—and least of all about the lady in question, who is undoubtedly eccentric."

Instead of being annoyed, Orsino felt his curiosity growing, and made a rash vow to find out the truth at any price. It was inconceivable, he thought, that Spicca should still have perfect control of his faculties, considering the extent of his potations. The second flask was growing light, and Orsino himself had not taken more than two or three glasses. Now a Chianti flask never holds less than two quarts. Moreover Spicca was generally a very moderate man. He would assuredly not resist the confusing effects of the wine much longer and he would probably become confidential.

But Orsino had mistaken his man. Spicca's nerves, overwrought by some unknown disturbance in his affairs, were in that state in which far stronger stimulants than Tuscan wine have little or no effect upon the brain. Orsino looked at him and wondered, as many had wondered already, what sort of life the man had led, outside and beyond the social existence which every one could see. Few men had been dreaded like the famous duellist, who had played with the best swordsmen in Europe as a cat plays with a mouse. And yet he had been respected, as well as feared. There had been that sort of fatality in his quarrels which had saved him from the imputation of having sought them. He had never been a gambler, as reputed duellists often are. He had never refused to stand second for another man out of personal dislike or prejudice. No one had ever asked his help in vain, high or low, rich or poor, in a reasonably good cause. His acts of kindness came to light accidentally after many years. Yet most people fancied that he hated mankind, with that sort of generous detestation which never stoops to take a mean advantage. In his duels he had always shown the utmost consideration for his adversary and the utmost indifference to his own interest when conditions had to be made. Above all, he had never killed a man by accident. That is a crime which society does not forgive. But he had not failed, either, when he had meant to kill. His speech was often bitter, but never spiteful, and, having nothing to fear, he was a very truthful man. He was also reticent, however, and no one could boast of knowing the story which every one agreed in saying had so deeply influenced his life. He had often been absent from Rome for long periods, and had been heard of as residing in more than one European capital. He had always been supposed to be rich, but during the last three years it had become clear to his friends that he was poor. That is all, roughly speaking, which was known of John Nepomucene, Count Spicca, by the society in which he had spent more than half his life.

Orsino, watching the pale and melancholy face, compared himself with his companion, and wondered whether any imaginable series of events could turn him into such a man at the same age. Yet he admired Spicca, besides respecting him. Boy-like, he envied the great duellist his reputation, his unerring skill, his unfaltering nerve; he even envied him the fear he inspired in those whom he did not like. He thought less highly of his sayings now, perhaps, than when he had first been old enough to understand them. The youthful affectation of cynicism had agreed well with the old man's genuine bitterness, but the pride of growing manhood was inclined to put away childish things and had not yet suffered so as to understand real suffering. Six months had wrought a change in Orsino, and so far the change was for the better. He had been fortunate in finding success at the first attempt, and his passing passion for Maria Consuelo had left little trace beyond a certain wondering regret that it had not been greater, and beyond the recollection of her sad face at their parting and of the sobs he had overheard. Though he could only give those tears one meaning, he realised less and less as the months passed that they had been shed for him.

That Maria Consuelo should often be in his thoughts was no proof that he still loved her in the smallest degree. There had been enough odd circumstances about their acquaintance to rouse any ordinary man's interest, and just at present Spicca's strange hints and half confidences had excited an almost unbearable curiosity in his hearer. But Spicca did not seem inclined to satisfy it any further.

One or two points, at least, were made clear. Maria Consuelo was not insane, as the maid had pretended. Her marriage with the deceased Aranjuez had been a marriage only in name, if it had even amounted to that. Finally, it was evident that she stood in some very near relation to Spicca and that neither she nor he wished the fact to be known. To all appearance they had carefully avoided meeting during the preceding winter, and no one in society was aware that they were even acquainted. Orsino recalled more than one occasion when each had been mentioned in the presence of the other. He had a good memory and he remembered that a scarcely perceptible change had taken place in the manner or conversation of the one who heard the other's name. It even seemed to him that at such moments Maria Consuelo had shown an infinitesimal resentment, whereas Spicca had faintly exhibited something more like impatience. If this were true, it argued that Spicca was more friendly to Maria Consuelo than she was to him. Yet on this particular evening Spicca had spoken somewhat bitterly of her—but then, Spicca was always bitter. His last remark was to the effect that she was eccentric. After a long silence, during which Orsino hoped that his friend would say something more, he took up the point.

"I wish I knew what you meant by eccentric," he said. "I had the advantage of seeing Madame d'Aranjuez frequently, and I did not notice any eccentricity about her."

"Ah—perhaps you are not observant. Or perhaps, as you say, we do not mean the same thing."

"That is why I would like to hear your definition," observed Orsino.

"The world is mad on the subject of definitions," answered Spicca. "It is more blessed to define than to be defined. It is a pleasant thing to say to one's enemy, 'Sir, you are a scoundrel.' But when your enemy says the same thing to you, you kill him without hesitation or regret—which proves, I suppose, that you are not pleased with his definition of you. You see definition, after all, is a matter of taste. So, as our tastes might not agree, I would rather not define anything this evening. I believe I have finished that flask. Let us take our coffee. We can define that beforehand, for we know by daily experience how diabolically bad it is."

Orsino saw that Spicca meant to lead the conversation away in another direction.

"May I ask you one serious question?" he inquired, leaning forward.

"With a little ingenuity you may even ask me a dozen, all equally serious, my dear Orsino. But I cannot promise to answer all or any particular one. I am not omniscient, you know."

"My question is this. I have no sort of right to ask it. I know that. Are you nearly related to Madame d'Aranjuez?"

Spicca looked curiously at him.

"Would the information be of any use to you?" he asked. "Should I be doing you a service in telling you that we are, or are not related?"

"Frankly, no," answered Orsino, meeting the steady glance without wavering.

"Then I do not see any reason whatever for telling you the truth," returned Spicca quietly. "But I will give you a piece of general information. If harm comes to that lady through any man whomsoever, I will certainly kill him, even if I have to be carried upon the ground."

There was no mistaking the tone in which the threat was uttered. Spicca meant what he said, though not one syllable was spoken louder than another. In his mouth the words had a terrific force, and told Orsino more of the man's true nature than he had learnt in years. Orsino was not easily impressed, and was certainly not timid, morally or physically; moreover he was in the prime of youth and not less skilful than other men in the use of weapons. But he felt at that moment that he would infinitely rather attack a regiment of artillery single-handed than be called upon to measure swords with the cadaverous old invalid who sat on the other side of the table.

"It is not in my power to do any harm to Madame d'Aranjuez," he answered proudly enough, "and you ought to know that if it were, it could not possibly be in my intention. Therefore your threat is not intended for me."

"Very good, Orsino. Your father would have answered like that, and you mean what you say. If I were young I think that you and I should be friends. Fortunately for you there is a matter of forty years' difference between our ages, so that you escape the infliction of such a nuisance as my friendship. You must find it bad enough to have to put up with my company."

"Do not talk like that," answered Orsino. "The world is not all vinegar."

"Well, well—you will find out what the world is in time. And perhaps you will find out many other things which you want to know. I must be going, for I have letters to write. Checco! My bill."

Five minutes later they parted.

CHAPTER XVIII

Although Orsino's character was developing quickly in the new circumstances which he had created for himself, he was not of an age to be continually on his guard against passing impressions; still less could it be expected that he should be hardened against them by experience, as many men are by nature. His conversation with Spicca, and Spicca's own behaviour while it lasted, produced a decided effect upon the current of his thoughts, and he was surprised to find himself thinking more often and more seriously of Maria Consuelo than during the months which had succeeded her departure from Rome. Spicca's words had acted indirectly upon his mind. Much that the old man had said was calculated to rouse Orsino's curiosity, but Orsino was not naturally curious and though he felt that it would be very interesting to know Maria Consuelo's story, the chief result of the Count's half confidential utterances was to recall the lady herself very vividly to his recollection.

At first his memory merely brought back the endless details of his acquaintance with her, which had formed the central feature of the first season he had spent without interruption in Rome and in society. He was surprised at the extreme precision of the pictures evoked, and took pleasure in calling them up when he was alone and unoccupied. The events themselves had not, perhaps, been all agreeable, yet there was not one which it did not give him some pleasant sensation to remember. There was a little sadness in some of them, and more than once the sadness was mingled with something of humiliation. Yet even this last was bearable. Though he did not realise it, he was quite unable to think of Maria Consuelo without feeling some passing touch of happiness at the thought, for happiness can live with sadness when it is the greater of the two. He had no desire to analyse these sensations. Indeed the idea did not enter his mind that they were worth analysing. His intelligence was better employed with his work, and his reflexions concerning Maria Consuelo chiefly occupied his hours of rest.

The days passed quickly at first and then, as September came they seemed longer, instead of shorter. He was beginning to wish that the winter would come, that he might again see the woman of whom he was continually thinking. More than once he thought of writing to her, for he had the address which the maid had given him—an address in Paris which said nothing, a mere number with the name of a street. He wondered whether she would answer him, and when he had reached the self-satisfying conviction that she would, he at last wrote a letter, such as any person might write to another. He told her of the weather, of the dulness of Rome, of his hope that she would return early in the season, and of his own daily occupations. It was a simply expressed, natural and not at all emotional epistle, not at all like that of a man in the least degree in love with his correspondent, but Orsino felt an odd sensation of pleasure in writing it and was surprised by a little thrill of happiness as he posted it with his own hand.

He did not forget the letter when he had sent it, either, as one forgets the uninteresting letters one is obliged to write out of civility. He hoped for an answer. Even if she were in Paris, Maria Consuelo might not, and probably would not, reply by return of post. And it was not probable that she would be in town at the beginning of September. Orsino calculated the time necessary to forward the letter from Paris to the most distant part of frequented Europe, allowed her three days for answering and three days more for her letter to reach him. The interval elapsed, but nothing came. Then he was irritated, and at last he became anxious. Either something had happened to Maria Consuelo, or he had somehow unconsciously offended her by what he had written. He had no copy of the letter and could not recall a single phrase which could have displeased her, but he feared lest something might have crept into it which she might misinterpret. But this idea was too absurd to be tenable for long, and the conviction grew upon him that she must be ill or in some great trouble. He was amazed at his own anxiety.

Three weeks had gone by since he had written, and yet no word of reply had reached him. Then he sought out Spicca and asked him boldly whether anything had happened to Maria Consuelo, explaining that he had written to her and had got no answer. Spicca looked at him curiously for a moment.

"Nothing has happened to her, as far as I am aware," he said, almost immediately. "I saw her this morning."

"This morning?" Orsino was surprised almost out of words.

"Yes. She is here, looking for an apartment in which to spend the winter."

"Where is she?"

Spicca named the hotel, adding that Orsino would probably find her at home during the hot hours of the afternoon.

"Has she been here long?" asked the young man.

"Three days."

"I will go and see her at once. I may be useful to her in finding an apartment."

"That would be very kind of you," observed Spicca, glancing at him rather thoughtfully.

On the following afternoon, Orsino presented himself at the hotel and asked for Madame d'Aranjuez. She received him in a room not very different from the one of which she had had made her sitting-room during the winter. As always, one or two new books and the mysterious silver paper cutter were the only objects of her own which were visible. Orsino hardly noticed the fact, however, for she was already in the room when he entered, and his eyes met hers at once.

He fancied that she looked less strong than formerly, but the heat was great and might easily account for her pallor. Her eyes were deeper, and their tawny colour seemed darker. Her hand was cold.

She smiled faintly as she met Orsino, but said nothing and sat down at a distance from the windows.

"I only heard last night that you were in Rome," he said.

"And you came at once to see me. Thanks. How did you find it out?"

"Spicca told me. I had asked him for news of you."

"Why him?" inquired Maria Consuelo with some curiosity.

"Because I fancied he might know," answered Orsino passing lightly over the question. He did not wish even Maria Consuelo to guess that Spicca had spoken of her to him. "The reason why I was anxious about you was that I had written you a letter. I wrote some weeks ago to your address in Paris and got no answer."

"You wrote?" Maria Consuelo seemed surprised. "I have not been in Paris. Who gave you the address? What was it?"

Orsino named the street and the number.

"I once lived there a short time, two years ago. Who gave you the address? Not Count Spicca?"

"No."

Orsino hesitated to say more. He did not like to admit that he had received the address from Maria Consuelo's maid, and it might seem incredible that the woman should have given the information unasked. At the same time the fact that the address was to all intents and purposes a false one tallied with the maid's spontaneous statement in regard to her mistress's mental alienation.

"Why will you not tell me?" asked Maria Consuelo.

"The answer involves a question which does not concern me. The address was evidently intended to deceive me. The person who gave it attempted to deceive me about a far graver matter, too. Let us say no more about it. Of course you never got the letter?"

"Of course not."

A short silence followed which Orsino felt to be rather awkward. Maria Consuelo looked at him suddenly.

"Did my maid tell you?" she asked.

"Yes—since you ask me. She met me in the corridor after my last visit and thrust the address upon me."

"I thought so," said Maria Consuelo.

"You have suspected her before?"

"What was the other deception?"

"That is a more serious matter. The woman is your trusted servant. At least you must have trusted her when you took her—"

"That does not follow. What did she try to make you believe?"

"It is hard to tell you. For all I know, she may have been instructed—you may have instructed her yourself. One stumbles upon odd things in life, sometimes."

"You called yourself my friend once, Don Orsino."

"If you will let me, I will call myself so still."

"Then, in the name of friendship, tell me what the woman said!" Maria Consuelo spoke with sudden energy, touching his arm quickly with an unconscious gesture.

"Will you believe me?"

"Are you accustomed to being doubted, that you ask?"

"No. But this thing is very strange."

"Do not keep me waiting—it hurts me!"

"The woman stopped me as I was going away. I had never spoken to her. She knew my name. She told me that you were—how shall I say?—mentally deranged."

Maria Consuelo started and turned very pale.

"She told you that I was mad?" Her voice sank to a whisper.

"That is what she said."

Orsino watched her narrowly. She evidently believed him. Then she sank back in her chair with a stifled cry of horror, covering her eyes with her hands.

"And you might have believed it!" she exclaimed. "You might really have believed it—you!"

The cry came from her heart and would have shown Orsino what weight she still attached to his opinion had he not himself been too suddenly and deeply interested in the principal question to pay attention to details.

"She made the statement very clearly," he said. "What could have been her object in the lie?"

"What object? Ah—if I knew that—"

Maria Consuelo rose and paced the room, her head bent and her hands nervously clasping and unclasping. Orsino stood by the empty fireplace, watching her.

"You will send the woman away of course?" he said, in a questioning tone.

But she shook her head and her anxiety seemed to increase.

"Is it possible that you will submit to such a thing from a servant?" he asked in astonishment.

"I have submitted to much," she answered in a low voice.

"The inevitable, of course. But to keep a maid whom you can turn away at any moment—"

"Yes—but can I?" She stopped and looked at him. "Oh, if I only could—if you knew how I hate the woman—"

"But then—"

"Yes?"

"Do you mean to tell me that you are in some way in her power, so that you are bound to keep her always?"

Maria Consuelo hesitated a moment.

"Are you in her power?" asked Orsino a second time. He did not like the idea and his black brows bent themselves rather angrily.

"No—not directly. She is imposed upon me."

"By circumstances?"

"No, again. By a person who has the power to impose much upon me—but this! Oh this is almost too much! To be called mad!"

"Then do not submit to it."

Orsino spoke decisively, with a kind of authority which surprised himself. He was amazed and righteously angry at the situation so suddenly revealed to him, undefined as it was. He saw that he was touching a great trouble and his natural energy bid him lay violent hands on it and root it out if possible.

For some minutes Maria Consuelo did not speak, but continued to pace the room, evidently in great anxiety. Then she stopped before him.

"It is easy for you to say, 'do not submit,' when you do not understand," she said. "If you knew what my life is, you would look at this in another way. I must submit—I cannot do otherwise."

"If you would tell me something more, I might help you," answered Orsino.

"You?" She paused. "I believe you would, if you could," she added, thoughtfully.

"You know that I would. Perhaps I can, as it is, in ignorance, if you will direct me."

A sudden light gleamed in Maria Consuelo's eyes and then died away as quickly as it had come.

"After all, what could you do?" she asked with a change of tone, as though she were somehow disappointed. "What could you do that others would not do as well, if they could, and with a better right?"

"Unless you will tell me, how can I know?"

"Yes—if I could tell you."

She went and sat down in her former seat and Orsino took a chair beside her. He had expected to renew the acquaintance in a very different way, and that he should spend half an hour with Maria Consuelo in talking about apartments, about the heat and about the places she had visited. Instead, circumstances had made the conversation an intimate one full of an absorbing interest to both. Orsino found that he had forgotten much which pleased him strangely now that it was again brought before him. He had forgotten most of all, it seemed, that an unexplained sympathy attracted him to her, and her to him. He wondered at the strength of it, and found it hard to understand that last meeting with her in the spring.

"Is there any way of helping you, without knowing your secret?" he asked in a low voice.

"No. But I thank you for the wish."

"Are you sure there is no way? Quite sure?"

"Quite sure."

"May I say something that strikes me?"

"Say anything you choose."

"There is a plot against you. You seem to know it. Have you never thought of plotting on your side?"

"I have no one to help me."

"You have me, if you will take my help. And you have Spicca. You might do better, but you might do worse. Between us we might accomplish something."

Maria Consuelo had started at Spicca's name. She seemed very nervous that day.

"Do you know what you are saying?" she asked after a moment's thought.

"Nothing that should offend you, at least."

"No. But you are proposing that I should ally myself with the man of all others whom I have reason to hate."

"You hate Spicca?" Orsino was passing from one surprise to another.

"Whether I hate him or not, is another matter. I ought to."

"At all events he does not hate you."

"I know he does not. That makes it no easier for me. I could not accept his help."

"All this is so mysterious that I do not know what to say," said Orsino, thoughtfully. "The fact remains, and it is bad enough. You need help urgently. You are in the power of a servant who tells your friends that you are insane and thrusts false addresses upon them, for purposes which I cannot explain."

"Nor I either, though I may guess."

"It is worse and worse. You cannot even be sure of the motives of this woman, though you know the person or persons by whom she is forced upon you. You cannot get rid of her yourself and you will not let any one else help you."

"Not Count Spicca."

"And yet I am sure that he would do much for you. Can you not even tell me why you hate him, or ought to hate him?"

Maria Consuelo hesitated and looked into Orsino's eyes for a moment.

"Can I trust you?" she asked.

"Implicitly."

"He killed my husband."

Orsino uttered a low exclamation of horror. In the deep silence which followed he heard Maria Consuelo draw her breath once or twice sharply through her closed teeth, as though she were in great pain.

"I do not wish it known," she said presently, in a changed voice. "I do not know why I told you."

"You can trust me."

"I must—since I have spoken."

In the surprise caused by the startling confidence, Orsino suddenly felt that his capacity for sympathy had grown to great dimensions. If he had been a woman, the tears would have stood in his eyes. Being what he was, he felt them in his heart. It was clear that she had loved the dead man very dearly. In the light of this evident fact, it was hard to explain her conduct towards Orsino during the winter and especially at their last meeting.

For a long time neither spoke again. Orsino, indeed, had nothing to say at first, for nothing he could say could reasonably be supposed to be of any use. He had learned the existence of something like a tragedy in Maria Consuelo's life, and he seemed to be learning the first lesson of friendship, which teaches sympathy. It was not an occasion for making insignificant phrases expressing his regret at her loss, and the language he needed in order to say what he meant was unfamiliar to his lips. He was silent, therefore, but his young face was grave and thoughtful, and his eyes sought hers from time to time as though trying to discover and forestall her wishes. At last she glanced at him quickly, then looked down, and at last spoke to him.

"You will not make me regret having told you this—will you?" she asked.

"No. I promise you that."

So far as Orsino could understand the words meant very little. He was not very communicative, as a rule, and would certainly not tell what he had heard, so that the promise was easily given and easy to keep. If he did not break it, he did not see that she could have any further cause for regretting her confidence in him. Nevertheless, by way of reassuring her, he thought it best to repeat what he had said in different words.

"You may be quite sure that whatever you choose to tell me is in safe keeping," he said. "And you may be sure, too, that if it is in my power to do you a service of any kind, you will find me ready, and more than ready, to help you."

"Thank you," she answered, looking earnestly at him.

"Whether the matter be small or great," he added, meeting her eyes.

Perhaps she expected to find more curiosity on his part, and fancied that he would ask some further question. He did not understand the meaning of her look.

"I believe you," she said at last. "I am too much in need of a friend to doubt you."

"You have found one."

"I do not know. I am not sure. There are other things—" she stopped suddenly and looked away.

"What other things?"

But Maria Consuelo did not answer. Orsino knew that she was thinking of all that had once passed between them. He wondered whether, if he led the way, she would press him as she had done at their last meeting. If she did, he wondered what he should say. He had been very cold then, far colder than he was now. He now felt drawn to her, as in the first days of their acquaintance. He felt always that he was on the point of understanding her, and yet that he was waiting, for something which should help him to pass that point.

"What other things?" he asked, repeating his question. "Do you mean that there are reasons which may prevent me from being a good friend of yours?"

"I am afraid there are. I do not know."

"I think you are mistaken, Madame. Will you name some of those reasons—or even one?"

Maria Consuelo did not answer at once. She glanced at him, looked down, and then her eyes met his again.

"Do you think that you are the kind of man a woman chooses for her friend?" she asked at length, with a faint smile.

"I have not thought of the matter—"

"But you should—before offering your friendship."

"Why? If I feel a sincere sympathy for your trouble, if I am—" he hesitated, weighing his words—"if I am personally attached to you, why can I not help you? I am honest, and in earnest. May I say as much as that of myself?"

"I believe you are."

"Then I cannot see that I am not the sort of man whom a woman might take for a friend when a better is not at hand."

"And do you believe in friendship, Don Orsino?" asked Maria Consuelo quietly.

"I have heard it said that it is not wise to disbelieve anything nowadays," answered Orsino.

"True—and the word 'friend' has such a pretty sound!" She laughed, for the first time since he had entered the room.

"Then it is you who are the unbeliever, Madame. Is not that a sign that you need no friend at all, and that your questions are not seriously meant?"

"Perhaps. Who knows?"

"Do you know, yourself?"

"No." Again she laughed a little, and then grew suddenly grave.

"I never knew a woman who needed a friend more urgently than you do," said Orsino. "I do not in the least understand your position. The little you have told me makes it clear enough that there have been and still are unusual circumstances in your life. One thing I see. That woman whom you call your maid is forced upon you against your will, to watch you, and is privileged to tell lies about you which may do you a great injury. I do not ask why you are obliged to suffer her presence, but I see that you must, and I guess that you hate it. Would it be an act of friendship to free you from her or not?"

"At present it would not be an act of friendship," answered Maria Consuelo, thoughtfully.

"That is very strange. Do you mean to say that you submit voluntarily—"

"The woman is a condition imposed upon me. I cannot tell you more."

"And no friend, no friendly help can change the condition, I suppose."

"I did not say that. But such help is beyond your power, Don Orsino," she added turning towards him rather suddenly. "Let us not talk of this any more. Believe me, nothing can be done. You have sometimes acted strangely with me, but I really think you would help me if you could. Let that be the state of our acquaintance. You are willing, and I believe that you are. Nothing more. Let that be our compact. But you can perhaps help me in another way—a smaller way. I want a habitation of some kind for the winter, for I am tired of camping out in hotels. You who know your own city so well can name some person who will undertake the matter."

"I know the very man," said Orsino promptly.

"Will you write out the address for me?"

"It is not necessary. I mean myself."

"I could not let you take so much trouble," protested Maria Consuelo.

But she accepted, nevertheless, after a little hesitation. For some time they discussed the relative advantages of the various habitable quarters of the city, both glad, perhaps, to find an almost indifferent subject of conversation, and both relatively happy merely in being together. The talk made one of those restful interludes which are so necessary, and often so hard to produce, between two people whose thoughts run upon a strong common interest, and who find it difficult to exchange half a dozen words without being led back to the absorbing topic.

What had been said had produced a decided effect upon Orsino. He had come expecting to take up the acquaintance on a new footing, but ten minutes had not elapsed before he had found himself as much interested as ever in Maria Consuelo's personality, and far more interested in her life than he had ever been before. While talking with more or less indifference about the chances of securing a suitable apartment for the winter, Orsino listened with an odd sensation of pleasure to every tone of his companion's voice and watched every changing expression of the striking face. He wondered whether he were not perhaps destined to love her sincerely as he had already loved her in a boyish, capricious fashion which would no longer be natural to him now. But for the present he was sure that he did not love her, and that he desired nothing but her sympathy for himself, and to feel sympathy for her. Those were the words he used, and he did not explain them to his own intelligence in any very definite way. He was conscious, indeed, that they meant more than formerly, but the same was true of almost everything that came into his life, and he did not therefore attach any especial importance to the fact. He was altogether much more in earnest than when he had first met Maria Consuelo; he was capable of deeper feeling, of stronger determination and of more decided action in all matters, and though he did not say so to himself he was none the less aware of the change.

"Shall we make an appointment for to-morrow?" he asked, after they had been talking some time.

"Yes—but there is one thing I wanted to ask you—"

"What is that?" inquired Orsino, seeing that she hesitated.

The faint colour rose in her cheeks, but she looked straight into his eyes, with a kind of fearless expression, as though she were facing a danger.

"Tell me," she said, "in Rome, where everything is known and every one talks so much, will it not be thought strange that you and I should be driving about together, looking for a house for me? Tell me the truth."

"What can people say?" asked Orsino.

"Many things. Will they say them?"

"If they do, I can make them stop talking."

"That means that they will talk, does it not? Would you like that?"

There was a sudden change in her face, with a look of doubt and anxious perplexity. Orsino saw it and felt that she was putting him upon his honour, and that whatever the doubt might be it had nothing to do with her trust in him. Six months earlier he would not have hesitated to demonstrate that her fears were empty—but he felt that six months earlier she might not have yielded to his reasoning. It was instinctive, but his instinct was not mistaken.

"I think you are right," he said slowly. "We should not do it. I will send my architect with you."

There was enough regret in the tone to show that he was making a considerable sacrifice. A little delicacy means more when it comes from a strong man, than when it is the natural expression of an over-refined and somewhat effeminate character. And Orsino was rapidly developing a strength of which other people were conscious. Maria Consuelo was pleased, though she, too, was perhaps sorry to give up the projected plan.

"After all," she said, thoughtlessly, "you can come and see me here, if—"

She stopped and blushed again, more deeply this time; but she turned her face away and in the half light the change of colour was hardly noticeable.

"You were going to say 'if you care to see me,'" said Orsino. "I am glad you did not say it. It would not have been kind."

"Yes—I was going to say that," she answered quietly. "But I will not."

"Thank you."

"Why do you thank me?"

"For not hurting me."

"Do you think that I would hurt you willingly, in any way?"

"I would rather not think so. You did once."

The words slipped from his lips almost before he had time to realise what they meant. He was thinking of the night when she had drawn up the carriage window, leaving him standing on the pavement, and of her repeated refusals to see him afterwards. It seemed long ago, and the hurt had not really been so sharp as he now fancied that it must have been, judging from what he now felt. She looked at him quickly as though wondering what he would say next.

"I never meant to be unkind," she said. "I have often asked myself whether you could say as much."

It was Orsino's turn to change colour. He was young enough for that, and the blood rose slowly in his dark cheeks. He thought again of their last meeting, and of what he had heard as he shut the door after him on that day. Perhaps he would have spoken, but Maria Consuelo was sorry for what she had said, and a little ashamed of her weakness, as indeed she had some cause to be, and she immediately turned back to a former point of the conversation, not too far removed from what had last been said.

"You see," said she, "I was right to ask you whether people would talk. And I am grateful to you for telling me the truth. It is a first proof of friendship—of something better than our old relations. Will you send me your architect to-morrow, since you are so kind as to offer his help?"

After arranging for the hour of meeting Orsino rose to take his leave.

"May I come to-morrow?" he asked. "People will not talk about that," he added with a smile.

"You can ask for me. I may be out. If I am at home, I shall be glad to see you."

She spoke coldly, and Orsino saw that she was looking over his shoulder. He turned instinctively and saw that the door was open and Spicca was standing just outside, looking in and apparently waiting for a word from Maria Consuelo before entering.

CHAPTER XIX

As Orsino had no reason whatever for avoiding Spicca he naturally waited a moment instead of leaving the room immediately. He looked at the old man with a new interest as the latter came forward. He had never seen and probably would never see again a man taking the hand of a woman whose husband he had destroyed. He stood a little back and Spicca passed him as he met Maria Consuelo. Orsino watched the faces of both.

Madame d'Aranjuez put out her hand mechanically and with evident reluctance, and Orsino guessed that but for his own presence she would not have given it. The expression in her face changed rapidly from that which had been there when they had been alone, hardening very quickly until it reminded Orsino of a certain mask of the Medusa which had once made an impression upon his imagination. Her eyes were fixed and the pupils grew small while the singular golden yellow colour of the iris flashed disagreeably. She did not bend her head as she silently gave her hand.

Spicca, too, seemed momentarily changed. He was as pale and thin as ever, but his face softened oddly; certain lines which contributed to his usually bitter and sceptical expression disappeared, while others became visible which changed his look completely. He bowed with more deference than he affected with other women, and Orsino fancied that he would have held Maria Consuelo's hand a moment longer, if she had not withdrawn it as soon as it had touched his.

If Orsino had not already known that Spicca often saw her, he would have been amazed at the count's visit, considering what she had said of the man. As it was, he wondered what power Spicca had over her to oblige her to receive him, and he wondered in vain. The conclusion which forced itself before him was that Spicca was the person who imposed the serving woman upon Maria Consuelo. But her behaviour towards him, on the other hand, was not that of a person obliged by circumstances to submit to the caprices and dictation of another. Judging by the appearance of the two, it seemed more probable that the power was on the other side, and might be used mercilessly on occasion.

"I hope I am not disturbing your plans," said Spicca, in a tone which was almost humble, and very unlike his usual voice. "Were you going out together?"

He shook hands with Orsino, avoiding his glance, as the young man thought.

"No," answered Maria Consuelo briefly. "I was not going out."

"I am just going away," said Orsino by way of explanation, and he made as though he would take his leave.

"Do not go yet," said Maria Consuelo. Her look made the words imperative.

Spicca glanced from one to the other with a sort of submissive protest, and then all three sat down. Orsino wondered what part he was expected to play in the trio, and wished himself away in spite of the interest he felt in the situation.

Maria Consuelo began to talk in a careless tone which reminded him of his first meeting with her in Gouache's studio. She told Spicca that Orsino had promised her his architect as a guide in her search for a lodging.

"What sort of person is he?" inquired Spicca, evidently for the sake of making conversation.

"Contini is a man of business," Orsino answered. "An odd fellow, full of talent, and a musical genius. One would not expect very much of him at first, but he will do all that Madame d'Aranjuez needs."

"Otherwise you would not have recommended him, I suppose," said Spicca.

"Certainly not," replied Orsino, looking at him.

"You must know, Madame," said Spicca, "that Don Orsino is an excellent judge of men."

He emphasised the last word in a way that seemed unnecessary. Maria Consuelo had recovered all her equanimity and laughed carelessly.

"How you say that!" she exclaimed. "Is it a warning?"

"Against what?" asked Orsino.

"Probably against you," she said. "Count Spicca likes to throw out vague hints—but I will do him the credit to say that they generally mean something." She added the last words rather scornfully.

An expression of pain passed over the old man's face. But he said nothing, though it was not like him to pass by a challenge of the kind. Without in the least understanding the reason of the sensation, Orsino felt sorry for him.

"Among men, Count Spicca's opinion is worth having," he said quietly.

Maria Consuelo looked at him in some surprise. The phrase sounded like a rebuke, and her eyes betrayed her annoyance.

"How delightful it is to hear one man defend another!" she laughed.

"I fancy Count Spicca does not stand much in need of defence," replied Orsino, without changing his tone.

"He himself is the best judge of that."

Spicca raised his weary eyes to hers and looked at her for a moment, before he answered.

"Yes," he said. "I think I am the best judge. But I am not accustomed to being defended, least of all against you, Madame. The sensation is a new one."

Orsino felt himself out of place. He was more warmly attached to Spicca than he knew, and though he was at that time not far removed from loving Maria Consuelo, her tone in speaking to the old man, which said far more than her words, jarred upon him, and he could not help taking his friend's part. On the other hand the ugly truth that Spicca had caused the death of Aranjuez more than justified Maria Consuelo in her hatred. Behind all, there was evidently some good reason why Spicca came to see her, and there was some bond between the two which made it impossible for her to refuse his visits. It was clear too, that though she hated him he felt some kind of strong affection for her. In her presence he was very unlike his daily self.

Again Orsino moved and looked at her, as though asking her permission to go away. But she refused it with an imperative gesture and a look of annoyance. She evidently did not wish to be left alone with the old man. Without paying any further attention to the latter she began to talk to Orsino. She took no trouble to conceal what she felt and the impression grew upon Orsino that Spicca would have gone away after a quarter of an hour, if he had not either possessed a sort of right to stay or if he had not had some important object in view in remaining.

"I suppose there is nothing to do in Rome at this time of year," she said.

Orsino told her that there was absolutely nothing to do. Not a theatre was open, not a friend was in town. Rome was a wilderness. Rome was an amphitheatre on a day when there was no performance, when the lions were asleep, the gladiators drinking, and the martyrs unoccupied. He tried to say something amusing and found it hard.

Spicca was very patient, but evidently determined to outstay Orsino. From time to time he made a remark, to which Maria Consuelo paid very little attention if she took any notice of it at all. Orsino could not make up his mind whether to stay or to go. The latter course would evidently displease Maria Consuelo, whereas by remaining he was clearly annoying Spicca and was perhaps causing him pain. It was a nice question, and while trying to make conversation he weighed the arguments in his mind. Strange to say he decided in favour of Spicca. The decision was to some extent an index of the state of his feelings towards Madame d'Aranjuez. If he had been quite in love with her, he would have stayed. If he had wished to make her love him, he would have stayed also. As it was, his friendship for the old count went before other considerations. At the same time he hoped to manage matters so as not to incur Maria Consuelo's displeasure. He found it harder than he had expected. After he had made up his mind, he continued to talk during three or four minutes and then made his excuse.

"I must be going," he said quietly. "I have a number of things to do before night, and I must see Contini in order to give him time to make a list of apartments for you to see to-morrow."

He took his hat and rose. He was not prepared for Maria Consuelo's answer.

"I asked you to stay," she said, coldly and very distinctly.

Spicca did not allow his expression to change. Orsino stared at her.

"I am very sorry, Madame, but there are many reasons which oblige me to disobey you."

Maria Consuelo bit her lip and her eyes gleamed angrily. She glanced at Spicca as though hoping that he would go away with Orsino. But he did not move. It was more and more clear that he had a right to stay if he pleased. Orsino was already bowing before her. Instead of giving her hand she rose quickly and led him towards the door. He opened it and they stood together on the threshold.

"Is this the way you help me?" she asked, almost fiercely, though in a whisper.

"Why do you receive him at all?" he inquired, instead of answering.

"Because I cannot refuse."

"But you might send him away?"

She hesitated, and looked into his eyes.

"Shall I?"

"If you wish to be alone—and if you can. It is no affair of mine."

She turned swiftly, leaving Orsino standing in the door and went to Spicca's side. He had risen when she rose and was standing at the other side of the room, watching.

"I have a bad headache," she said coldly. "You will forgive me if I ask you to go with Don Orsino."

"A lady's invitation to leave her house, Madame, is the only one which a man cannot refuse," said Spicca gravely.

He bowed and followed Orsino out of the room, closing the door behind him. The scene had produced a very disagreeable impression upon Orsino. Had he not known the worst part of the secret and consequently understood what good cause Maria Consuelo had for not wishing to be alone with Spicca, he would have been utterly revolted and for ever repelled by her brutality. No other word could express adequately her conduct towards the count. Even knowing what he did, he wished that she had controlled her temper better and he was more than ever sorry for Spicca. It did not even cross his mind that the latter might have intentionally provoked Aranjuez and killed him purposely. He felt somehow that Spicca was in a measure the injured party and must have been in that position from the beginning, whatever the strange story might be. As the two descended the steps together Orsino glanced at his companion's pale, drawn features and was sure that the man was to be pitied. It was almost a womanly instinct, far too delicate for such a hardy nature, and dependent perhaps upon that sudden opening of his sympathies which resulted from meeting Maria Consuelo. I think that, on the whole, in such cases, though the woman's character may be formed by intimacy with man's, with apparent results, the impression upon the man is momentarily deeper, as the woman's gentler instincts are in a way reflected in his heart.

Spicca recovered himself quickly, however. He took out his case and offered Orsino a cigarette.

"So you have renewed your acquaintance," he said quietly.

"Yes—under rather odd circumstances," answered Orsino. "I feel as though I owed you an apology, Count, and yet I do not see what there is to apologise for. I tried to go away more than once."

"You cannot possibly make excuses to me for Madame d'Aranjuez's peculiarities, my friend. Besides, I admit that she has a right to treat me as she pleases. That does not prevent me from going to see her every day."

"You must have strong reasons for bearing such treatment."

"I have," answered Spicca thoughtfully and sadly. "Very strong reasons. I will tell you one of those which brought me to-day. I wished to see you two together."

Orsino stopped in his walk, after the manner of Italians, and he looked at Spicca. He was hot tempered when provoked, and he might have resented the speech if it had come from any other man. But he spoke quietly.

"Why do you wish to see us together?" he asked.

"Because I am foolish enough to think sometimes that you suit one another, and might love one another."

Probably nothing which Spicca could have said could have surprised Orsino more than such a plain statement. He grew suspicious at once, but Spicca's look was that of a man in earnest.

"I do not think I understand you," answered Orsino. "But I think you are touching a subject which is better left alone."

"I think not," returned Spicca unmoved.

"Then let us agree to differ," said Orsino a little more warmly.

"We cannot do that. I am in a position to make you agree with me, and I will. I am responsible for that lady's happiness. I am responsible before God and man."

Something in the words made a deep impression upon Orsino. He had never heard Spicca use anything approaching to solemn language before. He knew at least one part of the meaning which showed Spicca's remorse for having killed Aranjuez, and he knew that the old man meant what he said, and meant it from his heart.

"Do you understand me now?" asked Spicca, slowly inhaling the smoke of his cigarette.

"Not altogether. If you desire the happiness of Madame d'Aranjuez why do you wish us to fall in love with each other? It strikes me that—" he stopped.

"Because I wish you would marry her."

"Marry her!" Orsino had not thought of that, and his words expressed a surprise which was not calculated to please Spicca.

The old man's weary eyes suddenly grew keen and fierce and Orsino could hardly meet their look. Spicca's nervous fingers seized the young man's tough arm and closed upon it with surprising force.

"I would advise you to think of that possibility before making any more visits," he said, his weak voice suddenly clearing. "We were talking together a few weeks ago. Do you remember what I said I would do to any man by whom harm comes to her? Yes, you remember well enough. I know what you answered, and I daresay you meant it. But I was in earnest, too."

"I think you are threatening me, Count Spicca," said Orsino, flushing slowly but meeting the other's look with unflinching coolness.

"No. I am not. And I will not let you quarrel with me, either, Orsino. I have a right to say this to you where she is concerned—a right you do not dream of. You cannot quarrel about that."

Orsino did not answer at once. He saw that Spicca was very much in earnest, and was surprised that his manner now should be less calm and collected than on the occasion of their previous conversation, when the count had taken enough wine to turn the heads of most men. He did not doubt in the least the statement Spicca made. It agreed exactly with what Maria Consuelo herself had said of him. And the statement certainly changed the face of the situation. Orsino admitted to himself that he had never before thought of marrying Madame d'Aranjuez. He had not even taken into consideration the consequences of loving her and of being loved by her in return. The moment he thought of a possible marriage as the result of such a mutual attachment, he realised the enormous difficulties which stood in the way of such a union, and his first impulse was to give up visiting her altogether. What Spicca said was at once reasonable and unreasonable. Maria Consuelo's husband was dead, and she doubtless expected to marry again. Orsino had no right to stand in the way of others who might present themselves as suitors. But it was beyond belief that Spicca should expect Orsino to marry her himself, knowing Rome and the Romans as he did.

The two had been standing still in the shade. Orsino began to walk forward again before he spoke. Something in his own reflexions shocked him. He did not like to think that an impassable social barrier existed between Maria Consuelo and himself. Yet, in his total ignorance of her origin and previous life the stories which had been circulated about her recalled themselves with unpleasant distinctness. Nothing that Spicca had said when they had dined together had made the matter any clearer, though the assurance that the deceased Aranjuez had come to his end by Spicca's instrumentality sufficiently contradicted the worst, if also the least credible, point in the tales which had been repeated by the gossips early in the previous winter. All the rest belonged entirely to the category of the unknown. Yet Spicca spoke seriously of a possible marriage and had gone to the length of wishing that it might be brought about. At last Orsino spoke.

"You say that you have a right to say what you have said," he began. "In that case I think I have a right to ask a question which you ought to answer. You talk of my marrying Madame d'Aranjuez. You ought to tell me whether that is possible."

"Possible?" cried Spicca almost angrily. "What do you mean?"

"I mean this. You know us all, as you know me. You know the enormous prejudices in which we are brought up. You know perfectly well that although I am ready to laugh at some of them, there are others at which I do not laugh. Yet you refused to tell me who Madame d'Aranjuez was, when I asked you, the other day. I do not even know her father's name, much less her mother's—"

"No," answered Spicca. "That is quite true, and I see no necessity for telling you either. But, as you say, you have some right to ask. I will tell you this much. There is nothing in the circumstances of her birth which could hinder her marriage into any honourable family. Does that satisfy you?"

Orsino saw that whether he were satisfied or not he was to get no further information for the present. He might believe Spicca's statement or not, as he pleased, but he knew that whatever the peculiarities of the melancholy old duellist's character might be, he never took the trouble to invent a falsehood and was as ready as ever to support his words. On this occasion no one could have doubted him, for there was an unusual ring of sincere feeling in what he said. Orsino could not help wondering what the tie between him and Madame d'Aranjuez could be, for it evidently had the power to make Spicca submit without complaint to something worse than ordinary unkindness and to make him defend on all occasions the name and character of the woman who treated him so harshly. It must be a very close bond, Orsino thought. Spicca acted very much like a man who loves very sincerely and quite hopelessly. There was something very sad in the idea that he perhaps loved Maria Consuelo, at his age, broken down as he was, and old before his time. The contrast between them was so great that it must have been grotesque if it had not been pathetic.

Little more passed between the two men on that day, before they separated. To Spicca, Orsino seemed indifferent, and the older man's reticence after his sudden outburst did not tend to prolong the meeting.

Orsino went in search of Contini and explained what was needed of him. He was to make a brief list of desirable apartments to let and was to accompany Madame d'Aranjuez on the following morning in order to see them.

Contini was delighted and set out about the work at once. Perhaps he secretly hoped that the lady might be induced to take a part of one of the new houses, but the idea had nothing to do with his satisfaction. He was to spend several hours in the sole society of a lady, of a genuine lady who was, moreover, young and beautiful. He read the little morning paper too assiduously not to have noticed the name and pondered over the descriptions of Madame d'Aranjuez on the many occasions when she had been mentioned by the reporters during the previous year. He was too young and too thoroughly Italian not to appreciate the good fortune which now fell into his way, and he promised himself a morning of uninterrupted enjoyment. He wondered whether the lady could be induced, by excessive fatigue and thirst to accept a water ice at Nazzari's, and he planned his list of apartments in such a way as to bring her to the neighbourhood of the Piazza di Spagna at an hour when the proposition, might seem most agreeable and natural.

Orsino stayed in the office during the hot September morning, busying himself with the endless details of which he was now master, and thinking from time to time of Maria Consuelo. He intended to go and see her in the afternoon, and he, like Contini, planned what he should do and say. But his plans were all unsatisfactory, and once he found himself staring at the blank wall opposite his table in a state of idle abstraction long unfamiliar to him.

Soon after twelve o'clock, Contini came back, hot and radiant. Maria Consuelo had refused the water ice, but the charm of her manner had repaid the architect for the disappointment. Orsino asked whether she had decided upon any dwelling.

"She has taken the apartment in the Palazzo Barberini," answered Contini. "I suppose she will bring her family in the autumn."

"Her family? She has none. She is alone."

"Alone in that place! How rich she must be!" Contini found the remains of a cigar somewhere and lighted it thoughtfully.

"I do not know whether she is rich or not," said Orsino. "I never thought about it."

He began to work at his books again, while Contini sat down and fanned himself with a bundle of papers.

"She admires you very much, Don Orsino," said the latter, after a pause. Orsino looked up sharply.

"What do you mean by that?" he asked.

"I mean that she talked of nothing but you, and in the most flattering way."

In the oddly close intimacy which had grown up between the two men it did not seem strange that Orsino should smile at speeches which he would not have liked if they had come from any one but the poor architect.

"What did she say?" he asked with idle curiosity.

"She said it was wonderful to think what you had done. That of all the Roman princes you were the only one who had energy and character enough to throw over the old prejudices and take an occupation. That it was all the more creditable because you had done it from moral reasons and not out of necessity or love of money. And she said a great many other things of the same kind."

"Oh!" ejaculated Orsino, looking at the wall opposite.

"It is a pity she is a widow," observed Contini.

"Why?"

"She would make such a beautiful princess."

"You must be mad, Contini!" exclaimed Orsino, half-pleased and half-irritated. "Do not talk of such follies."

"All well! Forgive me," answered the architect a little humbly. "I am not you, you know, and my head is not yours—nor my name—nor my heart either."

Contini sighed, puffed at his cigar and took up some papers. He was already a little in love with Maria Consuelo, and the idea that any man might marry her if he pleased, but would not, was incomprehensible to him.

The day wore on. Orsino finished his work as thoroughly as though he had been a paid clerk, put everything in order and went away. Late in the afternoon he went to see Maria Consuelo. He knew that she would usually be already out at that hour, and he fancied that he was leaving something to chance in the matter of finding her, though an unacknowledged instinct told him that she would stay at home after the fatigue of the morning.

"We shall not be interrupted by Count Spicca to-day," she said, as he sat down beside her.

In spite of what he knew, the hard tone of her voice roused again in Orsino that feeling of pity for the old man which he had felt on the previous day.

"Does it not seem to you," he asked, "that if you receive him at all, you might at least conceal something of your hatred for him?"

"Why should I? Have you forgotten what I told you yesterday?"

"It would be hard to forget that, though you told me no details. But it is not easy to imagine how you can see him at all if he killed your husband deliberately in a duel."

"It is impossible to put the case more plainly!" exclaimed Maria Consuelo.

"Do I offend you?"

"No. Not exactly."

"Forgive me, if I do. If Spicca, as I suppose, was the unwilling cause of your great loss, he is much to be pitied. I am not sure that he does not deserve almost as much pity as you do."

"How can you say that—even if the rest were true?"

"Think of what he must suffer. He is devotedly attached to you."

"I know he is. You have told me that before, and I have given you the same answer. I want neither his attachment nor his devotion."

"Then refuse to see him."

"I cannot."

"We come back to the same point again," said Orsino.

"We always shall, if you talk about this. There is no other issue. Things are what they are and I cannot change them."

"Do you know," said Orsino, "that all this mystery is a very serious hindrance to friendship?"

Maria Consuelo was silent for a moment.

"Is it?" she asked presently. "Have you always thought so?"

The question was a hard one to answer.

"You have always seemed mysterious to me," answered Orsino. "Perhaps that is a great attraction. But instead of learning the truth about you, I am finding out that there are more and more secrets in your life which I must not know."

"Why should you know them?"

"Because—" Orsino checked himself, almost with a start.

He was annoyed at the words which had been so near his lips, for he had been on the point of saying "because I love you"—and he was intimately convinced that he did not love her. He could not in the least understand why the phrase was so ready to be spoken. Could it be, he asked himself, that Maria Consuelo was trying to make him say the words, and that her will, with her question, acted directly on his mind? He scouted the thought as soon as it presented itself, not only for its absurdity, but because it shocked some inner sensibility.

"What were you going to say?" asked Madame d'Aranjuez almost carelessly.

"Something that is best not said," he answered.

"Then I am glad you did not say it."

She spoke quietly and unaffectedly. It needed little divination on her part to guess what the words might have been. Even if she wished them spoken, she would not have them spoken too lightly, for she had heard his love speeches before, when they had meant very little.

Orsino suddenly turned the subject, as though he felt unsure of himself. He asked her about the result of her search, in the morning. She answered that she had determined to take the apartment in the Palazzo Barberini.

"I believe it is a very large place," observed Orsino, indifferently.

"Yes," she answered in the same tone. "I mean to receive this winter. But it will be a tiresome affair to furnish such a wilderness."

"I suppose you mean to establish yourself in Rome for several years." His face expressed a satisfaction of which he was hardly conscious himself. Maria Consuelo noticed it.

"You seem pleased," she said.

"How could I possibly not be?" he asked.

Then he was silent. All his own words seemed to him to mean too much or too little. He wished she would choose some subject of conversation and talk that he might listen. But she also was unusually silent.

He cut his visit short, very suddenly, and left her, saying that he hoped to find her at home as a general rule at that hour, quite forgetting that she would naturally be always out at the cool time towards evening.

He walked slowly homewards in the dusk, and did not remember to go to his solitary dinner until nearly nine o'clock. He was not pleased with himself, but he was involuntarily pleased by something he felt and would not have been insensible to if he had been given the choice. His old interest in Maria Consuelo was reviving, and yet was turning into something very different from what it had been.

He now boldly denied to himself that he was in love and forced himself to speculate concerning the possibilities of friendship. In his young system, it was absurd to suppose that a man could fall in love a second time with the same woman. He scoffed at himself, at the idea and at his own folly, having all the time a consciousness amounting to certainty, of something very real and serious, by no means to be laughed at, overlooked nor despised.

CHAPTER XX

It was to be foreseen that Orsino and Maria Consuelo would see each other more often and more intimately now than ever before. Apart from the strong mutual attraction which drew them nearer and nearer together, there were many new circumstances which rendered Orsino's help almost indispensable to his friend. The details of her installation in the apartment she had chosen were many, there was much to be thought of and there were enormous numbers of things to be bought, almost each needing judgment and discrimination in the choice. Had the two needed reasonable excuses for meeting very often they had them ready to their hand. But neither of them were under any illusion, and neither cared to affect that peculiar form of self-forgiveness which finds good reasons always for doing what is always pleasant. Orsino, indeed, never pressed his services and was careful not to be seen too often in public with Maria Consuelo by the few acquaintances who were in town. Nor did Madame d'Aranjuez actually ask his help at every turn, any more than she made any difficulty about accepting it. There was a tacit understanding between them which did away with all necessity for inventing excuses on the one hand, or for the affectation of fearing to inconvenience Orsino on the other. During some time, however, the subjects which both knew to be dangerous were avoided, with an unspoken mutual consent for which Maria Consuelo was more grateful than for all the trouble Orsino was giving himself on her account. She fancied, perhaps, that he had at last accepted the situation, and his society gave her too much happiness to allow of her asking whether his discretion would or could last long.

It was an anomalous relation which bound them together, as is often the case at some period during the development of a passion, and most often when the absence of obstacles makes the growth of affection slow and regular. It was a period during which a new kind of intimacy began to exist, as far removed from the half-serious, half-jesting intercourse of earlier days as it was from the ultimate happiness to which all those who love look forward with equal trust, although few ever come near it and fewer still can ever reach it quite. It was outwardly a sort of frank comradeship which took a vast deal for granted on both sides for the mere sake of escaping analysis, a condition in which each understood all that the other said, while neither quite knew what was in the other's heart, a state in which both were pleased to dwell for a time, as though preferring to prolong a sure if imperfect happiness rather than risk one moment of it for the hope of winning a life-long joy. It was a time during which mere friendship reached an artificially perfect beauty, like a summer fruit grown under glass in winter, which in thoroughly unnatural conditions attains a development almost impossible even where unhelped nature is most kind. Both knew, perhaps, that it could not last, but neither wished it checked, and neither liked to think of the moment when it must either begin to wither by degrees, or be suddenly absorbed into a greater and more dangerous growth.

At that time they were able to talk fluently upon the nature of the human heart and the durability of great affections. They propounded the problems of the world and discussed them between the selection of a carpet and the purchase of a table. They were ready at any moment to turn from the deepest conversation to the consideration of the merest detail, conscious that they could instantly take up the thread of their talk. They could separate the major proposition from the minor, and the deduction from both, by a lively argument concerning the durability of a stuff or the fitness of a piece of furniture, and they came back each time with renewed and refreshed interest to the consideration of matters little less grave than the resurrection of the dead and the life of the world to come. That their conclusions were not always logical nor even very sensible has little to do with the matter. On the contrary, the discovery of a flaw in their own reasoning was itself a reason for opening the question again at their next meeting.

At first their conversation was of general things, including the desirability of glory for its own sake, the immortality of the soul and the principles of architecture. Orsino was often amazed to find himself talking, and, as he fancied, talking well, upon subjects of which he had hitherto supposed with some justice that he knew nothing. By and by they fell upon literature and dissected the modern novel with the keen zest of young people who seek to learn the future secrets of their own lives from vivid descriptions of the lives of others. Their knowledge of the modern novel was not so limited as their acquaintance with many other things less amusing, if more profitable, and they worked the vein with lively energy and mutual satisfaction.

Then, as always, came the important move. They began to talk of love. The interest ceased to be objective or in any way vicarious and was transferred directly to themselves.

These steps are not, I think, to be ever thought of as stages in the development of character in man or woman. They are phases in the intercourse of man and woman. Clever people know them well and know how to produce them at will. The end may or may not be love, but an end of some sort is inevitable. According to the persons concerned, according to circumstances, according to the amount of available time, the progression from general subjects to the discussion of love, with self-application of the conclusions, more or less sincere, may occupy an hour, a month or a year. Love is the one subject which ultimately attracts those not too old to talk about it, and those who consider that they have reached such an age are few.

In the case of Orsino and Maria Consuelo, neither of the two was making any effort to lead up to a certain definite result, for both felt a real dread of reaching that point which is ever afterwards remembered as the last moment of hardly sustained friendship and the first of something stronger and too often less happy. Orsino was inexperienced, but Maria Consuelo was quite conscious of the tendency in a fixed direction. Whether she had made up her mind, or not, she tried as skilfully as she could to retard the movement, for she was very happy in the present and probably feared the first stirring of her own ardently passionate nature.

As for Orsino, indeed, his inexperience was relative. He was anxious to believe that he was only her friend, and pretended to his own conscience that he could not explain the frequency with which the words "I love you" presented themselves. The desire to speak them was neither a permanent impulse of which he was always conscious nor a sudden strong emotion like a temptation, giving warning of itself by a few heart-beats before it reached its strength. The words came to his lips so naturally and unexpectedly that he often wondered how he saved himself from pronouncing them. It was impossible for him to foresee when they would crave utterance. At last he began to fancy that they rang in his mind without a reason and without a wish on his part to speak them, as a perfectly indifferent tune will ring in the ear for days so that one cannot get rid of it.

Maria Consuelo had not intended to spend September and October altogether in Rome. She had supposed that it would be enough to choose her apartment and give orders to some person about the furnishing of it to her taste, and that after that she might go to the seaside until the heat should be over, coming up to the city from time to time as occasion required. But she seemed to have changed her mind. She did not even suggest the possibility of going away.

She generally saw Orsino in the afternoon. He found no difficulty in making time to see her, whenever he could be useful, but his own business naturally occupied all the earlier part of the day. As a rule, therefore, he called between half-past four and five, and so soon as it was cool enough they went together to the Palazzo Barberini to see what progress the upholsterers were making and to consider matters of taste. The great half-furnished rooms with the big windows overlooking the little garden before the palace were pleasant to sit in and wander in during the hot September afternoons. The pair were not often quite alone, even for a quarter of an hour, the place being full of workmen who came and went, passed and repassed, as their occupations required, often asking for orders and probably needing more supervision than Maria Consuelo bestowed upon them.

On a certain evening late in September the two were together in the large drawing-room. Maria Consuelo was tired and was leaning back in a deep seat, her hands folded upon her knee, watching Orsino as he slowly paced the carpet, crossing and recrossing in his short walk, his face constantly turned towards her. It was excessively hot. The air was sultry with thunder, and though it was past five o'clock the windows were still closely shut to keep out the heat. A clear, soft light filled the room, not reflected from a burning pavement, but from grass and plashing water.

They had been talking of a chimneypiece which Maria Consuelo wished to have placed in the hall. The style of what she wanted suggested the sixteenth century, Henry Second of France, Diana of Poitiers and the durability of the affections. The transition from fireplaces to true love had been accomplished with comparative ease, the result of daily practice and experience. It is worth noting, for the benefit of the young, that furniture is an excellent subject for conversation for that very reason, nothing being simpler than to go in three minutes from a table to an epoch, from an epoch to an historical person and from that person to his or her love story. A young man would do well to associate the life of some famous lover or celebrated and unhappy beauty with each style of woodwork and upholstery. It is always convenient. But if he has not the necessary preliminary knowledge he may resort to a stratagem.

"What a comfortable chair!" says he, as he deposits his hat on the floor and sits down.

"Do you like comfortable chairs?"

"Of course. Fancy what life was in the days of stiff wooden seats, when you had to carry a cushion about with you. You know that sort of thing—twelfth century, Francesca da Rimini and all that."

"Poor Francesca!"

If she does not say "Poor Francesca!" as she probably will, you can say it yourself, very feelingly and in a different tone, after a short pause. The one kiss which cost two lives makes the story particularly useful. And then the ice is broken. If Paolo and Francesca had not been murdered, would they have loved each other for ever? As nobody knows what they would have done, you can assert that they would have been faithful or not, according to your taste, humour or personal intentions. Then you can talk about the husband, whose very hasty conduct contributed so materially to the shortness of the story. If you wish to be thought jealous, you say he was quite right; if you desire to seem generous, you say with equal conviction that he was quite wrong. And so forth. Get to generalities as soon as possible in order to apply them to your own case.

Orsino and Maria Consuelo were the guileless victims of furniture, neither of them being acquainted with the method just set forth for the instruction of the innocent. They fell into their own trap and wondered how they had got from mantelpieces to hearts in such an incredibly short time.

"It is quite possible to love twice," Orsino was saying.

"That depends upon what you mean by love," answered Maria Consuelo, watching him with half-closed eyes.

Orsino laughed.

"What I mean by love? I suppose I mean very much what other people mean by it—or a little more," he added, and the slight change in his voice pleased her.

"Do you think that any two understand the same thing when they speak of love?" she asked.

"We two might," he answered, resuming his indifferent tone. "After all, we have talked so much together during the last month that we ought to understand each other."

"Yes," said Maria Consuelo. "And I think we do," she added thoughtfully.

"Then why should we think differently about the same thing? But I am not going to try and define love. It is not easily defined, and I am not clever enough." He laughed again. "There are many illnesses which I cannot define—but I know that one may have them twice."

"There are others which one can only have once—dangerous ones, too."

"I know it. But that has nothing to do with the argument."

"I think it has—if this is an argument at all."

"No. Love is not enough like an illness—it is quite the contrary. It is a recovery from an unnatural state— that of not loving. One may fall into that state and recover from it more than once."

"What a sophism!"

"Why do you say that? Do you think that not to love is the normal condition of mankind?"

Maria Consuelo was silent, still watching him.

"You have nothing to say," he continued, stopping and standing before her. "There is nothing to be said. A man or woman who does not love is in an abnormal state. When he or she falls in love it is a recovery. One may recover so long as the heart has enough vitality. Admit it—for you must. It proves that any properly constituted person may love twice, at least."

"There is an idea of faithlessness in it, nevertheless," said Maria Consuelo, thoughtfully. "Or if it is not faithless, it is fickle. It is not the same to oneself to love twice. One respects oneself less."

"I cannot believe that."

"We all ought to believe it. Take a case as an instance. A woman loves a man with all her heart, to the point of sacrificing very much for him. He loves her in the same way. In spite of the strongest opposition, they agree to be married. On the very day of the marriage he is taken from her—for ever—loving her as he has always loved her, and as he would always have loved her had he lived. What would such a woman feel, if she found herself forgetting such a love as that after two or three years, for another man? Do you think she would respect herself more or less? Do you think she would have the right to call herself a faithful woman?"

Orsino was silent for a moment, seeing that she meant herself by the example. She, indeed, had only told him that her husband had been killed, but Spicca had once said of her that she had been married to a man who had never been her husband.

"A memory is one thing—real life is quite another," said Orsino at last, resuming his walk.

"And to be faithful cannot possibly mean to be faithless," answered Maria Consuelo in a low voice.

She rose and went to one of the windows. She must have wished to hide her face, for the outer blinds and the glass casement were both shut and she could see nothing but the green light that struck the painted wood. Orsino went to her side.

"Shall I open the window?" he asked in a constrained voice.

"No—not yet. I thought I could see out."

Still she stood where she was, her face almost touching the pane, one small white hand resting upon the glass, the fingers moving restlessly.

"You meant yourself, just now," said Orsino softly.

She neither spoke nor moved, but her face grew pale. Then he fancied that there was a hardly perceptible movement of her head, the merest shade of an inclination. He leaned a little towards her, resting against the marble sill of the window.

"And you meant something more—" he began to say. Then he stopped short.

His heart was beating hard and the hot blood throbbed in his temples, his lips closed tightly and his breathing was audible.

Maria Consuelo turned her head, glanced at him quickly and instantly looked back at the smooth glass before her and at the green light on the shutters without. He was scarcely conscious that she had moved. In love, as in a storm at sea, matters grow very grave in a few moments.

"You meant that you might still—" Again he stopped. The words would not come.

He fancied that she would not speak. She could not, any more than she could have left his side at that moment. The air was very sultry even in the cool, closed room. The green light on the shutters darkened suddenly. Then a far distant peal of thunder rolled its echoes slowly over the city. Still neither moved from the window.

"If you could—" Orsino's voice was low and soft, but there was something strangely overwrought in the nervous quality of it. It was not hesitation any longer that made him stop.

"Could you love me?" he asked. He thought he spoke aloud. When he had spoken, he knew that he had whispered the words.

His face was colourless. He heard a short, sharp breath, drawn like a gasp. The small white hand fell from the window and gripped his own with sudden, violent strength. Neither spoke. Another peal of thunder, nearer and louder, shook the air. Then Orsino heard the quick-drawn breath again, and the white hand went nervously to the fastening of the window. Orsino opened the casement and thrust back the blinds. There was a vivid flash, more thunder, and a gust of stifling wind. Maria Consuelo leaned far out, looking up, and a few great drops of rain, began to fall.

The storm burst and the cold rain poured down furiously, wetting the two white faces at the window. Maria Consuelo drew back a little, and Orsino leaned against the open casement, watching her. It was as though the single pressure of their hands had crushed out the power of speech for a time.

For weeks they had talked daily together during many hours. They could not foresee that at the great moment there would be nothing left for them to say. The rain fell in torrents and the gusty wind rose and buffeted the face of the great palace with roaring strength, to sink very suddenly an instant later in the steadily rushing noise of the water, springing up again without warning, rising and falling, falling and rising, like a great sobbing breath. The wind and the rain seemed to be speaking for the two who listened to it.

Orsino watched Maria Consuelo's face, not scrutinising it, nor realising very much whether it were beautiful or not, nor trying to read the thoughts that were half expressed in it—not thinking at all, indeed, but only loving it wholly and in every part for the sake of the woman herself, as he had never dreamed of loving any one or anything.

At last Maria Consuelo turned very slowly and looked into his eyes. The passionate sadness faded out of the features, the faint colour rose again, the full lips relaxed, the smile that came was full of a happiness that seemed almost divine.

"I cannot help it," she said.

"Can I?"

"Truly?"

Her hand was lying on the marble ledge. Orsino laid his own upon it, and both trembled a little. She understood more than any word could have told her.

"For how long?" she asked.

"For all our lives now, and for all our life hereafter."

He raised her hand to his lips, bending his head, and then he drew her from the window, and they walked slowly up and down the great room.

"It is very strange," she said presently, in a low voice.

"That I should love you?"

"Yes. Where were we an hour ago? What is become of that old time—that was an hour ago?"

"I have forgotten, dear—that was in the other life."

"The other life! Yes—how unhappy I was—there, by that window, a hundred years ago!"

She laughed softly, and Orsino smiled as he looked down at her.

"Are you happy now?"

"Do not ask me—how could I tell you?"

"Say it to yourself, love—I shall see it in your dear face."

"Am I not saying it?"

Then they were silent again, walking side by side, their arms locked and pressing one another.

It began to dawn upon Orsino that a great change had come into his life, and he thought of the consequences of what he was doing. He had not said that he was happy, but in the first moment he had felt it more than she. The future, however, would not be like the present, and could not be a perpetual continuation of it. Orsino was not at all of a romantic disposition, and the practical side of things was always sure to present itself to his mind very early in any affair. It was a part of his nature and by no means hindered him from feeling deeply and loving sincerely. But it shortened his moments of happiness.

"Do you know what this means to you and me?" he asked, after a time.

Maria Consuelo started very slightly and looked up at him.

"Let us think of to-morrow—to-morrow," she said. Her voice trembled a little.

"Is it so hard to think of?" asked Orsino, fearing lest he had displeased her.

"Very hard," she answered, in a low voice.

"Not for me. Why should it be? If anything can make to-day more complete, it is to think that to-morrow will be more perfect, and the next day still more, and so on, each day better than the one before it."

Maria Consuelo shook her head.

"Do not speak of it," she said.

"Will you not love me to-morrow?" Orsino asked. The light in his face told how little earnestly he asked the question, but she turned upon him quickly.

"Do you doubt yourself, that you should doubt me?" There was a ring of terror in the words that startled him as he heard them.

"Beloved—no—how can you think I meant it?"

"Then do not say it." She shivered a little, and bent down her head.

"No—I will not. But—dear—do you know where we are?"

"Where we are?" she repeated, not understanding.

"Yes—where we are. This was to have been your home this year."

"Was to have been?" A frightened look came into her face.

"It will not be, now. Your home is not in this house."

Again she shook her head, turning her face away.

"It must be," she said.

Orsino was surprised beyond expression by the answer.

"Either you do not know what you are saying, or you do not mean it, dear," he said. "Or else you will not understand me."

"I understand you too well."

Orsino made her stop and took both her hands, looking down into her eyes.

"You will marry me," he said.

"I cannot marry you," she answered.

Her face grew even paler than it had been when they had stood at the window, and so full of pain and sadness that it hurt Orsino to look at it. But the words she spoke, in her clear, distinct tones, struck him like a blow unawares. He knew that she loved him, for her love was in every look and gesture, without attempt at concealment. He believed her to be a good woman. He was certain that her husband was dead. He could not understand, and he grew suddenly angry. An older man would have done worse, or a man less in earnest.

"You must have a reason to give me—and a good one," he said gravely.

"I have."

She turned slowly away and began to walk alone. He followed her.

"You must tell it," he said.

"Tell it? Yes, I will tell it to you. It is a solemn promise before God, given to a man who died in my arms— to my husband. Would you have me break such a vow?"

"Yes." Orsino drew a long breath. The objection seemed insignificant enough compared with the pain it had cost him before it had been explained.

"Such promises are not binding," he continued, after a moment's pause. "Such a promise is made hastily, rashly, without a thought of the consequences. You have no right to keep it."

"No right? Orsino, what are you saying! Is not an oath an oath, however it is taken? Is not a vow made ten times more sacred when the one for whom it was taken is gone? Is there any difference between my promise and that made before the altar by a woman who gives up the world? Should I be any better, if I broke mine, than the nun who broke hers?"

"You cannot be in earnest?" exclaimed Orsino in a low voice.

Maria Consuelo did not answer. She went towards the window and looked at the splashing rain. Orsino stood where he was, watching her. Suddenly she came back and stood before him.

"We must undo this," she said.

"What do you mean?" He understood well enough.

"You know. We must not love each other. We must undo to-day and forget it."

"If you can talk so lightly of forgetting, you have little to remember," answered Orsino almost roughly.

"You have no right to say that."

"I have the right of a man who loves you."

"The right to be unjust?"

"I am not unjust." His tone softened again. "I know what it means, to say that I love you—it is my life, this love. I have known it a long time. It has been on my lips to say it for weeks, and since it has been said, it cannot be unsaid. A moment ago you told me not to doubt you. I do not. And now you say that we must not love each other, as though we had a choice to make—and why? Because you once made a rash promise—"

"Hush!" interrupted Maria Consuelo. "You must not—"

"I must and will. You made a promise, as though you had a right at such a moment to dispose of all your life—I do not speak of mine—as though you could know what the world held for you, and could renounce it all beforehand. I tell you you had no right to make such an oath, and a vow taken without the right to take it is no vow at all—"

"It is—it is! I cannot break it!"

"If you love me you will. But you say we are to forget. Forget! It is so easy to say. How shall we do it?"

"I will go away—"

"If you have the heart to go away, then go. But I will follow you. The world is very small, they say—it will not be hard for me to find you, wherever you are."

"If I beg you—if I ask it as the only kindness, the only act of friendship, the only proof of your love—you will not come—you will not do that—"

"I will, if it costs your soul and mine."

"Orsino! You do not mean it—you see how unhappy I am, how I am trying to do right, how hard it is!"

"I see that you are trying to ruin both our lives. I will not let you. Besides, you do not mean it."

Maria Consuelo looked into his eyes and her own grew deep and dark. Then as though she felt herself yielding, she turned away and sat down in a chair that stood apart from the rest. Orsino followed her, and tried to take her hand, bending down to meet her downcast glance.

"You do not mean it, Consuelo," he said earnestly. "You do not mean one hundredth part of what you say."

She drew her fingers from his, and turned her head sideways against the back of the chair so that she could not see him. He still bent over her, whispering into her ear.

"You cannot go," he said. "You will not try to forget—for neither you nor I can—nor ought, cost what it might. You will not destroy what is so much to us—you would not, if you could. Look at me, love—do not turn away. Let me see it all in your eyes, all the truth of it and of every word I say."

Still she turned her face from him. But she breathed quickly with parted lips and the colour rose slowly in her pale cheeks.

"It must be sweet to be loved as I love you, dear," he said, bending still lower and closer to her. "It must be some happiness to know that you are so loved. Is there so much joy in your life that you can despise this? There is none in mine, without you, nor ever can be unless we are always together—always, dear, always, always."

She moved a little, and the drooping lids lifted almost imperceptibly.

"Do not tempt me, dear one," she said in a faint voice. "Let me go—let me go."

Orsino's dark face was close to hers now, and she could see his bright eyes. Once she tried to look away, and could not. Again she tried, lifting her head from the cushioned chair. But his arm went round her neck and her cheek rested upon his shoulder.

"Go, love," he said softly, pressing her more closely. "Go—let us not love each other. It is so easy not to love."

She looked up into his eyes again with a sudden shiver, and they both grew very pale. For ten seconds neither spoke nor moved. Then their lips met.

CHAPTER XXI

When Orsino was alone that night, he asked himself more than one question which he did not find it easy to answer. He could define, indeed, the relation in which he now stood to Maria Consuelo, for though she had ultimately refused to speak the words of a promise, he no longer doubted that she meant to be his wife and that her scruples were overcome for ever. This was, undeniably, the most important point in the whole affair, so far as his own satisfaction was concerned, but there were others of the gravest import to be considered and elucidated before he could even weigh the probabilities of future happiness.

He had not lost his head on the present occasion, as he had formerly done when his passion had been anything but sincere. He was perfectly conscious that Maria Consuelo was now the principal person concerned in his life and that the moment would inevitably have come, sooner or later, in which he must have told her so as he had done on this day. He had not yielded to a sudden impulse, but to a steady and growing pressure from which there had been no means of escape, and which he had not sought to elude. He was not in one of those moods of half-senseless, exuberant spirits, such as had come upon him more than once during the winter after he had been an hour in her society and had said or done something more than usually rash. On the contrary, he was inclined to look the whole situation soberly in the face, and to doubt whether the love which dominated him might not prove a source of unhappiness to Maria Consuelo as well as to himself. At the same time he knew that it would be useless to fight against that domination, for he knew that he was now absolutely sincere.

But the difficulties to be met and overcome were many and great. He might have betrothed himself to almost any woman in society, widow or spinster, without anticipating one hundredth part of the opposition which he must now certainly encounter. He was not even angry beforehand with the prejudice which would animate his father and mother, for he admitted that it was hardly a prejudice at all, and certainly not one peculiar to them, or to their class. It would be hard to find a family, anywhere, of any respectability, no matter how modest, that would accept without question such a choice as he had made. Maria Consuelo was one of those persons about whom the world is ready to speak in disparagement, knowing that it will not be easy to find defenders for them. The world indeed, loves its own and treats them with consideration, especially in the matter of passing follies, and after it had been plain to society that Orsino had fallen under Maria Consuelo's charm, he had heard no more disagreeable remarks about her origin nor the circumstances of her widowhood. But he remembered what had been said before that, when he himself had listened indifferently enough, and he guessed that ill-natured people called her an adventuress or little better. If anything could have increased the suffering which this intuitive knowledge caused him, it was the fact that he possessed no proof of her right to rank with the best, except his own implicit faith in her, and the few words Spicca had chosen to let fall. Spicca was still thought so dangerous that people hesitated to contradict him openly, but his mere assertion, Orsino thought, though it might be accepted in appearance, was not of enough weight to carry inward conviction with it in the minds of people who had no interest in being convinced. It was only too plain that, unless Maria Consuelo, or Spicca, or both, were willing to tell the strange story in its integrity, there were not proof enough to convince the most willing person of her right to the social position she occupied after that had once been called into question. To Orsino's mind the very fact that it had been questioned at all demonstrated sufficiently a carelessness on her own part which could only proceed from the certainty of possessing that right beyond dispute. It would doubtless have been possible for her to provide herself from the first with something in the nature of a guarantee for her identity. She could surely have had the means, through some friend of her own elsewhere, of making the acquaintance of some one in society, who would have vouched for her and silenced the carelessly spiteful talk concerning her which had gone the rounds when she first appeared. But she had seemed to be quite indifferent. She had refused Orsino's pressing offer to bring her into relations with his mother, whose influence would have been enough to straighten a reputation far more doubtful than Maria Consuelo's, and she had almost wilfully thrown herself into a sort of intimacy with the Countess Del Ferice.

But Orsino, as he thought of these matters, saw how futile such arguments must seem to his own people, and how absurdly inadequate they were to better his own state of mind, since he needed no conviction himself but sought the means of convincing others. One point alone gave him some hope. Under the existing laws the inevitable legal marriage would require the production of documents which would clear the whole story at once. On the other hand, that fact could make Orsino's position no easier with his father and mother until the papers were actually produced. People cannot easily be married secretly in Rome, where the law requires the publication of banns by posting them upon the doors of the Capitol, and the name of Orsino Saracinesca would not be easily overlooked. Orsino was aware of course that he was not in need of his parents' consent for his marriage, but he had not been brought up in a way to look upon their acquiescence as unnecessary. He was deeply attached to them both, but especially to his mother who had been his staunch friend in his efforts to do something for himself, and to whom he naturally looked for sympathy if not for actual help. However certain he might be of the ultimate result of his marriage, the idea of being married in direct opposition to her wishes was so repugnant to him as to be almost an insurmountable barrier. He might, indeed, and probably would, conceal his engagement for some time, but solely with the intention of so preparing the evidence in favour of it as to make it immediately acceptable to his father and mother when announced.

It seemed possible that, if he could bring Maria Consuelo to see the matter as he saw it, she might at once throw aside her reticence and furnish him with the information he so greatly needed. But it would be a delicate matter to bring her to that point of view, unconscious as she must be of her equivocal position. He could not go to her and tell her that in order to announce their engagement he must be able to tell the world who and what she really was. The most he could do would be to tell her exactly what papers were necessary for her marriage and to prevail upon her to procure them as soon as possible, or to hand them to him at once if they were already in her possession. But in order to require even this much of her, it was necessary to push matters farther than they had yet gone. He had certainly pledged himself to her, and he firmly believed that she considered herself bound to him. But beyond that, nothing definite had passed.

They had been interrupted by the entrance of workmen asking for orders, and he had thought that Maria Consuelo had seemed anxious to detain the men as long as possible. That such a scene could not be immediately renewed where it had been broken off was clear enough, but Orsino fancied that she had not wished even to attempt a renewal of it. He had taken her home in the dusk, and she had refused to let him enter the hotel with her. She said that she wished to be alone, and he had been fain to be satisfied with the pressure of her hand and the look in her eyes, which both said much while not saying half of what he longed to hear and know.

He would see her, of course, at the usual hour on the following day, and he determined to speak plainly and strongly. She could not ask him to prolong such a state of uncertainty. Considering how gradual the steps had been which had led up to what had taken place on that rainy afternoon it was not conceivable, he thought, that she would still ask for time to make up her mind. She would at least consent to some preliminary agreement upon a line of conduct for both to follow.

But impossible as the other case seemed, Orsino did not neglect it. His mind was developing with his character and was acquiring the habit of foreseeing difficulties in order to forestall them. If Maria Consuelo returned suddenly to her original point of view maintaining that the promise given to her dying husband was still binding, Orsino determined that he would go to Spicca in a last resort. Whatever the bond which united them, it was clear that Spicca possessed some kind of power over Maria Consuelo, and that he was so far acquainted with all the circumstances of her previous life as to be eminently capable of giving Orsino advice for the future.

He went to his office on the following morning with little inclination for work. It would be more just, perhaps, to say that he felt the desire to pursue his usual occupation while conscious that his mind was too much disturbed by the events of the previous afternoon to concentrate itself upon the details of accounts and plans. He found himself committing all sorts of errors of oversight quite unusual with him. Figures seemed to have lost their value and plans their meaning. With the utmost determination he held himself to his task, not willing to believe that his judgment and nerve could be so disturbed as to render him unfit for any serious business. But the result was contemptible as compared with the effort.

Andrea Contini, too, was inclined to take a gloomy view of things, contrary to his usual habit. A report was spreading to the effect that a certain big contractor was on the verge of bankruptcy, a man who had hitherto been considered beyond the danger of heavy loss. There had been more than one small failure of late, but no one had paid much attention to such accidents which were generally attributed to personal causes rather than to an approaching turn in the tide of speculation. But Contini chose to believe that a crisis was not far off. He possessed in a high degree that sort of caution which is valuable rather in an assistant than in a chief. Orsino was little inclined to share his architect's despondency for the present.

"You need a change of air," he said, pushing a heap of papers away from him and lighting a cigarette. "You ought to go down to Porto d'Anzio for a few days. You have been too long in the heat."

"No longer than you, Don Orsino," answered Contini, from his own table.

"You are depressed and gloomy. You have worked harder than I. You should really go out of town for a day or two."

"I do not feel the need of it."

Contini bent over his table again and a short silence followed. Orsino's mind instantly reverted to Maria Consuelo. He felt a violent desire to leave the office and go to her at once. There was no reason why he should not visit her in the morning if he pleased. At the worst, she might refuse to receive him. He was thinking how she would look, and wondering whether she would smile or meet him with earnest half regretful eyes, when Contini's voice broke into his meditations again.

"You think I am despondent because I have been working too long in the heat," said the young man, rising and beginning to pace the floor before Orsino. "No. I am not that kind of man. I am never tired. I can go on for ever. But affairs in Rome will not go on for ever. I tell you that, Don Orsino. There is trouble in the air. I wish we had sold everything and could wait. It would be much better."

"All this is very vague, Contini."

"It is very clear to me. Matters are going from bad to worse. There is no doubt that Ronco has failed."

"Well, and if he has? We are not Ronco. He was involved in all sorts of other speculations. If he had stuck to land and building he would be as sound as ever."

"For another month, perhaps. Do you know why he is ruined?"

"By his own fault, as people always are. He was rash."

"No rasher than we are. I believe that the game is played out. Ronco is bankrupt because the bank with which he deals cannot discount any more bills this week."

"And why not?"

"Because the foreign banks will not take any more of all this paper that is flying about. Those small failures in the summer have produced their effect. Some of the paper was in Paris and some in Vienna. It turned out worthless, and the foreigners have taken fright. It is all a fraud, at best—or something very like it."

"What do you mean?"

"Tell me the truth, Don Orsino—have you seen a centime of all these millions which every one is dealing with? Do you believe they really exist? No. It is all paper, paper, and more paper. There is no cash in the business."

"But there is land and there are houses, which represent the millions substantially."

"Substantially! Yes—as long as the inflation lasts. After that they will represent nothing."

"You are talking nonsense, Contini. Prices may fall, and some people will lose, but you cannot destroy real estate permanently."

"Its value may be destroyed for ten or twenty years, which is practically the same thing when people have no other property. Take this block we are building. It represents a large sum. Say that in the next six months there are half a dozen failures like Ronco's and that a panic sets in. We could then neither sell the houses nor let them. What would they represent to us? Nothing. Failure—like the failure of everybody else. Do you know where the millions really are? You ought to know better than most people. They are in Casa Saracinesca and in a few other great houses which have not dabbled in all this business, and perhaps they are in the pockets of a few clever men who have got out of it all in time. They are certainly not in the firm of Andrea Contini and Company, which will assuredly be bankrupt before the winter is out."

Contini bit his cigar savagely, thrust his hands into his pockets and looked out of the window, turning his back on Orsino. The latter watched his companion in surprise, not understanding why his dismal forebodings should find such sudden and strong expression.

"I think you exaggerate very much," said Orsino. "There is always risk in such business as this. But it strikes me that the risk was greater when we had less capital."

"Capital!" exclaimed the architect contemptuously and without turning round. "Can we draw a cheque—a plain unadorned cheque and not a draft—for a hundred thousand francs to-day? Or shall we be able to draw it to-morrow? Capital! We have a lot of brick and mortar in our possession, put together more or less symmetrically according to our taste, and practically unpaid for. If we manage to sell it in time we shall get the difference between what is paid and what we owe. That is our capital. It is problematical, to say the least of it. If we realise less than we owe we are bankrupt."

He came back suddenly to Orsino's table as he ceased speaking and his face showed that he was really disturbed. Orsino looked at him steadily for a few seconds.

"It is not only Ronco's failure that frightens you, Contini. There must be something else."

"More of the same kind. There is enough to frighten any one."

"No, there is something else. You have been talking with somebody."

"With Del Ferice's confidential clerk. Yes—it is quite true. I was with him last night."

"And what did he say? What you have been telling me, I suppose."

"Something much more disagreeable—something you would rather not hear."

"I wish to hear it."

"You should, as a matter of fact."

"Go on."

"We are completely in Del Ferice's hands."

"We are in the hands of his bank."

"What is the difference? To all intents and purposes he is our bank. The proof is that but for him we should have failed already."

Orsino looked up sharply.

"Be clear, Contini. Tell me what you mean."

"I mean this. For a month past the bank could not have discounted a hundred francs' worth of our paper. Del Ferice has taken it all and advanced the money out of his private account."

"Are you sure of what you are telling me?" Orsino asked the question in a low voice, and his brow contracted.

"One can hardly have better authority than the clerk's own statement."

"And he distinctly told you this, did he?"

"Most distinctly."

"He must have had an object in betraying such a confidence," said Orsino. "It is not likely that such a man would carelessly tell you or me a secret which is evidently meant to be kept."

He spoke quietly enough, but the tone of his voice was changed and betrayed how greatly he was moved by the news. Contini began to walk up and down again, but did not make any answer to the remark.

"How much do we owe the bank?" Orsino asked suddenly.

"Roughly, about six hundred thousand."

"How much of that paper do you think Del Ferice has taken up himself?"

"About a quarter, I fancy, from what the clerk told me."

A long silence followed, during which Orsino tried to review the situation in all its various aspects. It was clear that Del Ferice did not wish Andrea Contini and Company to fail and was putting himself to serious inconvenience in order to avert the catastrophe. Whether he wished, in so doing, to keep Orsino in his power, or whether he merely desired to escape the charge of having ruined his old enemy's son out of spite, it was hard to decide. Orsino passed over that question quickly enough. So far as any sense of humiliation was concerned he knew very well that his mother would be ready and able to pay off all his liabilities at the shortest notice. What Orsino felt most deeply was profound disappointment and utter disgust at his own folly. It seemed to him that he had been played with and flattered into the belief that he was a serious man of business, while all along he had been pushed and helped by unseen hands. There was nothing to prove that Del Ferice had not thus deceived him from the first; and, indeed, when he thought of his small beginnings early in the year and realised the dimensions which the business had now assumed, he could not help believing that Del Ferice had been at the bottom of all his apparent success and that his own earnest and ceaseless efforts had really had but little to do with the development of his affairs. His vanity suffered terribly under the first shock.

He was bitterly disappointed. During the preceding months he had begun to feel himself independent and able to stand alone, and he had looked forward in the near future to telling his father that he had made a fortune for himself without any man's help. He had remembered every word of cold discouragement to which he had been forced to listen at the very beginning, and he had felt sure of having a success to set against each one of those words. He knew that he had not been idle and he had fancied that every hour of work had produced its permanent result, and left him with something more to show. He had seen his mother's pride in him growing day by day in his apparent success, and he had been confident of proving to her that she was not half proud enough. All that was gone in a moment. He saw, or fancied that he saw, nothing but a series of failures which had been bolstered up and inflated into seeming triumphs by a man whom his father despised and hated and whom, as a man, he himself did not respect. The disillusionment was complete.

At first it seemed to him that there was nothing to be done but to go directly to Saracinesca and tell the truth to his father and mother. Financially, when the wealth of the family was taken into consideration there was nothing very alarming in the situation. He would borrow of his father enough to clear him with Del Ferice and would sell the unfinished buildings for what they would bring. He might even induce his father to help him in finishing the work. There would be no trouble about the business question. As for Contini, he should not lose by the transaction and permanent occupation could doubtless be found for him on one of the estates if he chose to accept it.

He thought of the interview and his vanity dreaded it. Another plan suggested itself to him. On the whole, it seemed easier to bear his dependence on Del Ferice than to confess himself beaten. There was nothing dishonourable, nothing which could be called so at least, in accepting financial accommodation from a man whose business it was to lend money on security. If Del Ferice chose to advance sums which his bank would not advance, he did it for good reasons of his own and certainly not in the intention of losing by it in the end. In case of failure Del Ferice would take the buildings for the debt and would certainly in that case get them for much less than they were worth. Orsino would be no worse off than when he had begun, he would frankly confess that though he had lost nothing he had not made a fortune, and the matter would be at an end. That would be very much easier to bear than the humiliation of confessing at the present moment that he was in Del Ferice's power and would be bankrupt but for Del Ferice's personal help. And again he repeated to himself that Del Ferice was not a man to throw money away without hope of recovery with interest. It was inconceivable, too, that Ugo should have pushed him so far merely to flatter a young man's vanity. He meant to make use of him, or to make money out of his failure. In either case Orsino would be his dupe and would not be under any obligation to him. Compared with the necessity of acknowledging the present state of his affairs to his father, the prospect of being made a tool of by Del Ferice was bearable, not to say attractive.

"What had we better do, Contini?" he asked at length.

"There is nothing to be done but to go on, I suppose, until we are ruined," replied the architect. "Even if we had the money, we should gain nothing by taking off all our bills as they fall due, instead of renewing them."

"But if the bank will not discount any more—"

"Del Ferice will, in the bank's name. When he is ready for the failure, we shall fail and he will profit by our loss."

"Do you think that is what he means to do?"

Contini looked at Orsino in surprise.

"Of course. What did you expect? You do not suppose that he means to make us a present of that paper, or to hold it indefinitely until we can make a good sale."

"And he will ultimately get possession of all the paper himself."

"Naturally. As the old bills fall due we shall renew them with him, practically, and not with the bank. He knows what he is about. He probably has some scheme for selling the whole block to the government, or to some institution, and is sure of his profit beforehand. Our failure will give him a profit of twenty-five or thirty per cent."

Orsino was strangely reassured by his partner's gloomy view. To him every word proved that he was free from any personal obligation to Del Ferice and might accept the latter's assistance without the least compunction. He did not like to remember that a man of Ugo's subtle intelligence might have something more important in view than a profit of a few hundred thousand francs, if indeed the sum should amount to that. Orsino's brow cleared and his expression changed.

"You seem to like the idea," observed Contini rather irritably.

"I would rather be ruined by Del Ferice than helped by him."

"Ruin means so little to you, Don Orsino. It means the inheritance of an enormous fortune, a princess for a wife and the choice of two or three palaces to live in."

"That is one way of putting it," answered Orsino, almost laughing. "As for yourself, my friend, I do not see that your prospects are so very bad. Do you suppose that I shall abandon you after having led you into this scrape, and after having learned to like you and understand your talent? You are very much mistaken. We have tried this together and failed, but as you rightly say I shall not be in the least ruined by the failure. Do you know what will happen? My father will tell me that since I have gained some experience I should go and manage one of the estates and improve the buildings. Then you and I will go together."

Contini smiled suddenly and his bright eyes sparkled. He was profoundly attached to Orsino, and thought perhaps as much of the loss of his companionship as of the destruction of his material hopes in the event of a liquidation.

"If that could be, I should not care what became of the business," he said simply.

"How long do you think we shall last?" asked Orsino after a short pause.

"If business grows worse, as I think it will, we shall last until the first bill that falls due after the doors and windows are put in."

"That is precise, at least."

"It will probably take us into January, or perhaps February."

"But suppose that Del Ferice himself gets into trouble between now and then. If he cannot discount any more, what will happen?"

"We shall fail a little sooner. But you need not be afraid of that. Del Ferice knows what he is about better than we do, better than his confidential clerk, much better than most men of business in Rome. If he fails, he will fail intentionally and at the right moment."

"And do you not think that there is even a remote possibility of an improvement in business, so that nobody will fail at all?"

"No," answered Contini thoughtfully. "I do not think so. It is a paper system and it will go to pieces."

"Why have you not said the same thing before? You must have had this opinion a long time."

"I did not believe that Ronco could fail. An accident opens the eyes."

Orsino had almost decided to let matters go on but he found some difficulty in actually making up his mind. In spite of Contini's assurances he could not get rid of the idea that he was under an obligation to Del Ferice. Once, at least, he thought of going directly to Ugo and asking for a clear explanation of the whole affair. But Ugo was not in town, as he knew, and the impossibility of going at once made it improbable that Orsino would go at all. It would not have been a very wise move, for Del Ferice could easily deny the story, seeing that the paper was all in the bank's name, and he would probably have visited the indiscretion upon the unfortunate clerk.

In the long silence which followed, Orsino relapsed into his former despondency. After all, whether he confessed his failure or not, he had undeniably failed and been played upon from the first, and he admitted it to himself without attempting to spare his vanity, and his self-contempt was great and painful. The fact that he had grown from a boy to a man during his experience did not make it easier to bear such wounds, which are felt more keenly by the strong than by the weak when they are real.

As the day wore on the longing to see Maria Consuelo grew upon him until he felt that he had never before wished to be with her as he wished it now. He had no intention of telling her his trouble but he needed the assurance of an ever ready sympathy which he so often saw in her eyes, and which was always there for him when he asked it. When there is love there is reliance, whether expressed or not, and where there is reliance, be it ever so slender, there is comfort for many ills of body, mind and soul.

CHAPTER XXII

Orsino felt suddenly relieved when he had left his office in the afternoon. Contini's gloomy mood was contagious, and so long as Orsino was with him it was impossible not to share the architect's view of affairs. Alone, however, things did not seem so bad. As a matter of fact it was almost impossible for the young man to give up all his illusions concerning his own success in one moment, and to believe himself the dupe of his own blind vanity instead of regarding himself as the winner in the fight for independence of thought and action. He could not deny the facts Contini alleged. He had to admit that he was apparently in Del Ferice's power, unless he appealed to his own people for assistance. He was driven to acknowledge that he had made a great mistake. But he could not altogether distrust himself and he fancied that after all, with a fair share of luck, he might prove a match for Ugo on the financier's own ground. He had learned to have confidence in his own powers and judgment, and as he walked away from the office every moment strengthened his determination to struggle on with such resources as he might be able to command, so long as there should be a possibility of action of any sort. He felt, too, that more depended upon his success than the mere satisfaction of his vanity. If he failed, he might lose Maria Consuelo as well as his self-respect: He had that sensation, familiar enough to many young men when extremely in love, that in order to be loved in return one must succeed, and that a single failure endangers the stability of a passion which, if it be honest, has nothing to do with failure or success. At Orsino's age, and with his temper, it is hard to believe that pity is more closely akin to love than admiration.

Gradually the conviction reasserted itself that he could fight his way through unaided, and his spirits rose as he approached the more crowded quarters of the city on his way to the hotel where Maria Consuelo was stopping. Not even the yells of the newsboys affected him, as they announced the failure of the great contractor Ronco and offered, in a second edition, a complete account of the bankruptcy. It struck him indeed that before long the same brazen voices might be screaming out the news that Andrea Contini and Company had come to grief. But the idea lent a sense of danger to the situation which Orsino did not find unpleasant. The greater the difficulty the greater the merit in overcoming it, and the greater therefore the admiration he should get from the woman he loved. His position was certainly an odd one, and many men would not have felt the excitement which he experienced. The financial side of the question was strangely indifferent to him, who knew himself backed by the great fortune of his family, and believed that his ultimate loss could only be the small sum with which he had begun his operations. But the moral risk seemed enormous and grew in importance as he thought of it.

He found Maria Consuelo looking pale and weary. She evidently had no intention of going out that day, for she wore a morning gown and was established upon a lounge with books and flowers beside her as though she did not mean to move. She was not reading, however. Orsino was startled by the sadness in her face.

She looked fixedly into his eyes as she gave him her hand, and he sat down beside her.

"I am glad you are come," she said at last, in a low voice. "I have been hoping all day that you would come early."

"I would have come this morning if I had dared," answered Orsino.

She looked at him again, and smiled faintly.

"I have a great deal to say to you," she began. Then she hesitated as though uncertain where to begin.

"And I—" Orsino tried to take her hand, but she withdrew it.

"Yes, but do not say it. At least, not now."

"Why not, dear one? May I not tell you how I love you? What is it, love? You are so sad to-day. Has anything happened?"

His voice grew soft and tender as he spoke, bending to her ear. She pushed him gently back.

"You know what has happened," she answered. "It is no wonder that I am sad."

"I do not understand you, dear. Tell me what it is."

"I told you too much yesterday—"

"Too much?"

"Far too much."

"Are you going to unsay it?"

"How can I?"

She turned her face away and her fingers played nervously with her laces.

"No—indeed, neither of us can unsay such words," said Orsino. "But I do not understand you yet, darling. You must tell me what you mean to-day."

"You know it all. It is because you will not understand—"

Orsino's face changed and his voice took another tone when he spoke.

"Are you playing with me, Consuelo?" he asked gravely.

She started slightly and grew paler than before.

"You are not kind," she said. "I am suffering very much. Do not make it harder."

"I am suffering, too. You mean me to understand that you regret what happened yesterday and that you wish to take back your words, that whether you love me or not, you mean to act and appear as though you did not, and that I am to behave as though nothing had happened. Do you think that would be easy? And do you think I do not suffer at the mere idea of it?"

"Since it must be—"

"There is no must," answered Orsino with energy. "You would ruin your life and mine for the mere shadow of a memory which you choose to take for a binding promise. I will not let you do it."

"You will not?" She looked at him quickly with an expression of resistance.

"No—I will not," he repeated. "We have too much at stake. You shall not lose all for both of us."

"You are wrong, dear one," she said, with sudden softness. "If you love me, you should believe me and trust me. I can give you nothing but unhappiness—"

"You have given me the only happiness I ever knew—and you ask me to believe that you could make me unhappy in any way except by not loving me! Consuelo—my darling—are you out of your senses?"

"No. I am too much in them. I wish I were not. If I were mad I should—"

"What?"

"Never mind. I will not even say it. No—do not try to take my hand, for I will not give it to you. Listen, Orsino—be reasonable, listen to me—"

"I will try and listen."

But Maria Consuelo did not speak at once. Possibly she was trying to collect her thoughts.

"What have you to say, dearest?" asked Orsino at length. "I will try to understand."

"You must understand. I will make it all clear to you and then you will see it as I do."

"And then—what?"

"And then we must part," she said in a low voice.

Orsino said nothing, but shook his head incredulously.

"Yes," repeated Maria Consuelo, "we must not see each other any more after this. It has been all my fault. I shall leave Rome and not come back again. It will be best for you and I will make it best for me."

"You talk very easily of parting."

"Do I? Every word is a wound. Do I look as though I were indifferent?"

Orsino glanced at her pale face and tearful eyes.

"No, dear," he said softly.

"Then do not call me heartless. I have more heart than you think—and it is breaking. And do not say that I do not love you. I love you better than you know—better than you will be loved again when you are older—and happier, perhaps. Yes, I know what you want to say. Well, dear—you love me, too. Yes, I know it. Let there be no unkind words and no doubts between us to-day. I think it is our last day together."

"For God's sake, Consuelo—"

"We shall see. Now let me speak—if I can. There are three reasons why you and I should not marry. I have thought of them through all last night and all to-day, and I know them. The first is my solemn vow to the dying man who loved me so well and who asked nothing but that—whose wife I never was, but whose name I bear. Think me mad, superstitious—what you will—I cannot break that promise. It was almost an oath not to love, and if it was I have broken it. But the rest I can keep, and will. The next reason is that I am older than you. I might forget that, I have forgotten it more than once, but the time will come soon when you will remember it."

Orsino made an angry gesture and would have spoken, but she checked him.

"Pass that over, since we are both young. The third reason is harder to tell and no power on earth can explain it away. I am no match for you in birth, Orsino—"

The young man interrupted her now, and fiercely.

"Do you dare to think that I care what your birth may be?" he asked.

"There are those who do care, even if you do not, dear one," she answered quietly.

"And what is their caring to you or me?"

"It is not so small a matter as you think. I am not talking of a mere difference in rank. It is worse than that. I do not really know who I am. Do you understand? I do not know who my mother was nor whether she is alive or dead, and before I was married I did not bear my father's name."

"But you know your father—you know his name at least?"

"Yes."

"Who is he?" Orsino could hardly pronounce the words of the question.

"Count Spicca."

Maria Consuelo spoke quietly, but her fingers trembled nervously and she watched Orsino's face in evident distress and anxiety. As for Orsino, he was almost dumb with amazement.

"Spicca! Spicca your father!" he repeated indistinctly.

In all his many speculations as to the tie which existed between Maria Consuelo and the old duellist, he had never thought of this one.

"Then you never suspected it?" asked Maria Consuelo.

"How should I? And your own father killed your husband—good Heavens! What a story!"

"You know now. You see for yourself how impossible it is that I should marry you."

In his excitement Orsino had risen and was pacing the room. He scarcely heard her last words, and did not say anything in reply. Maria Consuelo lay quite still upon the lounge, her hands clasped tightly together and straining upon each other.

"You see it all now," she said again. This time his attention was arrested and he stopped before her.

"Yes. I see what you mean. But I do not see it as you see it. I do not see that any of these things you have told me need hinder our marriage."

Maria Consuelo did not move, but her expression changed. The light stole slowly into her face and lingered there, not driving away the sadness but illuminating it.

"And would you have the courage, in spite of your family and of society, to marry me, a woman practically nameless, older than yourself—"

"I not only would, but I will," answered Orsino.

"You cannot—but I thank you, dear," said Maria Consuelo.

He was standing close beside her. She took his hand and tenderly touched it with her lips. He started and drew it back, for no woman had ever kissed his hand.

"You must not do that!" he exclaimed, instinctively.

"And why not, if I please?" she asked, raising her eyebrows with a little affectionate laugh.

"I am not good enough to kiss your hand, darling—still less to let you kiss mine. Never mind—we were talking—where were we?"

"You were saying—" But he interrupted her.

"What does it matter, when I love you so, and you love me?" he asked passionately.

He knelt beside her as she lay on the lounge and took her hands, holding them and drawing her towards him. She resisted and turned her face away.

"No—no! It matters too much—let me go, it only makes it worse!"

"Makes what worse?"

"Parting—"

"We will not part. I will not let you go!"

But still she struggled with her hands and he, fearing to hurt them in his grasp, let them slip away with a lingering touch.

"Get up," she said. "Sit here, beside me—a little further—there. We can talk better so."

"I cannot talk at all—"

"Without holding my hands?"

"Why should I not?"

"Because I ask you. Please, dear—"

She drew back on the lounge, raised herself a little and turned her face to him. Again, as his eyes met hers, he leaned forward quickly, as though he would leave his seat. But she checked him, by an imperative glance and a gesture. He was unreasonable and had no right to be annoyed, but something in her manner chilled him and pained him in a way he could not have explained. When he spoke there was a shade of change in the tone of his voice.

"The things you have told me do not influence me in the least," he said with more calmness than he had yet shown. "What you believe to be the most important reason is no reason at all to me. You are Count Spicca's daughter. He is an old friend of my father—not that it matters very materially, but it may make everything easier. I will go to him to-day and tell him that I wish to marry you—"

"You will not do that!" exclaimed Maria Consuelo in a tone of alarm.

"Yes, I will. Why not? Do you know what he once said to me? He told me he wished we might take a fancy to each other, because, as he expressed it, we should be so well matched."

"Did he say that?" asked Maria Consuelo gravely.

"That or something to the same effect. Are you surprised? What surprises me is that I should never have guessed the relation between you. Now your father is a very honourable man. What he said meant something, and when he said it he meant that our marriage would seem natural to him and to everybody. I will go and talk to him. So much for your great reason. As for the second you gave, it is absurd. We are of the same age, to all intents and purposes."

"I am not twenty-three years old."

"And I am not quite two and twenty. Is that a difference? So much for that. Take the third, which you put first. Seriously, do you think that any intelligent being would consider you bound by such a promise? Do you mean to say that a young girl—you were nothing more—has a right to throw away her life out of sentiment by making a promise of that kind? And to whom? To a man who is not her husband, and never can be, because he is dying. To a man just not indifferent to her, to a man—"

Maria Consuelo raised herself and looked full at Orsino. Her face was extremely pale and her eyes were suddenly dark and gleamed.

"Don Orsino, you have no right to talk to me in that way. I loved him—no one knows how I loved him!"

There was no mistaking the tone and the look. Orsino felt again and more strongly, the chill and the pain he had felt before. He was silent for a moment. Maria Consuelo looked at him a second longer, and then let her head fall back upon the cushion. But the expression which had come into her face did not change at once.

"Forgive me," said Orsino after a pause. "I had not quite understood. The only imaginable reason which could make our marriage impossible would be that. If you loved him so well—if you loved him in such a way as to prevent you from loving me as I love you—why then, you may be right after all."

In the silence which followed, he turned his face away and gazed at the window. He had spoken quietly enough and his expression, strange to say, was calm and thoughtful. It is not always easy for a woman to understand a man, for men soon learn to conceal what hurts them but take little trouble to hide their happiness, if they are honest. A man more often betrays himself by a look of pleasure than by an expression of disappointment. It was thought manly to bear pain in silence long before it became fashionable to seem indifferent to joy.

Orsino's manner displeased Maria Consuelo. It was too quiet and cold and she thought he cared less than he really did.

"You say nothing," he said at last.

"What shall I say? You speak of something preventing me from loving you as you love me. How can I tell how much you love me?"

"Do you not see it? Do you not feel it?" Orsino's tone warmed again as he turned towards her, but he was conscious of an effort. Deeply as he loved her, it was not natural for him to speak passionately just at that moment, but he knew she expected it and he did his best. She was disappointed.

"Not always," she answered with a little sigh.

"You do not always believe that I love you?"

"I did not say that. I am not always sure that you love me as much as you think you do—you imagine a great deal."

"I did not know it."

"Yes—sometimes. I am sure it is so."

"And how am I to prove that you are wrong and I am right?"

"How should I know? Perhaps time will show."

"Time is too slow for me. There must be some other way."

"Find it then," said Maria Consuelo, smiling rather sadly.

"I will."

He meant what he said, but the difficulty of the problem perplexed him and there was not enough conviction in his voice. He was thinking rather of the matter itself than of what he said. Maria Consuelo fanned herself slowly and stared at the wall.

"If you doubt so much," said Orsino at last, "I have the right to doubt a little too. If you loved me well enough you would promise to marry me. You do not."

There was a short pause. At last Maria Consuelo closed her fan, looked at it and spoke.

"You say my reason is not good. Must I go all over it again? It seems a good one to me. Is it incredible to you that a woman should love twice? Such things have happened before. Is it incredible to you that, loving one person, a woman should respect the memory of another and a solemn promise given to that other? I should respect myself less if I did not. That it is all my fault I will admit, if you like—that I should never have received you as I did—I grant it all—that I was weak yesterday, that I am weak to-day, that I should be weak to-morrow if I let this go on. I am sorry. You can take a little of the blame if you are generous enough, or vain enough. You have tried hard to make me love you and you have succeeded, for I love you very much. So much the worse for me. It must end now."

"You do not think of me, when you say that."

"Perhaps I think more of you than you know—or will understand. I am older than you—do not interrupt me! I am older, for a woman is always older than a man in some things. I know what will happen, what will certainly happen in time if we do not part. You will grow jealous of a shadow and I shall never be able to tell you that this same shadow is not dear to me. You will come to hate what I have loved and love still, though it does not prevent me from loving you too—"

"But less well," said Orsino rather harshly.

"You would believe that, at least, and the thought would always be between us."

"If you loved me as much, you would not hesitate. You would marry me living, as you married him dead."

"If there were no other reason against it—" She stopped.

"There is no other reason," said Orsino insisting.

Maria Consuelo shook her head but said nothing and a long silence followed. Orsino sat still, watching her and wondering what was passing in her mind. It seemed to him, and perhaps rightly, that if she were really in earnest and loved him with all her heart, the reasons she gave for a separation were far from sufficient. He had not even much faith in her present obstinacy and he did not believe that she would really go away. It was incredible that any woman could be so capricious as she chose to be. Her calmness, or what appeared to him her calmness, made it even less probable, he thought, that she meant to part from him. But the thought alone was enough to disturb him seriously. He had suffered a severe shock with outward composure but not without inward suffering, followed naturally enough by something like angry resentment. As he viewed the situation, Maria Consuelo had alternately drawn him on and disappointed him from the very beginning; she had taken delight in forcing him to speak out his love, only to chill him the next moment, or the next day, with the certainty that she did not love him sincerely. Just then he would have preferred not to put into words the thoughts of her that crossed his mind. They would have expressed a disbelief in her character which he did not really feel and an opinion of his own judgment which he would rather not have accepted.

He even went so far, in his anger, as to imagine what would happen if he suddenly rose to go. She would put on that sad look of hers and give him her hand coldly. Then just as he reached the door she would call him back, only to send him away again. He would find on the following day that she had not left town after all, or, at most, that she had gone to Florence for a day or two, while the workmen completed the furnishing of her apartment. Then she would come back and would meet him just as though there had never been anything between them.

The anticipation was so painful to him that he wished to have it realised and over as soon as possible, and he looked at her again before rising from his seat. He could hardly believe that she was the same woman who had stood with him, watching the thunderstorm, on the previous afternoon.

He saw that she was pale, but she was not facing the light and the expression of her face was not distinctly visible. On the whole, he fancied that her look was one of indifference. Her hands lay idly upon her fan and by the drooping of her lids she seemed to be looking at them. The full, curved lips were closed, but not drawn in as though in pain, nor pouting as though in displeasure. She appeared to be singularly calm. After hesitating another moment Orsino rose to his feet. He had made up his mind what to say, for it was little enough, but his voice trembled a little.

"Good-bye, Madame."

Maria Consuelo started slightly and looked up, as though to see whether he really meant to go at that moment. She had no idea that he really thought of taking her at her word and parting then and there. She did not realise how true it was that she was much older than he and she had never believed him to be as impulsive as he sometimes seemed.

"Do not go yet," she said, instinctively.

"Since you say that we must part—" he stopped, as though leaving her to finish the sentence in imagination.

A frightened look passed quickly over Maria Consuelo's face. She made as though she would have taken his hand, then drew back her own and bit her lip, not angrily but as though she were controlling something.

"Since you insist upon our parting," Orsino said, after a short, strained silence, "it is better that it should be got over at once." In spite of himself his voice was still unsteady.

"I did not—no—yes, it is better so."

"Then good-bye, Madame."

It was impossible for her to understand all that had passed in his mind while he had sat beside her, after the previous conversation had ended. His abruptness and coldness were incomprehensible to her.

"Good-bye, then—Orsino."

For a moment her eyes rested on his. It was the sad look he had anticipated, and she put out her hand now. Surely, he thought, if she loved him she would not let him go so easily. He took her fingers and would have raised them to his lips when they suddenly closed on his, not with the passionate, loving pressure of yesterday, but firmly and quietly, as though they would not be disobeyed, guiding him again to his seat close beside her. He sat down.

"Good-bye, then, Orsino," she repeated, not yet relinquishing her hold. "Good-bye, dear, since it must be good-bye—but not good-bye as you said it. You shall not go until you can say it differently."

She let him go now and changed her own position. Her feet slipped to the ground and she leaned with her elbow upon the head of the lounge, resting her cheek against her hand. She was nearer to him now than before and their eyes met as they faced each other. She had certainly not chosen her attitude with any second thought of her own appearance, but as Orsino looked into her face he saw again clearly all the beauties that he had so long admired, the passionate eyes, the full, firm mouth, the broad brow, the luminous white skin—all beauties in themselves though not, together, making real beauty in her case. And beyond these he saw and felt over them all and through them all the charm that fascinated him, appealing as it were to him in particular of all men as it could not appeal to another. He was still angry, disturbed out of his natural self and almost out of his passion, but he felt none the less that Maria Consuelo could hold him if she pleased, as long as a shadow of affection for her remained in him, and perhaps longer. When she spoke, he knew what she meant, and he did not interrupt her nor attempt to answer.

"I have meant all I have said to-day," she continued. "Do not think it is easy for me to say more. I would give all I have to give to take back yesterday, for yesterday was my great mistake. I am only a woman and you will forgive me. I do what I am doing now, for your sake—God knows it is not for mine. God knows how hard it is for me to part from you. I am in earnest, you see. You believe me now."

Her voice was steady but the tears were already welling over.

"Yes, dear, I believe you," Orsino answered softly. Women's tears are a great solvent of man's ill temper.

"As for this being right and best, this parting, you will see it as I do sooner or later. But you do believe that I love you, dearly, tenderly, very—well, no matter how—you believe it?"

"I believe it—"

"Then say 'good-bye, Consuelo'—and kiss me once—for what might have been."

Orsino half rose, bent down and kissed her cheek.

"Good-bye, Consuelo," he said, almost whispering the words into her ear. In his heart he did not think she meant it. He still expected that she would call him back.

"It is good-bye, dear—believe it—remember it!" Her voice shook a little now.

"Good-bye, Consuelo," he repeated.

With a loving look that meant no good-bye he drew back and went to the door. He laid his hand on the handle and paused. She did not speak. Then he looked at her again. Her head had fallen back against a cushion and her eyes were half closed. He waited a second and a keen pain shot through him. Perhaps she was in earnest after all. In an instant he had recrossed the room and was on his knees beside her trying to take her hands.

"Consuelo—darling—you do not really mean it! You cannot, you will not—"

He covered her hands with kisses and pressed them to his heart. For a few moments she made no movement, but her eyelids quivered. Then she sprang to her feet, pushing him back violently as he rose with her, and turning her face from him.

"Go—go!" she cried wildly. "Go—let me never see you again—never, never!"

Before he could stop her, she had passed him with a rush like a swallow on the wing and was gone from the room.

CHAPTER XXIII

Orsino was not in an enviable frame of mind when he left the hotel. It is easier to bear suffering when one clearly understands all its causes, and distinguishes just how great a part of it is inevitable and how great a part may be avoided or mitigated. In the present case there was much in the situation which it passed his power to analyse or comprehend. He still possessed the taste for discovering motives in the actions of others as well as in his own, but many months of a busy life had dulled the edge of the artificial logic in which he had formerly delighted, while greatly sharpening his practical wit. Artificial analysis supplies from the imagination the details lacking in facts, but common sense needs something more tangible upon which to work. Orsino felt that the chief circumstance which had determined Maria Consuelo's conduct had escaped him, and he sought in vain to detect it.

He rejected the supposition that she was acting upon a caprice, that she had yesterday believed it possible to marry him, while a change of humour made marriage seem out of the question to-day. She was as capricious as most women, perhaps, but not enough so for that. Besides, she had been really consistent. Not even yesterday had she been shaken for a moment in her resolution not to be Orsino's wife. To-day had confirmed yesterday therefore. However Orsino might have still doubted her intention when he had gone to her side for the last time, her behaviour then and her final words had been unmistakable. She meant to leave Rome at once.

Yet the reasons she had given him for her conduct were not sufficient in his eyes. The difference of age was so small that it could safely be disregarded. Her promise to the dying Aranjuez was an engagement, he thought, by which no person of sense should expect her to abide. As for the question of her birth, he relied on that speech of Spicca's which he so well remembered. Spicca might have spoken the words thoughtlessly, it was true, and believing that Orsino would never, under any circumstances whatever, think seriously of marrying Maria Consuelo. But Spicca was not a man who often spoke carelessly, and what he said generally meant at least as much as it appeared to mean.

It was doubtless true that Maria Consuelo was ignorant of her mother's name. Nevertheless, it was quite possible that her mother had been Spicca's wife. Spicca's life was said to be full of strange events not generally known. But though his daughter might, and doubtless did believe herself a nameless child, and, as such, no match for the heir of the Saracinesca, Orsino could not see why she should have insisted upon a parting so sudden, so painful and so premature. She knew as much yesterday and had known it all along. Why, if she possessed such strength of character, had she allowed matters to go so far when she could easily have interrupted the course of events at an earlier period? He did not admit that she perhaps loved him so much as to have been carried away by her passion until she found herself on the point of doing him an injury by marrying him, and that her love was strong enough to induce her to sacrifice herself at the critical moment. Though he loved her much he did not believe her to be heroic in any way. On the contrary, he said to himself that if she were sincere, and if her love were at all like his own, she would let no obstacle stand in the way of it. To him, the test of love must be its utter recklessness. He could not believe that a still better test may be, and is, the constant forethought for the object of love, and the determination to protect that object from all danger in the present and from all suffering in the future, no matter at what cost.

Perhaps it is not easy to believe that recklessness is a manifestation of the second degree of passion, while the highest shows itself in painful sacrifice. Yet the most daring act of chivalry never called for half the bravery shown by many a martyr at the stake, and if courage be a measure of true passion, the passion which will face life-long suffering to save its object from unhappiness or degradation is greater than the passion which, for the sake of possessing its object, drags it into danger and the risk of ruin. It may be that all this is untrue, and that the action of these two imaginary individuals, the one sacrificing himself, the other endangering the loved one, is dependent upon the balance of the animal, intellectual and moral elements in each. We do not know much about the causes of what we feel, in spite of modern analysis; but the heart rarely deceives us, when we can see the truth for ourselves, into bestowing the more praise upon the less brave of two deeds. But we do not often see the truth as it is. We know little of the lives of others, but we are apt to think that other people understand our own very well, including our good deeds if we have done any, and we expect full measure of credit for these, and the utmost allowance of charity for our sins. In other words we desire our neighbour to combine a power of forgiveness almost divine with a capacity for flattery more than parasitic. That is why we are not easily satisfied with our acquaintances and that is why our friends do not always turn out to be truthful persons. We ask too much for the low price we offer, and if we insist we get the imitation.

Orsino loved Maria Consuelo with all his heart, as much as a young man of little more than one and twenty can love the first woman to whom he is seriously attached. There was nothing heroic in the passion, perhaps, nothing which could ultimately lead to great results. But it was a strong love, nevertheless, with much, of devotion in it and some latent violence. If he did not marry Maria Consuelo, it was not likely that he would ever love again in exactly the same way. His next love would be either far better or far worse, far nobler or far baser—perhaps a little less human in either case.

He walked slowly away from the hotel, unconscious of the people in the street and not thinking of the direction he took. His brain was in a whirl and his thoughts seemed to revolve round some central point upon which they could not concentrate themselves even for a second. The only thing of which he was sure was that Maria Consuelo had taken herself from him suddenly and altogether, leaving him with a sense of loneliness which he had not known before. He had gone to her in considerable distress about his affairs, with the certainty of finding sympathy and perhaps advice. He came away, as some men have returned from a grave accident, apparently unscathed it may be, but temporarily deprived of some one sense, of sight, or hearing, or touch. He was not sure that he was awake, and his troubled reflexions came back by the same unvarying round to the point he had reached the first time—if Maria Consuelo really loved him, she would not let such obstacles as she spoke of hinder her union with him.

For a time Orsino was not conscious of any impulse to act. Gradually, however, his real nature asserted itself, and he remembered how he had told her not long ago that if she went away he would follow her, and how he had said that the world was small and that he would soon find her again. It would undoubtedly be a simple matter to accompany her, if she left Rome. He could easily ascertain the hour of her intended departure and that alone would tell him the direction she had chosen. When she found that she had not escaped him she would very probably give up the attempt and come back, her humour would change and his own eloquence would do the rest.

He stopped in his walk, looked at his watch and glanced about him. He was at some distance from the hotel and it was growing dusk, for the days were already short. If Maria Consuelo really meant to leave Rome precipitately, she might go by the evening train to Paris and in that case the people of the hotel would have been informed of her intended departure.

Orsino only admitted the possibility of her actually going away while believing in his heart that she would remain. He slowly retraced his steps, and it was seven o'clock before he asked the hotel porter by what train Madame d'Aranjuez was leaving. The porter did not know whether the lady was going north or south, but he called another man, who went in search of a third, who disappeared for some time.

"Is it sure that Madame d'Aranjuez goes to-night?" asked Orsino trying to look indifferent.

"Quite sure. Her rooms will be free to-morrow."

Orsino turned away and slowly paced up and down the marble pavement between the tall plants, waiting for the messenger to come back.

"Madame d'Aranjuez leaves at nine forty-five," said the man, suddenly reappearing.

Orsino hesitated a moment, and then made up his mind.

"Ask Madame if she will receive me for a moment," he said, producing a card.

The servant went away and again Orsino walked backwards and forwards, pale now and very nervous. She was really going, and was going north—probably to Paris.

"Madame regrets infinitely that she is not able to receive the Signor Prince," said the man in black at Orsino's elbow. "She is making her preparations for the journey."

"Show me where I can write a note," said Orsino, who had expected the answer.

He was shown into the reading-room and writing materials were set before him. He hurriedly wrote a few words to Maria Consuelo, without form of address and without signature.

"I will not let you go without me. If you will not see me, I will be in the train, and I will not leave you, wherever you go. I am in earnest."

He looked at the sheet of note-paper and wondered that he should find nothing more to say. But he had said all he meant, and sealing the little note he sent it up to Maria Consuelo with a request for an immediate answer. Just then the dinner bell of the hotel was rung. The reading-room was deserted. He waited five minutes, then ten, nervously turning over the newspapers and reviews on the long table, but quite unable to read even the printed titles. He rang and asked if there had been no answer to his note. The man was the same whom he had sent before. He said the note had been received at the door by the maid who had said that Madame d'Aranjuez would ring when her answer was ready. Orsino dismissed the servant and waited again. It crossed his mind that the maid might have pocketed the note and said nothing about it, for reasons of her own. He had almost determined to go upstairs and boldly enter the sitting-room, when the door opposite to him opened and Maria Consuelo herself appeared.

She was dressed in a dark close-fitting travelling costume, but she wore no hat. Her face was quite colourless and looked if possible even more unnaturally pale by contrast with her bright auburn hair. She shut the door behind her and stood still, facing Orsino in the glare of the electric lights.

"I did not mean to see you again," she said, slowly. "You have forced me to it."

Orsino made a step forward and tried to take her hand, but she drew back. The slight uncertainty often visible in the direction of her glance had altogether disappeared and her eyes met Orsino's directly and fearlessly.

"Yes," he answered. "I have forced you to it. I know it, and you cannot reproach me if I have. I will not leave you. I am going with you wherever you go."

He spoke calmly, considering the great emotion he felt, and there was a quiet determination in his words and tone which told how much he was in earnest. Maria Consuelo half believed that she could dominate him by sheer force of will, and she would not give up the idea, even now.

"You will not go with me, you will not even attempt it," she said.

It would have been difficult to guess from her face at that moment that she loved him. Her face was pale and the expression was almost hard. She held her head high as though she were looking down at him, though he towered above her from his shoulders.

"You do not understand me," he answered, quietly. "When I say that I will go with you, I mean that I will go."

"Is this a trial of strength?" she asked after a moment's pause.

"If it is, I am not conscious of it. It costs me no effort to go—it would cost me much to stay behind—too much."

He stood quite still before her, looking steadily into her eyes. There was a short silence, and then she suddenly looked down, moved and turned away, beginning to walk slowly about. The room was large, and he paced the floor beside her, looking down at her bent head.

"Will you stay if I ask you to?"

The question came in a lower and softer tone than she had used before.

"I will go with you," answered Orsino as firmly as ever.

"Will you do nothing for my asking?"

"I will do anything but that."

"But that is all I ask."

"You are asking the impossible."

"There are many reasons why you should not come with me. Have you thought of them all?"

"No."

"You should. You ought to know, without being told by me, that you would be doing me a great injustice and a great injury in following me. You ought to know what the world will say of it. Remember that I am alone."

"I will marry you."

"I have told you that it is impossible—no, do not answer me! I will not go over all that again. I am going away to-night. That is the principal thing—the only thing that concerns you. Of course, if you choose, you can get into the same train and pursue me to the end of the world. I cannot prevent you. I thought I could, but I was mistaken. I am alone. Remember that, Orsino. You know as well as I what will be said— and the fact is sure to be known."

"People will say that I am following you—"

"They will say that we are gone together, for every one will have reason to say it. Do you suppose that nobody is aware of our—our intimacy during the last month?"

"Why not say our love?"

"Because I hope no one knows of that—well, if they do—Orsino, be kind! Let me go alone—as a man of honour, do not injure me by leaving Rome with me, nor by following me when I am gone!"

She stopped and looked up into his face with an imploring glance. To tell the truth, Orsino had not foreseen that she might appeal to his honour, alleging the danger to her reputation. He bit his lip and avoided her eyes. It was hard to yield, and to yield so quickly, as it seemed to him.

"How long will you stay away?" he asked in a constrained voice.

"I shall not come back at all."

He wondered at the firmness of her tone and manner. Whatever the real ground of her resolution might be, the resolution itself had gained strength since they had parted little more than an hour earlier. The belief suddenly grew upon him again that she did not love him.

"Why are you going at all?" he asked abruptly. "If you loved me at all, you would stay."

She drew a sharp breath and clasped her hands nervously together.

"I should stay if I loved you less. But I have told you—I will not go over it all again. This must end—this saying good-bye! It is easier to end it at once."

"Easier for you—"

"You do not know what you are saying. You will know some day. If you can bear this, I cannot."

"Then stay—if you love me, as you say you do."

"As I say I do!"

Her eyes grew very grave and sad as she stopped and looked at him again. Then she held out both her hands.

"I am going, now. Good-bye."

The blood came back to Orsino's face. It seemed to him that he had reached the crisis of his life and his instinct was to struggle hard against his fate. With a quick movement he caught her in his arms, lifting her from her feet and pressing her close to him.

"You shall not go!"

He kissed her passionately again and again, while she fought to be free, straining at his arms with her small white hands and trying to turn her face from him.

"Why do you struggle? It is of no use." He spoke in very soft deep tones, close to her ear.

She shook her head desperately and still did her best to slip from him, though she might as well have tried to break iron clamps with her fingers.

"It is of no use," he repeated, pressing her still more closely to him.

"Let me go!" she cried, making a violent effort, as fruitless as the last.

"No!"

Then she was quite still, realising that she had no chance with him.

"Is it manly to be brutal because you are strong?" she asked. "You hurt me."

Orsino's arms relaxed, and he let her go. She drew a long breath and moved a step backward and towards the door.

"Good-bye," she said again. But this time she did not hold out her hand, though she looked long and fixedly into his face.

Orsino made a movement as though he would have caught her again. She started and put out her hand behind her towards the latch. But he did not touch her. She softly opened the door, looked at him once more and went out.

When he realised that she was gone he sprang after her, calling her by name.

"Consuelo!"

There were a few people walking in the broad passage. They stared at Orsino, but he did not heed them as he passed by. Maria Consuelo was not there, and he understood in a moment that it would be useless to seek her further. He stood still a moment, entered the reading-room again, got his hat and left the hotel without looking behind him.

All sorts of wild ideas and schemes flashed through his brain, each more absurd and impracticable than the last. He thought of going back and finding Maria Consuelo's maid—he might bribe her to prevent her mistress's departure. He thought of offering the driver of the train an enormous sum to do some injury to his engine before reaching the first station out of Rome. He thought of stopping Maria Consuelo's carriage on her way to the tram and taking her by main force to his father's house. If she were compromised in such a way, she would be almost obliged to marry him. He afterwards wondered at the stupidity of his own inventions on that evening, but at the time nothing looked impossible.

He bethought him of Spicca. Perhaps the old man possessed some power over his daughter after all and could prevent her flight if he chose. There were yet nearly two hours left before the train started. If worst came to worst, Orsino could still get to the station at the last minute and leave Rome with her.

He took a passing cab and drove to Spicca's lodgings. The count was at home, writing a letter by the light of a small lamp. He looked up in surprise as Orsino entered, then rose and offered him a chair.

"What has happened, my friend?" he asked, glancing curiously at the young man's face.

"Everything," answered Orsino. "I love Madame d'Aranjuez, she loves me, she absolutely refuses to marry me and she is going to Paris at a quarter to ten. I know she is your daughter and I want you to prevent her from leaving. That is all, I believe."

Spicca's cadaverous face did not change, but the hollow eyes grew bright and fixed their glance on an imaginary point at an immense distance, and the thin hand that lay on the edge of the table closed slowly upon the projecting wood. For a few moments he said nothing, but when he spoke he seemed quite calm.

"If she has told you that she is my daughter," he said, "I presume that she has told you the rest. Is that true?"

Orsino was impatient for Spicca to take some immediate action, but he understood that the count had a right to ask the question.

"She has told me that she does not know her mother's name, and that you killed her husband."

"Both these statements are perfectly true at all events. Is that all you know?"

"All? Yes—all of importance. But there is no time to be lost. No one but you can prevent her from leaving Rome to-night. You must help me quickly."

Spicca looked gravely at Orsino and shook his head. The light that had shone in his eyes for a moment was gone, and he was again his habitual, melancholy, indifferent self.

"I cannot stop her," he said, almost listlessly.

"But you can—you will, you must!" cried Orsino laying a hand on the old man's thin arm. "She must not go—"

"Better that she should, after all. Of what use is it for her to stay? She is quite right. You cannot marry her."

"Cannot marry her? Why not? It is not long since you told me very plainly that you wished I would marry her. You have changed your mind very suddenly, it seems to me, and I would like to know why. Do you remember all you said to me?"

"Yes, and I was in earnest, as I am now. And I was wrong in telling you what I thought at the time."

"At the time! How can matters have changed so suddenly?"

"I do not say that matters have changed. I have. That is the important thing. I remember the occasion of our conversation very well. Madame d'Aranjuez had been rather abrupt with, me, and you and I went away together. I forgave her easily enough, for I saw that she was unhappy—then I thought how different her life might be if she were married to you. I also wished to convey to you a warning, and it did not strike me that you would ever seriously contemplate such a marriage."

"I think you are in a certain way responsible for the present situation," answered Orsino. "That is the reason why I come to you for help."

Spicca turned upon the young man rather suddenly.

"There you go too far," he said. "Do you mean to tell me that you have asked that lady to marry you because I suggested it?"

"No, but—"

"Then I am not responsible at all. Besides, you might have consulted me again, if you had chosen. I have not been out of town. I sincerely wish that it were possible—yes, that is quite another matter. But it is not. If Madame d'Aranjuez thinks it is not, from her point of view there are a thousand reasons why I should consider it far more completely out of the question. As for preventing her from leaving Rome I could not do that even were I willing to try."

"Then I will go with her," said Orsino, angrily.

Spicca looked at him in silence for a few moments. Orsino rose to his feet and prepared to go.

"You leave me no choice," he said, as though Spicca had protested.

"Because I cannot and will not stop her? Is that any reason why you should compromise her reputation as you propose to do?"

"It is the best of reasons. She will marry me then, out of necessity."

Spicca rose also, with more alacrity than generally characterised his movements. He stood before the empty fireplace, watching the young man narrowly.

"It is not a good reason," he said, presently, in quiet tones. "You are not the man to do that sort of thing. You are too honourable."

"I do not see anything dishonourable in following the woman I love."

"That depends on the way in which you follow her. If you go quietly home to-night and write to your father that you have decided to go to Paris for a few days and will leave to-morrow, if you make your arrangements like a sensible being and go away like a sane man, I have nothing to say in the matter—"

"I presume not—" interrupted Orsino, facing the old man somewhat fiercely.

"Very well. We will not quarrel yet. We will reserve that pleasure for the moment when you cease to understand me. That way of following her would be bad enough, but no one would have any right to stop you."

"No one has any right to stop me, as it is."

"I beg your pardon. The present circumstances are different. In the first instance the world would say that you were in love with Madame d'Aranjuez and were pursuing her to press your suit—of whatever nature that might be. In the second case the world will assert that you and she, not meaning to be married, have adopted the simple plan of going away together. That implies her consent, and you have no right to let any one imply that. I say, it is not honourable to let people think that a lady is risking her reputation for you and perhaps sacrificing it altogether, when she is in reality trying to escape from you. Am I right, or not?"

"You are ingenious, at all events. You talk as though the whole world were to know in half an hour that I have gone to Paris in the same train with Madame d'Aranjuez. That is absurd!"

"Is it? I think not. Half an hour is little, perhaps, but half a day is enough. You are not an insignificant son of an unknown Roman citizen, nor is Madame d'Aranjuez a person who passes unnoticed. Reporters watch people like you for items of news, and you are perfectly well known by sight. Apart from that, do you think that your servants will not tell your friends' servants of your sudden departure, or that Madame d'Aranjuez' going will not be observed? You ought to know Rome better than that. I ask you again, am I right or wrong?"

"What difference will it make, if we are married immediately?"

"She will never marry you. I am convinced of that."

"How can you know? Has she spoken to you about it?"

"I am the last person to whom she would come."

"Her own father—"

"With limitations. Besides, I had the misfortune to deprive her of the chosen companion of her life, and at a critical moment. She has not forgotten that."

"No she has not," answered Orsino gloomily. The memory of Aranjuez was a sore point. "Why did you kill him?" he asked, suddenly.

"Because he was an adventurer, a liar and a thief—three excellent reasons for killing any man, if one can. Moreover he struck her once—with that silver paper cutter which she insists on using—and I saw it from a distance. Then I killed him. Unluckily I was very angry and made a little mistake, so that he lived twelve hours, and she had time to get a priest and marry him. She always pretends that he struck her in play, by accident, as he was showing her something about fencing. I was in the next room and the door was open—it did not look like play. And she still thinks that he was the paragon of all virtues. He was a handsome devil—something like you, but shorter, with a bad eye. I am glad I killed him."

Spicca had looked steadily at Orsino while speaking. When he ceased, he began to walk about the small room with something of his old energy. Orsino roused himself. He had almost begun to forget his own position in the interest of listening to the count's short story.

"So much for Aranjuez," said Spicca. "Let us hear no more of him. As for this mad plan of yours, you are convinced, I suppose, and you will give it up. Go home and decide in the morning. For my part, I tell you it is useless. She will not marry you. Therefore leave her alone and do nothing which can injure her."

"I am not convinced," answered Orsino doggedly.

"Then you are not your father's son. No Saracinesca that I ever knew would do what you mean to do—would wantonly tarnish the good name of a woman—of a woman who loves him too—and whose only fault is that she cannot marry him."

"That she will not."

"That she cannot."

"Do you give me your word that she cannot?"

"She is legally free to marry whom she pleases, with or without my consent."

"That is all I want to know. The rest is nothing to me—"

"The rest is a great deal. I beg you to consider all I have said, and I am sure that you will, quite sure. There are very good reasons for not telling you or any one else all the details I know in this story—so good that I would rather go to the length of a quarrel with you than give them all. I am an old man, Orsino, and what is left of life does not mean much to me. I will sacrifice it to prevent your opening this door unless you tell me that you give up the idea of leaving Rome to-night."

As he spoke he placed himself before the closed door and faced the young man. He was old, emaciated, physically broken down, and his hands were empty. Orsino was in his first youth, tall, lean, active and very strong, and no coward. He was moreover in an ugly humour and inclined to be violent on much smaller provocation than he had received. But Spicca imposed upon him, nevertheless, for he saw that he was in earnest. Orsino was never afterwards able to recall exactly what passed through his mind at that moment. He was physically able to thrust Spicca aside and to open the door, without so much as hurting him. He did not believe that, even in that case, the old man would have insisted upon the satisfaction of arms, nor would he have been afraid to meet him if a duel had been required. He knew that what withheld him from an act of violence was neither fear nor respect for his adversary's weakness and age. Yet he was quite unable to define the influence which at last broke down his resolution. It was in all probability only the resultant of the argument Spicca had brought to bear and which Maria Consuelo had herself used in the first instance, and of Spicca's calm, undaunted personality.

The crisis did not last long. The two men faced each other for ten seconds and then Orsino turned away with an impatient movement of the shoulders.

"Very well," he said. "I will not go with her."

"It is best so," answered Spicca, leaving the door and returning to his seat.

"I suppose that she will let you know where she is, will she not?" asked Orsino.

"Yes. She will write to me."

"Good-night, then."

"Good-night."

Without shaking hands, and almost without a glance at the old man, Orsino left the room.

CHAPTER XXIV

Orsino walked slowly homeward, trying to collect his thoughts and to reach some distinct determination with regard to the future. He was oppressed by the sense of failure and disappointment and felt inclined to despise himself for his weakness in yielding so easily. To all intents and purposes he had lost Maria Consuelo, and if he had not lost her through his own fault, he had at least tamely abandoned what had seemed like a last chance of winning her back. As he thought of all that had happened he tried to fix some point in the past, at which he might have acted differently, and from which another act of consequence might have begun. But that was not easy. Events had followed each other with a certain inevitable logic, which only looked unreasonable because he suspected the existence of facts beyond his certain knowledge. His great mistake had been in going to Spicca, but nothing could have been more natural, under the circumstances, than his appeal to Maria Consuelo's father, nothing more unexpected than the latter's determined refusal to help him. That there was weight in the argument used by both Spicca and Maria Consuelo herself, he could not deny; but he failed to see why the marriage was so utterly impossible as they both declared it to be. There must be much more behind the visible circumstances than he could guess.

He tried to comfort himself with the assurance that he could leave Rome on the following day, and that Spicca would not refuse to give him Maria Consuelo's address in Paris. But the consolation he derived from the idea was small. He found himself wondering at the recklessness shown by the woman he loved in escaping from him. His practical Italian mind could hardly understand how she could have changed all her plans in a moment, abandoning her half-furnished apartment without a word of notice even to the workmen, throwing over her intention of spending the winter in Rome as though she had not already spent many thousands in preparing her dwelling, and going away, probably, without as much as leaving a representative to wind up her accounts. It may seem strange that a man as much in love as Orsino was should think of such details at such a moment. Perhaps he looked upon them rather as proofs that she meant to come back after all; in any case he thought of them seriously, and even calculated roughly the sum she would be sacrificing if she stayed away.

Beyond all he felt the dismal loneliness which a man can only feel when he is suddenly and effectually parted from the woman he dearly loves, and which is not like any other sensation of which the human heart is capable.

More than once, up to the last possible moment, he was tempted to drive to the station and leave with Maria Consuelo after all, but he would not break the promise he had given Spicca, no matter how weak he had been in giving it.

On reaching his home he was informed, to his great surprise, that San Giacinto was waiting to see him. He could not remember that his cousin had ever before honoured him with a visit and he wondered what could have brought him now and induced him to wait, just at the hour when most people were at dinner.

The giant was reading the evening paper, with the help of a particularly strong cigar.

"I am glad you have come home," he said, rising and taking the young man's outstretched hand. "I should have waited until you did."

"Has anything happened?" asked Orsino nervously. It struck him that San Giacinto might be the bearer of some bad news about his people, and the grave expression on the strongly marked face helped the idea.

"A great deal is happening. The crash has begun. You must get out of your business in less than three days if you can."

Orsino drew a breath of relief at first, and then grew grave in his turn, realising that unless matters were very serious such a man as San Giacinto would not put himself to the inconvenience of coming. San Giacinto was little given to offering advice unasked, still less to interfering in the affairs of others.

"I understand," said Orsino. "You think that everything is going to pieces. I see."

The big man looked at his young cousin with something like pity.

"If I only suspected, or thought—as you put it—that there was to be a collapse of business, I should not have taken the trouble to warn you. The crash has actually begun. If you can save yourself, do so at once."

"I think I can," answered the young man, bravely. But he did not at all see how his salvation was to be accomplished. "Can you tell me a little more definitely what is the matter? Have there been any more failures to-day?"

"My brother-in-law Montevarchi is on the point of stopping payment," said San Giacinto calmly.

"Montevarchi!"

Orsino did not conceal his astonishment.

"Yes. Do not speak of it. And he is in precisely the same position, so far as I can judge of your affairs, as you yourself, though of course he has dealt with sums ten times as great. He will make enormous sacrifices and will pay, I suppose, after all. But he will be quite ruined. He also has worked with Del Fence's bank."

"And the bank refuses to discount any more of his paper?"

"Precisely. Since this afternoon."

"Then it will refuse to discount mine to-morrow."

"Have you acceptances due to-morrow?"

"Yes—not much, but enough to make the trouble. It will be Saturday, too, and we must have money for the workmen."

"Have you not even enough in reserve for that?"

"Perhaps. I cannot tell. Besides, if the bank refuses to renew I cannot draw a cheque."

"I am sorry for you. If I had known yesterday how near the end was, I would have warned you."

"Thanks. I am grateful as it is. Can you give me any advice?"

Orsino had a vague idea that his rich cousin would generously propose to help him out of his difficulties. He was not quite sure whether he could bring himself to accept such assistance, but he more than half expected that it would be offered. In this, however, he was completely mistaken. San Giacinto had not the smallest intention of offering anything more substantial than his opinion. Considering that his wife's brother's liabilities amounted to something like five and twenty millions, this was not surprising. The giant bit his cigar and folded his long arms over his enormous chest, leaning back in the easy chair which creaked under his weight.

"You have tried yourself in business by this time, Orsino," he said, "and you know as well as I what there is to be done. You have three modes of action open to you. You can fail. It is a simple affair enough. The bank will take your buildings for what they will be worth a few months hence, on the day of liquidation. There will be a big deficit, which your father will pay for you and deduct from your share of the division at his death. That is one plan, and seems to me the best. It is perfectly honourable, and you lose by it. Secondly, you can go to your father to-morrow and ask him to lend you money to meet your acceptances and to continue the work until the houses are finished and can be sold. They will ultimately go for a quarter of their value, if you can sell them at all within the year, and you will be in your father's debt, exactly as in the other case. You would avoid the publicity of a failure, but it would cost you more, because the houses will not be worth much more when they are finished than they are now."

"And the third plan—what is it?" inquired Orsino.

"The third way is this. You can go to Del Ferice, and if you are a diplomatist you may persuade him that it is in his interest not to let you fail. I do not think you will succeed, but you can try. If he agrees it will be because he counts on your father to pay in the end, but it is questionable whether Del Ferice's bank can afford to let out any more cash at the present moment. Money is going to be very tight, as they say."

Orsino smoked in silence, pondering over the situation. San Giacinto rose.

"You are warned, at all events," he said. "You will find a great change for the worse in the general aspect of things to-morrow."

"I am much obliged for the warning," answered Orsino. "I suppose I can always find you if I need your advice—and you will advise me?"

"You are welcome to my advice, such as it is, my dear boy. But as for me, I am going towards Naples to-night on business, and I may not be back again for a day or two. If you get into serious trouble before I am here again, you should go to your father at once. He knows nothing of business, and has been sensible enough to keep out of it. The consequence is that he is as rich as ever, and he would sacrifice a great deal rather than see your name dragged into the publicity of a failure. Good-night, and good luck to you."

Thereupon the Titan shook Orsino's hand in his mighty grip and went away. As a matter of fact he was going down to look over one of Montevarchi's biggest estates with a view to buying it in the coming cataclysm, but it would not have been like him to communicate the smallest of his intentions to Orsino, or to any one, not excepting his wife and his lawyer.

Orsino was left to his own devices and meditations. A servant came in and inquired whether he wished to dine at home, and he ordered strong coffee by way of a meal. He was at the age when a man expects to find a way out of his difficulties in an artificial excitement of the nerves.

Indeed, he had enough to disturb him, for it seemed as though all possible misfortunes had fallen upon him at once. He had suffered on the same day the greatest shock to his heart, and the greatest blow to his vanity which he could conceive possible. Maria Consuelo was gone and the failure of his business was apparently inevitable. When he tried to review the three plans which San Giacinto had suggested, he found himself suddenly thinking of the woman he loved and making schemes for following her; but so soon as he had transported himself in imagination to her side and was beginning to hope that he might win her back, he was torn away and plunged again into the whirlpool of business at home, struggling with unheard of difficulties and sinking deeper at every stroke.

A hundred times he rose from his chair and paced the floor impatiently, and a hundred times he threw himself down again, overcome by the hopelessness of the situation. Occasionally he found a little comfort in the reflexion that the night could not last for ever. When the day came he would be driven to act, in one way or another, and he would be obliged to consult his partner, Contini. Then at last his mind would be able to follow one connected train of thought for a time, and he would get rest of some kind.

Little by little, however, and long before the day dawned, the dominating influence asserted itself above the secondary one and he was thinking only of Maria Consuelo. Throughout all that night she was travelling, as she would perhaps travel throughout all the next day and the second night succeeding that. For she was strong and having once determined upon the journey would very probably go to the end of it without stopping to rest. He wondered whether she too were waking through all those long hours, thinking of what she had left behind, or whether she had closed her eyes and found the peace of sleep for which he longed in vain. He thought of her face, softly lighted by the dim lamp of the railway carriage, and fancied he could actually see it with the delicate shadows, the subdued richness of colour, the settled look of sadness. When the picture grew dim, he recalled it by a strong effort, though he knew that each time it rose before his eyes he must feel the same sharp thrust of pain, followed by the same dull wave of hopeless misery which had ebbed and flowed again so many times since he had parted from her.

At last he roused himself, looked about him as though he were in a strange place, lighted a candle and betook himself to his own quarters. It was very late, and he was more tired than he knew, for in spite of all his troubles he fell asleep and did not awake till the sun was streaming into the room.

Some one knocked at the door, and a servant announced that Signor Contini was waiting to see Don Orsino. The man's face expressed a sort of servile surprise when he saw that Orsino had not undressed for the night and had been sleeping on the divan. He began to busy himself with the toilet things as though expecting Orsino to take some thought for his appearance. But the latter was anxious to see Contini at once, and sent for him.

The architect was evidently very much disturbed. He was as pale as though he had just recovered from a long illness and he seemed to have grown suddenly emaciated during the night. He spoke in a low, excited tone.

In substance he told Orsino what San Giacinto had said on the previous evening. Things looked very black indeed, and Del Ferice's bank had refused to discount any more of Prince Montevarchi's paper.

"And we must have money to-day," Contini concluded.

When he had finished speaking his excitement disappeared and he relapsed into the utmost dejection. Orsino remained silent for some time and then lit a cigarette.

"You need not be so down-hearted, Contini," he said at last. "I shall not have any difficulty in getting money—you know that. What I feel most is the moral failure."

"What is the moral failure to me?" asked Contini gloomily. "It is all very well to talk of getting money. The bank will shut its tills like a steel trap and to-day is Saturday, and there are the workmen and others to be paid, and several bills due into the bargain. Of course your family can give you millions—in time. But we need cash to-day. That is the trouble."

"I suppose the state telegraph is not destroyed because Prince Montevarchi cannot meet his acceptances," observed Orsino. "And I imagine that our steward here in the house has enough cash for our needs, and will not hesitate to hand it to me if he receives a telegram from my father ordering him to do so. Whether he has enough to take up the bills or not, I do not know; but as to-day is Saturday we have all day to-morrow to make arrangements. I could even go out to Saracinesca and be back on Monday morning when the bank opens."

"You seem to take a hopeful view."

"I have not the least hope of saving the business. But the question of ready money does not of itself disturb me."

This was undoubtedly true, but it was also undeniable that Orsino now looked upon the prospect of failure with more equanimity than on the previous evening. On the other hand he felt even more keenly than before all the pain of his sudden separation from Maria Consuelo. When a man is assailed, by several misfortunes at once, twenty-four hours are generally enough to sift the small from the great and to show him plainly which is the greatest of all.

"What shall we do this morning?" inquired Contini.

"You ask the question as though you were going to propose a picnic," answered Orsino. "I do not see why this morning need be so different from other mornings."

"We must stop the works instantly—"

"Why? At all events we will change nothing until we find out the real state of business. The first thing to be done is to go to the bank as usual on Saturdays. We shall then know exactly what to do."

Contini shook his head gloomily and went away to wait in another room while Orsino dressed. An hour later they were at the bank. Contini grew paler than ever. The head clerk would of course inform them that no more bills would be discounted, and that they must meet those already out when they fell due. He would also tell them that the credit balance of their account current would not be at their disposal until their acceptances were met. Orsino would probably at last believe that the situation was serious, though he now looked so supremely and scornfully indifferent to events.

They waited some time. Several men were engaged in earnest conversation, and their faces told plainly enough that they were in trouble. The head clerk was standing with them, and made a sign to Orsino, signifying that they would soon go. Orsino watched him. From time to time he shook his head and made gestures which indicated his utter inability to do anything for them. Contini's courage sank lower and lower.

"I will ask for Del Ferice at once," said Orsino.

He accordingly sought out one of the men who wore the bank's livery and told him to take his card to the count.

"The Signor Commendatore is not coming this morning," answered the man mysteriously.

Orsino went back to the head clerk, interrupting his conversation with the others. He inquired if it were true that Del Ferice were not coming.

"It is not probable," answered the clerk with a grave face. "They say that the Signora Contessa is not likely to live through the day."

"Is Donna Tullia ill?" asked Orsino in considerable astonishment.

"She returned from Naples yesterday morning, and was taken ill in the afternoon—it is said to be apoplexy," he added in a low voice. "If you will have patience Signor Principe, I will be at your disposal in five minutes."

Orsino was obliged to be satisfied and sat down again by Contini. He told him the news of Del Ferice's wife.

"That will make matters worse," said Contini.

"It will not improve them," answered Orsino indifferently. "Considering the state of affairs I would like to see Del Ferice before speaking with any of the others."

"Those men are all involved with Prince Montevarchi," observed Contini, watching the group of which the head clerk was the central figure. "You can see by their faces what they think of the business. The short, grey haired man is the steward—the big man is the architect. The others are contractors. They say it is not less than thirty millions."

Orsino said nothing. He was thinking of Maria Consuelo and wishing that he could get away from Rome that night, while admitting that there was no possibility of such a thing. Meanwhile the head clerk's gestures to his interlocutors expressed more and more helplessness. At last they went out in a body.

"And now I am at your service, Signor Principe," said the grave man of business coming up to Orsino and Contini. "The usual accommodation, I suppose? We will just look over the bills and make out the new ones. It will not take ten minutes. The usual cash, I suppose, Signor Principe? Yes, to-day is Saturday and you have your men to pay. Quite as usual, quite as usual. Will you come into my office?"

Orsino looked at Contini, and Contini looked at Orsino, grasping the back of a chair to steady himself.

"Then there is no difficulty about discounting?" stammered Contini, turning his face, now suddenly flushed, towards the clerk.

"None whatever," answered the latter with an air of real or affected surprise. "I have received the usual instructions to let Andrea Contini and Company have all the money they need."

He turned and led the way to his private office. Contini walked unsteadily. Orsino showed no astonishment, but his black eyes grew a little brighter than usual as he anticipated his next interview with San Giacinto. He readily attributed his good fortune to the supposed well-known prosperity of the firm, and he rose in his own estimation. He quite forgot that Contini, who had now lost his head, had but yesterday clearly foreseen the future when he had said that Del Ferice would not let the two partners fail until they had fitted the last door and the last window in the last of their houses. The conclusion had struck him as just at the time. Contini was the first to recall it.

"It will turn out, as I said," he began, when they were driving to their office in a cab after leaving the bank. "He will let us live until we are worth eating."

"We will arrange matters on a firmer basis before that," answered Orsino confidently. "Poor old Donna Tullia! Who would have thought that she could die! I will stop and ask for news as we pass."

He stopped the cab before the gilded gate of the detached house. Glancing up, he saw that the shutters were closed. The porter came to the bars but did not show any intention of opening.

"The Signora Contessa is dead," he said solemnly, in answer to Orsino's inquiry.

"This morning?"

"Two hours ago."

Orsino's face grew grave as he left his card of condolence and turned away. He could hardly have named a person more indifferent to him than poor Donna Tullia, but he could not help feeling an odd regret at the thought that she was gone at last with all her noisy vanity, her restless meddlesomeness and her perpetual chatter. She had not been old either, though he called her so, and there had seemed to be still a superabundance of life in her. There had been yet many years of rattling, useless, social life before her. To-morrow she would have taken her last drive through Rome—out through the gate of Saint Lawrence to the Campo Varano, there to wait many years perhaps for the pale and half sickly Ugo, of whom every one had said for years that he could not live through another twelve month with the disease of the heart which threatened him. Of late, people had even begun to joke about Donna Tullia's third husband. Poor Donna Tullia!

Orsino went to his office with Contini and forced himself through the usual round of work. Occasionally he was assailed by a mad desire to leave Rome at once, but he opposed it and would not yield. Though his affairs had gone well beyond his expectation the present crisis made it impossible to abandon his business, unless he could get rid of it altogether. And this he seriously contemplated. He knew however, or thought he knew, that Contini would be ruined without him. His own name was the one which gave the paper its value and decided Del Ferice to continue the advances of money. The time was past when Contini would gladly have accepted his partner's share of the undertaking, and would even have tried to raise funds to purchase it. To retire now would be possible only if he could provide for the final liquidation of the whole, and this he could only do by applying to his father or mother, in other words by acknowledging himself completely beaten in his struggle for independence.

The day ended at last and was succeeded by the idleness of Sunday. A sort of listless indifference came over Orsino, the reaction, no doubt, after all the excitement through which he had passed. It seemed to him that Maria Consuelo had never loved him, and that it was better after all that she should be gone. He longed for the old days, indeed, but as she now appeared to him in his meditations he did not wish her back. He had no desire to renew the uncertain struggle for a love which she denied in the end; and this mood showed, no doubt, that his own passion was less violent than he had himself believed. When a man loves with his whole nature, undividedly, he is not apt to submit to separations without making a strong effort to reunite himself, by force, persuasion or stratagem, with the woman who is trying to escape from him. Orsino was conscious of having at first felt the inclination to make such an attempt even more strongly than he had shown it, but he was conscious also that the interval of two days had been enough to reduce the wish to follow Maria Consuelo in such a way that he could hardly understand having ever entertained it.

Unsatisfied passion wears itself out very soon. The higher part of love may and often does survive in such cases, and the passionate impulses may surge up after long quiescence as fierce and dangerous as ever. But it is rarely indeed that two unsatisfied lovers who have parted by the will of the one or of both can meet again without the consciousness that the experimental separation has chilled feelings once familiar and destroyed illusions once more than dear. In older times, perhaps, men and women loved differently. There was more solitude in those days than now, for what is called society was not invented, and people generally were more inclined to sadness from living much alone. Melancholy is a great strengthener of faithfulness in love. Moreover at that time the modern fight for life had not begun, men as a rule had few interests besides love and war, and women no interests at all beyond love. We moderns should go mad if we were suddenly forced to lead the lives led by knights and ladies in the twelfth and thirteenth centuries. The monotonous round of such an existence in time of peace would make idiots of us, the horrors of that old warfare would make many of us maniacs. But it is possible that youths and maidens would love more faithfully and wait longer for each other than they will or can to-day. It is questionable whether Bayard would have understood a single page of a modern love story, Tancred would certainly not have done so; but Caesar would have comprehended our lives and our interests without effort, and Catullus could have described us as we are, for one great civilization is very like another where the same races are concerned.

In the days which followed Maria Consuelo's departure, Orsino came to a state of indifference which surprised himself. He remembered that when she had gone away in the spring he had scarcely missed her, and that he had not thought his own coldness strange, since he was sure that he had not loved her then. But that he had loved her now, during her last stay in Rome, he was sure, and he would have despised himself if he had not been able to believe that he loved her still. Yet, if he was not glad that she had quitted him, he was at least strangely satisfied at being left alone, and the old fancy for analysis made him try to understand himself. The attempt was fruitless, of course, but it occupied his thoughts.

He met Spicca in the street, and avoided him. He imagined that the old man must despise him for not having resisted and followed Maria Consuelo after all. The hypothesis was absurd and the conclusion vain, but he could not escape the idea, and it annoyed him. He was probably ashamed of not having acted recklessly, as a man should who is dominated by a master passion, and yet he was inwardly glad that he had not been allowed to yield to the first impulse.

The days succeeded each other and a week passed away, bringing Saturday again and the necessity for a visit to the bank. Business had been in a very bad state since it had been known that Montevarchi was ruined. So far, he had not stopped payment and although the bank refused discount he had managed to find money with which to meet his engagements. Probably, as San Giacinto had foretold, he would pay everything and remain a very poor man indeed. But, although many persons knew this, confidence was not restored. Del Ferice declared that he believed Montevarchi solvent, as he believed every one with whom his bank dealt to be solvent to the uttermost centime, but that he could lend no more money to any one on any condition whatsoever, because neither he nor the bank had any to lend. Every one, he said, had behaved honestly, and he proposed to eclipse the honesty of every one by the frank acknowledgment of his own lack of cash. He was distressed, he said, overcome by the sufferings of his friends and clients, ready to sell his house, his jewelry and his very boots, in the Roman phrase, to accommodate every one; but he was conscious that the demand far exceeded any supply which he could furnish, no matter at what personal sacrifice, and as it was therefore impossible to help everybody, it would be unjust to help a few where all were equally deserving.

In the meanwhile he proved the will of his deceased wife, leaving him about four and a half millions of francs unconditionally, and half a million more to be devoted to some public charity at Ugo's discretion, for the repose of Donna Tullia's unquiet spirit. It is needless to say that the sorrowing husband determined to spend the legacy magnificently in the improvement of the town represented by him in parliament. A part of the improvement would consist in a statue of Del Ferice himself—representing him, perhaps, as he had escaped from Rome, in the garb of a Capuchin friar, but with the addition of an army revolver to show that he had fought for Italian unity, though when or where no man could tell. But it is worth noting that while he protested his total inability to discount any one's bills, Andrea Contini and Company regularly renewed their acceptances when due and signed new ones for any amount of cash they required. The accommodation was accompanied with a request that it should not be mentioned. Orsino took the money indifferently enough, conscious that he had three fortunes at his back in case of trouble, but Contini grew more nervous as time went on and the sums on paper increased in magnitude, while the chances of disposing of the buildings seemed reduced to nothing in the stagnation which had already set in.

CHAPTER XXV

At this time Count Spicca received a letter from Maria Consuelo, written from Nice and bearing a postmark more recent than the date which headed the page, a fact which proved that the writer had either taken an unusually long time in the composition or had withheld the missive several days before finally despatching it.

"My father—I write to inform you of certain things which have recently taken place and which it is important that you should know, and of which I should have the right to require an explanation if I chose to ask it. Having been the author of my life, you have made yourself also the author of all my unhappiness and of all my trouble. I have never understood the cause of your intense hatred for me, but I have felt its consequences, even at a great distance from you, and you know well enough that I return it with all my heart. Moreover I have made up my mind that I will not be made to suffer by you any longer. I tell you so quite frankly. This is a declaration of war, and I will act upon it immediately.

"You are no doubt aware that Don Orsino Saracinesca has for a long time been among my intimate friends. I will not discuss the question, whether I did well to admit him to my intimacy or not. That, at least, does not concern you. Even admitting your power to exercise the most complete tyranny over me in other ways, I am and have always been free to choose my own acquaintances, and I am able to defend myself better than most women, and as well as any. I will be just, too. I do not mean to reproach you with the consequences of what I do. But I will not spare you where the results of your action towards me are concerned.

"Don Orsino made love to me last spring. I loved him from the first. I can hear your cruel laugh and see your contemptuous face as I write. But the information is necessary, and I can bear your scorn because this is the last opportunity for such diversion which I shall afford you, and because I mean that you shall pay dearly for it. I loved Don Orsino, and I love him still. You, of course, have never loved. You have hated, however, and perhaps one passion may be the measure of another. It is in my case, I can assure you, for the better I love, the better I learn to hate you.

"Last Thursday Don Orsino asked me to be his wife. I had known for some time that he loved me and I knew that he would speak of it before long. The day was sultry at first and then there was a thunderstorm. My nerves were unstrung and I lost my head. I told him that I loved him. That does not concern you. I told him, also, however, that I had given a solemn promise to my dying husband, and I had still the strength to say that I would not marry again. I meant to gain time, I longed to be alone, I knew that I should yield, but I would not yield blindly. Thank God, I was strong. I am like you in that, though happily not in any other way. You ask me why I should even think of yielding. I answer that I love Don Orsino better than I loved the man you murdered. There is nothing humiliating in that, and I make the confession without reserve. I love him better, and therefore, being human, I would have broken my promise and married him, had marriage been possible. But it is not, as you know. It is one thing to turn to the priest as he stands by a dying man and to say, Pronounce us man and wife, and give us a blessing, for the sake of this man's rest. The priest knew that we were both free, and took the responsibility upon himself, knowing also that the act could have no consequences in fact, whatever it might prove to be in theory. It is quite another matter to be legally married to Don Orsino Saracinesca, in the face of a strong opposition. But I went home that evening, believing that it could be done and that the opposition would vanish. I believed because I loved. I love still, but what I learned that night has killed my belief in an impossible happiness.

"I need not tell you all that passed between me and Lucrezia Ferris. How she knew of what had happened I cannot tell. She must have followed us to the apartment I was furnishing, and she must have overheard what we said, or seen enough to convince her. She is a spy. I suppose that is the reason why she is imposed upon me, and always has been, since I can remember—since I was born, she says. I found her waiting to dress me as usual, and as usual I did not speak to her. She spoke first. 'You will not marry Don Orsino Saracinesca,' she said, facing me with her bad eyes. I could have struck her, but I would not. I asked her what she meant. She told me that she knew what I was doing, and asked me whether I was aware that I needed documents in order to be married to a beggar in Rome, and whether I supposed that the Saracinesca would be inclined to overlook the absence of such papers, or could pass a law of their own abolishing the necessity for them, or, finally, whether they would accept such certificates of my origin as she could produce. She showed me a package. She had nothing better to offer me, she said, but such as she had, she heartily placed at my disposal. I took the papers. I was prepared for a shock, but not for the blow I received.

"You know what I read. The certificate of my birth as the daughter of Lucrezia Ferris, unmarried, by Count Spicca who acknowledged the child as his—and the certificate of your marriage with Lucrezia Ferris, dated—strangely enough a fortnight after my birth—and further a document legitimizing me as the lawful daughter of you two. All these documents are from Monte Carlo. You will understand why I am in Nice. Yes—they are all genuine, every one of them, as I have had no difficulty in ascertaining. So I am the daughter of Lucrezia Ferris, born out of wedlock and subsequently whitewashed into a sort of legitimacy. And Lucrezia Ferris is lawfully the Countess Spicca. Lucrezia Ferris, the cowardly spy-woman who more than half controls my life, the lying, thieving servant—she robs me at every turn—the common, half educated Italian creature,—she is my mother, she is that radiant being of whom you sometimes speak with tears in your eyes, she is that angel of whom I remind you, she is that sweet influence that softened and brightened your lonely life for a brief space some three and twenty years ago! She has changed since then.

"And this is the mystery of my birth which you have concealed from me, and which it was at any moment in the power of my vile mother to reveal. You cannot deny the fact, I suppose, especially since I have taken the trouble to search the registers and verify each separate document.

"I gave them all back to her, for I shall never need them. The woman—I mean my mother—was quite right. I shall not marry Don Orsino Saracinesca. You have lied to me throughout my life. You have always told me that my mother was dead, and that I need not be ashamed of my birth, though you wished it kept a secret. So far, I have obeyed you. In that respect, and only in that, I will continue to act according to your wishes. I am not called upon to proclaim to the world and my acquaintance that I am the daughter of my own servant, and that you were kind enough to marry your estimable mistress after my birth in order to confer upon me what you dignify by the name of legitimacy. No. That is not necessary. If it could hurt you to proclaim it I would do so in the most public way I could find. But it is folly to suppose that you could be made to suffer by so simple a process.

"Are you aware, my father, that you have ruined all my life from the first? Being so bad, you must be intelligent and you must realise what you have done, even if you have done it out of pure love of evil. You pretended to be kind to me, until I was old enough to feel all the pain you had in store for me. But even then, after you had taken the trouble to marry my mother, why did you give me another name? Was that necessary? I suppose it was. I did not understand then why my older companions looked askance at me in the convent, nor why the nuns sometimes whispered together and looked at me. They knew perhaps that no such name as mine existed. Since I was your daughter why did I not bear your name when I was a little girl? You were ashamed to let it be known that you were married, seeing what sort of wife you had taken, and you found yourself in a dilemma. If you had acknowledged me as your daughter in Austria, your friends in Rome would soon have found out my existence—and the existence of your wife. You were very cautious in those days, but you seem to have grown careless of late, or you would not have left those papers in the care of the Countess Spicca, my maid—and my mother. I have heard that very bad men soon reach their second childhood and act foolishly. It is quite true.

"Then, later, when you saw that I loved, and was loved, and was to be happy, you came between my love and me. You appeared in your own character as a liar, a slanderer and a traitor. I loved a man who was brave, honourable, faithful—reckless, perhaps, and wild as such men are—but devoted and true. You came between us. You told me that he was false, cowardly, an adventurer of the worst kind. Because I would not believe you, and would have married him in spite of you, you killed him. Was it cowardly of him to face the first swordsman in Europe? They told me that he was not afraid of you, the men who saw it, and that he fought you like a lion, as he was. And the provocation, too! He never struck me. He was showing me what he meant by a term in fencing—the silver knife he held grazed my cheek because I was startled and moved. But you meant to kill him, and you chose to say that he had struck me. Did you ever hear a harsh word from his lips during those months of waiting? When you had done your work you fled—like the murderer you were and are. But I escaped from the woman who says she is my mother—and is—and I went to him and found him living and married him. You used to tell me that he was an adventurer and little better than a beggar. Yet he left me a large fortune. It is as well that he provided for me, since you have succeeded in losing most of your own money at play—doubtless to insure my not profiting by it at your death. Not that you will die—men of your kind outlive their victims, because they kill them.

"And now, when you saw—for you did see it—when you saw and knew that Orsino Saracinesca and I loved each other, you have broken my life a second time. You might so easily have gone to him, or have come to me, at the first, with the truth. You know that I should never forgive you for what you had done already. A little more could have made matters no worse then. You knew that Don Orsino would have thanked you as a friend for the warning. Instead—I refuse to believe you in your dotage after all—you make that woman spy upon me until the great moment is come, you give her the weapons and you bid her strike when the blow will be most excruciating. You are not a man. You are Satan. I parted twice from the man I love. He would not let me go, and he came back and tried to keep me—I do not know how I escaped. God helped me. He is so brave and noble that if he had held those accursed papers in his hands and known all the truth he would not have given me up. He would have brought a stain on his great name, and shame upon his great house for my sake. He is not like you. I parted from him twice, I know all that I can suffer, and I hate you for each individual suffering, great and small.

"I have dismissed my mother from my service. How that would sound in Rome! I have given her as much money as she can expect and I have got rid of her. She said that she would not go, that she would write to you, and many other things. I told her that if she attempted to stay I would go to the authorities, prove that she was my mother, provide for her, if the law required it and have her forcibly turned out of my house by the aid of the same law. I am of age, married, independent, and I cannot be obliged to entertain my mother either in the character of a servant, or as a visitor. I suppose she has a right to a lodging under your roof. I hope she will take advantage of it, as I advised her. She took the money and went away, cursing me. I think that if she had ever, in all my life, shown the smallest affection for me— even at the last, when she declared herself my mother, if she had shown a spark of motherly feeling, of tenderness, of anything human, I could have accepted her and tolerated her, half peasant woman as she is, spy as she has been, and cheat and thief. But she stood before me with the most perfect indifference, watching my surprise with those bad eyes of hers. I wonder why I have borne her presence so long. I suppose it had never struck me that I could get rid of her, in spite of you, if I chose. By the bye, I sent for a notary when I paid her, and I got a legal receipt signed with her legal name, Lucrezia Spicca, ta Ferris. The document formally releases me from all further claims. I hope you will understand that you have no power whatsoever to impose her upon me again, though I confess that I am expecting your next move with interest. I suppose that you have not done with me yet, and have some new means of torment in reserve. Satan is rarely idle long.

"And now I have done. If you were not the villain you are, I should expect you to go to the man whose happiness I have endangered, if not destroyed. I should expect you to tell Don Orsino Saracinesca enough of the truth to make him understand my action. But I know you far too well to imagine that you would willingly take from my life one thorn of the many you have planted in it. I will write to Don Orsino myself. I think you need not fear him—I am sorry that you need not. But I shall not tell him more than is necessary. You will remember, I hope, that such discretion as I may show, is not shown out of consideration for you, but out of forethought for my own welfare. I have unfortunately no means of preventing you from writing to me, but you may be sure that your letters will never be read, so that you will do as well to spare yourself the trouble of composing them.

"MARIA CONSUELO D'ARANJUEZ."

Spicca received this letter early in the morning, and at mid-day he still sat in his chair, holding it in his hand. His face was very white, his head hung forward upon his breast, his thin fingers were stiffened upon the thin paper. Only the hardly perceptible rise and fall of the chest showed that he still breathed.

The clocks had already struck twelve when his old servant entered the room, a being thin, wizened, grey and noiseless as the ghost of a greyhound. He stood still a moment before his master, expecting that he would look up, then bent anxiously over him and felt his hands.

Spicca slowly raised his sunken eyes.

"It will pass, Santi—it will pass," he said feebly.

Then he began to fold up the sheets slowly and with difficulty, but very neatly, as men of extraordinary skill with their hands do everything. Santi looked at him doubtfully and then got a glass and a bottle of cordial from a small carved press in the corner. Spicca drank the liqueur slowly and set the glass steadily upon the table.

"Bad news, Signor Conte?" asked the servant anxiously, and in a way which betrayed at once the kindly relations existing between the two.

"Very bad news," Spicca answered sadly and shaking his head.

Santi sighed, restored the cordial to the press and took up the glass, as though he were about to leave the room. But he still lingered near the table, glancing uneasily at his master as though he had something to say, but was hesitating to begin.

"What is it, Santi?" asked the count.

"I beg your pardon, Signor Conte—you have had bad news—if you will allow me to speak, there are several small economies which could still be managed without too much inconveniencing you. Pardon the liberty, Signor Conte."

"I know, I know. But it is not money this time. I wish it were."

Santi's expression immediately lost much of its anxiety. He had shared his master's fallen fortunes and knew better than he what he meant by a few more small economies, as he called them.

"God be praised, Signor Conte," he said solemnly. "May I serve the breakfast?"

"I have no appetite, Santi. Go and eat yourself."

"A little something?" Santi spoke in a coaxing way. "I have prepared a little mixed fry, with toast, as you like it, Signor Conte, and the salad is good to-day—ham and figs are also in the house. Let me lay the cloth—when you see, you will eat—and just one egg beaten up with a glass of red wine to begin—that will dispose the stomach."

Spicca shook his head again, but Santi paid no attention to the refusal and went about preparing the meal. When it was ready the old man suffered himself to be persuaded and ate a little. He was in reality stronger than he looked, and an extraordinary nervous energy still lurked beneath the appearance of a feebleness almost amounting to decrepitude. The little nourishment he took sufficed to restore the balance, and when he rose from the table, he was outwardly almost himself again. When a man has suffered great moral pain for years, he bears a new shock, even the worst, better than one who is hard hit in the midst of a placid and long habitual happiness. The soul can be taught to bear trouble as the great self mortifiers of an earlier time taught their bodies to bear scourging. The process is painful but hardening.

"I feel better, Santi," said Spicca. "Your breakfast has done me good. You are an excellent doctor."

He turned away and took out his pocket-book—not over well garnished. He found a ten franc note. Then he looked round and spoke in a gentle, kindly tone.

"Santi—this trouble has nothing to do with money. You need a new pair of shoes, I am sure. Do you think that ten francs is enough?"

Santi bowed respectfully and took the money.

"A thousand thanks, Signor Conte," he said.

Santi was a strange man, from the heart of the Abruzzi. He pocketed the note, but that night, when he had undressed his master and was arranging the things on the dressing table, the ten francs found their way back into the black pocket-book. Spicca never counted, and never knew.

He did not write to Maria Consuelo, for he was well aware that in her present state of mind she would undoubtedly burn his letter unopened, as she had said she would. Late in the day he went out, walked for an hour, entered the club and read the papers, and at last betook himself to the restaurant where Orsino dined when his people were out of town.

In due time, Orsino appeared, looking pale and ill tempered. He caught sight of Spicca and went at once to the table where he sat.

"I have had a letter," said the young man. "I must speak to you. If you do not object, we will dine together."

"By all means. There is nothing like a thoroughly bad dinner to promote ill-feeling."

Orsino glanced at the old man in momentary surprise. But he knew his ways tolerably well, and was familiar with the chronic acidity of his speech.

"You probably guess who has written to me," Orsino resumed. "It was natural, perhaps, that she should have something to say, but what she actually says, is more than I was prepared to hear."

Spicca's eyes grew less dull and he turned an inquiring glance on his companion.

"When I tell you that in this letter, Madame d'Aranjuez has confided to me the true story of her origin, I have probably said enough," continued the young man.

"You have said too much or too little," Spicca answered in an almost indifferent tone.

"How so?"

"Unless you tell me just what she has told you, or show me the letter, I cannot possibly judge of the truth of the tale."

Orsino raised his head angrily.

"Do you mean me to doubt that Madame d'Aranjuez speaks the truth?" he asked.

"Calm yourself. Whatever Madame d'Aranjuez has written to you, she believes to be true. But she may have been herself deceived."

"In spite of documents—public registers—"

"Ah! Then she has told you about those certificates?"

"That—and a great deal more which concerns you."

"Precisely. A great deal more. I know all about the registers, as you may easily suppose, seeing that they concern two somewhat important acts in my own life and that I was very careful to have those acts properly recorded, beyond the possibility of denial—beyond the possibility of denial," he repeated very slowly and emphatically. "Do you understand that?"

"It would not enter the mind of a sane person to doubt such evidence," answered Orsino rather scornfully.

"No, I suppose not. As you do not therefore come to me for confirmation of what is already undeniable, I cannot understand why you come to me at all in this matter, unless you do so on account of other things which Madame d'Aranjuez has written you, and of which you have so far kept me in ignorance."

Spicca spoke with a formal manner and in cold tones, drawing up his bent figure a little. A waiter came to the table and both men ordered their dinner. The interruption rather favoured the development of a hostile feeling between them, than otherwise.

"I will explain my reasons for coming to find you here," said Orsino when they were again alone.

"So far as I am concerned, no explanation is necessary. I am content not to understand. Moreover, this is a public place, in which we have accidentally met and dined together before."

"I did not come here by accident," answered Orsino. "And I did not come in order to give explanations but to ask for one."

"Ah?" Spicca eyed him coolly.

"Yes. I wish to know why you have hated your daughter all her life, why you persecute her in every way, why you—"

"Will you kindly stop?"

The old man's voice grew suddenly clear and incisive, and Orsino broke off in the middle of his sentence. A moment's pause followed.

"I requested you to stop speaking," Spicca resumed, "because you were unconsciously making statements which have no foundation whatever in fact. Observe that I say, unconsciously. You are completely mistaken. I do not hate Madame d'Aranjuez. I love her with all my heart and soul. I do not persecute her in every way, nor in any way. On the contrary, her happiness is the only object of such life as I still have to live, and I have little but that life left to give her. I am in earnest, Orsino."

"I see you are. That makes what you say all the more surprising."

"No doubt it does. Madame d'Aranjuez has just written to you, and you have her letter in your pocket. She has told you in that letter a number of facts in her own life, as she sees them, and you look at them as she does. It is natural. To her and to you, I appear to be a monster of evil, a hideous incarnation of cruelty, a devil in short. Did she call me a devil in her letter?"

"She did."

"Precisely. She has also written to me, informing me that I am Satan. There is a directness in the statement and a general disregard of probability which is not without charm. Nevertheless, I am Spicca, and not Beelzebub, her assurances to the contrary notwithstanding. You see how views may differ. You know much of her life, but you know nothing of mine, nor is it my intention to tell you anything about myself. But I will tell you this much. If I could do anything to mend matters, I would. If I could make it possible for you to marry Madame d'Aranjuez—being what you are, and fenced in as you are, I would. If I could tell you all the rest of the truth, which she does not know, nor dream of, I would. I am bound by a very solemn promise of secrecy—by something more than a promise in fact. Yet, if I could do good to her by breaking oaths, betraying confidence and trampling on the deepest obligations which can bind a man, I would. But that good cannot be done any more. That is all I can tell you."

"It is little enough. You could, and you can, tell the whole truth, as you call it, to Madame d'Aranjuez. I would advise you to do so, instead of embittering her life at every turn."

"I have not asked for your advice, Orsino. That she is unhappy, I know. That she hates me, is clear. She would not be the happier for hating me less, since nothing else would be changed. She need not think of me, if the subject is disagreeable. In all other respects she is perfectly free. She is young, rich, and at liberty to go where she pleases and to do what she likes. So long as I am alive, I shall watch over her—"

"And destroy every chance of happiness which presents itself," interrupted Orsino.

"I gave you some idea, the other night, of the happiness she might have enjoyed with the deceased Aranjuez. If I made a mistake in regard to what I saw him do—I admit the possibility of an error—I was nevertheless quite right in ridding her of the man. I have atoned for the mistake, if we call it so, in a way of which you do not dream, nor she either. The good remains, for Aranjuez is buried."

"You speak of secret atonement—I was not aware that you ever suffered from remorse."

"Nor I," answered Spicca drily.

"Then what do you mean?"

"You are questioning me, and I have warned you that I will tell you nothing about myself. You will confer a great favour upon me by not insisting."

"Are you threatening me again?"

"I am not doing anything of the kind. I never threaten any one. I could kill you as easily as I killed Aranjuez, old and decrepit as I look, and I should be perfectly indifferent to the opprobrium of killing so young a man—though I think that, looking at us two, many people might suppose the advantage to be on your side rather than on mine. But young men nowadays do not learn to handle arms. Short of laying violent hands upon me, you will find it quite impossible to provoke me. I am almost old enough to be your grandfather, and I understand you very well. You love Madame d'Aranjuez. She knows that to marry you would be to bring about such a quarrel with your family as might ruin half your life, and she has the rare courage to tell you so and to refuse your offer. You think that I can do something to help you and you are incensed because I am powerless, and furious because I object to your leaving Rome in the same train with her, against her will. You are more furious still to-day because you have adopted her belief that I am a monster of iniquity. Observe—that, apart from hindering you from a great piece of folly the other day, I have never interfered. I do not interfere now. As I said then, follow her if you please, persuade her to marry you if you can, quarrel with all your family if you like. It is nothing to me. Publish the banns of your marriage on the doors of the Capitol and declare to the whole world that Madame d'Aranjuez, the future Princess Saracinesca, is the daughter of Count Spicca and Lucrezia Ferris, his lawful wife. There will be a little talk, but it will not hurt me. People have kept their marriages a secret for a whole lifetime before now. I do not care what you do, nor what the whole tribe of the Saracinesca may do, provided that none of you do harm to Maria Consuelo, nor bring useless suffering upon her. If any of you do that, I will kill you. That at least is a threat, if you like. Good-night."

Thereupon Spicca rose suddenly from his seat, leaving his dinner unfinished, and went out.

CHAPTER XXVI

Orsino did not leave Rome after all. He was not in reality prevented from doing so by the necessity of attending to his business, for he might assuredly have absented himself for a week or two at almost any time before the new year, without incurring any especial danger. From time to time, at ever increasing intervals, he felt strongly impelled to rejoin Maria Consuelo in Paris where she had ultimately determined to spend the autumn and winter, but the impulse always lacked just the measure of strength which would have made it a resolution. When he thought of his many hesitations he did not understand himself and he fell in his own estimation, so that he became by degrees more silent and melancholy of disposition than had originally been natural with him.

He had much time for reflection and he constantly brooded over the situation in which he found himself. The question seemed to be, whether he loved Maria Consuelo or not, since he was able to display such apparent indifference to her absence. In reality he also doubted whether he was loved by her, and the one uncertainty was fully as great as the other.

He went over all that had passed. The position had never been an easy one, and the letter which Maria Consuelo had written to him after her departure had not made it easier. It had contained the revelations concerning her birth, together with many references to Spicca's continued cruelty, plentifully supported by statements of facts. She had then distinctly told Orsino that she would never marry him, under any circumstances whatever, declaring that if he followed her she would not even see him. She would not ruin his life and plunge him into a life long quarrel with his family, she said, and she added that she would certainly not expose herself to such treatment as she would undoubtedly receive at the hands of the Saracinesca if she married Orsino without his parents' consent.

A man does not easily believe that he is deprived of what he most desires exclusively for his own good and welfare, and the last sentence quoted wounded Orsino deeply. He believed himself ready to incur the displeasure of all his people for Maria Consuelo's sake, and he said in his heart that if she loved him she should be ready to bear as much as he. The language in which she expressed herself, too, was cold and almost incisive.

Unlike Spicca Orsino answered this letter, writing in an argumentative strain, bringing the best reasons he could find to bear against those she alleged, and at last reproaching her with not being willing to suffer for his sake a tenth part of what he would endure for her. But he announced his intention of joining her before long, and expressed the certainty that she would receive him.

To this Maria Consuelo made no reply for some time. When she wrote at last, it was to say that she had carefully considered her decision and saw no good cause for changing it. To Orsino her tone seemed colder and more distant than ever. The fact that the pages were blotted here and there and that the handwriting was unsteady, was probably to be referred to her carelessness. He brooded over his misfortune, thought more than once of making a desperate effort to win back her love, and remained in Rome. After a long interval he wrote to her again. This time he produced an epistle which, under the circumstances, might have seemed almost ridiculous. It was full of indifferent gossip about society, it contained a few sarcastic remarks about his own approaching failure, with some rather youthfully cynical observations on the instability of things in general and the hollowness of all aspirations whatsoever.

He received no answer, and duly repented the flippant tone he had taken. He would have been greatly surprised could he have learned that this last letter was destined to produce a greater effect upon his life than all he had written before it.

In the meanwhile his father, who had heard of the increasing troubles in the world of business, wrote him in a constant strain of warning, to which he paid little attention. His mother's letters, too, betrayed her anxiety, but expressed what his father's did not, to wit the most boundless confidence in his power to extricate himself honourably from all difficulties, together with the assurance that if worst came to worst she was always ready to help him.

Suddenly and without warning old Saracinesca returned from his wanderings. He had taken the trouble to keep the family informed of his movements by his secretary during two or three months and had then temporarily allowed them to lose sight of him, thereby causing them considerable anxiety, though an occasional paragraph in a newspaper reassured them from time to time. Then, on a certain afternoon in November, he appeared, alone and in a cab, as though he had been out for a stroll.

"Well, my boy, are you ruined yet?" he inquired, entering Orsino's room without ceremony.

The young man started from his seat and took the old gentleman's rough hand, with an exclamation of surprise.

"Yes—you may well look at me," laughed the Prince. "I have grown ten years younger. And you?" He pushed his grandson into the light and scrutinised his face fiercely. "And you are ten years older," he concluded, in a discontented tone.

"I did not know it," answered Orsino with an attempt at a laugh.

"You have been at some mischief. I know it. I can see it."

He dropped the young fellow's arm, shook his head and began to move about the room. Then he came back all at once and looked up into Orsino's face from beneath his bushy eyebrows.

"Out with it, I mean to know!" he said, roughly but not unkindly. "Have you lost money? Are you ill? Are you in love?"

Orsino would certainly have resented the first and the last questions, if not all three, had they been put to him by his father. There was something in the old Prince's nature, something warmer and more human, which appealed to his own. Sant' Ilario was, and always had been, outwardly cold, somewhat measured in his speech, undemonstrative, a man not easily moved to much expression or to real sympathy except by love, but capable, under that influence, of going to great lengths. And Orsino, though in some respects resembling his mother rather than his father, was not unlike the latter, with a larger measure of ambition and less real pride. It was probably the latter characteristic which made him feel the need of sympathy in a way his father had never felt it and could never understand it, and he was thereby drawn more closely to his mother and to his grandfather than to Sant' Ilario.

Old Saracinesca evidently meant to be answered, as he stood there gazing into Orsino's eyes.

"A great deal has happened since you went away," said Orsino, half wishing that he could tell everything. "In the first place, business is in a very bad state, and I am anxious."

"Dirty work, business," grumbled Saracinesca. "I always told you so. Then you have lost money, you young idiot! I thought so. Did you think you were any better than Montevarchi? I hope you have kept your name out of the market, at all events. What in the name of heaven made you put your hand to such filth! Come—how much do you want? We will whitewash you and you shall start to-morrow and go round the world."

"But I am not in actual need of money at all—"

"Then what the devil are you in need of?"

"An improvement in business, and the assurance that I shall not ultimately be bankrupt."

"If money is not an assurance that you will not be bankrupt, I would like to learn what is. All this is nonsense. Tell me the truth, my boy—you are in love. That is the trouble."

Orsino shrugged his shoulders.

"I have been in love some time," he answered.

"Young? Old? Marriageable? Married? Out with it, I say!"

"I would rather talk about business. I think it is all over now."

"Just like your father—always full of secrets! As if I did not know all about it. You are in love with that Madame d'Aranjuez."

Orsino turned a little pale.

"Please do not call her 'that' Madame d'Aranjuez," he said, gravely.

"Eh? What? Are you so sensitive about her?"

"Yes."

"You are? Very well—I like that. What about her?"

"What a question!"

"I mean—is she indifferent, cold, in love with some one else?"

"Not that I am aware. She has refused to marry me and has left Rome, that is all."

"Refused to marry you!" cried old Saracinesca in boundless astonishment. "My dear boy, you must be out of your mind! The thing is impossible. You are the best match in Rome. Madame d'Aranjuez refuse you—absolutely incredible, not to be believed for a moment. You are dreaming. A widow—without much fortune—the relict of some curious adventurer—a woman looking for a fortune, a woman—"

"Stop!" cried Orsino, savagely.

"Oh yes—I forgot. You are sensitive. Well, well, I meant nothing against her, except that she must be insane if what you tell me is true. But I am glad of it, my boy, very glad. She is no match for you, Orsino. I confess, I wish you would marry at once. I would like to see my great grandchildren—but not Madame d'Aranjuez. A widow, too."

"My father married a widow."

"When you find a widow like your mother, and ten years younger than yourself, marry her if you can. But not Madame d'Aranjuez—older than you by several years."

"A few years."

"Is that all? It is too much, though. And who is Madame d'Aranjuez? Everybody was asking the question last winter. I suppose she had a name before she married, and since you have been trying to make her your wife, you must know all about her. Who was she?"

Orsino hesitated.

"You see!" cried, the old Prince. "It is not all right. There is a secret—there is something wrong about her family, or about her entrance into the world. She knows perfectly well that we would never receive her and has concealed it all from you—"

"She has not concealed it. She has told me the exact truth. But I shall not repeat it to you."

"All the stronger proof that everything is not right. You are well out of it, my boy, exceedingly well out of it. I congratulate you."

"I would rather not be congratulated."

"As you please. I am sorry for you, if you are unhappy. Try and forget all about it. How is your mother?"

At any other time Orsino would have laughed at the characteristic abruptness.

"Perfectly well, I believe. I have not seen her all summer," he answered gravely.

"Not been to Saracinesca all summer! No wonder you look ill. Telegraph to them that I have come back and let us get the family together as soon as possible. Do you think I mean to spend six months alone in your company, especially when you are away all day at that wretched office of yours? Be quick about it—telegraph at once."

"Very well. But please do not repeat anything of what I have told you to my father or my mother. That is the only thing I have to ask."

"Am I a parrot? I never talk to them of your affairs."

"Thanks. I am grateful."

"To heaven because your grandfather is not a parakeet! No doubt. You have good cause. And look here, Orsino—"

The old man took Orsino's arm and held it firmly, speaking in a lower tone.

"Do not make an ass of yourself, my boy—especially in business. But if you do—and you probably will, you know—just come to me, without speaking to any one else. I will see what can be done without noise. There—take that, and forget all about your troubles and get a little more colour into your face."

"You are too good to me," said Orsino, grasping the old Prince's hand. For once, he was really moved.

"Nonsense—go and send that telegram at once. I do not want to be kept waiting a week for a sight of my family."

With a deep, good humoured laugh he pushed Orsino out of the door in front of him and went off to his own quarters.

In due time the family returned from Saracinesca and the gloomy old palace waked to life again. Corona and her husband were both struck by the change in Orsino's appearance, which indeed contrasted strongly with their own, refreshed and strengthened as they were by the keen mountain air, the endless out-of-door life, the manifold occupations of people deeply interested in the welfare of those around them and supremely conscious of their own power to produce good results in their own way. When they all came back, Orsino himself felt how jaded and worn he was as compared with them.

Before twelve hours had gone by, he found himself alone with his mother. Strange to say he had not looked forward to the interview with pleasure. The bond of sympathy which had so closely united the two during the spring seemed weakened, and Orsino would, if possible, have put off the renewal of intimate converse which he knew to be inevitable. But that could not be done.

It would not be hard to find reasons for his wishing to avoid his mother. Formerly his daily tale had been one of success, of hope, of ever increasing confidence. Now he had nothing to tell of but danger and anxiety for the future, and he was not without a suspicion that she would strongly disapprove of his allowing himself to be kept afloat by Del Ferice's personal influence, and perhaps by his personal aid. It was hard to begin daily intercourse on a basis of things so different from that which had seemed solid and safe when they had last talked together. He had learned to bear his own troubles bravely, too, and there was something which he associated with weakness in the idea of asking sympathy for them now. He would rather have been left alone.

Deep down, too, was the consciousness of all that had happened between himself and Maria Consuelo since his mother's departure. Another suffering, another and distinctly different misfortune, to be borne better in silence than under question even of the most affectionate kind. His grandfather had indeed guessed at both truths and had taxed him with them at once, but that was quite another matter. He knew that the old gentleman would never refer again to what he had learned, and he appreciated the generous offer of help, of which he would never avail himself, in a way in which he could not appreciate an assistance even more lovingly proffered, perhaps, but which must be asked for by a confession of his own failure.

On the other hand, he was incapable of distorting the facts in any way so as to make his mother believe him more successful than he actually was. There was nothing dishonest, perhaps, in pretending to be hopeful when he really had little hope, but he could not have represented the condition of the business otherwise than as it really stood.

The interview was a long one, and Corona's dark face grew grave if not despondent as he explained to her one point after another, taking especial care to elucidate all that bore upon his relations with Del Ferice. It was most important that his mother should understand how he was placed, and how Del Ferice's continued advances of money were not to be regarded in the light of a personal favour, but as a speculation in which Ugo would probably get the best of the bargain. Orsino knew how sensitive his mother would be on such a point, and dreaded the moment when she should begin to think that he was laying himself under obligations beyond the strict limits of business.

Corona leaned back in her low seat and covered her eyes with one hand for a moment, in deep thought. Orsino waited anxiously for her to speak.

"My dear," she said at last, "you make it very clear, and I understand you perfectly. Nevertheless, it seems to me that your position is not very dignified, considering who you are, and what Del Ferice is. Do you not think so yourself?"

Orsino flushed a little. She had not put the point as he had expected, and her words told upon him.

"When I entered business, I put my dignity in my pocket," he answered, with a forced laugh. "There cannot be much of it in business, at the best."

His mother's black eyes seemed to grow blacker, and the delicate nostril quivered a little.

"If that is true, I wish you had never meddled in these affairs," she said, proudly. "But you talked differently last spring, and you made me see it all in another way. You made me feel, on the contrary that in doing something for yourself, in showing that you were able to accomplish something, in asserting your independence, you were making yourself more worthy of respect—and I have respected you accordingly."

"Exactly," answered Orsino, catching at the old argument. "That is just what I wished to do. What I said a moment since was in the way of a generality. Business means a struggle for money, I suppose, and that, in itself, is not dignified. But it is not dishonourable. After all, the means may justify the end."

"I hate that saying!" exclaimed Corona hotly. "I wish you were free of the whole affair."

"So do I, with all my heart!"

A short silence followed.

"If I had known all this three months ago," Corona resumed, "I would have taken the money and given it to you, to clear yourself. I thought you were succeeding and I have used all the funds I could gather to buy the Montevarchi's property between us and Affile and in planting eucalyptus trees in that low land of mine where the people have suffered so much from fever. I have nothing at my disposal unless I borrow. Why did you not tell me the truth in the summer, Orsino? Why have you let me imagine that you were prospering all along, when you have been and are at the point of failure? It is too bad—"

She broke off suddenly and clasped her hands together on her knee.

"It is only lately that business has gone so badly," said Orsino.

"It was all wrong from the beginning! I should never have encouraged you. Your father was right, as he always is—and now you must tell him so."

But Orsino refused to go to his father, except in the last extremity. He represented that it was better, and more dignified, since Corona insisted upon the point of dignity, to fight the battle alone so long as there was a chance of winning. His mother, on the other hand, maintained that he should free himself at once and at any cost. A few months earlier he could easily have persuaded her that he was right; but she seemed changed since he had parted from her, and he fancied that his father's influence had been at work with her. This he resented bitterly. It must be remembered, too, that he had begun the interview with a preconceived prejudice, expecting it to turn out badly, so that he was the more ready to allow matters to take an unfavourable turn.

The result was not a decided break in his relations with his mother, but a state of things more irritating than any open difference could have been. From that time Corona discouraged him, and never ceased to advise him to go to his father and ask frankly for enough money to clear him outright. Orsino, on his part, obstinately refused to apply to any one for help, as long as Del Ferice continued to advance him money.

In those months which followed there were few indeed who did not suffer in the almost universal financial cataclysm. All that Contini and others, older and wiser than he, had predicted, took place, and more also. The banks refused discount, even upon the best paper, saying with justice that they were obliged to hold their funds in reserve at such a time. The works stopped almost everywhere. It was impossible to raise money. Thousands upon thousands of workmen who had come from great distances during the past two or three years were suddenly thrown out of work, penniless in the streets and many of them burdened with wives and children. There were one or two small riots and there was much demonstration, but, on the whole, the poor masons behaved very well. The government and the municipality did what they could—what governments and municipalities can do when hampered at every turn by the most complicated and ill-considered machinery of administration ever invented in any country. The starving workmen were by slow degrees got out of the city and sent back to starve out of sight in their native places. The emigration was enormous in all directions.

The dismal ruins of that new city which was to have been built and which never reached completion are visible everywhere. Houses seven stories high, abandoned within a month of completion rise uninhabited and uninhabitable out of a rank growth of weeds, amidst heaps of rubbish, staring down at the broad, desolate streets where the vigorous grass pushes its way up through the loose stones of the unrolled metalling. Amidst heavy low walls which were to have been the ground stories of palaces, a few ragged children play in the sun, a lean donkey crops the thistles, or if near to a few occupied dwellings, a wine seller makes a booth of straw and chestnut boughs and dispenses a poisonous, sour drink to those who will buy. But that is only in the warm months. The winter winds blow the wretched booth to pieces and increase the desolation. Further on, tall façades rise suddenly up, the blue sky gleaming through their windows, the green moss already growing upon their naked stones and bricks. The Barbarini of the future, if any should arise, will not need to despoil the Colosseum to quarry material for their palaces. If, as the old pasquinade had it the Barbarini did what the Barbarians did not, how much worse than barbarians have these modern civilizers done!

The distress was very great in the early months of 1889. The satisfaction which many of the new men would have felt at the ruin of great old families was effectually neutralized by their own financial destruction. Princes, bankers, contractors and master masons went down together in the general bankruptcy. Ugo Del Ferice survived and with him Andrea Contini and Company, and doubtless other small firms which he protected for his own ends. San Giacinto, calm, far-seeing, and keen as an eagle, surveyed the chaos from the height of his magnificent fortune, unmoved and immovable, awaiting the lowest ebb of the tide. The Saracinesca looked on, hampered a little by the sudden fall in rents and other sources of their income, but still superior to events, though secretly anxious about Orsino's affairs, and daily expecting that he must fail.

And Orsino himself had changed, as was natural enough. He was learning to seem what he was not, and those who have learned that lesson know how it influences the real man whom no one can judge but himself. So long as there had been one person in his life with whom he could live in perfect sympathy he had given himself little trouble about his outward behaviour. So long as he had felt that, come what might, his mother was on his side, he had not thought it worth his while not to be natural with every one, according to his humour. He was wrong, no doubt, in fancying that Corona had deserted him. But he had already suffered a loss, in Maria Consuelo, which had at the time seemed the greatest conceivable, and the pain he had suffered then, together with, the deep though, unacknowledged wound to his vanity, had predisposed him to believe that he was destined to be friendless. The consequence was that a very slight break in the perfect understanding which had so long existed between him and his mother had produced serious results. He now felt that he was completely alone, and like most lonely men of sound character he acquired the habit of keeping his troubles entirely to himself, while affecting an almost unnaturally quiet and equable manner with those around him. On the whole, he found that his life was easier when he lived it on this principle. He found that he was more careful in his actions since he had a part to sustain, and that his opinion carried more weight since he expressed it more cautiously and seemed less liable to fluctuations of mood and temper. The change in his character was more apparent than real, perhaps, as changes of character generally are when not in the way of logical development; but the constant thought of appearances reacts upon the inner nature in the end, and much which at first is only put on, becomes a habit next, and ends by taking the place of an impulse.

Orsino was aware that his chief preoccupation was identical with that which absorbed his mother's thoughts. He wished to free himself from the business in which he was so deeply involved, and which still prospered so strangely in spite of the general ruin. But here the community of ideas ended. He wished to free himself in his own way, without humiliating himself by going to his father for help. Meanwhile, too, Sant' Ilario himself had his doubts concerning his own judgment. It was inconceivable to him that Del Ferice could be losing money to oblige Orsino, and if he had desired to ruin him he could have done so with ease a hundred times in the past months. It might be, he said to himself, that Orsino had after all, a surprising genius for affairs and had weathered the storm in the face of tremendous difficulties. Orsino saw the belief growing in his father's mind, and the certainty that it was there did not dispose him to throw up the fight and acknowledge himself beaten.

The Saracinesca were one of the very few Roman families in which there is a tradition in favour of non-interference with the action of children already of age. The consequence was that although the old Prince, Giovanni and his wife, all three felt considerable anxiety, they did nothing to hamper Orsino's action, beyond an occasionally repeated warning to be careful. That his occupation was distasteful to them, they did not conceal, but he met their expressions of opinion with perfect equanimity and outward good humour, even when his mother, once his staunch ally, openly advised him to give up business and travel for a year. Their prejudice was certainly not unnatural, and had been strengthened by the perusal of the unsavoury details published by the papers at each new bankruptcy during the year. But they found Orsino now always the same, always quiet, good-humoured and firm in his projects.

Andrea Contini had not been very exact in his calculation of the date at which the last door and the last window would be placed in the last of the houses which he and Orsino had undertaken to build. The disturbance in business might account for the delay. At all events it was late in April of the following year before the work was completed. Then Orsino went to Del Ferice.

"Of course," he said, maintaining the appearance of calm which had now become habitual with him, "I cannot expect to pay what I owe the bank, unless I can effect a sale of these buildings. You have known that, all along, as well as I. The question is, can they be sold?"

"You have no applicant, then?" Del Ferice looked grave and somewhat surprised.

"No. We have received no offer."

"You owe the bank a very large sum on these buildings, Don Orsino."

"Secured by mortgages on them," answered the young man quietly, but preparing for trouble.

"Just so. Secured by mortgages. But if the bank should foreclose within the next few months, and if the buildings do not realize the amount secured, Contini and Company are liable for the difference."

"I know that."

"And the market is very bad, Don Orsino, and shows no signs of improvement."

"On the other hand the houses are finished, habitable, and can be let immediately."

"They are certainly finished. You must be aware that the bank has continued to advance the sums necessary for two reasons. Firstly, because an expensive but habitable dwelling is better than a cheap one with no roof. Secondly, because in doing business with Andrea Contini and Company we have been dealing with the only really honest and economical firm in Rome."

Orsino smiled vaguely, but said nothing. He had not much faith in Del Ferice's flattery.

"But that," continued the latter, "does not dispense us from the necessity of realising what is owing to us—I mean the bank—either in money, or in an equivalent—or in an equivalent," he repeated, thoughtfully rolling a big silver pencil case backward and forward upon the table under his fat white hand.

"Evidently," assented Orsino. "Unfortunately, at the present time, there seems to be no equivalent for ready money."

"No—no—perhaps not," said Ugo, apparently becoming more and more absorbed in his own thoughts. "And yet," he added, after a little pause, "an arrangement may be possible. The houses certainly possess advantages over much of this wretched property which is thrown upon the market. The position is good and the work is good. Your work is very good, Don Orsino. You know that better than I. Yes—the houses have advantages, I admit. The bank has a great deal of waste masonry on its hands, Don Orsino—more than I like to think of."

"Unfortunately, again, the time for improving such property is gone by."

"It is never too late to mend, says the proverb," retorted Del Ferice with a smile. "I have a proposition to make. I will state it clearly. If it is not to our mutual advantage, I think neither of us will lose so much by it as we should lose in other ways. It is simply this. We will cry quits. You have a small account current with the bank, and you must sacrifice the credit balance—it is not much, I find—about thirty-five thousand."

"That was chiefly the profit on the first contract," observed Orsino.

"Precisely. It will help to cover the bank's loss on this. It will help, because when I say we will cry quits, I mean that you shall receive an equivalent for your houses—a nominal equivalent of course, which the bank nominally takes back as payment of the mortgages."

"That is not very clear," said Orsino. "I do not understand you."

"No," laughed Del Ferice. "I admit that it is not. It represented rather my own view of the transaction than the practical side. But I will explain myself beyond the possibility of mistake. The bank takes the houses and your cash balance and cancels the mortgages. You are then released from all debt and all obligation upon the old contract. But the bank makes one condition which, is important. You must buy from the bank, on mortgage of course, certain unfinished buildings which it now owns, and you—Andrea Contini and Company—must take a contract to complete them within a given time, the bank advancing you money as before upon notes of hand, secured by subsequent and successive mortgages."

Orsino was silent. He saw that if he accepted, Del Ferice was receiving the work of a whole year and more without allowing the smallest profit to the workers, besides absorbing the profits of a previous successfully executed contract, and besides taking it for granted that the existing mortgages only just covered the value of the buildings. If, as was probable, Del Ferice had means of either selling or letting the houses, he stood to make an enormous profit. He saw, too, that if he accepted now, he must in all likelihood be driven to accept similar conditions on a future occasion, and that he would be binding Andrea Contini and himself to work, and to work hard, for nothing and perhaps during years.

But he saw also that the only alternative was an appeal to his father, or bankruptcy which ultimately meant the same thing. Del Ferice spoke again.

"Whether you agree, or whether you prefer a foreclosure, we shall both lose. But we should lose more by the latter course. In the interests of the bank I trust that you will accept. You see how frankly I speak about it. In the interests of the bank. But then, I need not remind you that it would hardly be fair to let us lose heavily when you can make the loss relatively a slight one—considering how the bank has behaved to you, and to you alone, throughout this fatal year."

"I will give you an answer to-morrow," said Orsino.

He thought of poor Contini who would find that he had worked for nothing during a whole year. But then, it would be easy for Orsino to give Contini a sum of money out of his private resources. Anything was better than giving up the struggle and applying to his father.

CHAPTER XXVII

Orsino was to all intents and purposes without a friend. How far circumstances had contributed to this result and how far he himself was to blame for his lonely state, those may judge who have followed his history to this point. His grandfather had indeed offered him help and in a way to make it acceptable if he had felt that he could accept it at all. But the old Prince did not in the least understand the business nor the situation. Moreover a young fellow of two or three and twenty does not look for a friend in the person of a man sixty years older than himself. While maintaining the most uniformly good relations in his home, Orsino felt himself estranged from his father and mother. His brothers were too young, and were generally away from home at school and college, and he had no sisters. Beyond the walls of the Palazzo Saracinesca, San Giacinto was the only man whom he would willingly have consulted; but San Giacinto was of all men the one least inclined to intimacy with his neighbours, and, after all, as Orsino reflected, he would probably repeat the advice he had already given, if he vouchsafed counsel of any kind.

He thought of all his acquaintance and came to the conclusion that he was in reality in terms more closely approaching to friendship with Andrea Contini than with any man of his own class. Yet he would have hesitated to call the architect his friend, as he would have found it impossible to confide in him concerning any detail of his own private life.

At a time when most young men are making friends, Orsino had been hindered, from the formation of such ties by the two great interests which had absorbed his existence, his attachment and subsequent love for Maria Consuelo, and the business at which he had worked so steadily. He had lost Maria Consuelo, in whom he would have confided as he had often done before, and at the present important juncture he stood quite alone.

He felt that he was no match for Del Ferice. The keen banker was making use of him for his own purposes in a way which neither Orsino nor Contini had ever suspected. It could not be supposed that Ugo had foreseen from the first the advantage he might reap from the firm he had created and which was so wholly dependent on him. Orsino might have turned out ignorant and incapable. Contini might have proved idle and even dishonest. But, instead of this, the experiment had succeeded admirably and Ugo found himself possessed of an instrument, as it were, precisely adapted to his end, which was to make worthless property valuable at the smallest possible expense, in fact, at the lowest cost price. He had secured a first-rate architect and a first-rate accountant, both men of spotless integrity, both young, energetic and unusually industrious. He paid nothing for their services and he entirely controlled their expenditure. It was clear that he would do his utmost to maintain an arrangement so immensely profitable to himself. If Orsino had realised exactly how profitable it was, he might have forced Del Ferice to share the gain with him, and would have done so for the sake of Contini, if not for his own. He suspected, indeed, that Ugo was certain beforehand, in each case, of selling or letting the houses, but he had no proof of the fact. Ugo did not leave everything to his confidential clerk, and the secrets he kept to himself were well kept.

Orsino consulted Contini, as a matter of necessity, before accepting Del Ferice's last offer. The architect went into a tragic-comic rage, bit his cigar through several times, ground his teeth, drank several glasses of cold water, talked of the blood of Cola di Rienzo, vowed vengeance on Del Ferice and finally submitted.

The signing of the new contract determined the course of Orsino's life for another year. It is surprising to see, in the existence of others, how periods of monotonous calm succeed seasons of storm and danger. In our own they do not astonish us so much, if at all. Orsino continued to work hard, to live regularly and to do all those things which, under the circumstances he ought to have done and earned the reputation of being a model young man, a fact which surprised him on one or two occasions when it came to his ears. Yet when he reflected upon it, he saw that he was in reality not like other young men, and that his conduct was undoubtedly abnormally good as viewed by those around him. His grandfather began to look upon him as something almost unnatural, and more than once hinted to Giovanni that the boy, as he still called him, ought to behave like other boys.

"He is more like San Giacinto than any of us," said Giovanni, thoughtfully. "He has taken after that branch."

"If that is the case, he might have done worse," answered the old man. "I like San Giacinto. But you always judge superficially, Giovanni—you always did. And the worst of it is, you are always perfectly well satisfied with your own judgments."

"Possibly. I have certainly not accepted those of others."

"And the result is that you are turning into an oyster—and Orsino has begun to turn into an oyster, too, and the other boys will follow his example—a perfect oyster-bed! Go and take Orsino by the throat and shake him—"

"I regret to say that I am physically not equal to that feat," said Giovanni with a laugh.

"I should be!" exclaimed the aged Prince, doubling his hard hand and bringing it down on the table, while his bright eyes gleamed. "Go and shake him, and tell him to give up this dirty building business—make him give it up, buy him out of it, put plenty of money into his pockets and send him off to amuse himself! You and Corona have made a prig of him, and business is making an oyster of him, and he will be a hopeless idiot before you realise it! Stir him, shake him, make him move! I hate your furniture-man—who is always in the right place and always ready to be sat upon!"

"If you can persuade him to give up affairs I have no objection."

"Persuade him! I never knew a man worth speaking to who could be persuaded to anything he did not like. Make him—that is the way."

"But since he is behaving himself and is occupied—that is better than the lives all these young fellows are leading."

"Do not argue with me, Giovanni, I hate it. Besides, your reason is worth nothing at all. Did I spend my youth over accounts, in the society of an architect? Did I put water in my wine and sit up like a model little boy at my papa's table and spend my evenings in carrying my mamma's fan? Nonsense! And yet all that was expected in my day, in a way it is not expected now. Look at yourself. You are bad enough—dull enough, I mean. Did you waste the best years of your life in counting bricks and measuring mortar?"

"You say that you hate argument, and yet you are arguing. But Orsino shall please himself, as I did, and in his own way. I will certainly not interfere."

"Because you know you can do nothing with him!" retorted old Saracinesca contemptuously.

Giovanni laughed. Twenty years earlier he would have lost his temper to no purpose. But twenty years of unruffled existence had changed him.

"You are not the man you were," grumbled his father.

"No. I have been too happy, far too long, to be much like what I was at thirty."

"And do you mean to say I am not happy, and have not been happy, and do not mean to be happy, and do not wish everybody to be happy, so long as this old machine hangs together? What nonsense you talk, my boy. Go and make love to your wife. That is all you are fit for!"

Discussions of this kind were not unfrequent but of course led to nothing. As a matter of fact Sant' Ilario was quite right in believing interference useless. It would have been impossible. He was no more able to change Orsino's determination than he was physically capable of shaking him. Not that Sant' Ilario was weak, physically or morally, nor ever had been. But his son had grown up to be stronger than he.

Twelve months passed away. During that time the young man worked, as he had worked before, regularly and untiringly. But his object now was to free himself, and he no longer hoped to make a fortune or to do any thing beyond the strict execution of the contract he had in hand, determined if possible to avoid taking another. With a coolness and self-denial beyond his years, he systematically hoarded the allowance he received from his father, in order to put together a sum of money for poor Contini. He made economies everywhere, refused to go into society and spent his evenings in reading. His acquired manner stood him in good stead, but he could not bear more than a limited amount of the daily talk in the family. Being witty, rather than gay, if he could be said to be either, he found himself inclined rather to be bitter than amusing when he was wearied by the monotonous conversation of others. He knew this to be a mistake and controlled himself, taking refuge in solitude and books when he could control himself no longer.

Whether he loved Maria Consuelo still, or not, it was clear that he was not inclined to love any one else for the present. The tolerably harmless dissipation and wildness of the two or three years he had spent in England could not account for such a period of coldness as followed his separation from Maria Consuelo. He had by no means exhausted the pleasures of life and his capacity for enjoyment could not even be said to have reached its height. But he avoided the society of women even more consistently than he shunned the club and the card table.

More than a year had gone by since he had heard from Maria Consuelo. He met Spicca from time to time, looking now as though he had not a day to live, but neither of them mentioned past events. The Romans had talked a little of her sudden change of plans, for it had been known that she had begun to furnish a large apartment for the winter of the previous year, and had then very unaccountably changed her mind and left the place in the hands of an agent to be sub-let. People said she had lost her fortune. Then she had been forgotten in the general disaster that followed, and no one had taken the trouble to remember her since then. Even Gouache, who had once been so enthusiastic over her portrait, did not seem to know or care what had become of her. Once only, and quite accidentally, Orsino had authentic information of her whereabouts. He took up an English society journal one evening and glanced idly over the paragraphs. Maria Consuelo's name arrested his attention. A certain very high and mighty old lady of royal lineage was about to travel in Egypt during the winter. "Her Royal Highness," said the paper, "will be accompanied by the Countess d'Aranjuez d'Aragona." Orsino's hand shook a little as he laid the sheet aside, and he was pale when he rose a few moments later and went off to his own room. He could not help wondering why Maria Consuelo was styled by a title to which she certainly had a legal right, but which she had never before used, and he wondered still more why she travelled in Egypt with an old princess who was generally said to be anything but an agreeable companion, and was reported to be quite deaf. But on the whole he thought little of the information itself. It was the sight of Maria Consuelo's name which had moved him, and he was not altogether himself for several days. The impression wore off before long, and he followed the round of his monotonous life as before.

Early in the month of March in the year 1890, he was seated alone in his room one evening before dinner. The great contract he had undertaken was almost finished, and he knew that within two months he would be placed in the same difficult position from which he had formerly so signally failed to extricate himself. That he and Contini had executed the terms of the contract with scrupulous and conscientious nicety did not better the position. That they had made the most strenuous efforts to find purchasers for the property, as they had a right to do if they could, and had failed, made the position hopeless or almost as bad as that. Whether they liked it or not, Del Ferice had so arranged that the great mass of their acceptances should fall due about the time when the work would be finished. To mortgage on the same terms or anything approaching the same terms with any other bank was out of the question, so that they had no hope of holding the property for the purpose of leasing it. Even if Orsino could have contemplated for a moment such an act of bad faith as wilfully retarding the work in order to gain a renewal of the bills, such a course could have led to no actual improvement in the situation. The property was unsaleable and Del Ferice knew it, and had no intention of selling it. He meant to keep it for himself and let it, as a permanent source of income. It would not have cost him in the end one half of its actual value, and was exceptionally good property. Orsino saw how hopeless it was to attempt resistance, unless he would resign himself to voting an appeal to his own people, and this, as of old, he was resolved not to do.

He was reflecting upon his life of bondage when a servant brought him a letter. He tossed it aside without looking at it, but it chanced to slip from the polished table and fall to the ground. As he picked it up his attention was arrested by the handwriting and by the stamp. The stamp was Egyptian and the writing was that of Maria Consuelo. He started, tore open the envelope and took out a letter of many pages, written on thin paper. At first he found it hard to follow the characters, and his heart beat at a rate which annoyed him. He rose, walked the length of the room and back again, sat down in another seat close to the lamp and read the letter steadily from beginning to end.

"My Dear Friend—You may, perhaps, be surprised at hearing from me after so long a time. I received your last letter. How long ago was that? Twelve, fourteen, fifteen months? I do not know. It is as well to forget, since I at least would rather not remember what you wrote. And I write now—why? Simply because I have the impulse to do so. That is the best of all reasons. I wish to hear from you, which is selfish; and I wish to hear about you, which is not. Are you still working at that business in which you were so much interested? Or have you given it up and gone back to the life you used to hate so thoroughly? I would like to know. Do you remember how angry I was long ago, because you agreed to meet Del Ferice in my drawing-room? I was very wrong, for the meeting led to many good results. I like to think that you are not quite like all the young men of your set, who do nothing—and cannot even do that gracefully. I think you used those very words about yourself, once upon a time. But you proved that you could live a very different life if you chose. I hope you are living it still.

"And so poor Donna Tullia is dead—has been dead a year and a half! I wrote Del Ferice a long letter when I got the news. He answered me. He is not as bad as you used to think, for he was terribly pained by his loss—I could see that well enough in what he wrote though there was nothing exaggerated or desperate in the phrases. In fact there were no phrases at all. I wish I had kept the letter to send to you, but I never keep letters. Poor Donna Tullia! I cannot imagine Rome without her. It would certainly not be the same place to me, for she was uniformly kind and thoughtful where I was concerned, whatever she may have been to others.

"Echoes reach me from time to time in different parts of the world, as I travel, and Rome seems to be changed in many ways. They say the ruin was dreadful when the crash came. I suppose you gave up business then, as was natural, since they say there is no more business to do. But I would be glad to know that nothing disagreeable happened to you in the financial storm. I confess to having felt an unaccountable anxiety about you of late. Perhaps that is why I write and why I hope for an answer at once. I have always looked upon presentiments and forewarnings and all such intimations as utterly false and absurd, and I do not really believe that anything has happened or is happening to distress you. But it is our woman's privilege to be inconsistent, and we should be still more inconsistent if we did not use it. Besides I have felt the same vague disquietude about you more than once before and have not written. Perhaps I should not write even now unless I had a great deal more time at my disposal than I know what to do with. Who knows? If you are busy, write a word on a post-card, just to say that nothing is the matter. Here in Egypt we do not realise what time means, and certainly not that it can ever mean money.

"It is an idle life, less idle for me perhaps than for some of those about me, but even for me not over-full of occupations. The climate occupies all the time not actually spent in eating, sleeping and visiting ruins. It is fair, I suppose, to tell you something of myself since I ask for news of you. I will tell you what I can.

"I am travelling with an old lady, as her companion—not exactly out of inclination and yet not exactly out of duty. Is that too mysterious? Do you see me as Companion and general amuser to an old lady— over seventy years of age? No. I presume not. And I am not with her by necessity either, for I have not suffered any losses. On the contrary, since I dismissed a certain person—an attendant, we will call her— from my service, it seems to me that my income is doubled. The attendant, by the bye, has opened a hotel on the Lake of Como. Perhaps you, who are so good a man of business, may see some connexion between these simple facts. I was never good at managing money, nor at understanding what it meant. It seems that I have not inherited all the family talents.

"But I return to Egypt, to the Nile, to this dahabiyah, on board of which it has pleased the fates to dispose my existence for the present. I am not called a companion, but a lady in waiting, which would be only another term for the same thing, if I were not really very much attached to the Princess, old and deaf as she is. And that is saying a great deal. No one knows what deafness means who has not read aloud to a deaf person, which is what I do every day. I do not think I ever told you about her. I have known her all my life, ever since I was a little girl in the convent in Vienna. She used to come and see me and bring me good things—and books of prayers—I remember especially a box of candied fruits which she told me came from Kiew. I have never eaten any like them since. I wonder how many sincere affections between young and old people owe their existence originally to a confectioner!

"When I left Rome, I met her again in Nice. She was there with the Prince, who was in wretched health and who died soon afterwards. He never was so fond of me as she was. After his death, she asked me to stay with her as long as I would. I do not think I shall leave her again so long as she lives. She treats me like her own child—or rather, her grandchild—and besides, the life suits me very well. I am, really, perfectly independent, and yet I am perfectly protected. I shall not repeat the experiment of living alone for three years, until I am much older.

"It is a rather strange friendship. My Princess knows all about me—all that you know. I told her one day and she did not seem at all surprised. I thought I owed her the truth about myself, since I was to live with her, and since she had always been so kind to me. She says I remind her of her daughter, the poor young Princess Marie, who died nearly thirty years ago. In Nice, too, like her father, poor girl. She was only just nineteen, and very beautiful they say. I suppose the dear good old lady fancies she sees some resemblance even now, though I am so much older than her daughter was when she died. There is the origin of our friendship—the trivial and the tragic—confectionery and death—a box of candied fruits and an irreparable loss! If there were no contrasts what would the world be? All one or the other, I suppose. All death, or all Kiew sweetmeats.

"I suppose you know what life in Egypt is like. If you have not tried it yourself, your friends have and can describe it to you. I will certainly not inflict my impressions upon your friendship. It would be rather a severe test—perhaps yours would not bear it, and then I should be sorry.

"Do you know? I like to think that I have a friend in you. I like to remember the time when you used to talk to me of all your plans—the dear old time! I would rather remember that than much which came afterwards. You have forgiven me for all I did, and are glad, now, that I did it. Yes, I can fancy your smile. You do not see yourself, Prince Saracinesca, Prince Sant' Ilario, Duke of Whatever-it-may-be, Lord of ever so many What-are-their-names, Prince of the Holy Roman Empire, Grandee of Spain of the First Class, Knight of Malta and Hereditary Something to the Holy See—in short the tremendous personage you will one day be—you do not exactly see yourself as the son-in-law of the Signora Lucrezia Ferris, proprietor of a tourist's hotel on the Lake of Como! Confess that the idea was an absurdity! As for me, I will confess that I did very wrong. Had I known all the truth on that afternoon—do you remember the thunderstorm? I would have saved you much, and I should have saved myself—well—something. But we have better things to do than to run after shadows. Perhaps it is as well not even to think of them. It is all over now. Whatever you may think of it all, forgive your old friend,

Maria Consuelo d'A."

Orsino read the long letter to the end, and sat a while thinking over the contents. Two points in it struck him especially. In the first place it was not the letter of a woman who wished to call back a man she had dismissed. There was no sentiment in it, or next to none. She professed herself contented in her life, if not happy, and in one sentence she brought before him the enormous absurdity of the marriage he had once contemplated. He had more than once been ashamed of not making some further direct effort to win her again. He was now suddenly conscious of the great influence which her first letter, containing the statement of her parentage, had really exercised over him. Strangely enough, what she now wrote reconciled him, as it were, with himself. It had turned out best, after all.

That he loved her still, he felt sure, as he held in his hand the pages she had written and felt the old thrill he knew so well in his fingers, and the old, quick beating of the heart. But he acknowledged gladly—too gladly, perhaps—that he had done well to let her go.

Then came the second impression. "I like to remember the time when you used to talk to me of all your plans." The words rang in his ears and called up delicious visions of the past, soft hours spent by her side while she listened with something warmer than patience to the outpouring of his young hopes and aspirations. She, at least, had understood him, and encouraged him, and strengthened him with her sympathy. And why not now, if then? Why should she not understand him now, when he most needed a friend, and give him sympathy now, when he stood most in need of it? She was in Egypt and he in Rome, it was true. But what of that? If she could write to him, he could write to her, and she could answer him again. No one had ever felt with him as she had.

He did not hesitate long. On that same evening, after dinner, he went back to his own room and wrote to her. It was a little hard at first, but, as the ink flowed, he expressed himself better and more clearly. With an odd sort of caution, which had grown upon him of late, he tried to make his letter take a form as similar to hers as possible.

"MY DEAR FRIEND" (he wrote)—"If people always yielded to their impulses as you have done in writing to me, there would be more good fellowship and less loneliness in the world. It would not be easy for me to tell you how great a pleasure you have given me. Perhaps, hereafter, I may compare it to your own memory of the Kiew candied fruits! For the present I do not find a worthy comparison to my hand.

"You ask many questions. I propose to answer them all. Will you have the patience to read what I write? I hope so, for the sake of the time when I used to talk to you of all my plans—and which you say you like to remember. For another reason, too. I have never felt so lonely in my life as I feel now, nor so much in need of a friend—not a helping friend, but one to whom I can speak a little freely. I am very much alone. A sort of estrangement has grown up between my mother and me, and she no longer takes my side in all I want to do, as she did once.

"I will be quite plain. I will tell you all my troubles, because there is not another person in the world to whom I could tell them—and because I know that they will not trouble you. You will feel a little friendly sympathy, and that will be enough. But you will feel no pain. After all, I daresay that I exaggerate, and that there is nothing so very painful in the matter, as it will strike you. But the case is serious, as you will see. It involves my life, perhaps for many years to come.

"I am completely in Del Ferice's power. A year ago I had the possibility of freeing myself. What do you think that chance was? I could have gone to my grandfather and asked him to lay down a sum of money sufficient to liberate me, or I could have refused Del Ferice's new offer and allowed myself to be declared bankrupt. My abominable vanity stood in the way of my following either of those plans. In less than two months I shall be placed in the same position again. But the circumstances are changed. The sum of money is so considerable that I would not like to ask all my family, with their three fortunes, to contribute it. The business is enormous. I have an establishment like a bank and Contini—you remember Contini?—has several assistant architects. Moreover we stand alone. There is no other firm of the kind left, and our failure would be a very disagreeable affair. But so long as I remain Del Ferice's slave, we shall not fail. Do you know that this great and successful firm is carried on systematically without a centime of profit to the partners, and with the constant threat of a disgraceful failure, used to force me on? Do you think that if I chose the alternative, any one would believe, or that my tyrant would let any one believe, that Orsino Saracinesca had served Ugo Del Ferice for years—two years and a half before long—as a sort of bondsman? I am in a very unenviable position. I am sure that Del Ferice made use of me at first for his own ends—that is, to make money for him. The magnitude of the sums which pass through my hands makes me sure that he is now backed by a powerful syndicate, probably of foreign bankers who lost money in the Roman crash, and who see a chance of getting it back through Del Ferice's management. It is a question of millions. You do not understand? Will you try to read my explanation?"

And here Orsino summed up his position towards Del Ferice in a clear and succinct statement, which it is not necessary to reproduce here. It needed no talent for business on Maria Consuelo's part to understand that he was bound hand and foot.

"One of three things must happen" (Orsino continued). "I must cripple, if not ruin, the fortune of my family, or I must go through a scandalous bankruptcy, or I must continue to be Ugo Del Ferice's servant during the best years of my life. My only consolation is that I am unpaid. I do not speak of poor Contini. He is making a reputation, it is true, and Del Ferice gives him something which I increase as much as I can. Considering our positions, he is the more completely sacrificed of the two, poor fellow—and through my fault. If I had only had the courage to put my vanity out of the way eighteen months ago, I might have saved him as well as myself. I believed myself a match for Del Ferice—and I neither was nor ever shall be. I am a little desperate.

"That is my life, my dear friend. Since you have not quite forgotten me, write me a word of that good old sympathy on which I lived so long. It may soon be all I have to live on. If Del Ferice should have the bad taste to follow Donna Tullia to Saint Lawrence's, nothing could save me. I should no longer have the alternative of remaining his slave in exchange for safety from bankruptcy to myself and ruin—or something like it—to my father.

"But let us talk no more about it all. But for your kindly letter, no one would ever have known all this, except Contini. In your calm Egyptian life—thank God, dear, that your life is calm!—my story must sound like a fragment from an unpleasant dream. One thing you do not tell me. Are you happy, as well as peaceful? I would like to know. I am not.

"Pray write again, when you have time—and inclination. If there is anything to be done for you in Rome—any little thing, or great thing either—command your old friend,

"ORSINO SARACINESCA."

CHAPTER XXVIII

Orsino posted his letter with an odd sensation of relief. He felt that he was once more in communication with humanity, since he had been able to speak out and tell some one of the troubles that oppressed him. He had assuredly no reason for being more hopeful than before, and matters were in reality growing more serious every day; but his heart was lighter and he took a more cheerful view of the future, almost against his own better judgment.

He had not expected to receive an answer from Maria Consuelo for some time and was surprised when one came in less than ten days from the date of his writing. This letter was short, hurriedly written and carelessly worded, but there was a ring of anxiety for him in every line of it which he could not misinterpret. Not only did she express the deepest sympathy for him and assure him that all he did still had the liveliest interest for her, but she also insisted upon being informed of the state of his affairs as often as possible. He had spoken of three possibilities, she said. Was there not a fourth somewhere? There might often be an issue from the most desperate situation, of which no one dreamed. Could she not help him to discover where it lay in this case? Could they not write to each other and find it out together?

Orsino looked uneasily at the lines, and the blood rose to his temples. Did she mean what she said, or more, or less? He was overwrought and over-sensitive, and she had written thoughtlessly, as though not weighing her words, but only following an impulse for which she had no time to find the proper expression. She could not imagine that he would accept substantial help from her—still less that he would consent to marry her for the sake of the fortune which might save him. He grew very angry, then turned cold again, and then, reading the words again, saw that he had no right to attach any such meaning to them. Then it struck him that even if, by any possibility, she had meant to convey such an idea, he would have no right at all to resent it. Women, he reflected, did not look upon such matters as men did. She had refused to marry him when he was prosperous. If she meant that she would marry him now, to save him from ruin, he could not but acknowledge that she was carrying devotion near to its farthest limit. But the words themselves would not bear such an interpretation. He was straining language too far in suggesting it.

"And yet she means something," he said to himself. "Something which I cannot understand."

He wrote again, maintaining the tone of his first letter more carefully than she had done on her part, though not sparing the warmest expressions of heartfelt thanks for the sympathy she had so readily given. But there was no fourth way, he said. One of those three things which he had explained to her must happen. There was no hope, and he was resigned to continue his existence of slavery until Del Ferice's death brought about the great crisis of his life. Not that Del Ferice was in any danger of dying, he added, in spite of the general gossip about his bad health. Such men often outlasted stronger people, as Ugo had outlived Donna Tullia. Not that his death would improve matters, either, as they stood at present. That he had explained before. If the count died now, there were ninety-nine chances out of a hundred that Orsino would be ruined. For the present, nothing would happen. In little more than a month—in six weeks at the utmost—a new arrangement would be forced upon him, binding him perhaps for years to come. Del Ferice had already spoken to him of a great public undertaking, at least half of the contract for which could easily be secured or controlled by his bank. He had added that this might be a favourable occasion for Andrea Contini and Company to act in concert with the bank. Orsino knew what that meant. Indeed, there was no possibility of mistaking the meaning, which was clear enough. The fourth plan could only lie in finding beforehand a purchaser for buildings which could not be so disposed of, because they were built for a particular purpose, and could only be bought by those who had ordered them, namely persons whom Del Ferice so controlled that he could postpone their appearance if he chose and drive Orsino into a failure at any moment after the completion of the work. For instance, one of those buildings was evidently intended for a factory, and probably for a match factory. Del Ferice, in requiring that Contini and Company should erect what he had already arranged to dispose of, had vaguely remarked that there were no match factories in Rome and that perhaps some one would like to buy one. If Orsino had been less desperate he would willingly have risked much to resent the suave insolence. As it was, he had laughed in his tyrant's face, and bitterly enough; a form of insult, however, to which Ugo was supremely indifferent. These and many other details Orsino wrote to Maria Consuelo, pouring out his confidence with the assurance of a man who asks nothing but sympathy and is sure of receiving that in overflowing measure. He no longer waited for her answers, as the crucial moment approached, but wrote freely from day to day, as he felt inclined. There was little which he did not tell her in the dozen or fifteen letters he penned in the course of the month. Like many reticent men who have never taken up a pen except for ordinary correspondence or for the routine work of a business requiring accuracy, and who all at once begin to write the history of their daily lives for the perusal of one trusted person, Orsino felt as though he had found a new means of expression and abandoned himself willingly to the comparative pleasure of complete confidence. Like all such men, too, he unconsciously exhibited the chief fault of his character in his long, diary-like letters. That fault was his vanity. Had he been describing a great success he could and would have concealed it better; in writing of his own successive errors and disappointments he showed by the excessive blame he cast upon himself, how deeply that vanity of his was wounded. It is possible that Maria Consuelo discovered this. But she made no profession of analysis, and while appearing outwardly far colder than Orsino, she seemed much more disposed than he to yield to unexpected impulses when she felt their influence. And Orsino was quite unconscious that he might be exhibiting the defects of his moral nature to eyes keener than his own.

He wrote constantly therefore, with the utmost freedom, and in the moments while he was writing he enjoyed a faint illusion of increased safety, as though he were retarding the events of the future by describing minutely those of the past. More than once again Maria Consuelo answered him, and always in the same strain, doing her best, apparently, to give him hope and to reconcile him with himself. However much he might condemn his own lack of foresight, she said, no man who did his best according to his best judgment, and who acted honourably, was to be blamed for the result, though it might involve the ruin of thousands. That was her chief argument and it comforted him, and seemed to relieve him from a small part of the responsibility which weighed so heavily upon his shoulders, a burden now grown so heavy that the least lightening of it made him feel comparatively free until called upon to face facts again and fight with realities.

But events would not be retarded, and Orsino's own good qualities tended to hasten them, as they had to a great extent been the cause of his embarrassment ever since the success of his first attempt, in making him valuable as a slave to be kept from escaping at all risks. The system upon which the business was conducted was admirable. It had been good from the beginning and Orsino had improved it to a degree very uncommon in Rome. He had mastered the science of book-keeping in a short time, and had forced himself to an accuracy of detail and a promptness of ready reference which would have surprised many an old professional clerk. It must be remembered that from the first he had found little else to do. The technical work had always been in Contini's hands, and Del Ferice's forethought had relieved them both from the necessity of entering upon financial negotiations requiring time, diplomatic tact and skill of a higher order. The consequence was that Orsino had devoted the whole of his great energy and native talent for order to the keeping of the books, with the result that when a contract had been executed there was hardly any accountant's work to be done. Nominally, too, Andrea Contini and Company were not responsible to any one for their book-keeping; but in practice, and under pretence of rendering valuable service, Del Ferice sent an auditor from time to time to look into the state of affairs, a proceeding which Contini bitterly resented while Orsino expressed himself perfectly indifferent to the interference, on the ground that there was nothing to conceal. Had the books been badly kept, the final winding up of each contract would have been retarded for one or more weeks. But the more deeply Orsino became involved, the more keenly he felt the value and, at last, the vital importance, of the most minute accuracy. If worse came to worst and he should be obliged to fail, through Del Ferice's sudden death or from any other cause, his reputation as an honourable man might depend upon this very accuracy of detail, by which he would be able to prove that in the midst of great undertakings, and while very large sums of money were passing daily through his hands, he had never received even the very smallest share of the profits absorbed by the bank. He even kept a private account of his own expenditure on the allowance he received from his father, in order that, if called upon, he might be able to prove how large a part of that allowance he regularly paid to poor Contini as compensation for the unhappy position in which the latter found himself. If bankruptcy awaited him, his failure would, if the facts were properly made known, reckon as one of the most honourable on record, though he was pleased to look upon such a contingency as a certain source of scandal and more than possible disgrace.

Unconsciously his own determined industry in book-keeping gave him a little more confidence. In his great anxiety he was spared the terrible uncertainty felt by a man who does not precisely know his own financial position at a given critical moment. His studiously acquired outward calm also stood him in good stead. Even San Giacinto who knew the financial world as few men knew it watched his youthful cousin with curiosity and not without a certain sympathy and a very little admiration. The young man's face was growing stern and thoughtful like his own, lean, grave and strong. San Giacinto remembered that night a year and a half earlier when he had warned Orsino of the coming danger, and he was almost displeased with himself now for having taken a step which seemed to have been unnecessary. It was San Giacinto's principle never to do anything unnecessary, because a useless action meant a loss of time and therefore a loss of advantage over the adversary of the moment. San Giacinto, in different circumstances, would have made a good general—possibly a great one; his strange life had made him a financier of a type singular and wholly different from that of the men with whom he had to deal. He never sought to gain an advantage by a deception, but he won everything by superior foresight, imperturbable coolness, matchless rapidity of action and undaunted courage under all circumstances. It needs higher qualities to be a good man, but no others are needed to make a successful one. Orsino possessed something of the same rapidity and much of a similar coolness and courage, but he lacked the foresight. It was vanity, of the most pardonable kind, indeed, but vanity nevertheless which had led him to embark upon his dangerous enterprise—not in the determination to accomplish for the sake of accomplishing, still less in the direct desire for wealth as an ultimate object, but in the almost boyish longing to show to his own people that there was more in him than they suspected. The gift of foresight is generally weakened by the presence of vanity, but when vanity takes its place the result is as likely to be failure as not, and depends almost directly upon chance alone.

The crisis in Orsino's life was at hand, and what has here been finally said of his position at that time seemed necessary, as summing up the consequences to him of more than two years' unremitting labour, during which he had become involved in affairs of enormous consequence at an age when most young men are spending their time, more profitably perhaps and certainly more agreeably, in such pleasures and pursuits as mother society provides for her half-fledged nestlings.

On the day before his final interview with Del Ferice Orsino wrote a lengthy letter to Maria Consuelo. As she did not receive it until long afterwards it is quite unnecessary to give any account of its contents. Some time had passed since he had heard from her and he was not sure whether or not she were still in Egypt. But he wrote to her, nevertheless, drawing much fictitious comfort and little real advantage from the last clear statement of his difficulties. By this time, writing to her had become a habit and he resorted to it naturally when over wearied by work and anxiety.

On this same day also he had spent several hours in talking over the situation with Contini. The architect, strange to say, was more reconciled with his position than he had formerly been. He, at least, received a certain substantial remuneration. He, at least, loved his profession and rejoiced in the handling of great masses of brick and stone. He, too, was rapidly making a reputation and a name for himself, and, if business improved, was not prevented from entering into other enterprises besides the one in which he found himself so deeply interested. As a member of the firm, he could not free himself. As an architect, he could have an architect's office of his own and build for any one who chose to employ him. For his own part, he said, he might perhaps be more profitably employed upon less important work; but then, he might not, for business was very bad. The great works in which Del Ferice kept him engaged had the incalculable advantage of bringing him constantly before the public as an architect and of keeping his name, which was the name of the firm, continually in the notice of all men of business. He was deeply indebted to Orsino for the generous help given when the realities of profit were so greatly at variance with the appearances of prosperity. He would always regard repayment of the money so advanced to him as a debt of honour and he hoped to live long enough to extinguish it. He sympathised with Orsino in his desire to be freer and more independent, but reminded him that when the day of liberation came, he would not regret the comparatively short apprenticeship during which he had acquired so great a mastery of business. Business, he said, had been Orsino's ambition from the beginning, and business he had, in plenty, if not with profit. For his own part, he was satisfied.

Orsino felt that his partner could not be blamed, and he felt, too, that he would be doing Contini a great injury in involving him in a failure. But he regretted the time when their interests had coincided and they had cursed Del Ferice in common and with a good will. There was nothing to be done but to submit. He knew well enough what awaited him.

On the following morning, by appointment, he went with a heavy heart to meet Del Ferice at the bank. The latter had always preferred to see Orsino without Contini when a new contract was to be discussed. As a personal acquaintance he treated with Orsino on a footing of social equality, and the balance of outwardly agreeable relations would have been disturbed by the presence of a social inferior. Moreover, Del Ferice knew the Saracinesca people tolerably well, and though not so timid as many people supposed, he somewhat dreaded a sudden outbreak of the hereditary temper; if such a manifestation really took place, it would be more agreeable that there should be no witnesses of it.

Orsino was surprised to find that Ugo was out of town. Having made an appointment, he ought at least to have sent word to the Palazzo Saracinesca of his departure. He had indeed left a message for Orsino, which was correctly delivered, to the effect that he would return in twenty-four hours, and requesting him to postpone the interview until the following afternoon. In Orsino's humour this was not altogether pleasant. The young man felt little suspense indeed, for he knew how matters must turn out, and that he should be saddled with another contract. But he found it hard to wait with equanimity, now that he had made up his mind to the worst, and he resented Del Ferice's rudeness in not giving a civil warning of his intended journey.

The day passed somehow, at last, and towards evening Orsino received a telegram from Ugo, full of excuses, but begging to put off the meeting two days longer. The dispatch was from Naples whither Del Ferice often went on business.

It was almost unbearable and yet it must be borne. Orsino spent his time in roaming about the less frequented parts of the city, trying to make new plans for the future which was already planned for him, doing his best to follow out a distinct line of thought, if only to distract his own attention. He could not even write to Maria Consuelo, for he felt that he had said all there was to be said, in his last long letter.

On the morning of the fourth day he went to the bank again. Del Ferice was there and greeted him warmly, interweaving his phrases with excuses for his absence.

"You will forgive me, I am sure," he said, "though I have put you to very great inconvenience. The case was urgent and I could not leave it in the hands of others. Of course you could have settled the business with another of the directors, but I think—indeed, I know—that you prefer only to see me in these matters. We have worked together so long now, that we understand each other with half a word. Really, I am very sorry to have kept you waiting so long!"

"It is of no importance," answered Orsino coolly. "Pray do not speak of it."

"Of importance—no—perhaps not. That is, as you could not lose by it, it was not of financial importance. But when I have made an engagement, I like to keep it. In business, so much depends upon keeping small engagements—and they may mean quite as much in the relations of society. However, as you are so kind, we will not speak of it again. I have made my excuses and you have accepted them. Let that end the matter. To business, now, Don Orsino—to business!"

Orsino fancied that Del Ferice's manner was not quite natural. He was generally more quiet. His rather watery blue eyes did not usually look so wide awake, his fat white hands were not commonly so active in their gestures. Altogether he seemed more nervous, and at the same time better pleased with himself and with life than usual. Orsino wondered what had happened. He had perhaps made some very successful stroke in his affairs during the three days he had spent in Naples.

"So let us now have a look into your contracts, Don Orsino," he said. "Or rather, look into the state of the account yourself if you wish to do so, for I have already examined it."

"I am familiar enough with the details," answered the young man. "I do not need to look over everything. The books have been audited as you see. The only thing left to be done is to hand over the work to you, since it is executed according to the contract. You doubtless remember that verbal part of the agreement. You receive the buildings as they now stand and our credit cash if there is any, in full discharge of all the obligations of Andrea Contini and Company to the bank—acceptances coming due, balance of account if in debit, and mortgages on land and houses—and we are quits again, my firm being discharged of all obligation."

Del Ferice's expression changed a little and became more grave.

"Doubtless," he answered, "there was a tacit understanding to that effect. Yes—yes—I remember. Indeed it was not altogether tacit. A word was said about it, and a word is as good as a contract. Very well, Don Orsino—very well. Since you desire it, we will cry quits again. This kind of business is not very profitable to the bank—not very—but it is not actual loss."

"It is not profitable to us," observed Orsino. "If you do not wish any more of it, we do not."

"Really?"

Del Ferice looked at him rather curiously as though wishing that he would say more. Orsino met his glance steadily, expecting to be informed of the nature of the next contract to be forced upon him.

"So you really prefer to discontinue these operations—if I may call them so," said Del Ferice thoughtfully. "It is strange that you should, I confess. I remember that you much desired to take a part in affairs, to be an actor in the interesting doings of the day, to be a financial personage, in short. You have had your wish, Don Orsino. Your firm plays an important part in Rome. Do you remember our first interview on the steps of Monte Citorio? You asked me whether I could and would help you to enter business. I promised that I would, and I have kept my word. The sums mentioned in those papers, here, show that I have done all I promised. You told me that you had fifteen thousand francs at your disposal. From that small beginning I have shown you how to deal with millions. But you do not seem to care for business, after all, Don Orsino. You really do not seem to care for it, though I must confess that you have a remarkable talent. It is very strange."

"Is it?" asked Orsino with a shade of contempt. "You may remember that my business has not been profitable, in spite of what you call my talent, and in spite of what I know to have been hard work."

Del Ferice smiled softly.

"That is quite another matter," he answered. "If you had asked me whether you could make a fortune at this time, I would have told you that it was quite impossible without enormous capital. Quite impossible. Understand that, if you please. But, negatively, you have profited, because others have failed—hundreds of firms and contractors—while you have lost but the paltry fifteen thousand or so with which you began. And you have acquired great knowledge and experience. Therefore, on the whole, you have been the gainer. In balancing an account one takes but the sordid debit and credit and compares them—but in estimating the value of a firm one should consider its reputation and the goodwill it has created. The name of Andrea Contini and Company is a power in Rome. That is the result of your work, and it is not a loss."

Orsino said nothing, but leaned back in his chair, gloomily staring at the wall. He wondered when Del Ferice would come to the point, and begin to talk about the new contract.

"You do not seem to agree with me," observed Ugo in an injured tone.

"Not altogether, I confess," replied the young man with a contemptuous laugh.

"Well, well—it is no matter—it is of no importance—of no consequence whatever," said Del Fence, who seemed inclined to repeat himself and to lengthen, his phrases as though he wished to gain time. "Only this, Don Orsino. I would remind you that you have just executed a piece of work successfully, which no other firm in Rome could have carried out without failure, under the present depression. It seems to me that you have every reason to congratulate yourself. Of course, it was impossible for me to understand that you really cared for a large profit—for actual money—"

"And I do not," interrupted Orsino with more warmth than he had hitherto shown.

"But, in that case, you ought to be more than satisfied," objected Ugo suavely.

Orsino grew impatient at last and spoke out frankly.

"I cannot be satisfied with a position of absolute dependence, from which I cannot escape except by bankruptcy. You know that I am completely in your power. You know very well that while you are talking to me now you contemplate making your usual condition before crying quits, as you express it. You intend to impose another and probably a larger piece of work on me, which I shall be obliged to undertake on the same terms as before, because if I do not accept it, it is in your power to ruin me at once. And this state of things may go on for years. That is the enviable position of Andrea Contini and Company."

Del Ferice assumed an air of injured dignity.

"If you think anything of this kind you greatly misjudge me," he said.

"I do not see why I should judge otherwise," retorted Orsino. "That is exactly what took place on the last occasion, and what will take place now—"

"I think not," said Del Ferice very quietly, and watching him.

Orsino was somewhat startled by the words, but his face betrayed nothing. It was clear to him that Ugo had something new to propose, and it was not easy to guess the nature of the coming proposition.

"Will you kindly explain yourself?" he asked.

"My dear Don Orsino, there is nothing to explain," replied Del Ferice again becoming very bland.

"I do not understand."

"No? It is very simple. You have finished the buildings. The bank will take them over and consider the account closed. You stated the position yourself in the most precise terms. I do not see why you should suppose that the bank wishes to impose anything upon you which you are not inclined to accept. I really do not see why you should think anything of the kind."

In the dead silence which followed Orsino could hear his own heart beating loudly. He wondered whether he had heard aright. He wondered whether this were not some new manoeuvre on Del Ferice's part by which he must ultimately fall still more completely under the banker's domination. Ugo doubtless meant to qualify what he had just said by adding a clause. Orsino waited for what was to follow.

"Am I to understand that this does not suit your wishes?" inquired Ugo, presently.

"On the contrary, it would suit me perfectly," answered Orsino controlling his voice with some difficulty.

"In that case, there is nothing more to be said," observed Del Ferice. "The bank will give you a formal release—indeed, I think the notary is at this moment here. I am very glad to be able to meet your views, Don Orsino. Very glad, I am sure. It is always pleasant to find that amicable relations have been preserved after a long and somewhat complicated business connexion. The bank owes it to you, I am sure—"

"I am quite willing to owe that to the bank," answered Orsino with a ready smile. He was almost beside himself with joy.

"You are very good, I assure you," said Del Ferice, with much politeness. He touched a bell and his confidential clerk appeared.

"Cancel these drafts," he said, giving the man a small bundle of bills. "Direct the notary to prepare a deed of sale, transferring all this property, as was done before—" he hesitated. "I will see him myself in ten minutes," he added. "It will be simpler. The account of Andrea Contini is balanced and closed. Make out a preliminary receipt for all dues whatsoever and bring it to me."

The clerk stared for one moment as though he believed that Del Ferice were mad. Then he went out.

"I am sorry to lose you, Don Orsino," said Del Ferice, thoughtfully rolling his big silver pencil case on the table. "All the legal papers will be ready to-morrow afternoon."

"Pray express to the directors my best thanks for so speedily winding up the business," answered Orsino. "I think that, after all, I have no great talent for affairs."

"On the contrary, on the contrary," protested Ugo. "I have a great deal to say against that statement." And he eulogised Orsino's gifts almost without pausing for breath until the clerk returned with the preliminary receipt. Del Ferice signed it and handed it to Orsino with a smile.

"This was unnecessary," said the young man. "I could have waited until to-morrow."

"A matter of conscience, dear Don Orsino—nothing more."

CHAPTER XXIX

Orsino was free at last. The whole matter was incomprehensible to him, and almost mysterious, so that after he had at last received his legal release he spent his time in trying to discover the motives of Del Ferice's conduct. The simplest explanation seemed to be that Ugo had not derived as much profit from the last contract as he had hoped for, though it had been enough to justify him in keeping his informal engagement with Contini and Company, and that he feared a new and unfavourable change in business which made any further speculations of the kind dangerous. For some time Orsino believed this to have been the case, but events proved that he was mistaken. He dissolved his partnership with Contini, but Andrea Contini and Company still continued to exist. The new partner was no less a personage than Del Ferice himself, who was constantly represented in the firm by the confidential clerk who has been more than once mentioned in this history, and who was a friend of Contini's. What terms Contini made for himself, Orsino never knew, but it is certain that the architect prospered from that time and is still prosperous.

Late in the spring of that year 1890 Roman society was considerably surprised by the news of a most unexpected marriage. The engagement had been carefully kept a secret, the banns had been published in Palermo, the civil and religious ceremonies had taken place there, and the happy couple had already reached Paris before either of them thought of informing their friends and before any notice of the event appeared in the papers. Even then, society felt itself aggrieved by the laconic form in which the information was communicated.

The statement, indeed, left nothing to be desired on the score of plainness or conciseness of style. Count Del Ferice had married Maria Consuelo d'Aranjuez d'Aragona.

Two persons only received the intelligence a few days before it was generally made known. One was Orsino and the other was Spicca. The letters were characteristic and may be worth reproducing.

"MY FATHER" (Maria Consuelo wrote)—"I am married to Count Del Ferice, with whom I think that you are acquainted. There is no reason why I should enter into any explanation of my reasons for taking this step. There are plenty which everybody can see. My husband's present position and great wealth make him what the world calls a good match, and my fortune places me above the suspicion of having married him for his money. If his birth was not originally of the highest, it was at least as good as mine, and society will say that the marriage was appropriate in all its circumstances. You are aware that I could not be married without informing my husband and the municipal authorities of my parentage, by presenting copies of the registers in Nice. Count Del Ferice was good enough to overlook some little peculiarity in the relation between the dates of my birth and your marriage. We will therefore say no more about the matter. The object of this letter is to let you know that those facts have been communicated to several persons, as a matter of necessity. I do not expect you to congratulate me. I congratulate myself, however, with all my heart. Within two years I have freed myself from my worthy mother, I have placed myself beyond your power to injure me, and I have escaped ruining a man I loved by marrying him. I have laid the foundations of peace if not of happiness.

"The Princess is very ill but hopes to reach Normandy before the summer begins. My husband will be obliged to be often in Rome but will come to me from time to time, as I cannot leave the Princess at present. She is trying, however, to select among her acquaintance another lady in waiting—the more willingly as she is not pleased with my marriage. Is that a satisfaction to you? I expect to spend the winter in Rome.

"MARIA CONSUELO DEL FERICE."

This was the letter by which Maria Consuelo announced her marriage to the father whom she so sincerely hated. For cruelty of language and expression it was not to be compared with the one she had written to him after parting with Orsino. But had she known how the news she now conveyed would affect the old man who was to learn it, her heart might have softened a little towards him, even after all she had suffered. Very different were the lines Orsino received from her at the same time.

"My dear Friend—When you read this letter, which I write on the eve of my marriage, but shall not send till some days have passed, you must think of me as the wife of Ugo Del Ferice. To-night, I am still Maria Consuelo. I have something to say to you, and you must read it patiently, for I shall never say it again— and after all, it will not be much. Is it right of me to say it? I do not know. Until to-morrow I have still time to refuse to be married. Therefore I am still a free agent, and entitled to think freely. After to-morrow it will be different.

"I wish, dear, that I could tell you all the truth. Perhaps you would not be ashamed of having loved the daughter of Lucrezia Ferris. But I cannot tell you all. There are reasons why you had better never know it. But I will tell you this, for I must say it once. I love you very dearly. I loved you long ago, I loved you when I left you in Rome, I have loved you ever since, and I am afraid that I shall love you until I die.

"It is not foolish of me to write the words, though it may be wrong. If I love you, it is because I know you. We shall meet before long, and then meet, perhaps, hundreds of times, and more, for I am to live in Rome. I know that you will be all you should be, or I would not speak now as I never spoke before, at the moment when I am raising an impassable barrier between us by my own free will. If you ever loved me—and you did—you will respect that barrier in deed and word, and even in thought. You will remember only that I loved you with all my heart on the day before my marriage. You will forget even to think that I may love you still to-morrow, and think tenderly of you on the day after that.

"You are free now, dear, and can begin your real life. How do I know it? Del Ferice has told me that he has released you—for we sometimes speak of you. He has even shown me a copy of the legal act of release, which he chanced to find among the papers he had brought. An accident, perhaps. Or, perhaps he knows that I loved you. I do not care—I had a right to, then.

"So you are quite free. I like to think that you have come out of all your troubles quite unscathed, young, your name untarnished, your hands clean. I am glad that you answered the letter I wrote to you from Egypt and told me all, and wrote so often afterwards. I could not do much beyond give you my sympathy, and I gave it all—to the uttermost. You will not need any more of it. You are free now, thank God!

"If you think of me, wish me peace, dear—I do not ask for anything nearer to happiness than that. But I wish you many things, the least of which should make you happy. Most of all, I wish that you may some day love well and truly, and win the reality of which you once thought you held the shadow. Can I say more than that? No loving woman can.

"And so, good-bye—good-bye, love of all my life, good-bye dear, dear Orsino—I think this is the hardest good-bye of all—when we are to meet so soon. I cannot write any more. Once again, the last—the very last time, for ever—I love you.

"MARIA CONSUELO."

A strange sensation came over Orsino as he read this letter. He was not able at first to realise much beyond the fact that Maria Consuelo was actually married to Del Ferice—a match than which none imaginable could have been more unexpected. But he felt that there was more behind the facts than he was able to grasp, almost more than he dared to guess at. A mysterious horror filled his mind as he read and reread the lines. There was no doubting the sincerity of what she said. He doubted the survival of his own love much more. She could have no reason whatever for writing as she did, on the eve of her marriage, no reason beyond the irresistible desire to speak out all her heart once only and for the last time. Again and again he went over the passages which struck him as most strange. Then the truth flashed upon him. Maria Consuelo had sold herself to free him from his difficulties, to save him from the terrible alternatives of either wasting his life as Del Ferice's slave or of ruining his family.

With a smothered exclamation, between an oath and a groan of pain, Orsino threw himself upon the divan and buried his face in his hands. It is kinder to leave him there for a time, alone.

Poor Spicca broke down under this last blow. In vain old Santi got out the cordial from the press in the corner, and did his best to bring his master back to his natural self. In vain Spicca roused himself, forced himself to eat, went out, walked his hour, dragging his feet after him, and attempted to exchange a word with his friends at the club. He seemed to have got his death wound. His head sank lower on his breast, his long emaciated frame stooped more and more, the thin hands grew daily more colourless, and the deathly face daily more deathly pale. Days passed away, and weeks, and it was early June. He no longer tried to go out. Santi tried to prevail upon him to take a little air in a cab, on the Via Appia. It would be money well spent, he said, apologising for suggesting such extravagance. Spicca shook his head, and kept to his chair by the open window. Then, on a certain morning, he was worse and had not the strength to rise from his bed.

On that very morning a telegram came. He looked at it as though hardly understanding what he should do, as Santi held it before him. Then he opened it. His fingers did not tremble even now. The iron nerve of the great swordsman survived still.

"Ventnor—Rome. Count Spicca. The Princess is dead. I know the truth at last. God forgive me and bless you. I come to you at once.—Maria Consuelo."

Spicca read the few words printed on the white strip that was pasted to the yellow paper. Then his hands sank to his sides and he closed his eyes. Santi thought it was the end, and burst into tears as he fell to his knees by the bed.

Half an hour passed. Then Spicca raised his head, and made a gesture with his hand.

"Do not be a fool, Santi, I am not dead yet," he said, with kindly impatience. "Get up and send for Don Orsino Saracinesca, if he is still in Rome."

Santi left the room, drying his eyes and uttering incoherent exclamations of astonishment mingled with a singular cross fire of praise and prayer directed to the Saints and of imprecations upon himself for his own stupidity.

Before noon Orsino appeared. He was gaunt and pale, and more like San Giacinto than ever. There was a settled hardness in his face which was never again to disappear permanently. But he was horror-struck by Spicca's appearance. He had no idea that a man already so cadaverous could still change as the old man had changed. Spicca seemed little more than a grey shadow barely resting upon the white bed. He put the telegram into Orsino's hands. The young man read it twice and his face expressed his astonishment. Spicca smiled faintly, as he watched him.

"What does it mean?" asked Orsino. "Of what truth does she speak? She hated you, and now, all at once, she loves you. I do not understand."

"How should you?" The old man spoke in a clear, thin voice, very unlike his own. "You could not understand. But before I die, I will tell you."

"Do not talk of dying—"

"No. It is not necessary. I realise it enough, and you need not realise it at all. I have not much to tell you, but a little truth will sometimes destroy many falsehoods. You remember the story about Lucrezia Ferris? Maria Consuelo wrote it to you."

"Remember it! Could I forget it?"

"You may as well. There is not a word of truth in it. Lucrezia Ferris is not her mother."

"Not her mother!"

"No. I only wonder how you could ever have believed that a Piedmontese nurse could be the mother of Maria Consuelo. Nor am I Maria Consuelo's father. Perhaps that will not surprise you so much. She does not resemble me, thank Heaven!"

"What is she then? Who is she?" asked Orsino impatiently.

"To tell you that I must tell you the story. When I was young—very long before you were born—I travelled much, and I was well received. I was rich and of good family. At a certain court in Europe—I was at one time in the diplomacy—I loved a lady whom I could not have married, even had she been free. Her station was far above mine. She was also considerably older than I, and she paid very little attention to me, I confess. But I loved her. She is just dead. She was that princess mentioned in this telegram. Do you understand? Do you hear me? My voice is weak."

"Perfectly. Pray go on."

"Maria Consuelo is her grandchild—the granddaughter of the only woman I ever loved. Understand that, too. It happened in this way. My Princess had but one daughter, the Princess Marie, a mere child when I first saw her—not more than fourteen years old. We were all in Nice, one winter thirty years ago—some four years after I had first met the Princess. I travelled in order to see her, and she was always kind to me, though she did not love me. Perhaps I was useful, too, before that. People were always afraid of me, because I could handle the foils. It was thirty years ago, and the Princess Marie was eighteen. Poor child!"

Spicca paused a moment, and passed his transparent hand over his eyes.

"I think I understand," said Orsino.

"No you do not," answered Spicca, with unexpected sharpness. "You will not understand, until I have told you everything. The Princess Marie fell ill, or pretended to fall ill while we were at Nice. But she could not conceal the truth long—at least not from her mother. She had already taken into her confidence a little Piedmontese maid, scarcely older than herself—a certain Lucrezia Ferris—and she allowed no other woman to come near her. Then she told her mother the truth. She loved a man of her own rank and not much older—not yet of age, in fact. Unfortunately, as happens with such people, a marriage was diplomatically impossible. He was not of her nationality and the relations were strained. But she had married him nevertheless, secretly and, as it turned out, without any legal formalities. It is questionable whether the marriage, even then, could have been proved to be valid, for she was a Catholic and he was not, and a Catholic priest had married them without proper authorisation or dispensation. But they were both in earnest, both young and both foolish. The husband—his name is of no importance—was very far away at the time we were in Nice, and was quite unable to come to her. She was about to be a mother and she turned to her own mother in her extremity, with a full confession of the truth."

"I see," said Orsino. "And you adopted—"

"You do not see yet. The Princess came to me for advice. The situation was an extremely delicate one from all points of view. To declare the marriage at that moment might have produced extraordinary complications, for the countries to which, the two young people belonged were on the verge of a war which was only retarded by the extraordinary genius of one man. To conceal it seemed equally dangerous, if not more so. The Princess Marie's reputation was at stake—the reputation of a young girl, as people supposed her to be, remember that. Various schemes suggested themselves. I cannot tell what would have been done, for fate decided the matter—tragically, as fate does. The young husband was killed while on a shooting expedition—at least so it was stated. I always believed that he shot himself. It was all very mysterious. We could not keep the news from the Princess Marie. That night Maria Consuelo was born. On the next day, her mother died. The shock had killed her. The secret was now known to the old Princess, to me, to Lucrezia Ferris and to the French doctor—a man of great skill and discretion. Maria Consuelo was the nameless orphan child of an unacknowledged marriage—of a marriage which was certainly not legal, and which the Church must hesitate to ratify. Again we saw that the complications, diplomatic and of other kinds, which would arise if the truth were published, would be enormous. The Prince himself was not yet in Nice and was quite ignorant of the true cause of his daughter's sudden death. But he would arrive in forty-eight hours, and it was necessary to decide upon some course. We could rely upon the doctor and upon our two selves—the Princess and I. Lucrezia Ferris seemed to be a sensible, quiet girl, and she certainly proved to be discreet for a long time. The Princess was distracted with grief and beside herself with anxiety. Remember that I loved her—that explains what I did. I proposed the plan which was carried out and with which you are acquainted. I took the child, declared it to be mine, and married Lucrezia. The only legal documents in existence concerning Maria Consuelo prove her to be my daughter. The priest who had married the poor Princess Marie could never be found. Terrified, perhaps, at what he had done, he disappeared—probably as a monk in an Austrian monastery. I hunted him for years. Lucrezia Ferris was discreet for two reasons. She received a large sum of money, and a large allowance afterwards, and later on it appears that she further enriched herself at Maria Consuelo's expense. Avarice was her chief fault, and by it we held her. Secondly, however, she was well aware, and knows to-day, that no one would believe her story if she told the truth. The proofs are all positive and legal for Maria Consuelo's supposed parentage, and there is not a trace of evidence in favour of the truth. You know the story now. I am glad I have been able to tell it to you. I will rest now, for I am very tired. If I am alive to-morrow, come and see me—good-bye, in case you should not find me."

Orsino pressed the wasted hand and went out silently, more affected than he owned by the dying man's words and looks. It was a painful story of well-meant mistakes, he thought, and it explained many things which he had not understood. Linking it with all he knew besides, he had the whole history of Spicca's mysterious, broken life, together with the explanation of some points in his own which had never been clear to him. The old cynic of a duellist had been a man of heart, after all, and had sacrificed his whole existence to keep a secret for a woman whom he loved but who did not care for him. That was all. She was dead and he was dying. The secret was already half buried in the past. If it were told now, no one would believe it.

Orsino returned on the following day. He had sent for news several times, and was told that Spicca still lingered. He saw him again but the old man seemed very weak and only spoke a few words during the hour Orsino spent with him. The doctor had said that he might possibly live, but that there was not much hope.

And again on the next day Orsino came back. He started as he entered the room. An old Franciscan, a Minorite, was by the bedside, speaking in low tones. Orsino made as though he would withdraw, but Spicca feebly beckoned to him to stay, and the monk rose.

"Good-bye," whispered Spicca, following him with his sunken eyes.

Orsino led the Franciscan out. At the outer door the latter turned to Orsino with a strange look and laid a hand upon his arm.

"Who are you, my son?" he asked.

"Orsino Saracinesca."

"A friend of his?"

"Yes."

"He has done terrible things in his long life. But he has done noble things, too, and has suffered much, and in silence. He has earned his rest, and God will forgive him."

The monk bowed his head and went out. Orsino re-entered the room and took the vacant chair beside the bed. He touched Spicca's hand almost affectionately, but the latter withdrew it with an effort. He had never liked sympathy, and liked it least when another would have needed it most. For a considerable time neither spoke. The pale hand lay peacefully upon the pillows, the long, shadowy frame was wrapped in a gown of dark woollen material.

"Do you think she will come to-day?" asked the old man at length.

"She may come to-day—I hope so," Orsino answered.

A long pause followed.

"I hope so, too," Spicca whispered. "I have not much strength left. I cannot wait much longer."

Again there was silence. Orsino knew that there was nothing to be said, nothing at least which he could say, to cheer the last hours of the lonely life. But Spicca seemed contented that he should sit there.

"Give me that photograph," he said, suddenly, a quarter of an hour later.

Orsino looked about him but could not see what Spicca wanted.

"Hers," said the feeble voice, "in the next room."

It was the photograph in the little chiselled frame—the same frame which had once excited Donna Tullia's scorn. Orsino brought it quickly from its place over the chimney-piece, and held it before his friend's eyes. Spicca gazed at it a long time in silence.

"Take it away," he said, at last. "It is not like her."

Orsino put it aside and sat down again. Presently Spicca turned a little on the pillow and looked at him.

"Do you remember that I once said I wished you might marry her?" he asked.

"Yes."

"It was quite true. You understand now? I could not tell you then."

"Yes. I understand everything now."

"But I am sorry I said it."

"Why?" "Perhaps it influenced you and has hurt your life. I am sorry. You must forgive me."

"For Heaven's sake, do not distress yourself about such trifles," said Orsino, earnestly. "There is nothing to forgive."

"Thank you."

Orsino looked at him, pondering on the peaceful ending of the strange life, and wondering what manner of heart and soul the man had really lived with. With the intuition which sometimes comes to dying persons, Spicca understood, though it was long before he spoke again. There was a faint touch of his old manner in his words.

"I am an awful example, Orsino," he said, with the ghost of a smile. "Do not imitate me. Do not sacrifice your life for the love of any woman. Try and appreciate sacrifices in others."

The smile died away again.

"And yet I am glad I did it," he added, a moment later. "Perhaps it was all a mistake—but I did my best."

"You did indeed," Orsino answered gravely.

He meant what he said, though he felt that it had indeed been all a mistake, as Spicca suggested. The young face was very thoughtful. Spicca little knew how hard his last cynicism hit the man beside him, for whose freedom and safety the woman of whom Spicca was thinking had sacrificed so very much. He would die without knowing that.

The door opened softly and a woman's light footstep was on the threshold. Maria Consuelo came silently and swiftly forward with outstretched hands that had clasped the dying man's almost before Orsino realised that it was she herself. She fell on her knees beside the bed and pressed the powerless cold fingers to her forehead.

Spicca started and for one moment raised his head from the pillow. It fell back almost instantly. A look of supreme happiness flashed over the deathly features, followed by an expression of pain.

"Why did you marry him?" he asked in tones so loud that Orsino started, and Maria Consuelo looked up with streaming eyes.

She did not answer, but tried to soothe him, rising and caressing his hand, and smoothing his pillows.

"Tell me why you married him!" he cried again. "I am dying—I must know!"

She bent down very low and whispered into his ear. He shook his head impatiently.

"Louder! I cannot hear! Louder!"

Again she whispered, more distinctly this time, and casting an imploring glance at Orsino, who was too much disturbed to understand.

"Louder!" gasped the dying man, struggling to sit up. "Louder! O my God! I shall die without hearing you—without knowing—"

It would have been inhuman to torture the departing soul any longer. Then Maria Consuelo made her last sacrifice. She spoke in calm, clear tones.

"I married to save the man I loved."

Spicca's expression changed. For fully twenty seconds his sunken eyes remained fixed, gazing into hers. Then the light began to flash in them for the last time, keen as the lightning.

"God have mercy on you! God reward you!" he cried.

The shadowy figure quivered throughout its length, was still, then quivered again, then sprang up suddenly with a leap, and Spicca was standing on the floor, clasping Maria Consuelo in his arms. All at once there was colour in his face and the fire grew bright in his glance.

"Oh, my darling, I have loved you so!" he cried.

He almost lifted her from the ground as he pressed his lips passionately upon her forehead. His long thin hands relaxed suddenly, and the light broke in his eyes as when a mirror is shivered by a blow. For an instant that seemed an age, he stood upright, dead already, and then fell back all his length across the bed with wide extended arms.

There was a short, sharp sob, and then a sound of passionate weeping filled the silent room. Strongly and tenderly Orsino laid his dead friend upon the couch as he had lain alive but two minutes earlier. He crossed the hands upon the breast and gently closed the staring eyes. He could not have had Maria Consuelo see him as he had fallen, when she next looked up.

A little later they stood side by side, gazing at the calm dead face, in a long silence. How long they stood, they never knew, for their hearts were very full. The sun was going down and the evening light filled the room.

"Did he tell you, before he died—about me?" asked Maria Consuelo in a low voice.

"Yes. He told me everything."

Maria Consuelo went forward and bent over the face and kissed the white forehead, and made the sign of the Cross upon it. Then she turned and took Orsino's hand in hers.

"I could not help your hearing what I said, Orsino. He was dying, you see. You know all, now."

Orsino's fingers pressed hers desperately. For a moment he could not speak. Then the agonised words came with a great effort, harshly but ringing from the heart.

"And I can give you nothing!"

He covered his face and turned away.

"Give me your friendship, dear—I never had your love," she said.

It was long before they talked together again.

This is what I know of young Orsino Saracinesca's life up to the present time. Maria Consuelo, Countess Del Ferice, was right. She never had his love as he had hers. Perhaps the power of loving so is not in him. He is, after all, more like San Giacinto than any other member of the family, cold, perhaps, and hard by nature. But these things which I have described have made a man of him at an age when many men are but boys, and he has learnt what many never learn at all—that there is more true devotion to be found in the world than most people will acknowledge. He may some day be heard of. He may some day fall under the great passion. Or he may never love at all and may never distinguish himself any more than his father has done. One or the other may happen, but not both, in all probability. The very greatest passion is rarely compatible with the very greatest success except in extraordinary good or bad natures. And Orsino Saracinesca is not extraordinary in any way. His character has been formed by the unusual circumstances in which he was placed when very young, rather than by anything like the self-development which we hear of in the lives of great men. From a somewhat foolish and affectedly cynical youth he has grown into a decidedly hard and cool-headed man. He is very much seen in society but talks little on the whole. If, hereafter, there should be anything in his life worth recording, another hand than mine may write it down for future readers.

If any one cares to ask why I have thought it worth the trouble to describe his early years so minutely, I answer that the young man of the Transition Period interests me. Perhaps I am singular in that. Orsino Saracinesca is a fair type, I think, of his class at his age. I have done my best to be just to him.

F. Marion Crawford – A Short Biography

Francis Marion Crawford was born in Bagni di Lucca, Italy on 2nd August, 1854, the only son of the American sculptor Thomas Crawford and Louisa Cutler Ward. His aunt was Julia Ward Howe, the American poet, most famous for the words to 'The Battle Hymn of the Republic'.

After his father's death in 1857, his mother remarried to Luther Terry, with whom she had Crawford's half-sister, Margaret Ward Terry.

Crawford's education began at St Paul's School, Concord, New Hampshire and then went on to Cambridge University, the University of Heidelberg and finally the University of Rome.

In 1879, Crawford went to India to study the ancient language of Sanskrit and to edit Allahabad, The Indian Herald.

Returning to America in February 1881, he enrolled at Harvard University for a year to continue his studies in Sanskrit. Crawford had no real career path at this time although for two years he contributed to various periodicals, mainly The Critic.

Early in 1882, Crawford established a close, lifelong friendship with Isabella Stewart Gardner, a noted and eccentric heiress from Boston who over the years built up a large and eclectic collection of art.

Crawford lived most of his time in Boston with his Aunt Julia and Uncle Sam. The family were concerned by his lack of ambition, prospects in general, and his financial ones in particular.

His mother had hoped he might train in Boston for a career as an operatic baritone based on his private renditions of Schubert lieder. With that in mind it was, in January 1882, that George Henschel, the conductor of the Boston Symphony Orchestra, was called in to assess young Crawford's talents. Henschel was direct and to the point. Crawford would 'never be able to sing in perfect tune'. His Uncle Sam, knowing that Crawford was keen on literary pursuits, proposed that his years in India might be good source material to write about. Crawford agreed. He set to work. Uncle Sam also set about developing contacts with a number of New York publishers.

Events moved very quickly. By December of that year Crawford had completed his first novel, 'Mr Isaacs', based on modern Anglo-Indian life flavoured with a touch of Oriental mystery. It was an immediate success. Crawford set about writing a second novel and the result was 'Dr Claudius' in 1883.

In October 1884 he married Elizabeth Berdan, the daughter of the Civil War Union General Hiram Berdan. The marriage would produce two sons; Harold and Bertram, and two daughters; Eleanor and Clara.

Crawford, buoyed by his excellent start, now decided to return to Italy and to live there permanently. The couple initially went to Sorrento and lived at the historic Hotel Cocumella during 1885 before moving permanently to Sant' Agnello, where the purchase of the Villa Renzi would now be rededicated as Villa Crawford.

As a writer Crawford had more than his fair share of detractors but, perhaps due to the physical distance between author and these detractors, they did not distract from his prolific output.

Each year seemed to bring a new F. Marion Crawford novel. His popularity was evident although some works, such as 1896's offering 'Adam Johnstone's Son', was described by his left-wing English contemporary, George Gissing, as "rubbish". Over half of his novels are set in Italy. He also wrote three long historical studies of Italy and was nearing completion on a history of Rome in the Middle Ages when he died.

His 'Saracinesca' series are considered his best works. The third in the series, 'Don Orsino' (1892) was told against the background of a real estate bubble and is especially effective. The volume immediately after was 'Corleone' (1897), and the first major treatment of the Mafia in literature.

Crawford himself was fondest of 'Khaled: A Tale of Arabia' (1891), a story of a genie who becomes human. 'A Cigarette-Maker's Romance' (1890) was dramatized, and had considerable popularity on the stage as well as in its novel form.

Towards the end of the 1890's Crawford ventured down another path with his writing. He began his historical works. 'Ave Roma Immortalis' was published in 1898, followed by 'Rulers of the South' (1900), and 'Gleanings from Venetian History' (1905). Most were re-titled with longer more explanatory titles for the American market. Within them all his careful and precise knowledge of the local Italian history together with his literary talents combined to great effect.

Whilst on an American Lecture tour in the winter of 1897-1898 Crawford was researching and gathering technical information for his historical work 'Marietta' (published 1901), that describes glass-making in late medieval Venice. Whilst visiting a glass-smelting plant in Colorado he suffered a severe lung injury when he inhaled toxic gasses. This would eventually contribute to his death a decade or so later.

Crawford's commercial popularity and appeal at the time was such that in 1901, the American Macmillan firm began a deluxe uniform edition of his novels as his works came up for re-printing. In 1904 the P. F. Collier Company in New York was authorized to publish a 25-volume edition (which was later expanded to 32 volumes).

In 1902 he wrote a stage play 'Francesca da Rimini', that was produced in Paris by his friend and legendary actress Sarah Bernhardt.

Towards the end of his life Hollywood had begun to realise that his works were a valuable source of stories and ideas and several were turned into movies and continued to be so for decades after his death.

Crawford also had a gift for pulling off excellent short stories. Several, such as 'The Upper Berth' (1886), 'For the Blood Is the Life' (1905, a vampiress tale), 'The Dead Smile' (1899), and 'The Screaming Skull' (1908), are among the most anthologized classics of the horror genre. After his death several collected volumes were published from various sources.

After most of his fictional works had been published, most had the view that he was a gifted narrator; and his books of fiction, were full of historic vitality and energy as well as dramatic characterization. He was widely popular among readers to whom literature was more for escapism than a confrontation with reality or pages of subjective analysis. In 'The Novel: What It Is' (1893), Crawford was both resolute and disarming in defending his literary approach, self-conceived as a combination of romanticism and realism, defining the art form in terms of its marketplace and audience. The novel, he wrote, is "a marketable commodity" and "intellectual artistic luxury" that "must amuse, indeed, but should amuse reasonably, from an intellectual point of view .... Its intention is to amuse and please, and certainly not to teach and preach; but in order to amuse well it must be a finely-balanced creation ...."

Francis Marion Crawford died at Sorrento on Good Friday 1909 at Villa Crawford of a heart attack.

F. Marion Crawford – A Concise Bibliography

Novels

Mr. Isaacs: A Tale of Modern India (1882)
Dr. Claudius (1883)

To Leeward (1884)
A Roman Singer (1884)
An American Politician (1884)
Zoroaster (1885)
A Tale of a Lonely Parish (1886)
Saracinesca (1887)
Marzio's Crucifix (1887)
Paul Patoff (1887)
With the Immortals (1888)
Greifenstein (1889)
Sant' Ilario (1889); sequel to Saracinesca
A Cigarette-Maker's Romance (1890)
Khaled: A Tale of Arabia (1891)
The Witch of Prague (1891)
The Three Fates (1892)
Don Orsino (1892); sequel to Sant' Ilario
The Children of the King (1893)
Pietro Ghisleri (1893)
Marion Darche (1893)
Katharine Lauderdale (1894)
The Upper Berth (1894); with "By the Waters of Paradise"
Love in Idleness (1894)
The Ralstons (1894); sequel to Katharine Lauderdale
Casa Braccio (1895); related to Katharine Lauderdale and The Ralstons.
Adam Johnstone's Son (1896)
Taquisara (1896)
A Rose of Yesterday (1897)
Corleone (1897)
Via Crucis (1899)
In the Palace of the King (1900)
Marietta (1901)
Cecilia (1902)
Man Overboard! (1903)
The Heart of Rome (1903)
Whosoever Shall Offend (1904)
Soprano (1905); U.S. title: Fair Margaret.
A Lady of Rome (1906)
Arethusa (1907)
The Little City of Hope (1907)
The Primadonna (1908); sequel to Soprano/Fair Margaret
The Diva's Ruby (1908); sequel to The Primadonna
The White Sister (1909)
Stradella (1909)
The Undesirable Governess (1910)
Wandering Ghosts; British title: Uncanny Tales.

Non-fiction

Our Silver (1881)
The Novel: What It Is (1893)
Constantinople (1895)
Bar Harbor (1896)
Ave Roma Immortalis (1898)
Rulers of the South (1900; 1905 in the U.S. as Southern Italy and Sicily and The Rulers of the South)
Gleanings from Venetian History (1905; in the U.S. as Salvae Venetia and in 1909 as Venice; the People and the Place)

Drama

In the Palace of the King (1900) with Lorrimer Stoddard.
Francesca da Rimini (1902) The piece was adapted into an opera by Franco Leoni in 1904.
Evelyn Hastings (1902) Unpublished typescript discovered in 2008.
The White Sister (1909) with Walter C. Hackett.

Filmography

A Cigarette-Maker's Romance, directed by Frank Wilson (UK, 1913, based on the novella)
The White Sister, directed by Fred E. Wright [it] (1915, based on the novel)
In the Palace of the King [it], directed by Fred E. Wright [it] (1915, based on the novel)
Whosoever Shall Offend, directed by Arrigo Bocchi (UK, 1919, based on the novel)
Il cuore di Roma, directed by Edoardo Bencivenga (Italy, 1919, based on the novel)
A Cigarette-Maker's Romance, directed by Tom Watts (UK, 1920, based on the novella)
Saracinesca [it], directed by Gaston Ravel (Italy, 1921, based on the novel)
Sant' Ilario [it], directed by Henry Kolker (Italy, 1923, based on the novel)
The White Sister, directed by Henry King (1923, based on the novel)
In the Palace of the King, directed by Emmett J. Flynn (1923, based on the novel)
Son of India, directed by Jacques Feyder (1931, based on the novel Mr. Isaacs)
The White Sister, directed by Victor Fleming (1933, based on the novel)
The Screaming Skull, directed by Alex Nicol (1958, named after the short story)
The White Sister, directed by Tito Davison (Mexico, 1960, based on the novel)